THE ASSISTANTS

TITLE

THE ASSISTANTS

ISBN 0-06-072386-6

A Novel

BY Robin Lynn Williams

REGAN BOOKS   / /   2004

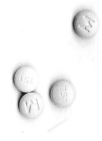

10 ReganBooks
Celebrating Ten Bestselling Years
An Imprint of HarperCollins*Publishers*

THE ASSISTANTS. Copyright © 2004 by Robin Lynn Williams. All rights reserved. Printed in the United States of America. No part of this book may be used or reproduced in any manner whatsoever without written permission except in the case of brief quotations embodied in critical articles and reviews. For information address HarperCollins Publishers Inc., 10 East 53rd Street, New York, NY 10022.

HarperCollins books may be purchased for educational, business, or sales promotional use. For information please write: Special Markets Department, HarperCollins Publishers Inc., 10 East 53rd Street, New York, NY 10022.

FIRST EDITION

Designed by Judith Stagnitto Abbate

Interior photographs by Patrick Hoelck

Printed on acid-free paper

Library of Congress Cataloging-in-Publication Data

Williams, Robin Lynn.
   The assistants : a novel / Robin Lynn Williams.—1st ed.
      p. cm.
   ISBN 0-06-072386-6 (acid-free paper)
      1. Hollywood (Los Angeles, Calif.)—Fiction. 2. Motion picture industry—Fiction. 3. Administrative   assistants—Fiction. 4. Revenge—Fiction. I. Title.

PS3623.I5625A94 2004
813'.6—dc22

2004041783

04 05 06 07 08 BVG/RRD 10 9 8 7 6 5 4 3 2 1

FOR ALL ASSISTANTS PAST, PRESENT, AND FUTURE

THE ASSISTANTS

Polaroid C20726A08611A

Michaela

Michaela

I FEEL LIKE I'm in an Old Navy commercial. You know, the ones where there's a bunch of hip minors dressed in similar outfits, dancing around merrily—as if their lives actually had meaning? Except here, nobody's dressed alike, nobody's dancing, and I'm the oldest one in the room—by more than a decade.

"Michaela Marsh?"

Everyone in the waiting area turns around and gawks. I raise my hand. "Right here."

Standing up always presents a challenge because the black slim skirt I'm wearing is very short and very tight, so tight I have to sit on the edge of my seat with my knees pressed firmly together to avoid giving away the goods. You see, the skirt is about the size of a washcloth, and it gives the illusion that I'm taller. At a whopping five-two, I need all the help I can get.

I extend my hand to the casting assistant. Stunned by my professionalism, a strange look appears on her pockmarked face. It's obvious that no one ever wants to shake her hand. After all, she is *just* the assistant. She offers her hand anyway and shakes mine limply. She definitely has to work on the handshake.

What's even more disturbing than the limp handshake, however, is that the assistant looks sixteen. In fact, everyone at this casting call seems extremely juvenile. They belong in a tenth-grade geometry class if anywhere, certainly not *here*, competing with *me*.

I can't help shuddering when I think of my own age, but then I quickly put it out of my mind. *Bad vibes.* I won't let anything distract me. This audition for *Coral Gables* (or *The CG*, for those of us in the know) is way too important. I hand the assistant my head shot and résumé.

"Follow me," she instructs, leading me into a barren windowless office that's ablaze in fluorescent light. *Great.* I can't begin to tell you how horribly pale and decrepit I look under this light. The few tiny lines on my face—and I stress *few*—probably look like they were drawn with a Sharpie fine-point. To make matters worse, one of the bulbs is flickering like a strobe.

A woman and two men sit behind a conference table. In the middle of the room, a young tan guy with highlighted curly hair sits in a chair, flipping through slides. Directly facing him is an empty chair. I study it, trying to figure out how I'm going to ease in and out of it in my tight skirt.

"This is Michaela Marsh," the assistant announces as she hands over my headshot.

"Hello, Michaela," the panel murmur in unison, glancing at the photo. When they look up at me, I smile a perfect I'm-not-desperate smile. And I'm *not* desperate. Not even a teensy bit. I have classic Southern Californian looks: tan, with blue eyes and shoulder-length blonde hair. Traveling southward, I have perky breasts and a flawless, rock-hard body. I'm basically a midget Tai Bo Barbie. It's definitely too much perfection for one person. Too bad I'm completely man-made. Only the best for daddy's little girl.

The woman clears her throat. "My name's Erin Malone. I'm casting this pilot. On my right is Jason Carr, the executive producer of *The CG*, and on my left is Bill Bond, head writer."

Both men nod their heads and smile. I smile more broadly—a perfect, toothpaste-commercial smile filled with white, bonded teeth. And it has the added benefit of stretching my skin just enough to hide the few lines in my face. I had to practice in the mirror for several days to get it just right.

"This is Brandon East, who plays Rico, the lead of this show," Erin continues.

Brandon's legs are stretched out in front of him and he looks bored, stoned, or both. He gives me a nonchalant "Hey."

I hold that winning smile, trying to convey that I'm perfect for the show, which is about a bunch of twentysomething students at the University of Miami. But I'm also nervous, admittedly. I met this same casting director many years ago, at the early auditions for—gulp!—*Beverly Hills 90210*. Will she remember me? Suddenly I feel like Grandma Walton.

"Which part are you reading?" Erin asks. She looks like a Jenny Craig client who cheats. "Celeste or Simone?"

"Either one," I say with a confident smile. "I've memorized both roles."

Impressed, Jason Carr and Bill Bond nod their heads, then the three of them huddle together to discuss the situation. I stand there politely with my hands at my sides and right foot turned outward. This is the classic beauty contestant stance. I learned it when I Jon Bene*ted* my way through the Miss Southern California pageant. Please don't get me wrong. I believe, as strongly as the next educated person, that pageants are unnecessary, demeaning, and extremely cheesy. And I'm almost sure Michelle Pfeiffer felt exactly the same way. But look what pageants did for her.

Every few seconds, the threesome look at me in wide-eyed wonderment, then return to their discussion. Now I'm really freaked. They're trying to decide if they've seen me before. That could be because I'm a working actress, as opposed to nonworking, thank you very much. My credits include guest shots as Jerry's girlfriend on *Seinfeld*, a district attorney on *Law & Order*, Hooker #3 on *NYPD Blue*, and a host of commercials—including Denny's, Pizza Hut, Miller Lite, and Playtex. I hate to rendezvous in the Land of Negativity, but there should be something else on my résumé that's not. It's too painful. I costarred in a little TV pilot once. I had been in countless pilots already, but NBC actually picked this one up for thirteen episodes, and everyone knew it was special. Here's the part that sucks, though. Two weeks before the season premiere, the producers told me they were going in a different direction—which in L.A.-speak means, *Bend over, this is going to hurt.* They said they envisioned another "look" for the character. They wanted someone taller, with longer hair. So I had to call everybody I've ever known and tell them I wasn't playing Phoebe on a new show called *Friends*. A week later I was on Prozac.

So here I am, in front of these people like an item from *Antiques Roadshow*. Erin checks me out with narrowed eyes and pursed lips. Bill stares, too, but he's a little moony-eyed. He must be a new producer and not yet immune to beautiful actresses. He's wondering how to get in touch with me. Jason studies my mouth with great intensity. My lips are more Julia, less Angelina, courtesy of my close friend the collagen injection. He's probably wondering if I give good head. I do. I'm really gifted in that department.

Erin's eyes light up and my worst fear is realized. I can almost hear the cog click in her mind. She remembers that long-ago *90210* casting call. I can see her brain heating up as it goes into overdrive. *Exactly how old is this Michaela person? If 90210 was a decade ago, then she has to be—oh, the horror—thirtysomething?!*

That would be the end of that. Bye, bye. See ya. Sayonara.

Meanwhile, Surfer Boy stops flipping through his sides and suddenly becomes fixated on his forearm.

Jason smiles. "Why don't you read Celeste's part?"

"Great." I perch myself on the edge of the seat and notice a dried, dime-sized brown scab on Brandon's arm. He begins to pick at it.

Erin clears her throat loudly. "Uh, Brandon . . . Page twelve please."

Brandon snaps out of his trance and turns to the appropriate page.

"Perhaps we should tell you exactly what we're looking for," Jason says.

I bat my eyelashes ever so slightly. "Yes, that would be very helpful."

Jason gets up and paces in front of the conference table. "Celeste is a complex character. She's had a privileged life but she wants to make her way in the world without her parents' help. She's a student by day and an aspiring R&B singer at night. She's beautiful, intense, intelligent, and has the voice of an angel."

"She's got the sexy soul of Beyoncé," Bill says.

"The attitude of Pink," Jason says.

"The youthfulness of Avril," Bill adds.

"And of course, the girl-next-door wholesomeness of the first *American Idol* winner, whatever her name is," Jason says.

I smile on the outside but grimace on the inside. What the hell am I doing here? Beyoncé? Pink? Avril? *American Idol!!* Fetuses. Zygotes. I'm old enough to be their . . . their . . . very big sister.

"Now in this scene, Rico and Celeste are meeting for the very first time. They're on her parents' yacht, in the marina. She's in the kitchen cleaning the oven. Because she's simply dressed and wearing rubber gloves, Rico, who has been hired to mop the decks, assumes she works on the boat, too. And she's so stunning that he simply must move in for a closer look."

"Michaela, can you start from the top?" Erin asks.

I nod. I know the scene by heart, so I look directly at Brandon before delivering it.

"If you get any closer, you'll be on top of me."

Brandon does not return eye contact. Bored stiff, he looks down at his sides and murmurs, *"Maybe that's not such a bad idea."*

I'm forced to stare at a blossoming whitehead in the crease of his nose. *"What's your name, boat boy?"*

Brandon's words are slow and stilted: *"The name's Rico. And I'm not a boy. I'm a man. I was thinking we could go to my place after work."*

"Do you make a habit of harassing all the women you work with?" I say to the whitehead.

"No," Brandon says listlessly. *"Only the ones that are as hot as you."*

"I don't work here," I say sternly. *"I live here. And my father will probably want to know exactly what kind of boy he's hired. You're the epitome of a male chauvinist pig."*

Erin suddenly interrupts, "Thanks. We'll be in touch."

Brandon goes back to picking his scab. Jason and Bill look at Erin curiously, wondering why she's so quick to dismiss me. Apparently she and I are the only ones who know what's going on. I stand carefully and manage a pleasant smile.

"It was a pleasure to meet all of you," I say.

"Same here," the table of three respond as Brandon's scab seeps blood.

I am completely humiliated, but I manage to hold my head high as I leave the room, and I linger outside only just long enough to eavesdrop.

"What's going on?" Bill says. "That girl can act."

"That girl is over thirty," Erin states.

"*Thirty?*" Brandon exclaims. "I'm only nineteen!"

"We're well aware of that," Erin sniffs.

"She doesn't look anywhere close to thirty," Jason says.

"Trust me. She auditioned when I was casting *90210*."

Jason slaps his palm on the table. "That's who she looks like. Jennie Garth."

"Who?" Brandon asks.

"That's another reason she's not right. You don't want *90210* lookalikes on your show," Erin says.

"She was the best Celeste we've seen all day," Bill says. "She's the only one who pronounced *epitome* correctly."

Jason disagrees. "We decided this would be breakthrough television. We're only casting actors that are the same age as the characters they play."

"And casting thirty-year-olds kind of defeats the purpose, doesn't it?" Erin says.

Bill nods. "I guess you're right."

"So who's next?" Erin says.

Tʜᴀɴᴋ ɢᴏᴅ Pʀᴏᴢᴀᴄ keeps the depression in check, because I'm constantly told the same thing: "You're too old" or "You look too much like (enter perky blonde *du jour*)." For years it was Jennie Garth. Lately it's been Gwyneth, Cameron, Reese, or Kirsten. The only person I don't resemble is Lisa Kudrow, which sucks because then I could have kept that job. It's so ironic: I go to all the trouble of changing my looks to turn out exactly like someone else. I would have been better off staying just the way I was.

Nah. Then everyone would have said I look too much like Janeane Garofalo, or Velma from *Scooby-Doo*.

Since I have only ten minutes to get to an office that's twenty minutes away, I speed up. My face begins to flush and my blood pressure rises. Take a deep breath. Inhale. Exhale. Relax. Remember everything you learned in yoga. Expel the negativity. I light up a smoke. I'll get there soon enough. No sense getting into an accident. Although if that were to happen, I know I have the talent to pull a Halle Berry: *I hit someone? How's that possible, officer? Surely I would know if I hit someone!*

Victoria Rush can wait. And so can her annoying husband, Lorne *I'll-Fuck-Anything* Henderson. Still, just in case, I turn my cell phone back on. And instantly it rings.

"Michaela, where are you?" asks a panic-stricken Courtney Collins, Lorne's assistant.

"I'm stuck in traffic," I lie.

"Victoria and Lorne are both looking for you," she says.

Bad vibe. I overturn my satchel and glance at two neatly typed schedules. "Lorne is supposed to be getting a massage and Victoria is on her way to the studio. Why are they looking for me?"

"Mary got fired," Courtney says.

I slam on the brakes and go into a skid, barely missing the car next to me.

"When are you getting here?" she asks.

I lie again. "I should be there in less than five minutes."

"Victoria's making me go to the studio until we hire someone new."

"Tell her we'll have someone hired by the end of the week."

"It'll take that long?"

"We have to run an ad and interview people."

Courtney huffs. "I'm Lorne's assistant, not hers. Why do I have to do work for her?"

Because you're fucking her husband, is what I want to say, but I don't. That's me all the way: too nice for my own good. "Hang in there," I say. "I'll be there soon."

After ending the call, I swerve into the fast lane and start weaving in and out of traffic. I can't believe this is happening, and today of all days, when I knew I'd be late. In the eight months I've been running the Victoria Rush/Lorne Henderson empire, I've watched at least twenty employees get fired. I wonder if I'm next.

I arrive in Brentwood in nine minutes flat, a record. I speed through the neighborhood, turn onto Beechwood Lane, and park a few houses down the street. I pull my hair back into a ponytail and retrieve a large button-down shirt and long skirt from the back seat. In a matter of seconds, I'm transformed from a blonde goddess to the type of girl who only gets picked up about thirty seconds before the bar closes. I'm searching for my glasses, the thick, red ones immortalized by Sally Jessy Raphael, when the phone rings again, scaring the shit out of me.

"I'll be right in," I shout half-hysterically into the phone.

"Michaela, it's Jeb."

Jeb is my agent's assistant. Maybe he's calling with good news.

"Having a bad day?" he chuckles. He's a creepy guy and there's something about him that makes me nervous.

"Did Randall hear from the producers of *The CG?*" I ask. Maybe they changed their minds. Maybe my age wasn't a factor. Maybe they want me to come back and read for the part of Simone, the innocent virgin.

"Randall says they decided to go with someone a little younger," he says. "And they thought you looked too much like Jennie Garth."

"Great," I say, grimacing. "Thank you for your brutal honesty."

"You still look very hot to me, Michaela."

"Thanks." I find my prop glasses in the bottom of my bag.

"Randall wants to meet you for lunch Wednesday. Are you free?"

Bad vibe. What does my agent want to discuss? I hate to be paranoid, but I always have the feeling he wants to dump me as a client. He never does, though, because I can be *very* convincing when I want to be.

"Sure. What time?"

"One," Jeb says. "He said you know where to meet him."

"Perfect."

I hang up, place the Sally Jessys on my face, and spring out of the car. I dash to the entrance, punch in the alarm code, and wait for the large, ornate gates to open. And that's when I remember my teeth. I fumble in my bag for them. They were made by a dentist friend of my dad's and were professionally discolored to the perfect shade of iced-tea brown. I pop them in my mouth and scurry through the gates toward the house, a woman transformed.

Polaroid C20786A08611A

Jeb.

INT. OUTCOME TALENT AGENCY—DAY (SLOW MOTION)

It's a typically posh Hollywood agency, filled with desks, ringing phones, high-powered agents—and all of their lowly, miserable assistants.

ME, early twenties, handsome, rock-hard, wearing black shades and black clothes, looking very Neo from *The Matrix*. My tolerance for bullshit is zero. I saunter into the office with an AK-47 and go Columbine on everybody's ass. Bullets splay through walls, desks, and doors—and through the bodies of some of the most powerful agents in town. Heads explode like melons, limbs are blown off, and . . . wait. I'm missing something. Strippers. Maybe a chick with a dick, real or strap-on. But you can't actually tell because she's in the background. Two of the others are completely nude. No G-strings or pasties, NAKED. Except for high heels. Five-inch black patent-leather fuck-me pumps. Yeah, strippers in a workplace massacre scene! That should give it the old Oliver Stone what-the-fuck-is-that-in-there-for? feel.

So there I am, doing my best disgruntled-employee-from-hell impression. I throw my head back and cackle maniacally. I remove a nose or two, nice clean shots, do my own version of a rhinoplasty. Maybe expose some brains à la JFK. Nah, too much Stone. EXTREME CLOSE-UP: RANDOM CROTCH. I pump several rounds to the groin, clean out the old prostate. But after a few bangs to the balls, no cocks are flying, and the CAMERA ZOOMS IN to reveal that the agents have no genitalia. Nothing, squat. CAMERA PANS BACK and we see a big bloody empty office of splattered Ken dolls that never had any balls in the first place. I stand in the middle of the carnage and raise my arms in victory.

CUT TO:

Helicopter shot of me walking from the building, hands overhead, then kneeling as the cops rush in to cuff me. The CAMERA TILTS DOWN to street level. I'm shoved through an angry mob toward a police cruiser and find Johnny Cochran waiting for me in the back seat. They shove me in.

> JOHNNY
> Watch your head.

I think we all know what happens next. KA-CHING! A million-dollar script sale, with two actual gross points. None of those monkey points for this writer. Actors would kill for the lead. KA-CHING KA-CHING! I can hear the critics now: "Makes *The Player* seem like a student film." I am a fucking genius!

> BLUME (O.S.)
> Jeb!

CUT TO:
INT. OUTCOME AGENCY—DAY

"Get me Bob Bush on the line."

I'll never understand why these jerks can't make their own phone calls. What are they, quadriplegics? Why the middleman? I pick up the phone and dial the producer's number. Bob Bush is hot at the moment, having produced a handheld-camera-shot lesbian vampire flick that premiered at Sundance and ended up grossing fifty million dollars. He's a moron and probably won't last another year, but for the time being I know his number by heart.

His assistant answers on the first ring. "Bob Bush's office."

"Jane, Jeb."

She sighs.

I have no idea why she doesn't like me. "What are you wearing?"

"W-what can I help you with?" she stammers.

I met Jane once when she hand-delivered a script. She's one of those prissy Vassar chicks. A little narrow in the anal cavity. Probably lived by the *Preppie Handbook*. She's rarely seen the veins.

"I was hoping I could give you a massage," I say. "With my tongue."

"That's not funny, Jeb. Why are you calling?"

"I already told you."

"I'm serious. I don't have time for this. "

Stem cell researcher she is not. "Why do I ever call? Is Bob in for Blume?"

"Please hold. I'll see if he's available."

Of course he's available. Producers are always available. They have squat to do. As I wait to connect with Bob, I find myself tapping my pen to the beat of some Creed bullshit. I stop when I realize what I'm doing and glance over at Jim's desk. That's where the offensive music is coming from. He hums along as he types a letter. Jim works for Parker King, a senior agent, and he's brand-new and wide-eyed and bushy tailed. He has no idea that his days are numbered. He's about to be shitcanned right along with Parker. Apparently Parker is fucking one of the partner's whores. Turns out these guys are very protective of their high-dollar snatch. Who'da thunk it?

Jane returns to the line. "Jeb, I've got Bob on the line."

I buzz Blume's office. "Bob's on Line One."

Whenever he takes a phone call with a producer or any other power prick, I press the mute button on my phone and stay on the line. I believe a man's education should be ongoing, especially in this business.

He picks up his phone. "Bob, how are you?"

"Great, just great. We finally have a green light on that Elian Gonzales movie. We landed Jonathan Lipnicki."

"Lipnicki. Interesting choice."

"I know, I know. He'll have to lose the specs, learn Spanish, and spend some time in the sun, but we're psyched. The kid's got talent."

"*Kid?* Isn't he about nineteen now?"

"He can play much younger."

"Good for you, then. Congratulations are in order."

"Yes, they are. To *you*. For making *Entertainment Weekly's* Power Issue at Number Seventy-Eight."

"Thanks."

"I bet you break the Top Fifty next year."

"Enough about me," Blume says, though he is his own favorite subject. "I hear you have the pitch of a lifetime."

"I sure do!" Bush yaps. He sounds like a chihuahua on crack. "The studio's ready to greenlight on the strength of the idea alone, if we can get the right star."

"I'm all ears."

Bob takes a deep breath and plunges in: "There's a gigantic meteoroid the size of Texas hurtling toward Earth—"

"Been done," Blume says, cutting him off. "Twice. *Armageddon* and *Deep Impact*."

"No. That was an asteroid and a comet, respectively. This is a *meteoroid*."

There's a pause. Then Blume says, "I see. Continue."

"Okay, so there's a gigantic meteoroid the size of Texas hurtling toward Earth . . ." Bob stops. Nothing but silence.

"And?"

"That's all I have so far. But this has Travis Trask written all over it."

"Christ, Bob," Blume says with disgust. "Can't you at least complete a sentence? Doesn't anybody work in this town?"

This from the laziest agent in Hollywood.

"Stay with me, Randall," Bob says, sounding winded. "I'm working on making your boy a big star."

"He's already a big star."

"A big *action* star. So far he's starred in—what?—two teen flicks and an art house stinker. Think of the possibilities here. We're looking at a teenage Schwarzenegger. Big budget, big box office, big paydays all around."

Blume mulls it over. "Who's directing?"

"Take your pick. It's an action movie. Any idiot can direct action."

"So what's the story? He's gotta stop the comet?"

You're brilliant, Blume! How did you figure that out?

"Meteoroid," Bob corrects.

"Whatever."

"A special team of scientists—" Bob says.

"Scientists are boring."

"You're right," Bob says. "How about this? This is not your average meteoroid. This broke from the sun, so it's literally a ball of fire. And how do you put out a fire? With a giant hose! The main characters could be a special team of firefighters, and they've been secretly training for this very day. And everybody loves firefighters, right?"

"Maybe. But there's no water in space."

How did the jackass know that?

Blume's comment stumps Bob for a second, but he keeps rolling. "Forget the hose. Let's make it a team of architects and engineers. They build a giant wall to put in its path."

"Travis is an architect now? At his age?"

"Who cares?!" Bob whines. "Maybe he was always great with Legos."

"That's not bad."

"They put a giant wall in its path, diverting the comet into a black hole and saving the world."

"I don't know," Blume says. "I hate architects. You should meet the asshole who did our house."

"For God's sake, Blume—what does it matter? It's Travis Trask. I'm just trying to make a movie here . . . Blume? You there?"

"It needs a good title," Blume says. "How about *Doomsday*?"

"No, I've already got our title: *Fire in the Hole*."

"Perfect," Blume says. "So far, that's the only thing I like about the entire project. That and Travis."

That's when I hang up. These jacklicks don't have a creative bone in their bodies, let alone the ability to recognize an original idea if it urinated on them in an Industrial Light & Magic special effect.

"Great tie."

I look up. It's that loser, Jim. "Thanks."

He waves a sheet of paper in my face. "Can I interest you in a little March Madness?"

Jim has xeroxed the NCAA championship tournament brackets from *USA Today*. I search for my alma mater, the University of Wyoming, but they're a no-show. Figures. The cowboys have always sucked at b-ball.

"Everyone puts in twenty bucks," he explains. "I'm hoping for a two-hundred-dollar pot."

You'll need it, buddy. Since your ass won't have a job.

"No, thanks."

He frowns like I farted on him. "Well, if you know anybody that wants to play, let me know."

"Sure, Jim."

I watch him skip down the hall to recruit more gamblers. He knows full well I have no intention of spreading the word.

"Water!" Blume suddenly yells.

As I hurry into the so-called lounge, I think of all the things I could put in Blume's drink . . . piss, spit, roofies, or my personal fave: Visine. A flight attendant who once saw the veins told me about it. Just a couple of drops and presto! Instant diarrhea.

Christ, this assistant bullshit blows. But I have no choice. I wasn't privileged enough to attend Harvard and write for the campus humor magazine. Come up with an idea like a "humor magazine" in Laramie, Wyoming, and you'll find yourself bloodied, beaten, and tied to a fence. And résumé-building is out because I don't have any connections. I know dick. Nobody, zilch. That leaves the old *start-at-the-bottom-and-claw-my-way-up* strategy. I did the mailroom thing. Hollywood is the only town where a blue-collar job requires white-collar qualifications: B.A. from a good school, high GPA, Greek affiliation. I was eventually promoted to assistant, and that's where I've stayed. I never seem to last very long at these jobs. I've worked at William Morris, CAA, Gersh, and ICM, but inevitably something always goes wrong. Apparently I have an attitude problem. My only consolation is that I'm bigger and stronger than most of the pimps I've worked for. I bench 350. They need to know that if provoked, I will snap their backs and make them call me "sir."

CUT TO:
INT. LOUNGE—DAY

Typical office fare: fridge with unidentifiable leftovers, water cooler, round table with four chairs. A chick named Tess loiters. She's a partner's assistant and looks like a POW—pale, malnourished, skanky. She's never seen anyone's veins. I kind of startle her and she jumps like she has shell shock.

"Oh, hi, Jeb," she whines.

That's when I notice her eyes are filled with tears. She's about to break down at any moment. I immediately turn my back and open the fridge. No doubt about it. She's definitely crying. She's sniffling and trying to catch her breath. I grab a bottle of Evian and shut the door.

"Jack is such an asshole," she says, whimpering. I don't want to look at her, but I have to. Shit. Now I wish I hadn't. She's a total wreck. Mascara down her face, snot dripping from her nose, that white crap accumulating in the corners of her mouth. Disgusting.

"He threw his laptop at me because I dry-cleaned a shirt instead of having it laundered," she sobs. "He missed my head by two inches."

I muster up as much sincerity as I can and give her a sympathetic look—caring eyes, tilted head, downturned mouth. But this only makes her think I give a shit. I'm on my way out when she whines, "What am I going to do?"

I don't turn around. Keep moving. I learned a long time ago that you don't roll around in other people's shit. I don't mean to be insensitive. But come on, she's just a stick and only a dog wants a bone.

I walk down the hallway trying not to make eye contact with anyone. The name of this agency should be spelled Outcum because everybody's fucking everybody. Junior agents are fucking senior agents. Senior agents are fucking the partners. The partners fuck each other. They leave the assistants alone because we're human placebos, inert matter, nonentities. The agency has a suite at the Four Seasons that's supposed to be for big NY clients, but it's actually a private fuck pen. The senior agents and partners have keys. An assistant keeps a schedule so they don't double-book. Blume is fucking two of the partners and has even ventured outside the office to fuck a couple of his clients, including Michaela. That gal has the veins committed to memory. But then again, it's all about fucking in this town. If you're not fucking someone, literally, then you better hope you're fucking them figuratively.

The only good thing about working at Outcome is that Randall Blume is semitolerable and agreed to read my script—after I saved his life. It was lunchtime at The Source and he had a grape lodged in his throat. Everyone stared, frozen: the Von Bulow family picnic. Except for me. Had to give him the Heimlich. Not only did I score the assistant gig, but I got what I really wanted: someone to read my goddamn script. You'd think that reading a great script wouldn't be too much to ask in a town that's desperate for new material. But you have a better shot at a ménage a trois with the Hilton sisters than getting someone to read your spec.

The truth is, I was feeling as if I'd finally caught a real break. Randall

15

Blume wasn't going to bail on me: I'd saved his life. He'd read my script, right? It wasn't too much to ask.

And he will. I know it. It's sitting in his briefcase, in the side pocket. I show him where it is every evening as he leaves for home. I know he'll be reading it soon. Maybe I'll give him one of my menacing looks today. Flex a muscle or two. I'll make him keep his word.

Kecia

D

AMN. THIS BOY'S crazy.

Partying up in here like Robert Downey Jr. straight out of rehab. I can't even park because five cars are blocking the driveway. So I park on the street. It's 10:00 A.M. and the stereo's loud enough to wake the whole 'hood. *Insane in the membrane, insane in the brain!* The bass might as well be vibrating the picture window out the front of the house. I grab his breakfast—a twelve-pack of Mountain Dew and a dozen Krispy Kreme donuts—and make my way toward the house. And no, I'm not working for *The Fly*. I work for nineteen-year-old Travis Trask, the hottest teen heart-throb to come along since that other white boy called Leo.

"Hey, girl."

"Get off the property, Lou."

"Technically, the curb is not his property," he says. Lou is as dark as espresso and just as bold. He's got muscles in all the right places and his long dreads are pulled back in a ponytail. A massive camera with a tele-photo lens hangs from his neck.

"Tell it to the cops."

"Come on. Why ya gotta be like that?"

Did I mention his Denzel smile? I have to admit he's kinda cute.

"Why don't you stake out Justin Timberlake or some other no-rhythm, lip-synching boy of the moment?" I say.

"Justin won't bring as much money as Travis Trask."

"What's your sign?" I ask him.

My question catches him off guard. He grins wide. "I'm a Leo, baby."

"Figures," I grunt. "Overconfident, overbearing, and self-centered."

"What sign are you?"

"None of your business," I say, turning my back on him. I'm a Pisces. Water signs and fire signs don't mix. Know what I'm saying?

"Girl, I don't know why you gotta be like that. You help me get a picture of the man, I'll split the money with you sixty-forty."

"I'm not selling my boss out."

"You have a good day, then," he says. I'll give him props for being polite.

I work my way past the cars and toward the front door. The house has five bedrooms, three baths, a swimming pool, and a view of the valley. This place was built in the early 1970s, so it's more than a little run-down. But this is in Encino, one of the phatter neighborhoods in the area, which makes it a 2.2-million-dollar spread.

The music gets louder at the front door. When I unlock it and step through, it's like I released a dam. The power almost knocks me off my feet. It's a rap song with a very pleasant lyric, "Nigga, nigga, pull that trigga." The rapper's named Ah'ight—that's *All right* for all the nonblack folks. *Take Whitey Down* is the name of the CD, and some other tunes include *"Cap da Cracker," "My Crib's on Fire,"* and *"F*@k the #%&* ers."*

I don't get this whole hip-hop craze. Now, most brothers and sisters would say I need to have my African-American card revoked, but I can't help the way I feel. My musical taste is more refined. I prefer jazz. It's in the blood. My daddy was the famous Eddie Christy, piano player and founder of the Eddie Christy Quartet. They cut more albums than any other jazz group in the late 1950s and early 1960s. Daddy was a close personal friend of Sammy Davis Jr. and Nat King Cole. But I never met them—barely knew my daddy. He died when I was six. Only thing I recall is a tall, mocha-colored man with a thin mustache who always smelled like Cuban cigars and brandy. He had large hands with slender fingers, exactly like mine.

The house smells like a bar at closing time. Nobody's in sight as I creep around the corner into the living room. The modern furniture does not go with the *Brady Bunch* interior. The couch and chairs are chrome and suede. The coffee table has a granite base and a kidney-shaped glass top. There are two large metal sculptures that double as furniture. They're not too sturdy, though. I sat down on the "ottoman" once and fell on my padded ass.

Fruit-flavored Stoli bottles and empty beer cans are all over the gold shag carpet. Cool Ranch Doritos bags and In and Out burger wrappers lie on the coffee table, next to a metal tray containing a pile of pot. Next to that I see Travis's blue glass bong, some rolling papers, and several lines of coke just waiting for a hungry nostril.

The bass in the den is rumbling the room like an aftershock. I open up the stereo cabinet to turn off the music. It's an all-digital home entertainment system comprised of top-of-the-line components: a Sony DVD player, Yamaha amp and tuner, Nakamichi cassette deck, Denon home CD jukebox, and Bose subwoofer and tweeters. Damn! I always forget how to turn it off. I begin pressing buttons. The bass gets louder and threatens to rattle pictures off the wall. I manage to kill the bass, but then the treble gets so high I think my ears are gonna bleed. When I switch the treble off, I accidentally hit the radio button. Ah'ight is gone but now Howard Stern's gabbing at full volume, giving the business to a porn star. Where *is* the volume button? There's no knob. Just a bunch of buttons and blue lights. I try another button, but now I'm listening to dialogue from *Pulp Fiction*. Samuel L. is telling me to be cool like the Fonz. Right before I'm about to lose my own damn cool, I finally spot the power button. I hit it and everything goes eerily quiet. Way off in the distance, a neighbor's dog barks.

I'm starving. On my way to the kitchen, I almost trip over two nude bodies passed out behind the couch. I recognize the guy right away. His name is Pokey and he's Travis's main man. The nickname refers to his habit of poking anything in a skirt. He has dirty blond hair wrapped in a red bandanna and a tattoo of a decapitated woman on his right forearm. Pokey's obvious hatred for women does not deter him from cozying up with the nude girl next to him. I'm no Christie Love, but the girl's hoochie mama look and those breasts—standing up straight and proud like orange road cones—can only mean one thing: stripper. I glance down at Pokey's wrinkled penis and wonder how large it actually got. Probably not very, I figure. I sneak one more peek before leaving the room.

I enter the kitchen at exactly the same time as Marta. She's the housekeeper, a tiny Mexican woman in her sixties who wears her thinning gray hair in a stylish shag. She's also a fan of large, colorful earrings. Today a miniature hot pink car key dangles from each lobe. We go way back, Marta and I. In fact, she pretty much raised me single-handed. Mama was never there and OD'd in a Vegas motel room before I had even learned to walk. And when Daddy died, some years later, Marta became my legal guardian.

"The area behind the couch needs vacuuming," I say.

Marta purses her lips. "Party every day, this boy. Not healthy. *No es bueno.*"

"You know it, girl."

Marta disappears toward the utility room, mumbling to herself. I place the Mountain Dew and donuts on the counter and fight the urge to open the box. As a Pisces, I tend to overindulge myself, and I tend to retain water, so I'm a little overweight. I've promised myself to cut out sweets, but I can't seem to stop salivating. I finger the edges of the box, then I squeeze those few extra inches on my waist to remind myself exactly where those little donuts will end up. Still, I've only got fifteen pounds to lose. It's not like I'm Star Jones big. That sister looks like a black leather sofa wearing a wig. Besides, I'm a tall girl. Not WNBA-tall, exactly—I don't cross a basketball court and get asked if I got game—but pretty respectable at five-nine. So what if I've got a few pounds to shed? Today my horoscope said, *"Don't be ashamed; personal change comes slowly, but it is definitely worth the effort."*

I decide to stay strong and quickly leave the kitchen. Marta's in the living room, standing over Pokey and the bimbo. She's got the vacuum an inch away from his head. With her eyes all a-twinkle, she looks at me, then quickly switches it on. The loudass noise rattles them out of sleep.

"What the . . ." Pokey says.

The girl beside him sits up and rubs her eyes. When she sees Marta standing over her, she covers her breasts with her arms and looks around for her clothes. Pokey isn't so modest. He picks himself up off the floor, slowly, stretches his arms way above his head, and struts down the hall—his johnson swinging in the wind. The girl finds her tank top and skirt wadded up under a couch cushion. She shields herself with the clothes and follows Pokey like a well-trained dog. They disappear into one of the bedrooms and slam the door behind them.

I spot someone else passed out in the backyard near the pool. His name is Frog and he has green spiked hair and bad skin. He's lying facedown on one of the lounge chairs, looking like a corpse. I look at Marta. "The weeds need trimming."

Marta nods her head and disappears into the garage. A few moments later, she reappears near the pool with the weed-cutter. It's attached to a long orange cord. She stands a few feet away from Frog and turns it on. The boy barely turns over, so she edges closer. When it's just a few inches from his head, making *me* nervous, Frog groans, yawns, and eases himself out of the lounge chair. He pauses to vomit into the swimming pool, then wipes his mouth with the back of his hand and heads toward the house. Marta turns off the weed eater and returns it to the garage.

I make my way to the office. This job is much different from my old one. I have a degree in social work and used to work at the DMV. Didn't mind the job, but it didn't pay squat. I feel around the back of the bookcase for the switch and flip on the light. As usual, there ain't nothing going on. The room is lined with floor-to-ceiling bookshelves and has a fax machine, Xerox copier, computer, and three-line phone system. I turn on the computer to check my e-mail. The nasty stench from the living room has managed to follow me. I hate working here. It's better when Travis stars in a movie and I can work alongside other professionals. Well, it's not like I actually *work*. I really only answer the phone and take messages, get him food or drinks whenever he asks, and order drugs from his dealer. If Travis wants company on the set, I make arrangements for his friends to visit. Mostly I hang out. Sometimes I help the production assistants with their jobs. Or I help the catering crew. Now that I think of it, that probably wasn't so good for my diet.

After his last movie, Travis took a few weeks off to chill, but a few weeks turned into six months. So now I'm here in this house with nothing but time on my hands. To keep busy, I usually read scripts submitted by Travis's agency, Outcome. In fact, there's ten piled on my desk right now, and those are just the ones I read *this* week. Every last one stank. Still, in the grand scheme of things, I can't complain much. Travis is a decent boss for someone five years younger than me. He's a little on the dumb side, but he's also harmless. I just wish he'd get himself some new friends.

There are no messages on the answering machine. Then again, people know better than to call Travis Trask before noon, whether he's here or not. I flip open the appointment book and the only thing scheduled for the week is a meeting on Thursday with his management. The phone rings.

"Hello?"

"Is Kecia Christy there?"

I don't recognize the voice, though I have a pretty good idea who it belongs to. "She's not in. May I take a message?"

"This is Joseph Sanders from the IRS. She can reach me at 376-4231."

"I'll let her know," I say and hang up. Damn! They tracked me down at work.

My stomach grumbles and my thoughts go right back to those donuts. I leave the office to join Marta on the back patio. She brings two cups of coffee and the Krispy Kreme box. In the pool, Frog's chunky vomit slick floats on top of the water. Thank Jesus the pool man's coming later. We sit down on the wrought-iron patio furniture and stare at the haze hanging over the San Fernando Valley. Marta opens the box. "Donut?"

"Sure." I reach across the table and help myself to a little something.

GRIFFIN

SOUTHERN CALIFORNIA in the spring is unparalleled: azure sky, sunshine, buoyant breeze, annual review for promotion and salary boost . . . It's the small things that make me content, although I sincerely hope that my raise and promotion will be anything but diminutive.

I turn off Sunset Boulevard and pull into the underground garage of the Gem Building. I head for one of six spaces marked JTE, which stands for Johnny Treadway Enterprises, and park next to the man's black Mercedes sedan. I grab my belongings and stroll into the building, careful not to spill the cardboard drink tray containing two cups of tea.

"Good morning!" It's the security guard, Stu. "Have you had a chance to read my script?"

I push the elevator button. "Yes, I have."

"Do you think Travis will like it?"

"I'm not sure it's right for him. We're trying to steer him away from snuff films."

Disappointment cascades over his face.

"But, hey," I say reassuringly. "That doesn't mean it wouldn't be right for someone else."

He nods. "Maybe another draft. You have a great day."

"You too, Stu," I say, and I step into the elevator.

Once the doors close, I shake my head and smirk. Everybody in this town has a screenplay. Unfortunately, most of them are atrocious—and those are the ones being produced. I couldn't possibly fathom all the rubbish that never gets beyond the preliminary stages. With current budgets routinely pushing past the $100 million mark, you'd think the studios could produce better product. But most of these high-budget movies seem to exist only to explore that ancient, unsolved mystery: how many ways can you blow things up and kick ass? I don't mind encouraging Stu, because everyone should pursue his or her dreams, no matter how unrealistic. My motivation may be slightly selfish, too, since you never know when you might unearth that diamond in the rough.

On the fifth floor, I proceed down a long hall, passing Trolley Records, Dr. Marcos Santos, D.D.S., and Bud & Bud, C.P.A. At Suite 525, I swing open the door and Lucy, the receptionist, greets me. She's Hispanic, in her forties, and the mother of three teenagers. She sneezes and grabs a tissue.

"Good morning, Griffin."

"Good morning." I place my briefcase on a stone-colored leather chair. "How long has he been here?"

She looks at her watch. "Eight minutes."

I hand her one of the cups. "It's called Wellness Tea."

"Ooh. What's in it?"

"Jasmine, ginseng, and flower extracts. Should zap the flu right out of your body."

"Mmmm. Smells good," Lucy says as she removes the lid. "Thank you."

"You're welcome," I wink. "You must get well because I don't know what I'd do without you. It's your radiant bonhomie that keeps me going."

"Oh, Griffin," she smiles.

I spin the plastic lazy susan where messages are kept. "Any calls?"

"Michaela called. Victoria fired Mary."

"You're kidding?"

I'm not surprised. After all, the poor girl had the misfortune of working for Victoria Rush. How long did this one last? A month? Three weeks?

I rub my chin. "The woman's incorrigible, like someone else we know."

"I know that's right," Lucy agrees.

"Would you mind calling *Variety* and have them run the classified?"

"I already took care of it."

"That's why I'm enamored of you." I pick up my tea and briefcase and approach the gargantuan door that separates the reception area from the rest of the office. "If you need me, you know where I'll be."

"Sure thing," Lucy smiles.

I push open the door with my backside and proceed straight to my desk. After putting down my things, I tiptoe toward Johnny's mammoth office, crane my neck, and listen. The only sound is the familiar hum of the Tropical Rays tanning bed. Knowing he'll be tied up for at least twelve minutes more, I sit down at my desk and glance at the calendar. I'm officially one month and one day away from my big raise and promotion. I'm more than ready to be promoted from assistant to a full-fledged manager. To say my tenure here has been grueling is an understatement.

What does a manager do? Defining the job in simple terms is difficult because of its protean nature. Main duties include troubleshooting all potential problems before they come up, handholding, giving counsel, and monitoring the other people each client employs. I'm here to make sure that all battles are won and that the best course of action is always pursued in the name of the client. In exchange for all this cosseting, I am rewarded with 15% of the client's gross salary. Actually, I don't receive the 15% because I'm not a manager—yet. At $300 a week, with zero benefits, I'm a handful of pocket change from utter indigence.

Searching for the next *big* thing takes up the majority of my spare time. I flip through *L.A. Weekly,* scanning each page carefully and jotting down notes with the Mark Cross pen my brother gave me for graduation. All of the information is recorded in a three-by-five notebook that is kept on my person. In it, I have the names and addresses of every venue in town where you can see plays, comedy, or alternative performances. Checking out something new at least once a week has become a priority. At a later date, I will return to observe those same artists to see if my hunch was correct. I must be 1000% certain before recommending anyone to Johnny Treadway, supermanager to the stars. Actually, "supermanager" might be a bit of an exaggeration. His constellation only consists of two stars: sitcom diva Victoria Rush and Hollywood's new wonder boy, Travis Trask. I discovered Travis in a one-act play in Venice. At the time, he was one bad day away from homelessness, and none too clean. Nevertheless, there was something special about him, a quiet energy beneath an Adonis guise. Currently I have my eye on another potential client. His name is Bart

Abelman and he's a stand-up comic. I caught his act at the The Improv on Melrose and was more than impressed. Perhaps the proverbial lightning can strike twice.

Johnny's voice bellows from his office. "Griffin!"

I grab my notepad and the appointment book and enter Johnny's domain. It's thirty feet long with récherché furnishings and a huge picture window looking out onto Sunset Boulevard. Johnny lies in his tanning bed, wearing blue plastic eye protectors and a Speedo thong. He has dyed-black, slicked-back hair, cheek implants to give his face more definition, and a perpetual tan, courtesy of the device that now entombs him.

"Spritz!" he says.

I grab the spray bottle filled with Evian and squirt him three times.

"I've got a question for you," he says.

"Shoot."

"I was riding behind a lesbo this morning and she had a big rainbow sticker in the back window. What does that mean?"

Aware of my sexual orientation since day one, Johnny has anointed me the doyen of homosexuality.

"How do you know she was gay? Maybe she likes rainbows."

"She had a bumper sticker that said, *Everybody cheer, I'm black and I'm queer.*" He shakes his head in amazement. "Can you imagine? She should put a bullet in her head."

Irascible and boastful bully that he is, nothing brings him more joy than this type of comment. I glance out the window. The morning haze has yet to burn off and everything appears monochromatic.

"You didn't answer my question," he says.

"I have no idea. But I can certainly find out for you."

"Somebody should know more about their heritage."

Johnny often refers to me as *"Somebody"*. Like when he says, *"Somebody* needs to get so-and-so on the line." Or, *"Somebody* needs to wash my car." Or, *"Somebody* needs to make a reservation . . ." I'm thinking, *Somebody should kick his Royal Highness's ass.*

The timer dings. I raise the lid as Johnny sits up and removes his eye protectors. He hands them to me and I offer him a maroon Ralph Lauren towel. He wraps it tightly around his tanned bottom and moves behind his grand, polished walnut desk. I'm not allowed to sit until invited. When he feels like it, he says, "Have a seat. What's on tap this week?"

I sit and open the appointment book. "You have a hot crème manicure at noon. Tomorrow you have an aromatherapy massage. On Wednesday you have a lunch meeting with Randall Blume, and Thursday you have a business meeting with Travis Trask. Friday, you're free."

"It's a busy week," he says as he leans back in the chair, places his hands behind his head, and shows off his pec implants. "I'm thirsty."

This is my cue to get up and walk over to the minifridge, twelve inches behind Johnny's chair. I remove a Capri Sun Wild Cherry fruit drink, puncture it with the attached straw, and squeeze the packet from bottom to top, pumping the drink into a Waterford crystal wine goblet. After handing it to him, over his left shoulder, I return to my seat.

He gulps half the beverage before asking, "What's the status with Travis?"

"He hasn't committed to any projects yet."

"Every studio in town is willing to give him twenty mil and the idiot can't make a decision?!"

"He's opting to take a break."

"A *break?* The kid's only been in three pictures!"

I try not to cringe when Johnny uses the word *kid.* Who did he think he was? Louis B. Mayer? He was right, though. Travis Trask had starred in only three films . . . but all had ridiculously low budgets and each of them made over $50 million, thanks solely to the appeal of our nineteen-year-old star.

"They *were* back-to-back," I offer.

"Doesn't he realize people will soon forget he exists?"

"I've explained that to him, Johnny. He says he's waiting for the right project."

He waves his arms around. "He wants to fucking party. Remember when DiCaprio went that route? He made two shitty movies and got fat and bloated."

Johnny props his elbows on the desk and wiggles his fingers in front of his face as if he were playing an imaginary clarinet. This is Johnny's deep-thinking ritual. His fingers move rapidly until he has an epiphany. Or a *thought*, anyway. And often a not-very-good thought. He slams both hands on the desk. "You have to talk to him. You're young. You can relate to him better, except when it comes to pussy, of course. Tell him he *has* to pick a project."

"Or what?"

"Why are you questioning me?" Johnny growls. "I have bills to pay."

Truth be told, Johnny loathes his clients. Once they've signed on the dotted line—for a minimum of three years—he passes the real work off to his underling: me. With virtually no responsibility, he has created quite the sinecure for himself.

He picks up a script that's lying on his desk. "Here's one. I read the coverage last night. It really moved me."

The words *Shotgun High* are written on the cover. I'm almost afraid to ask, but I ask anyway: "What's it about?"

"Remember that Colorado school shooting? Travis is perfect for one of the killers. Ashton Kutcher is considering the role of his friend. There's also a great little role for someone a few years older: the teacher who risks his life to save the kids."

I know what that means. Johnny wants to be in the movie. Ever since a large bribe bought him a walk-on role in Travis's last film, he has gone thespian.

"As intriguing as that project sounds, I thought the plan was to steer Travis into serious films," I say.

Obviously puzzled by my brashness, Johnny raises his eyebrows. They are bushy and unruly, with individual hairs fanning out in various directions. I suddenly recall that the "serious film" plan was my idea, not his.

"The plan is for me to make money. Lots of it. He can star in *Leprechaun 8* for all I care. I want my fifteen percent management fee, my producing fee, my consulting fee, and I want my SAG card—if there happens to be a part for me, of course."

In a sudden volte-face, I chirp, "Of course. I'll certainly show this script to Travis and see how he feels."

"For Christ's sake. Bribe him. Tell him the studio will throw him the biggest party he's ever seen. He can fly in all his friends. We'll get him blow, hookers, whatever it takes." He looks at my lap. "*Somebody* might want to jot this down."

"Travis prefers marijuana or mushrooms," I reply, and write "FUCK-ING PINHEAD" in big bold caps in my notebook.

"We must get this done. In this business, you have to keep working or they assume you died. That's something you might want to pass on to that little shit."

I nod my head and write "MOTHERFUCKER" on the pad.

"Speaking of money, did you go by the bank this morning?" he asks.

"Yes. The deposit slip's on my desk."

He shakes his head. "Call my broker and tell him to buy more IBM."

I jot down "BITE ME."

"Now, where are the ratings?" he asks.

I sift through my papers until I find the overnight Nielsen ratings sheet. "Victoria was last in her time slot again."

Johnny sighs and studies his fingers again. "How many weeks has it been?"

"Eight."

"It's bad enough they pulled her for sweeps. I was afraid of this. The broad's too old. Nobody gives a shit about Victoria Rush anymore. Hell, *I* don't give a shit about her anymore."

"I think she still has a loyal following."

"Well, if there was a *gay* demographic, that might matter."

"Oh, but there is," I quip. "Who do you think propelled *JAG* into the top twenty?"

He looks at me blankly. "These numbers make Travis all the more important to me," he says. "He needs to commit to something."

"Certainly."

He wipes his face with the edge of the towel. "Is there anything else?"

"Bart Abelman is on Leno tonight."

"Who?"

"The comic I told you about. I showed you his tape."

"I'm not interested in comedians."

I persist. "He's quite remarkable. He went up on a random showcase for the *Tonight* show and walked away with the gig. I think we should try to get him into the Aspen Comedy Festival. With enough attention, he has a shot at a development deal. There's a dearth of funny people out there."

"Look. Not everybody has what it takes to make it in this business. And comics are a dime a dozen. Besides, no one's been funny since Emo Phillips. And he's dead."

"Emo Phillips isn't dead."

Johnny's stunned. "He's not?"

"I think it would be worth your while to come to the showcase and check out Bart's show. I was right about Travis."

He waves me off. "I have no interest in comedians. They're all exactly the same: fucked-up Jewish guys who think they had lousy childhoods. Is there anything else?"

I glance at the appointment book. A woman's name is penciled in at nine o'clock that evening. "You have a date tonight at nine. I made reservations at Asia de Cuba."

A salacious grin crosses Johnny's lips. "What's her name again?"

"Volaria."

His eyes roll back in his head. "Vola- what?"

I enunciate carefully, "Vo-lar-ia."

"Why can't models have normal names?" He looks up at the ceiling, trying to place her. "Blonde with big tits?"

"Brunette with medium-sized breasts. You met her at that cancer benefit last week. She's twenty-two and originally from Memphis." When this doesn't register, I add, "Tennessee."

My comment draws a sharp rejoinder: "I know where fucking Memphis is."

I retrieve a Victoria's Secret catalog off an end table and flip through it until I find her picture. "Here."

Johnny stares at the long-limbed brunette. She's wearing a lilac lace teddy with stockings. "Oh, yeah."

In an attempt to jar his memory, I continue, "She goes to USC and is studying to be a veterinarian." He lifts the catalog close to his face and studies it.

"Is there something wrong?" I ask.

"I can see her bush." He tosses me the catalog. "Look, right there."

"Maybe it's a shadow."

Johnny snorts. "Shadow, my ass. You know, if you look close enough, you can sometimes see their nipples."

"I never knew that."

He sneers. "So you think this chick's hot?"

"She's a very attractive woman."

"She'd be hotter if she had a cock. That's what you're thinking."

"Actually, that wasn't what I was thinking at all."

"Yeah, sure. I know *your kind.* You only think about one thing."

"How would you know?" I snap, knowing full well that I'm treading on a precarious fault line.

His expression turns grim. "What did you say?"

Raise. Promotion. Raise. Promotion. I decide to back down. There's no sense in getting upset over an obtuse comment. I stand up quickly. "She's a beautiful girl. I'm sure you'll have a wonderful time."

He stares me down like a bull in a ring. "Anything else?"

I clear my throat. "That's pretty much your day in a nutshell."

"See! What did I tell you?" Johnny says. "You had to go and bring up *nuts.*" And, with a disgusted wave of the hand, he dismisses me.

Rachel

"THE WORKING TITLE is *The Days and Nights of Puerto Vallarta*," the weird girl says as she stands in front of the classroom. She's real skinny, has greasy hair, and wears wrinkled thrift shop clothing. I hate to judge a book by its cover, but I worry that she might be a heroin or crack addict. Of course, I've never actually seen a heroin or crack addict in real life, so I can't be completely sure. Or maybe she's one of those hippie types who noodles at Fish, smells like vitamins, doesn't shave, and only eats vegetables. There's lots of vegetarians out here, I guess because everybody's concerned about their health, being that it's Hollywood and all. I heard there's now these *really* radical vegetarians who avoid anything that comes from an animal, including milk and cheese. They're called *vegans*. Doesn't that sound like a *Star Trek* character?

I'm not the only one staring at the poor, weird girl. When she hands in her synopsis, the whole class can see that it's handwritten. It's supposed to be typed. I glance at my friend Maleek, the only black guy in the class. He wears one of those brown, green, and red African necklaces. He's shaking his head and grumbling, which is not unusual, since he pretty much gets annoyed with all white people, except me for some reason.

"Uh, Janice, it's a new millennium, how about typing the next thing you submit?" Professor Burrows says from the back of the classroom. So *that* was her name. Funny, she doesn't look like a Janice. I knew a girl called Janice in Sugarland. She was half-Indian. That's what she said, anyway. But then someone told me she just had a skin condition.

"I don't like machines," Janice says. "They besmirch the purity of the creative process."

Professor Burrows is not amused. "Then proceed. I cannot wait to discuss this brilliant piece of writing."

A few people chuckle. Burrows can be very sarcastic at times, which is not a good quality in a teacher. Still, I feel for him. He looks like the ugly guy from *Fargo*—my favorite character, bless his heart—and he hasn't come to terms with it. And none of his screenplays have ever been produced. He had a couple optioned, of course, but he has never made enough money as a writer to quit teaching. I think he is also disturbed by the fact that he doesn't even teach at a real university, like USC or UCLA. He teaches at Santa Monica College, which is just a community college, also known as thirteenth and fourteenth grade. But I don't think there's anything wrong with that. I think teaching is very honorable, at any level.

"This screenplay is about a love triangle between two women and a man," Janice begins. "I like to think of it as *Three's Company* meets *9 1/2 Weeks*, except all the characters are Mennonites."

"What's a Mennonite?" someone asks, which is helpful because I don't know, either.

"They're kind of like the Amish," Janice says. "Except they use electricity, drive cars, and listen to the radio."

Suddenly my screenplay about a deeply sensitive small-town Texas girl who abandons her alcoholic mother to try to make it as a writer in Hollywood doesn't seem all that bizarre.

Janice reads from her synopsis. "Unable to control her lesbian desires, Ruth coaxes Esther into having sex in the barn. Jebediah walks in. At first he is angry but soon finds himself getting aroused. He joins in and they all fall in love, but realize they must run away to avoid being shunned by their people. The three end up in Mexico, where they are accepted by the simple, lazy Mexican people, and they spend the rest of their lives in a bungalow on the beach, loving each other in perfect, harmonic convergence."

"This has Oscar written all over it," Professor Burrows says. "Any comments, class?"

Maleek raises his hand. "Are there any brothers in this movie?"

Just from the way he says it, I know he's getting ready to go off again.

"Not every story needs to be turned into a civil rights issue, Maleek," the professor says. "And there are so many things wrong with this idea that racism would be the last thing on the list."

But Maleek's on a roll. "Racism exists in every film made today. With the exception of the musical *Chicago*, which ain't a real movie anyway, look at the past few Oscar winners. *Lord of the Rings.* Not a brother in all of Middle Earth. *A Beautiful Mind.* Not a brother on the whole campus. *American Beauty.* Not a brother in the whole 'hood."

"Wait a minute," a guy in back volunteers. "There was a black guy in *Gladiator.*"

"And what was that brother playing?" Maleek snaps. "A damn slave!"

"I see," Professor Burrows remarks. "Affirmative action in the movies. Interesting concept."

"Every director has his own perspective. If he doesn't envision a black actor in a role, he shouldn't feel obligated to include one," a stocky guy in the first row says.

"That's exactly the kind of Aryan attitude I'm talking about," Maleek gripes.

The stocky guy stands up. "Are you calling me a skinhead?"

Before things get too hairy, Professor Burrows interrupts, "Perhaps you two can continue this debate on *Springer.*"

He strolls to the front of the classroom with a grim look on his face and motions for Janice to take her seat. He looks up at the ceiling for a while before speaking.

"As interesting as this discussion is, I have to say, it's all rather pointless. When you look at the big picture, you need to forget about your little 'triumph of the human spirit' projects. The soulless studio executives who call the shots don't give a shit about artistic merit, racial harmony, or goodwill to your fellow man." He paces back and forth, his voice getting louder with each step.

"Their target audience is a prepubescent video game addict with a perpetual hard-on. He decides what kind of films get made today. So give him car chases, explosions, blood, guts, gratuitous nudity, and The Rock." His face is red and his fists are clenched. "Any questions?"

No one in the class dares to raise a hand. I'm afraid to make eye contact with him. He has that crazed serial killer look like that Jesse Dahmer. The professor scans the room, looking into all of our faces, thinking long and hard about what he should say next. He's probably hoping we'll carry the advice with us forever.

"Oh, what's the point!" he says, near tears, then turns and gathers his things and leaves the classroom."

"I REFUSE TO believe what he said about the target audience," I tell Maleek on our way out of the class. "He makes it sound as if there are no good people in Hollywood."

"There aren't."

"That's not possible. I cannot accept that. I'm here because I love writing, and because I want to create something that genuinely touches people."

"I'm here for the M-O-N-E-Y. This is the only town in the world where your entire life can change on the basis of one screenplay. That kid in the mailroom at William Morris could be driving a Carrera Four tomorrow."

I don't understand his motivation, especially the part about the car. We all get stuck in the same traffic, right? Maleek wasn't tell me anything I didn't know already. I've read countless stories about people who started as nobodies and were now *somebody* in Hollywood, wheeling and dealing.

"Wanna grab a bite?" he says.

"Sorry," I say. "I can't. I need to find a job."

I PULL MY two-toned primer-and-gold Dodge Colt into a Union 76 gas station. The driver's-side door doesn't open, so I crawl over the emergency brake and exit from the passenger side. I reach into my front shorts pocket and give the attendant two dollars, then remove the wadded-up rag that functions as the gas cap and begin pumping. Today is my anniversary. California has been my home for exactly three months and I'm officially broke. Up until now, I've been living off the money I saved working at Starbucks in my hometown of Sugarland, Texas. I worked there for two years and honestly thought the money would last longer. But then again, Los Angeles is a whole 'nother world altogether. When I've pumped two dollars' worth of gas, I replace the nozzle and stuff the rag back in its place.

I get in the passenger side and crawl over my knapsack to get behind the wheel. The engine turns over several times before cranking. I notice a lady in a Lexus staring at me like I'm a freak. I'm used to the looks I receive for driving such an ugly car, a junkyard reject actually. Uncle Dwayne gave it to me for my sixteenth birthday. He's an auto mechanic and his specialty is building whole cars from random parts. This might explain the permanently locked driver's door. But, hey—five years and 100,000 miles later and the car is still running. Recently, though, parts have fallen off for no apparent reason. And it's loud. I think I lost part of the muffler on Pico Boulevard last week.

I still can't believe I'm a Los Angeleno. It's always been my dream to work in Hollywood. And all because of a little tiny movie called *Sugarland Express*, that was made before I was even born. It was Mr. Steven Spielberg's first feature film, and it put our quiet little hometown on the map. Imagine how excited everybody was when a whole crew arrived to film a *real* movie in our podunk town. Many of the residents got to be extras, and most of them are still talking about it to this day. Goldie Hawn sightings were also a very big deal, especially when she went to the Hairport to get her famous tresses trimmed.

I originally came to L.A. to attend the UCLA Film and Television School. God, isn't the name alone intimidating? *The UCLA Film and Television School.* It's really, really competitive. They only pick, like, fifty people out of, like, eight hundred. I've already applied once before and got turned down. So my plan was to move out here, take classes at a community college, and keep applying until I got in. Any day now I'll be hearing from them. Even if I do get accepted, the program doesn't start until the fall, so guess who needs a job? But there's one sticking point: I won't do just anything. I know it's not right to be picky when you're two cents away from starvation, but I can't help it. I definitely know I don't want to waitress, nanny, or return to Starbucks. It's not that I don't like Starbucks. I actually loved it. At Starbucks, you're not just an employee, you're a partner. And since I'd been Employee of the Month two times, which was twice as often as the next best employee, I was practically guaranteed a job at any Starbucks worldwide. At least according to my old manager. But no: I don't want to go back to coffee just yet. I'd feel like that was a giant backward step, and I want to move *forward*. So I scour the trades every Wednesday, when the new listings come out. I love saying "trades." It feels so *inside*. It's very important to know the lingo here in Tinseltown.

Which reminds me: today is Wednesday. I pull over at the next news-stand and start flipping through *Variety*. There's nothing there. Then I grab *The Hollywood Reporter*. The little Indian man who runs the newsstand is looking at me because I never buy any magazines from him, but I don't think he's going to say anything mean. Foreigners in this country have sure taken a beating since 9-11.

I quickly flip to the back of the *Reporter* and check out the ads. Right away, the words "personal assistant" jump out at me. They are in bold print above an ad that reads: *Help wanted by busy, high-profile Hollywood couple. Duties include answering telephones, faxing, running errands, and multitasking. Must have own car and valid driver's license. College student preferred.*

I suck in my breath. I know in my heart that this is it.

Michaela

I SPEND WAY TOO much time figuring out who to fuck to get ahead. I can't help it. I'm obsessed with becoming a successful actress. Sleeping my way to the top was never on my agenda. When I first came to L.A., I did everything on the up-and-up. Casting directors and producers hit on me all the time, but I refused their advances. I was not about to jeopardize my self-respect to get a part. It took me one year to figure out how the game is played. Once I started granting sexual favors, I started getting roles. So now my attitude is, BRING IT ON! If this is what it takes, then I'm ready for anything and everything.

I'm sitting in the office at Victoria's, awaiting instruction. The office is located in the basement of your standard mansion, the part that was formerly a wine cellar. For all the grandeur of the rest of the house, they sure scrimped when it came to the employees' digs. The room is ten-by-ten, dank, and dark. Sophisticated surveillance equipment takes up most of the room. Filling an entire wall, ten thirteen-inch television screens spy on various locations around the property. A computer, laser printer, fax machine, and elaborate phone and intercom system are crowded together on a desk the size of an end table. A mound of wires resembling an overturned colander of spaghetti bulges from an extension cord that hangs from the ceiling. A bookshelf conceals a safe where we keep Victoria's medication. There are enough pills inside it to run a M.A.S.H. unit. She had a little problem that two tours of duty at Betty Ford couldn't remedy. Sometimes, on really stressful days, I help myself to a Xanax or two.

I blow into my hands and rub them together. Did I mention the temperature? Lorne always wants his environment to be 60 degrees, and since the wine cellar is ten degrees cooler than the rest of the house, I'm forced to wear a parka. I rub my arms together and resist the urge to put on my hood. I take out my compact to put on some Chap Stick. I still scare myself with this disguise. My fake brown teeth are horrid and the glasses are a little too *Tootsie-ish*. Wearing the disguise enables me to keep working here. If I looked like my normal fabulous self, Lorne would be all over me. I'd fuck him if I thought it would get me somewhere. But since it won't, I don't need any distractions. I need this job. It's only ten bucks an hour, but it pays my cheap rent. It's hard to imagine I left Park Avenue to live in a studio above my landlord's garage in Mar Vista. I apply the Chap Stick and check to see if there are any more lines on my face. The phone rings. I pick up my headset. "Hello?"

"Michaela?" asks the panic-stricken voice of Mary Jane Gay, Victoria's latest publicist.

"A&E will not do a *Biography* on Victoria," she says.

This development is not good. The producers have repeatedly snubbed Victoria. "They've done Meredith Baxter, for Christ's sake!" she's fond of saying. And I must admit that I see her point.

"They have all their shows for the rest of the year. They said they couldn't even consider her until maybe next year."

I pinch the bridge of my nose. "Consider her?"

"On the other hand, Lifetime's on board. They want to do an *Intimate Portrait*. That's good, right?"

The telephone wire seems to crackle with her nervousness. Mary Jane's days are numbered. Victoria has been trying to get A&E to do her life story for as long as I've been here. She's already gone through five publicists. And she thinks Lifetime—or Vagina Vision, as she calls it—is the network of last resort. She will not be pleased.

"Tell her I'm sorry," Mary Jane says desperately. "And tell her I'll keep trying."

"I'll let Victoria know," I say, and I reach into the safe for my first Xanax of the day.

When I hang up, Lorne's assistant, Courtney, comes into the office. She's barely twenty-one and already has the breasts of a forty-year-old woman with five kids.

"I am so sick, sick, sick, and tired of Victoria's crap!" she huffs and flings herself into a chair.

"We'll have someone hired by the end of the week."

"She's just soooo mean. Poor Lorne. I don't know why he stays married to her. She's old and icky. He could do way better."

I nod my head.

She throws her hands in the air. "I mean, I don't get it. He says he wants a divorce but he hasn't done anything about it!"

I cock my brows. "He told you he wants a divorce?"

She knows she's revealed something she wasn't supposed to. Her face turns pink. "Uh, no. I'm just guessing. I mean, why *wouldn't* he want a divorce?"

"And you think this why, exactly?"

She looks at me crossly. "I just do, is all."

"Where is Lorne?" I ask.

She glances at her watch. "He's with *her* right now. But we're supposed to go shopping later."

"Shopping?"

"He needs some new clothes. I'm going to help him pick them out."

"I see."

She stands. "I don't know what's keeping him. I better go find out."

As she marches up the stairs, I roll my eyes and decide to go outside and get a breath of fresh air. I pass the tennis court, black-bottomed pool with an elaborate waterfall rock formation, gazebo, and koi pond, which is home to ten speckled goldfish the size of salmon. I take off my parka and sit down on a wrought-iron bench in the English garden, remove my glasses and headset, and pull my hair out of the ponytail and shake it out. I remove my long-sleeved Oxford shirt and sit there in my tank top. I'm thinking about something kinky that I can do to get my next gig when Lorne walks by.

"Michaela?"

I quickly put my glasses back on.

"Can I help you?" I say.

He leers at me for at least thirty seconds before saying, "I had no idea how attractive you were."

Shit! He's going *Ah-nold* on me. I put my shirt back on and start buttoning it up.

He walks over to me. "No, I mean it. Take off those glasses."

Having no choice but to geek it up, I squint at him like Mr. Magoo.

"You have beautiful eyes. Have you ever thought about LASIK surgery?"

I scrunch up my face and resist the urge to use a weird voice. "I can't. My corneas are too sensitive."

His eyes have already undressed and molested me even though I'd give Urkel a run for his money.

"Do you work out?"

I force myself to turn red and snort, "No."

"I bet you've got a great body. But you hide it under all those clothes."

I cover my mouth like I'm embarrassed.

"Maybe we can get together sometime. I'll take you shopping."

"Okay," I say and give him a big wide smile that reveals all of my stained teeth. Startled by the hideousness of my mouth, he jumps back and tramples a row of geraniums, lady's mantle, and catmint. Suddenly he's not so interested in getting together with me.

Courtney walks up. "Lorne!"

He shoots her a look. "Are you ready?"

Once they're gone, I reach into my pocket for my cigarettes and light up a smoke. I can finally relax . . . until Victoria needs something. And sure enough, right on cue, her voice booms over the intercom, echoing into the farthest reaches of the property. I throw my cigarette down and head toward the house. I'm going to break the bad news about *Biography*, and I'm not looking forward to it. My big regret is that I didn't pocket another Xanax. Shit.

GRIFFIN

T HE VALET at Chaya Brasserie is not impressed with Johnny's $100,000 black Mercedes. I've chauffeured him to the restaurant for his lunch meeting with Randall Blume, an Outcome agent extraordinaire. As Johnny exits his chariot, he's greeted by the maître d', Don Hardy, a man so plugged in he's a fire hazard.

"Good afternoon, Mr. Treadway," Don beams.

Johnny's rule for conversing is simple. He only speaks to celebrities and studio heads. Everyone else gets ignored, and Don is no exception. He fervently scans the scene for Randall Blume, but to no avail. Their appointment was for noon. A cursory glance at his watch confirms 12:15. Johnny purposely arrives late to all meetings. He believes that arriving first puts one at a decided disadvantage in any negotiation.

He glares at me. "Where is he?"

Don intervenes. "May I be of assistance?"

Johnny looks at Don with curiosity and loathing. He can't believe the nerve of this peon! How dare he address him?

"He had a noon appointment with Randall Blume," I explain. I whip out my cell phone and begin dialing.

Johnny's cold shoulder does not deter Don. "Would you like to be seated, Mr. Treadway? As soon as Mr. Blume arrives, I'll show him to your table."

Johnny would rather have rectal surgery than sit alone at a table. Men in power are never alone. "We'll wait at the bar," I say.

"If he's not here in five minutes, he's fired," Johnny informs me. "There're some pricks at CAA who would love to rep Travis."

The only person who can fire Randall is Travis Trask, but this doesn't stop Johnny from making idle threats. Johnny stalks to an area of the bar where no one will notice he's by himself.

"I see Mr. Treadway is his usual charming self," Don says. "And I thought Ovitz was an asshole."

I nod, the phone glued to my ear. Jeb answers on the second ring.

"Where is he?" I ask.

"The jacklick's not there yet?" Jeb asks.

"Not yet."

"Hold on. I'll call him on the other line."

Johnny tries his best to be inconspicuous as he stands next to a ficus plant. He waves me over.

"I'm on hold," I mouth. He snaps his fingers and points to the floor as if telling an animal to heel. I swagger over, coolly pretending I wasn't summoned.

"Send Mr. Weinstein one of whatever he's drinking," Johnny mumbles. Across the bar, Harvey Weinstein chats with another man. I instruct the bartender and watch as he carries out my wishes. Harvey looks at the bartender, then glances at us with disdain. It seems that Peter Biskind's highly critical book has done nothing to alter Harvey's undisguised contempt for humanity.

Johnny smirks and holds up his demitasse. "What's he saying?"

One of my many talents is reading lips. As a child I always wanted to know what the adults were whispering about, so I began watching intently. As time passed, this little game became almost Pavlovian. Unfortunately, I made the mistake of telling Johnny about this gift, and he often calls upon me to perform.

Harvey utters to his friend, "Who the hell is that?"

The friend smiles and lifts his glass. "I have no idea."

Johnny murmurs, "Well?"

"They have no idea who you are," I say.

"Fat bastard," Johnny grimaces as he turns around and throws back the rest of his drink.

Jeb clicks back over. "He's out front."

"Thanks." I turn around and see the agent enter the restaurant.

The intrepid Randall Blume floats in with his trademark shit-eating grin. It's a look conveying he knows something you don't, which is probably true but still monumentally effective. He looks like someone's accountant rather than one of the most puissant agents in town. He's wearing an immaculately pressed navy Armani suit, Gucci loafers, and Dolce & Gabbana titanium-rimmed glasses. At the age of thirty, he's already a member of the Hair Club for Men.

I meet Randall halfway. He smiles and extends his hand. "Is he pissed?"

I shake his hand. "Yep."

"Good." Randall winks and makes his way to the bar. The two men greet each other like they're long-lost buddies: all smiles, handshakes, and slaps on the back. After the hellos, they preen like peacocks admiring each other's plumes.

"Looking good, Johnny." Randall smiles. "Nice suit."

"Nice is the wrong word. Giorgio Armani, black label. Five grand."

Randall fingers his lapel. "Prada. Seventy-five hundred dollars. Who's your guy?"

"Pepe from Barney's," Johnny says proudly.

Randall frowns. "I had to give up on Pepe. He was always trying to dress me in passé designers. I think he still wears Obsession."

Visibly alarmed, Johnny feigns indifference. "Who do you go to now?"

"Pablo, at Prada."

Don interrupts the floor show to guide them to a primo table. Johnny glides about the room like Jesus walking on water. He's glad-handing, winking, and promising to do lunch with those who matter and ignoring those who don't. I take a seat at the bar with an unobstructed view of both men and order a club soda.

Don returns and sits down beside me. "Hey, Griffin."

"How's it going?"

"You know, the usual. Shootin' hoops with Nelly, gamblin' with Affleck."

"You're a busy man."

"You're telling me." He smiles and leans in. "But listen. I've got a great idea for Travis. It's pretty big and I don't want to share it with just anyone."

Like a million other changelings, Don wanted to produce—the best paid, least skilled job in the biz. I sip from my drink. "What's your idea?"

He drags his bar stool closer and whispers, "Remember how popular *Shakespeare in Love* was? What about *Hitler in Love*? Suppose he was a charming young man—sans mustache—who was desperately in love with a woman he couldn't have? And here's the kicker. She's Jewish."

I raise my eyebrows. "So the Holocaust was the result of unrequited love?"

He slaps his hands on the bar. "Exactly!"

"As intriguing as that sounds," I say, "I don't think that will go over too well in this town."

"You're right," he says, nodding unhappily. "Too many Hebes. Well, I'll keep thinking."

"You do that, Don."

AFTER GORGING on organic baby lettuce salads, Johnny and Randall settle into their postprandial business chat. They gossip about weekend grosses, what studio head's job is in jeopardy, and who's fucking whom. Before long, their conversation becomes vapid. Or, rather, *more* vapid.

"So what else you got for me?" Johnny asks listlessly.

"How's Victoria?" Randall asks.

Johnny grimaces. "About to be canceled. The old gray mare ain't what she used to be."

"No doubt."

"Where's some of that Hollywood age discrimination when you need it?" Johnny waves his hand in front of him like he's clearing a bad smell. "Let's talk about Travis."

Randall smiles. "I've got the inside track on a couple of projects that would be perfect for him."

"Such as?" Johnny asks, glancing around the room. He makes eye contact with Martin Scorsese and smiles.

"A prequel to *The Last Emperor*. Everyone's very excited about it."

Johnny raises his eyebrows. "Everyone?"

"Only those that know, of course," Randall says as he backpedals, which pleases Johnny to no end. Retreating is a loser's defense.

An ebullient Randall continues, "It has everything. Sweeping epic, exotic locale, costumes, foreign accents, tons of blood."

"What's it called?"

"*Next to the Last Emperor*."

"It's not really moving me. What else ya got?"

I can see the follicles on Randall's head loosen up. He knows what Johnny's getting at. He's holding out for a project that has a part for him. "There's a meteoroid movie being developed right now."

"Meteoroid?" Johnny repeats.

"A meteoroid threatens to destroy Earth and a group of experts are sent into space to try and divert it into a black hole."

Johnny resists the urge to wriggle his fingers. He never flutters his hands in public. Definitive sign of weakness. "Hmm. Certainly sounds original."

"It's called *Fire in the Hole*."

Johnny slaps his hand on the table and laughs, "Sounds like this redhead I know."

Randall chortles as if he's actually amused, then continues, "It'll be the event movie of next summer, a genuine tent pole. We're talking big budget, big special effects, big marketing campaign—and action figures across the board." He pauses to let that sink in and then goes for the kill. "Lots of good secondary parts, too."

Johnny's fingers waver ever so slightly. He imagines what he'd look like as an action figure. G.I. Joe would have nothing on him.

"We're thinking Travis for the lead, with maybe Catherine Zeta-Jones to co-star."

"Are you fucking kidding me? She's old enough to be his mother. Let's get that tasty little thing from *Pirates of the Caribbean*."

Johnny glances around the room again and exhales. An action-packed extravaganza is the project to launch his career as an actor. As a featured player, he'd surely be involved in action sequences. He'd insist on doing all his own stunts. If Steven Seagal could do them, so could he. After all, Seagal was just an aikido instructor before he was handed his first movie—thanks to Ovitz, his least talented student—and went on to stultify audiences the world over with his irrepressible talent.

Randall sees the wheels turning in Johnny's brain. If the producers want Travis, they'll have to cast this self-centered prick. Naturally they'd balk, but they'd have the youngest number-one box office star. Money in the fucking bank.

Johnny restrains a smile. Never let them know how much you like anything. "Get me a script."

BACK IN THE car, Johnny says excitedly, "We've got to get Travis in *Fire in the Hole*."

I glance at him in the rearview mirror. "Ashton's not available?"

"They want Travis. This is *our* movie for *our* client."

The man is so transparent.

"Tell Travis about it today," he says. "Get him to commit on a pitch."

What else am I going to get him to commit on? There's no script.

"I'll do my best," I say. Then I realize that Johnny has already forgotten about that Other Really Important Project. He has the attention span of a gnat. "What about *Shotgun High*?"

"Fuck *Shotgun High*," he says.

"Done," I say.

"And get me an appointment with Pablo at Prada, today if possible."

JEB PICKS UP on the first ring. "Yeah?"

"*Fire in the Hole*? You've got to be kidding me." I'm leaving the parking garage in my own car after dropping Johnny off.

"Sounds like a porn flick about a redhead with a nuclear pussy."

"Who came up with this piece of crap?"

"Bob Bush. He thinks he has a twist. Stay away from the old farts: Affleck, Damon, Will Smith, and get a younger cast."

"Naturally. Well, Johnny wants you to get a copy of it to Travis, ASAP."

"A copy of what?" Jeb asks. "There's no script."

"Isn't there a treatment? An outline?"

"No. Right now it's just a title."

"Can you write a page of fake coverage?"

"I don't know. I'll clear it with Bob."

"It doesn't have to be very deep. *Action star saves the world*, gets the girl, blah blah blah. Just enough to get him excited."

"Okay," Jeb says, then lowers his voice to a conspiratorial whisper. "Listen, I found out about a hot new independent. They're finally making *Catcher in the Rye*."

"You're kidding?"

"A friend of a friend is producing. He knows Salinger's great-nephew. And guess who would be great for the lead?"

I've gotta hand it to that big lunkhead. This is definitely worthy of our client.

Kecia

$\mathbf{I}$'M KICKING IT on the patio with a couple of chocolate iced crullers when the phone rings. "Hello?"

"Kecia, it's Griffin. I'm on my way."

I swallow quickly and look at the time. It's 1:40. "Okay," I say but it comes out "Omkay."

"How is our young star doing?" Griffin asks.

"Had another party last night."

"Did he have spend-the-night company?"

"Don't he always?"

Griffin chuckles. "Aah. To be young, good-looking, rich, and famous."

"Must be nice," I mumble.

"What are you talking about? You're all of those things and more."

I wonder if the *and more* bit refers to my weight, but I let it pass. Griffin's not like that. "I'm not famous," I say. "My daddy was. And if I was rich I wouldn't need this crappy job."

"Ouch!"

Today my horoscope said, *"There have been a lot of ups and downs in your financial affairs and you'd probably welcome a little stability."* Ain't that the damn truth?! The sliding-glass door opens and Marta steps out, shaking her head. Two miniature dice hang from her lobes. "Mr. Travis is up."

"Good news, Griffin," I say. "The man is conscious."

Crackling static invades our conversation. "See you when I get there."

I hang up and lick the donut crumbs off my fingers. Already had two and my stomach hasn't stopped grumbling. Those donuts got a spell on me. I found out there's about fifteen grams of fat in each one, give or take a few grams, depending on the *crème* and chocolate involved. Already ate two, so that's thirty grams, the recommended daily amount of fat for a dieter. If I eat one more, I'll be up to forty-five. That's not so bad because I'd still be under the recommended daily amount of fat for a nondieter: sixty grams. Technically, I'm not overeating as long as I don't eat nothing else for the rest of the day. I reach for another original glazed.

On my way back to the office, I pass the master bedroom and hear Travis and some girl talking about Eminem.

"Hey, Kecia!" Travis yells.

I stop right where I am, shove the rest of the donut in my mouth, and wipe my hands on my pants. "Mm-hmm?" I mumble, trying to gulp it down.

"Am I doing anything today?" he asks.

The bedroom door is cracked open and there he is having sex with the girl doggie-style. She grasps the headboard tightly.

I clear my throat. "Griffin's on his way."

His tight round butt shines like a piece of Chinette. He looks over his shoulder, "What for?"

I quickly step out of the doorway. "To talk about some projects."

"Do we have any Mountain Dew?"

"Yes," I say. Miss Thang starts moaning in pleasure and I'm dying to sneak another peek, but I can't bring myself to do it. I've seen enough already.

"Hey, Kecia. One other thing."

"Yeah?" I refuse to look in the room. Especially since they both start making grunting noises as their booties smack together loudly.

"Why don't you tell me later," I say.

"No!" he shouts. Then changes it to "Yes!"

The smacking flesh on flesh gets louder and quicker until suddenly Travis groans like a wounded boar and collapses on the bed next to her.

I exhale deeply and try to breathe normally. For some reason, my body's tingling all over. It's been a long-ass time, but you can't have the big O listening to somebody else get freaky. Or can you? I should walk away, but I can't move. My feet feel superglued to the floor.

"Kecia. Can you bring me the bong? It's on the coffee table."

"Sure," I say, relieved my feet can move again.

As I walk away, I hear him tell the girl, "That was almost good as The Viper at Magic Mountain."

T<small>RAVIS SITS ACROSS</small> the coffee table from Griffin and me. He's resting his elbows on his knees and holding his chin in his hands. He's wearing nothing except a pair of plaid Joe Boxers. It don't take a genius to figure out why this boy is plastered in every young girl's bedroom worldwide. He's not only phat, he is PHINE. He put the *mack* in Mack Daddy. But there's one drawback: too much sex, drugs, and rock and roll have really begun to mess him up. His skin is pasty and he has dark circles under his glassy, bloodshot eyes. His hay-colored bangs stick straight up off his forehead.

"Have you read any scripts that you like?" Griffin asks.

I grunt. As if Travis reads anything but liner notes on his favorite CDs. And he has trouble with *those*.

"Not really," Travis mumbles and reaches for a purple glass bong on the table in front of him.

Griffin looks at me. He's just as fine. He has gray-blue eyes and a sexy smile. And he's always wearing a sharp suit and tie. It's no secret I've been crushing on him for a long time. I feel a tingle down there. I don't know what's going on, but my hormones are all in an uproar.

"There's a project I think you would be great for," Griffin says.

Travis opens a large round Tupperware bowl and takes out a pinch of weed. The piney, skunky smell is so strong that Griffin and I both wrinkle our noses. He extends the bowl toward us. "Cannabis Cup?"

"What?" Griffin asks.

"This shit is the 1999 Cannabis Cup winner. You know, from Amsterdam. It rocks."

"No, thank you," Griffin says.

"Ya sure?"

"I'm sure," Griffin says seriously. He probably never touched a drug in his life. "Like I was saying, there's a project that you would be great for. It's called *Catcher in the Rye*."

Travis loads the weed into the bong bowl. "Baseball movie?"

Griffin makes a face. "No. It's one of the classic books of all time. Everybody's read—"

"Do you know where my lighter is?" Travis asks, paying Griffin no mind. I locate it and slide it across the table. Travis places his mouth over the bong and lights the bowl. He inhales deeply and offers the bong to Griffin.

Griffin holds up both hands. "No. Really. I like it here, on Planet Earth." Then he gets on with his pitch. "As I was saying, *Catcher in the Rye* is the quintessential teen angst story. It's a day in the life of Holden Caulfield, the very day he gets expelled from prep school. For an independent, it has a pretty decent budget. And Miramax is producing, which is both the good news and the bad."

Travis takes another hit. I watch the smoke travel up the bong en route to his lungs.

"Gwyneth is considering a cameo," Griffin says.

This doesn't register with Travis, either.

Then Pokey decides to strut his sorry ass in the room. He's also in boxers, but his hair is wet, indicating a recent shower or—at the very least—a plunge into the swimming pool. Tiny droplets of water still dot his shoulders. "Hello, Pokey," Griffin says.

Pokey gives Griffin a chin nod and Travis a two-fingered high five, then plops down on the couch next to him and takes the bong. "Those chicks leave?"

"Yeah," Travis says.

"I'm not going to think about pussy for another hour," Pokey says. He takes a big hit. "I mean it. I know I can do it."

Griffin clears his throat. "Travis, we're in the middle of a meeting. Maybe Pokey can wait in the other room until we're finished."

"It's okay, he's cool," Travis says. Pokey starts coughing and Travis pounds on his back. "Dude, you all right?"

Griffin waits for Pokey to settle down before speaking. "The project I just described is a very hot property right now."

"What project?" Pokey asks.

"Some catcher movie," Travis says.

"Baseball blows," Pokey says, which sends Travis into a spasm of laughter. He loves his little buddy.

Griffin smiles uneasily. As a Gemini, he needs mental challenges to keep him stimulated on the job. Maybe he *should* try some Cannibus Cup. That way he can at least be on the same wavelength as Beavis and Butt-head.

"That idea's really not my scene," Travis says.

"It sucks, man," Pokey agrees.

Griffin looks at me again. I can tell they're getting on his last nerve. "Why don't you tell me what your scene *is*?"

"Something with guns or X-box," Pokey says, blowing smoke at Griffin.

Griffin waves the smoke out of his face.

"Dude, I've been meanin' to show you." Travis points excitedly toward the carpet in front of the TV. "See that worn-down spot on the carpet? I thought I must've put somethin' heavy there until it hit me: that's my damn butt print! I been playin' so much *Grand Theft Auto* I've left my ass outline on the floor."

Travis and Pokey howl uncontrollably, spitting and coughing.

Griffin waits, at a loss. Travis takes another hit off the bong. He holds the smoke and rasps, "I like gangs."

"Like the Bloods and the Grips," Pokey chips in.

"*Crips*," I say, correcting him.

"You know, like that Colorado school shooting where the dudes blew away all their classmates? I could play one of the killers."

Pokey sets the bong on the table. "Dude. *I* could play the other guy."

Travis smiles. "Yeah. You and I can shoot up everybody in the cafeteria and library." Then he turns to Griffin. "Pokey wants to be an actor."

Griffin forces himself to smile. "That's wonderful."

"I gotta look out for my main man," Travis says and thumps his chest in a ceremonial hip-hop Hail Caesar. I'll never understand why white boys wanna be black.

Griffin smiles big and fake. "Let me make a few calls. Maybe someone would like to develop this idea. I'll see what I can come up with."

Travis and Pokey high-five each other. I glance over at Griffin, my eyebrows raised.

"So what ever happened to those dudes in real life?" Pokey asks.

"They killed themselves," Griffin says.

"Can we change the ending in the movie version?" Travis asks.

"YOU'RE HUMORING HIM again," I say to Griffin as I walk him to his car.

Griffin shakes his head, "No, I'm not. Take a look at this." He reaches into his briefcase and hands me a script called *Shotgun High.*

I shake my head. "Damn."

"And that's not the best part. I was supposed to convince Travis to do a meteoroid movie."

"Say what?"

"You know, meteoroid threatens Earth, Earth fights back."

"Haven't they done that already?" I ask.

"They've done a comet and an asteroid."

"Isn't that the same thing?"

Griffin nods. "Can you believe Johnny wants him to do that piece of crap?"

"What are you going to do?"

"You heard Travis. He wants to shoot people."

"But you said he has the potential to be a really good actor."

"He does," Griffin says, sighing. "He has a lot of talent. I'm trying to help him make the right decisions, but I can't force him to do anything he doesn't want to do."

"A *comet* movie?" I repeat.

"Meteoroid," Griffin corrects. "My hands are tied. Johnny wants him in this film. And whatever Johnny wants—"

"Johnny gets."

"Bingo," he says. "Put me down for next week, same time. I'll wait till then to tell Travis about *Fire in the Hole.*"

I make a face. "That's what they're calling it? That's jacked."

"Tell me about it."

I'm looking at Griffin's teeth. He has straight square teeth that look like white peppermint Chiclets. Damn. Why are all the fine ones gay?

"You're getting your raise in a month and you don't want to piss any-one off," I say.

"You got it," Griffin says, brushing his cheek against mine. Geminis are always on the run.

Again I get the tingle.

"Are we still getting together this week?" I ask desperately. What's wrong with me? I need to chill.

Griffin climbs into his car. "Oh, sure, Thursday. Same time, same place."

"Great," I smile.

I watch him drive away, then walk down to check the mail.

"Nice guy," a voice comes from the bushes.

I roll my eyes as Lou steps out. He's got an even bigger telephoto lens than he had the day before. "He works for that hot-shit manager, what's his name? Johnny Treadway. Right?"

"Maybe." I open up the mailbox and retrieve a packet of coupons and a *High Times* magazine.

"He also manages Victoria Rush."

I close the mailbox. "Why don't you stake her out? She's a big star."

"America doesn't want to see pictures of her tired ass. They want to see pictures of my boy."

I tsk. "So now you're the voice of America?"

"I'm just tellin' you what sells."

I start up the driveway.

"Have you thought any more about my proposition?"

"There's nothing to think about," I say without even turning around.

"There's no way I can persuade you?"

I give him the hand and keep walking. But the brother's relentless. "Hey, you never told me what sign you are."

I don't answer.

"Come on, girl. We might be meant for each other."

His tired banter was getting as old as that *Wassup?* business. "Doubt it."

"What's a man gotta do?"

I turn around. "Stay out of my grill."

"Have a good day, then," he shouts.

I don't care how charming he tries to be. He's still the enemy. That's something I can't forget.

Polaroid C20786A08611A

Jeb.

INT. OUTCOME AGENCY—EARLY EVENING

It's 6:30 P.M. Most people have called it a day. But not me. Jacknut is still here, getting a manicure, and I can't duck out until he does. I pass the time filling out YOU'RE FIRED postcards. There's a long list of clients who are about to become nonclients. The postcards are actually quite personable. CLOSE-UP on a stack of postcards. They're preprinted with one simple line. _We regret to inform you that the agency is letting you go._ In other words, you suck, you have no talent, we couldn't make money off you, have a nice fucking life.

After Ming finishes buffing Jacknut's nails, she comes to me for payment. She's a nubile Mulan-looking chick. I wink when I hand her the envelope of bills. She blushes and looks down at the floor. The veins would make her cry. A geisha fantasy fills my head and I get instantly stiff. Then I realize I only have a few moments to talk to Blume before he leaves.

CUT TO:

INT. BLUME'S OFFICE—EARLY EVENING

I rap on his door. "Got a sec?"

Blume immediately jumps up and begins putting items into his brief-case, careful not to mess up his nails. He knows I'm going to ask about my script. He's got that look in on his face. The one that says, "Haven't read your spec and never intend to."

"I actually need to talk to you as well," he says.

This takes me off guard. Maybe he's already read it. I decide to go ahead and ask. "Have you read my script?"

"Yes, I have."

He pulls it out of his bag, avoiding eye contact with me. Not a good sign.

"And?"

He hands it to me. "Unfortunately, I know of three projects about the same subject."

I clench my fists ever so slightly. "You know of *three* stories about the only white man to play in the Negro leagues?"

Blume nods his Q-ball head. "It's very *in* right now. This whole reverse-discrimination thing. Was it registered at the Guild?"

I squeeze my fists tighter. "No. I was waiting for your feedback. I wanted to submit the cleanest possible copy."

He seems relieved. "Every rookie learns the hard way. Get it regis-tered. Screenplays get stolen all the time."

"Stolen? You're the only person who's seen my script."

"Jeb, I'm talking to you as a friend: you've gotta be careful in this town."

My biceps flex and my neck tenses up. He's a lying prick. He must have noticed the flexing because a worried look crosses his face. I can be an in-timidating motherfucker when I want to be.

He closes his briefcase and walks around his desk. "There's something else we need to talk about, and it's not very pleasant," he says. "I'm sure it's harder for me than it is for you."

"What?"

He glances at his freshly polished nails. "I was going to wait until to-morrow, but I might as well do it now."

I could bite his nose off. Chew it up and spit it back in his fucking face.

"We're letting you go."

I'm not sure I heard him correctly. "Excuse me?"

"We had a partners' meeting this morning. We have to make some cut-backs. We're going to restructure. Unfortunately, that means we have to lay off some assistants." Here he pauses for a self-disparaging chuckle. "You know, some of us are completely spoiled. We could do a lot of this stuff ourselves."

No shit, cocksucker.

Then he's back in serious mode. "But you're not the only one. Parker King's assistant is also being let go."

"Because of cutbacks?" I repeat and resist the urge to choke him.

"I'm sorry, Jeb. You were a great assistant." He slaps my shoulder on the way out of the office. Then he turns around. "And hey, if you need a reference, I'm there for you, buddy."

Polaroid C20786A08611A

Rachel

I KINDA FEEL sorry for the people who work at Kinko's. I go over to fax my résumé and of course the place is more crowded than *TRL* when Britney's on. I have to get in line behind like twenty other people, and none of the customers are being particularly patient. I wish they understood that working at Kinko's is not like the lifelong goal of Trixie and Langley, the only two people behind the counter. (They both have name tags: it's company policy.) And maybe Trixie shouldn't be on the phone all this time, but it looks to me like she's getting some bad news. Sure enough, she hangs up and hurries toward the back in tears.

"Where the hell's she going now?" some grumpy bald guy says. Everyone in line starts moaning and groaning.

Langley is trying to enlarge a picture of somebody's pet iguana, and he's having technical problems. This could take a while. But wait. Here's Trixie now. You can tell how bad she's been crying because she has black eyeliner boogers in the corners of both eyes. I want to rush over and hug her, but there are so many people in front of me that I'll probably get lynched before I reach the counter.

As I wait in line, I try to think positive thoughts about the job I'm applying for. And by the time I reach the counter, I am totally full of positive feelings. I am especially nice to Trixie. When she is done faxing my résumé, I smile a big smile and say, "You hang in there, okay? Tomorrow's another day."

"What the fuck's your problem?" she says.

I TURN DOWN Fifth Street and park under the little carport adjacent to my apartment building. I'm supposed to hear from UCLA any day now, but as I approach the mailbox I try not to get my hopes up. It could be today, tomorrow, the next day, or the day after that. It could be any day at all, come to think of it. Or it could be *never*. Still, when I check the mailbox and find nothing, it hurts. I feel strangely emptied out.

I fight the feeling and march up the rickety stairs and put my key into the lock. That's when I hear sex sounds coming from inside my apartment. That's my roommate, Dan. He's a wonderful boy, but he has some issues.

I knock on the door. "Dan! I'm home!"

"Don't come in!" he hollers.

I hear a pair of bodies scrambling around for a few secs, followed by the slamming of his bedroom door. Once inside, I see all the evidence of a seduction: four empty bottles of Zima on the coffee table, along with two of those midget candles. And ugh! An empty pack of Marlboro Lights next to an overflowing ashtray.

Dan's undies are on the couch. I move them aside and sit down and check my watch. Three more hours until Stone—that's Stone Phillips from *Dateline NBC*. I have a HUGE crush on him. He's so handsome! And smart! And tall!

I flip on the TV and *Ricki Lake* is just starting. *Go Ricki! Go Ricki!* I love that song.

Twenty minutes later, Dan comes out of his room with just a towel wrapped around his waist. "Sorry about the mess," he says.

"I thought we weren't going to let anyone smoke in the house." That was one of the House Rules. The other two were no eating or tooting on the couch.

"But this chick looks so sexy when she smokes. You should see it."

The door to Dan's room opens and a woman who looks like a forty-year-old version of that Blondie singer tiptoes into the room. Her makeup's smeared and she's not a real blonde because a two-inch dark stripe runs down her head like a skunk's. Dan escorts her outside and returns a few minutes later.

"How long have you known this one?" I ask without looking at him. I want him to know I'm very disappointed. I want him to know that I expect more from him.

He retrieves his undies. "About three hours. She bought some cologne for her husband."

I swear! He's just like Richard Gere in *American Gigolo,* except he doesn't get paid and he doesn't hang upside-down in those big booties. I've known him forever and love him like a brother, but he can be very annoying. Not to mention messy and supremely opinionated. And I don't think he should be working at Macy's. Dan was like the smartest kid at Sugarland High.

"Don't you get tired of sleeping with strange women?" I ask.

"No," he says, and goes off to take a shower.

People often think we're related. We actually look alike. He's five-ten, lanky like a swimmer, with long limbs, broad shoulders, and a firm chest. His dark brown hair is almost black, and his eyes are the color of a denim shirt. Except for two subtle differences—I'm four inches shorter and have no chest at all—we could have been twins.

He always said he'd get the hell out of Texas the moment he got a chance, and he swore he'd take me with him. And wouldn't you know it? Here we are! He dragged me away kicking and screaming. I didn't want to leave my mother behind; she's an alcoholic and I didn't think she could fend for herself. But Dan convinced me that it was for the best, and he was right . . . I think.

Our small two-bedroom apartment has green furry carpeting, grass cloth wallpaper, and blue Rubbermaid daisy appliqués on the tub. Venice is more than a little scary and run-down, and it seems like every night we hear police sirens and gunshots. But at least we're near the beach, a real beach with blue water. The only beach we ever knew was in Galveston, an hour from Houston, and it's lovely if you like oil slicks. At Venice Beach, we can actually *swim.* On *most* days. But our favorite thing to do is watch all the freaks. We especially love this old guy on roller skates who always wears a tutu and hunting cap. If I were brave enough, I'd go over and hug him and ask him to tell me all about his childhood.

When Dan gets out of the shower, he plops down on the couch next to me. "What's on *Ricki* today?"

I haven't been paying attention. He reads the screen. *Catholic priests and the women prisoners who love them.* Just then a woman wearing an orange jumpsuit pledges her love for Father Flanagan via satellite from the Little Rock county jail. "I will do anything for you, Father. *Anything.*"

"How's the job hunt coming?" Dan asks.

"I just faxed a résumé over to somebody famous," I say.

"Who?"

"I don't know, some Hollywood couple."

"If it doesn't work out, Rach, I can get you a job at Macy's tomorrow. Name your counter. Lancôme, Clinique, Estée Lauder. I have an in with all of them except M.A.C. Those M.A.C. women are bitches."

"I need to find a job that'll help me get my foot in the door," I say. "I think it's my only chance."

"How about an internship?"

"You have to know someone to get those internships."

"You have to know someone to get a job that doesn't pay?"

"Dan, we're not in Sugarland anymore."

Just then, Father Flanagan begins explaining the meaning of celibacy. He makes it sounds like a disease, and it's clear I'm a victim.

"Cheryl Lansing was in today," he says.

"Who?"

"She's like president of one of the studios. ABC, I think. She's very good-looking. I'd sleep with her if I felt it would do something for your career."

"That's very sweet," I say, and I try to make it sound ironic. I'm not very good at irony. I read an article once about how *over* irony was, but I didn't understand a word. Who'd want to live in a world with irony, anyway? Isn't life confusing enough without trying to figure out what people are really saying?

The phone rings. Dan is closer and he reaches for it and checks the caller ID. If it says "Out of Area," we know it's another telemarketer. They were supposed to stop calling when they passed that law, but some of them don't care. Dan refuses to take their calls, but I don't mind. I feel sorry that they were singled out for such harsh punishment by the federal government, when all they are trying to do is put food on the table for their loved ones.

"What's Holly Pond?" he asks.

"Oh my God!" I holler. "Did you say, *Holly Pond*?"

"Yes."

"I know who it is!" I say, jumping to my feet. "It's for me!"

Dan answers the phone before I can stop him. "Hello?" he says. "Yes, she is," he continues. "Let me see if she's available."

That was pretty good. Dan always comes through for me in a pinch. But I am *so* nervous.

He holds out the phone and I take it, shaking like a leaf. "Hello?" I can feel myself turning beet red, and my hands are sweating. Panic attack! Panic attack! I try to calm down. "Yes, this is Rachel."

Dan makes faces at me. I turn my back so I can concentrate.

The lady's voice is strong and stern. "My name is Michaela Marsh and I'm calling from Holly Pond Productions. I just received your résumé. When are you available for an interview?"

I take a breath. "Anytime."

"Will tomorrow at one P.M. work for you?"

"Yes, ma'am," I squeak.

"Great. Come to 162 Beechwood Lane in Brentwood."

I can't find a pen. Panic attack! Panic attack! We should always have a pen by the phone. I never learn! Dan taps me on the shoulder and hands me one. "One-sixty-two Beechwood Lane in Brentwood," I repeat, jotting it down.

"Do you know where that is?" the lady asks.

"Yes, ma'am," I lie.

"Very good. I'll see you tomorrow. And please—don't be late."

"Rest assured," I say, "I won't."

I hang up and turn to look at Dan. "*Rest assured*?" he says, making his Dan face. "Where did *that* come from?"

"I have an interview at Holly Pond Productions!" I squeal.

"What's that?"

"The ad said it was a 'busy showbiz couple,' but I know who it is! It's Victoria Rush and Lorne Henderson!"

I had seen the Holly Pond logo during the closing credits of Victoria's latest sitcom, *Mid-Life*, and when Dan saw the name on our caller ID—well, I immediately *knew*. I was so excited I had to fight the urge to run to the bathroom. Panic attack! Panic attack!

I have to pull myself together. My chances are not good. Holly Pond will be interviewing tons of other candidates, all of whom are probably more qualified than me. But none of them would work harder than me. If I actually got a chance to talk to the Queen of Television herself, in person, I might be able to convince her to pick me.

"Victoria Rush," Dan says, impressed. "I'd do her in a minute."

I ignore him and go into my bedroom and rummage through my closet, searching for something to wear to the big interview. I own nothing dressy, let alone professional. I remove a pair of black pants that I used to wear at Starbucks and try to decide what would look best with them. The only thing that looks halfway decent is a faded blue cotton shell with matching cardigan. Dan comes into the room and whistles loudly.

"Fashion police," he says holding his nose. "You're under arrest."

"This is all I have," I say.

"It can't be," he says, and begins searching through my closet. He takes every item out one by one, shakes his head with disappointment, and puts them back in their place. "You're right. You have nothing to wear."

I throw myself on the bed. "That's just great."

"Now don't have a cow. Let me work some magic." He goes back to the closet and finally decides on the black pants with the blue shell and the cardigan.

"What about shoes?" he says. "Not those worn black penny loafers?"

I nod glumly.

"You need new shoes."

"I need new everything."

He nods. "I hope you're not going to wear your hair like that."

I reach up and touch the barrette that keeps the bangs out of my face. "What's wrong with my hair?"

He unsnaps the barrette. "It looks so much better down." He grabs a brush off the dresser and runs it through my hair.

"I need to get it cut," I say.

"Hans will cut it."

"I don't want Hans to cut it."

Dan sucks in his breath. "How can you say that? He's one of the best hairdressers in L.A. He cuts Mickey Rourke's hair."

"I am so nervous. My stomach is cramping up."

"Relax, would you? I know you're going to get this job."

"You really think so?"

"I'd hire you."

That's one of the things I love most about Dan. He always knows what to say. And he believes in me. "Thanks, Dan. You're the best friend I ever had."

"I know," he says. "Now get some sleep." Then he lets himself out of the room and shuts the door.

Before I get under the covers, I say my prayers, like I do every night. First, I thank God for a wonderful day and all that he has given me. Then I ask Him to bless all my friends and relatives, especially my mom, who sometimes needs an extra helping or two. And on this particular night I can't help asking for one more favor: to let me be a personal assistant to one of the most famous people in the world! I can't believe this is really happening and I find myself starting to get excited all over again. I love Hollywood. Please, God, make Hollywood love me back!

GRIFFIN

"**H**ONEY, IS THAT YOU?"

"Yes, Mel." I step into our West Hollywood apartment, on the second floor of a two-story complex. There's a small rectangular pool in the courtyard, Melrose Place–style.

"I'm making your favorite again," Mel says. "Coq au vin blanc."

"Great." I take off the Calvin Klein suit jacket that I've had since college graduation and sort through the mail. There's the usual collection of credit card and department store bills. As I begin sifting through them, I hear a loud sigh. Mel is standing in the doorway in a white chef's apron and tall hat, courtesy of the California School of Culinary Arts.

"You're supposed to say, 'Hi, honey! I'm home!'" His bushy plump mustache is perched on his lip like a caterpillar.

"You look ridiculous," I say.

"I won't look so ridiculous when I have my own TV show. I'm calling it *The Bistro*. Has a nice ring to it, don't you think?"

I stroll into the living room and collapse on the couch.

He follows me. "Did somebody have a bad day at work?"

"Do me a favor. Don't call me that."

"Call you what?"

"*Somebody.*"

He looks at me strangely. "Okay."

"Johnny calls me that all the time."

"Sorry."

He sits on the arm of the couch with one leg crossed over the other, pats my back, and exhales deeply, the leading indicator of a lecture. "You're so smart. Why are you wasting your Stanford education on show business? You could have been a doctor or a lawyer," he says, sounding like a Jewish mother. "Better you should have been both!"

"No. I'm doing exactly what I want to do. There's something about discovering new talent, Mel. It's a rush—it's like nothing else in the world. You're panning for gold, painstakingly searching for weeks and months on end, and then there it is—the nugget you've been dreaming about. Magic, irresistible, luminous."

"My, we're feeling poetic this evening!"

"I find the process exhilarating," I tell him. "It's better than sex."

"You poor, misguided boy!" he says, shaking his head. "You're just like your brother, and just as passionate. I can't believe how much you remind me of him."

I'm stunned. I can't remember the last time someone compared me to Roger.

There's a picture of Mel and Roger on the mantel. It's from last winter when they were on vacation in Palm Springs, celebrating their fifth anniversary. "I miss him, Mel."

He squeezes my shoulder. "I do too, honey."

I don't discuss my brother. With anyone. Ever. It's too upsetting. I haven't seen my parents in over a year because they invariably bring Roger up when they criticize my career choice. But they'll see. "Someday I'll start my own management company," I say with conviction.

He runs his fingers through my hair and I feel it coming: the same discussion we have every week. "I'm worried about you, Griff. A straight man pretending to be gay is almost as bad as a gay man pretending to be straight. No, I take it back: it's worse."

"Johnny Treadway would never have hired me if I was straight. He finds heterosexuals threatening. He wants someone he can push around, and I'll be that someone for as long as it takes."

"I don't understand it. Bryan Lourd was a hugely successful straight agent, married to Carrie Fisher, and when he was at the top of his career he left her and ran off with a guy. And what about John Goldwyn at Paramount? I hear he had a huge coming-out party right on the lot when he left the woman he lived with."

"It was different then. That was before the Gay Mafia started wresting control from the powerful heterosexuals who used to run this town. I want to be part of David Geffen's circle. I want to hang out with Elton John."

He shakes his head. "What? Doesn't it bother you that your whole life is a lie?"

"I only lied about my sexuality to one person. I didn't think everybody would find out."

Mel nods. "Whenever we get a new member, we send out a newsletter. Maybe you really are gay and just don't know it?"

"Why do you guys always do that? Paul Newman? Gay. Bruce Willis? Gay. Clint Eastwood? Definitely gay."

"How do you know you won't like a man unless you've tried?"

"I know I wouldn't want anyone to urinate on me, and I haven't tried that, either."

"Ooh! Maybe we can start there!"

Someone knocks on the door. Mel crosses toward it and I continue thumbing through bills. "Hello, Ruby," I hear him say. Then, "Griffin, it's for you."

I go to the door and say hello to Ruby. She's close to ninety and looks like a bloodhound in a housecoat and slippers. Her eyebrows and lips are painted on her face, more or less where they'd be in real life. "We're playing poker tonight at eight," she says in her raspy smoker's voice. "You in or out?"

"I'll be there," I say. "With bells on."

"I'll let everybody know," she says, and hobbles off down the corridor.

When I shut the door, Mel says, "She's so Ruth Gordon from *Rosemary's Baby*."

"As opposed to Ruth Gordon in *Every Which Way but Loose*," I counter. We both laugh.

RUBY HAS a poker table set up in the middle of her living room. It has a green felt top and space for eight, but the only players sitting around it are four elderly women and me. I've taken my brother's place in the weekly game. The women all live in the complex and have known each other for over forty years. Widows now, they often regale me with stories of their brushes with fame as B movie actresses.

"It's Rose's deal," Ruby announces before sipping on her brandy. The sweet yet sickly aroma of perfume, cigarettes, and old age permeates the room.

Rose, at seventy, is the youngest gal in the group and always impeccably dressed. On this particular evening she's wearing a lavender suit with a white pillbox hat. She finishes shuffling and places the cards in front of Marge, who's sitting to her right.

"Cut," Rose says.

Marge, who looks like an aged walrus wearing a muumuu, has great peripheral vision. She rarely turns her head, needing only to look straight ahead or down. She cuts the cards and Rose begins dealing.

"Five-card stud. Last one down," Rose says. When an ace lands in front of Dell, Rose barks, "Dell, your bet."

Dell is black, skinny, and wears a red and yellow outfit. She resembles a Slim Jim. Prone to narcolepsy, she has dozed off again and her light snoring sounds like the droning hiss of a radiator. She awakens after Rose yells.

"One dollar," Dell says.

"Too rich for my blood," I say, folding.

"I'm with ya, Griffy," Ruby says.

Rose calls the bet. Marge has yet to make a decision. She slyly leans back in her chair.

"Keep your eyes to yourself, Marge," Rose says.

"I'm stretching my back," Marge says innocently.

"Only thing you stretching is the truth," Dell says.

"I call," Marge says.

After she throws in a chip, Rose continues to deal. Ruby elbows me. "I want you to meet my great-nephew."

I smile. "What for?"

"He hasn't come out yet, but I know he's gay," she says.

"How do you know he's gay?" Marge asks.

"He likes that new Cher song," Ruby says.

Marge throws in her cards. "I like the new Cher song. Does that mean

I'm a rug muncher?" Rose wins the pot. She scoops up her chips and passes the cards. "Dell! Wake up! It's your deal."

Dell opens her eyes and takes the cards. "Let's play follow the queen." She pats my arm. "No offense."

"None taken," I say.

As she deals the cards, someone knocks at the door. Ruby shoots me a look. "Would you mind getting that?"

"Not at all."

I open the door to see a young black kid standing out front, his hands in the pockets of his baggy jeans. He wears a one-carat diamond stud in his ear and an ornate jeweled cross on a long, thick gold chain. My first thought is, *How did Li'l Bow Wow—uh, excuse me, Bow Wow—find out about our game?*

"Is my Grams here?" he says.

"Dell, you've got company," I announce and hold the door open as he struts over to the poker table.

Dell turns around. "Is that my grandbaby? Come here and give me some sugar." She looks at us. "Kenvin's staying with me for awhile."

Kenvin gives Dell a quick squeeze but quickly steps backward. It's not cool to be hugging your grandma for more than a second or two.

"Kenvin is so smart," Dell says. "He's building me a computer."

"What do you need a computer for?" Ruby snaps.

"I'm going to find me a man, right, Kenvin?"

"That's right, Grams."

"They got a matchmaking site for just us black folks, though I'd consider a nice Jewish man, too."

"You build computers?" I ask Kenvin.

He nods shyly and studies the floor.

"That's pretty impressive," I say. "How old are you? Thirteen?"

He nods again.

"A man of few words, huh, Kenvin? Can I get you something? A Coke, a candy bar, some pants that fit?"

This gets a smile from Kenvin, albeit a small one. I rejoin the girls just as they bring another round to a close.

Rose turns her cards over. "Full house. Kings over sevens."

"We can *see* the damn cards," Marge sneers.

"Sure you can. You been stealing looks at them all night."

"Listen here, Rip Van *Wrinkle*," Marge blusters. "I suggest you take that back."

"Take it back?!" Dell says, rising from her seat—and the caterwauling begins. "Don't make me come over there, you bigass, hairy-mustached, lowdown, cheatin', no-good biddy—"

"Bring it on!" Marge says.

I look around the room and feel like I'm in the middle of a really bad TV series: *Golden Girls Gone to Seed.*

Michaela

I HATE LYING in the wet spot after sex. The thought of mixed bodily fluids soaking through the sheet and mattress pad is revolting, especially in a hotel room. Even in a suite at the Four Seasons, there's no telling whose DNA you're lying in.

Randall Blume comes out of the bathroom and retrieves his pants.

"Can't we stay longer?" I ask dreamily. We only ever stay half an hour, max, but I have to make him think I care. I'm sprawled out on the bed with the sheet strategically placed over my breasts, leaving my left nipple exposed.

Randall picks up his shirt. "I need to get back to the office."

I stare at the back of his pale, balding head. It's decorated with capillaries, small patches of discoloration, and a freckle or two. That's when it strikes me. Randall looks like his penis. "So, what do you think?" I ask him. "Should I go auburn or not?"

"Sure," Randall says, buttoning up his shirt. He doesn't care what color my hair is or what my name is, for that matter. All he cares about is the instant hard-on he gets whenever he sees me. My fabulous looks have nothing to do with why he gets so aroused. He gets a hard-on for one reason only. My BP. Or in layman terms: Bald Pussy. Every man loves easy access and a clean workspace, not to mention the porn factor—which goes without saying. My BP is the secret to my success. Every girl needs one. I should write a book.

"I might cut it shorter, too," I add. "Maybe I'll go with a bob."

Randall didn't mean to sleep with me again. We were only supposed to have a quick lunch. But how can he concentrate on business when all of the blood drains from his big head and concentrates in the little head? To be fair, it's not that little. He's a good six inches, not gigantic, but better than average.

"Uh-uh," Randall murmurs. He's not listening. He's too busy feeling guilty. After all, he has a wife and kid at home. A *rich* wife. But sometimes these primal urges just take over. What's a man to do?

"There's something on my mind," he says nonchalantly as he sits down on the edge of the bed and pulls on his socks.

Bad vibe. I know what he's going to say. *You don't have it anymore. You're old news. We have to cut our losses.* Here it is, The Big Dumpola. I have to act fast. Before he can say anything else, I sit up and let the sheet slip down to my waist. "Is everything okay?"

Randall turns around and looks at me. That's his first mistake. He's getting aroused as he stares directly at my perfect, teardrop-shaped breasts. "Not really."

"You're always thinking about work. You need to relax more," I purr, doing my best sultry Lauren Bacall.

He turns around and puts on his shoes. I won't let him blurt it out now. "Maybe we should go somewhere like Catalina. Stay in a little B&B." I place my hand on his thigh. "Or maybe we could drive up the coast to Monterrey?"

Randall hears me yammering, but he's oh, so distracted. "What?"

I move behind him and rub his shoulders. "Boy, you *are* preoccupied."

Then he utters, "We're letting you go. It wasn't my idea. It was the agency's. They want to move in a different direction. They only want to rep *working* actresses."

I jump out of the bed and stand in front of him. "I know I haven't booked anything in a few weeks—"

"Sixteen months," Randall says to my navel. He's afraid to look at my BP, and the effort to not look is killing him.

"I have this stupid job," I purr. "It's hard to get out to auditions."

"That's not my problem," Randall says coldly. He trying to tie his shoe, but I'm in his way.

"Okay. I'll start going to more auditions. Screw the job."

"More auditions would just mean more rejections." Randall steals a glance at my BP. He's weak. They all are.

"I know there's something out there for me. Look how close I got with *Friends*."

"That was a hundred years ago."

I wipe off the imaginary sweat that has accumulated on my hairline. "Does it feel warm in here to you?"

"Look. You're a beautiful girl with a great body. Maybe it's time to give up the dream and settle down and get married. Sometimes people have to realize that it's not going to happen for them. But they can still have a good life. They need to channel all that energy into something else. My advice to you, keep your day job."

"I love it when you look at me like that," I whisper.

"Michaela," he starts, but I place his hand between my legs.

"Look what you do to me."

Randall sighs. "I really need to get going."

I straddle him, pushing my breasts up against his chest. "You make me so hot." I kiss his neck tenderly. "Are you sure you have to go?"

"I'm sure," he says. His hands stay on the bed, but I can feel his erection underneath me. I wriggle my hips around on his lap until he can't take it anymore. He buries his face into my chest. "Maybe I can stay a little while longer."

"I'd really enjoy that," I whisper before running my tongue in and around his ear. Then I go in for the kill. "Give me some more time. I know I can book something."

"Okay," he says breathlessly as he begins ripping off his clothes.

I sigh with relief as I fall back on the bed. It's not easy being sleazy. Thank God he's a man. A penis is an actress's best friend.

I'M STARVING. Sex always gives me a big appetite. I reach into my bag for the can of Planter's peanuts. I'm on a low-carb vegan diet but I only eat nuts. I switch them up, though. Today, it's peanuts, tomorrow cashews, then walnuts and pistachios and macadamias. I guess you could say I'm on an all-nut diet. I put a handful in my mouth and chew slowly. It's important never to rush eating because it's bad for your digestive system. When I'm done, I gulp down a half-bottle of Evian. I'm still hungry but can't eat again for seven hours. I take a deep breath and will those hunger pangs away. Eating is all about control. And I'm *always* in control.

I have to have dinner with my father. He comes out to L.A. every six months to see how I'm doing, give me money, and beg me to go back to New York with him. My mother never accompanies him on these trips. She and I don't exactly get along. She doesn't know it, but she's an argument away from becoming estranged.

Dad loves to eat, and it shows. He's a squat, jolly man with a large waistline and a trim, gray beard. We always dine at trendy, expensive restaurants like Campanile, Patina, or Crustacean—the kind of places Victoria frequents. I keep telling myself that one day I will be successful enough to afford to eat nuts at the best eateries in town. We blend in easily with other patrons because we resemble that age-old cliché: the big-time Hollywood producer and his bimbo starlet. Our dinners always begin and end in exactly the same way. First, we talk about how skinny I am. "You look like a death camp survivor!" Dad is fond of saying. So I have to prove that I eat by forcing a big meal down, like a sour cream roast veal chop and tarte tatin with ice cream for dessert. (And lots of liquids, too, to make purging afterward easier.) Then we talk about my mother and all of the fund-raisers she drags him to. He hates all of her friends. If he has to have dinner with Herman and Mitzi Schwartz one more time, he tells me, he's going to end it all. He can't understand how I could leave him alone with that crazy woman.

Next, he talks about his plastic surgery practice, which he hopes to abandon soon so he can retire to Aspen. My mother doesn't like Aspen—she hates the cold—so he's considering going without her. He always lights up at the thought of living in a nice, manageable condo in the Colorado mountains, without Mom.

Toward the end of the evening, inevitably, Dad always gets around to that painful old question: "When are you going to give up this acting thing, honey?"

"You mean my acting career?" I smile through clenched teeth.

"Can you really call it a career if you've only worked eight times in ten years? If you were a business you'd already be bankrupt."

I look down and play with the napkin in my lap. My nails need new silk wraps.

"Why don't you move back home and settle down," he suggests, then lowers his voice. "You're not getting any younger, you know."

"Thanks, Dad," I grimace.

"Well, it's true. Just the other day your mother and I were talking about how old you are and we were shocked."

I look around nervously to see if anyone is listening.

"Then we realized how old *we* are. That's the *real* shocker."

"I don't want to move back to New York."

"Why not?"

"Because there's more opportunity for me out here. I had a very promising audition last Tuesday."

"I just hate to see you struggling, honey. If you come home, I'll buy you an apartment. I'll pay all your bills. You won't have to work as someone's assistant."

"I don't mind working for Victoria Rush," I lie. I pick up the shiny dessert spoon and check out my reflection.

He wants to say something else but changes his mind. Then he smiles broadly, "Guess who I ran into at Bergdorf's?"

I roll my eyes. "Ernie Finklestein?"

"How did you know?"

"Because every time you come out here you mention him."

"You should have seen him, Sylvie."

I cut him off. "Shh. It's Michaela now. How many times do I have to tell you?"

"Your mother and I really hate your stage name. We don't understand what was wrong with Sylvie. If it was good enough for your grandmother it should be good enough for you."

My cheeks feel warm. Luckily no one's listening.

"Little Ernie Finklestein. I remember when he used to come to your birthday parties and follow you around like a puppy. But you know what? He's not so little anymore. He's at least five-six, maybe five-seven. Full head of hair. You should've seen him. He was dressed in the sharpest-looking suit I've ever seen, and he was buying five more. He always had great taste. Got it from Ernie Senior, who had his own clothing shop in the garment district. But you know that, of course. Fine people, the Finklesteins."

I'm sure Ernie has yet to surgically remove the "L" from his forehead. He not only followed me around my birthday parties—he followed me around school, temple, and the entire neighborhood. There's a new word for that now: stalking.

"Dad, can we talk about something else?"

"Do you know how much money Ernie made last year?"

"I don't care how much money he made last year."

"Ten million!" Dad claps his hands.

"So?"

"He started an Internet company, one of the few that survived. And legitimate stuff, too! Not like those thieves at Enron. Or that horrible Martha Stewart. No, not Ernie. He's honest and a millionaire and very single and still pining for that little girl who used to be known as Sylvie Kirshbaum."

I sigh. "That's nice, dad. But Ernie Finklestein just doesn't do it for me. He never has."

"Did I tell you that he just bought a penthouse on Fifth Avenue?"

I want to crawl under the table.

"But here's the best part. He's coming out here for a visit and I gave him your number."

"Dad! Why did you do that? I don't want to see him."

"What's a little dinner?"

"I'm very busy. I have a job and acting class and auditions. I won't be able to squeeze anything in."

"Make time," he insists.

"Dad—"

"Do this for me, sweetie. I think you'll be pleasantly surprised."

He isn't going to give up. He's been trying to marry me off since I graduated high school. "Okay, fine."

He leans over and kisses me on the cheek. "I think you'll really enjoy yourself."

"It's just dinner. *Once*. Nothing else."

He dismisses me with his hand. "Don't put such limitations on yourself. You might want to see him several times while he's here."

I direct my gaze elsewhere. "I don't think so."

Dad ignores me and sits there with a satisfied smug on his face. He's probably already planning the wedding at the Waldorf-Astoria.

Polaroid C20786A08611A

Kecia

I

HATE WALKING into an empty, dark house—not 'cause I'm scared. It would just be nice if there were someone here to ask how my day went or give me a hug like at the Cosbys'—even though everybody knows that shit isn't real. Marta lives out back in the guesthouse and I spend most of my time over there. The only thing that greets me here is the answering machine. And it isn't too friendly. I've been walking into this house by myself for as long as I remember. It used to belong to Daddy—now it's all mine. As usual, the red zero is lit up on the answering machine. Nice to see you, too. I place a bill over it, but even then, its red glow tries to peek out from under the envelope.

That's when I notice what that envelope is. It's not just any bill. It's a bill from the IRS. And it isn't the first time they've sent it to me. They've been on my case for six months, saying I owe money for taxes my daddy didn't pay when he was alive. And even though he's not here, his estate is still responsible. The tab's pretty steep. With penalties and interest, they want upwards of $100,000. I don't have that kind of money. Don't know many people that do. It has to be a mistake. Or if it's not, why should I take their word for it? Daddy's not around here to defend himself. He might have had a very good reason for not paying those taxes. The situation was between him and them. I'm not getting involved.

The crib looks exactly the same as it did when Daddy lived here. It's got a 1960s funkadelic feel that Lenny Kravitz would probably dig. Never felt the need to change it. Don't want to. Sometimes I pretend Daddy and Mama are still here. I used to think that if things were kept just the same, they might come back.

I walk into the kitchen and get myself a Coke. I should be drinking Diet Coke, but I can't get used to the nasty aftertaste. I open up the cabinets and search for something to nibble on. I recently stocked up on rice cakes, pretzels, and air-popped popcorn. But I'm not in the mood. I get the jar of peanut butter out of the trash and remove a big scoop with my finger. I promise I'll only take one, and throw it away for real this time, but it's so smooth and tasty I can't stop. Still, something's missing. I get out the Hershey's chocolate syrup and squeeze a couple of large drops into the peanut butter jar. After another bite, a smile transforms my face. Now *that's* what you call comfort food.

I take my snack into the den, where Daddy's black baby grand sits in the corner. An orange plastic ashtray still rests on top, next to the water stains made by years of brandies on the rocks. The inside of the piano bench is filled with chewed-up pencils and music sheets with his scribbling. I reach for the last album he ever made and put it on the record player. I lay down on the couch and look up at the ceiling as the sounds of Daddy's quartet fill the room. I have every track memorized. It's easy to imagine I'm six again and Daddy's in the room with me, writing his sweet songs. Wasn't supposed to be disturbing him when he was working, but I'd hear him playing and be drawn to the music like a bear to the most delicious honey she's ever tasted. I'd sway in the doorway, intoxicated by the music and the smell of his cigar, watching the smoke hang over him like a halo. He'd be right in the middle of his composition and stop abruptly. Without turning around, he'd say in his deep, baritone voice: "I sense a little girl in the room." Busted, I'd suck in my breath and stand stiff as a statue.

Then he'd slide over and pat the space next to him. I'd tiptoe across the room and climb up on the piano bench. Daddy would start playing again, and I'd watch with fascination as his long, lean fingers danced gracefully across those ivories. My legs would be swinging back and forth as they dangled off the bench. I'd study his profile, his wide flat nose, his full lips, the short, trim mustache and round chin. When he liked the sound of something, he'd pick up his pencil and jot it down. Then he'd wink at me before taking a puff from the cigar burning in the ashtray.

"Kecia?"

I sit up. "In here, Marta," I say as she lets herself in the back door. She has changed out of her drab pink work smock and into a pair of shorts and a T-shirt.

"Dinner's almost ready," she says.

"All right," I say, taking another swig of Coke.

She looks at the peanut butter jar and makes a face. "That's not good for you."

"Nothing I like to eat is good for me."

She shakes her head, picks up the jar, and returns it to the kitchen. She notices the floor hasn't been washed in a longass time, and I can sense that she's about to lapse into one of her cleaning spells. That's when the doorbell rings. She walks back into the room and looks at me strangely. Nobody ever comes to visit—not even those door-to-door folks selling shit.

"Who do you think it is?" she asks.

"No idea," I say, but that's a damn lie. I move across the living room, with Marta close behind. I look through the peephole. Sure enough, it's the same brother who showed up last night around this time.

"Who is it?" Marta says.

"Shhh."

Must be the one calling me, too. He's tall with a short fade and a cheap suit that don't fit right. His looks are plain, like a baked potato without the cheese and sour cream. He rings the doorbell again and fiddles with his tie. After a few more seconds, he retrieves a business card from the pocket of his jacket and leaves it on the porch. I watch him walk back to the street, get in his Camry, and drive away.

"What's going on, Kecia?" Marta asks.

"Nothing," I say. "Just someone trying to sell me something I don't want or need."

She accepts my answer and walks back into the den to turn off the record player. "Come. Let's get a hot meal in your stomach."

Just the mention of a hot meal sends my stomach into all kinds of spasms, and I immediately forget all about Mr. IRS Man.

6A08611A

Rachel

WOW! HERE I AM in front of Victoria Rush's house. This is actually my second trip to Victoria's. The first was the night before with Dan, to practice. I even timed the trip and noted the mileage from our apartment. I am lucky, lucky that *the* Victoria Rush would be considering *me* for a job. And it just so happens that I know every single thing about her because I subscribe to *People* magazine. First of all, you'd have to be living under a rock for the last twenty-three years not to be on intimate terms with Victoria Rush. Her first series, back in the 1970s, was called, simply, *Victoria*. The show ran for ten years and it won a bunch of Emmys. In the 1980s, she starred in *Blue Belle* and won Emmys for that, too. *Mid-Life* is her third show, and it's not doing well. It's what they call a "midseason replacement," and the critics seem to think it's a real stinker, which is a first for Victoria. The show is about a group of divorcées who live in the same high-rise, kind of like *Friends*, but they're all pushing fifty. Initially the show scored good numbers, but a few episodes later *Mid-Life* was in trouble with a capital T.

Victoria Rush was married twice before she met husband number three, Lorne Henderson, who's twenty years younger. The relationship is a classic Hollywood love story. He was working as a valet at 21, opened the door of her Jag one fateful night, and fireworks happened. Before long, reporters were in Lorne's hometown, Kalamazoo, Michigan, digging up stories about his endless employment problems, alleged affair with his history teacher at the age of thirteen, and his six-month jail stay after a fifth DUI.

But their love survived the tabloids.

I still remember the wedding from *InStyle* magazine. The nuptials cost close to $1 million and were designed by that fancy wedding guy, Collin Whatever, and held at the posh Beverly Hills Hotel. Famous movie stars mingled with Lorne's white-trash relatives from Kalamazoo, sipping champagne under silk tents. It was all right there in *People*, page after page of glossy pictures, and I almost felt as if I were part of it.

And now look at me! Standing on the street where she lives! A little nobody from Sugarland, Texas, about to be whisked into the home of the flesh-and-blood Victoria Rush. Sometimes life works in mysterious ways. I know it's hard to believe, but it does.

You can barely see Victoria's house from the road. There's a tall brick wall out front, and beyond the wall several gigantic trees. I park down the street, per Michaela's instructions. Apparently Victoria doesn't want the help's cars junking up the front of her house, and who am I to argue?

I smooth down the new navy blue suit jacket I'm wearing and admire the matching dress pants. A brand new pair of black Kenneth Cole low-heeled pumps rounds out the ensemble. When I came home from screen-writing class this morning to change for the interview, the outfit was on my bed with a note:

R—

Now you have something to wear. Try not to spill anything on it and don't remove the tags. I'll return the clothes tomorrow. They'll never know.

Love, D

P.S. *The shoes are on me.*

I turn the rearview mirror to look at myself and it snaps off in my hand. But it doesn't even faze me. Because I'm going to meet Victoria Rush! I hold the mirror above my head to check out my hair. Maybe Dan's right. It does look better down. Mom used to say, *Bad hair means bad person*. At least that's what I *think* she was saying. When she drank, she mumbled. And she always drank.

I take one more deep breath, smooth down my hair, climb over the passenger seat, and crawl out of the car. In the driveway, a square alarm box rests on top of a metal pole. I press the buzzer and jump when a voice shrieks through the speaker, "Yes?"

I place my mouth as close to the speaker as possible and shout, "I have an appointment with Michaela."

"Come to the delivery entrance," the voice says, followed by a loud, buzzing noise. Then the gates begin to swing open all by themselves. As I walk up the driveway, I'm overwhelmed by wonderful smells. Victoria's front yard is like a miniversion of the Los Angeles botanical garden. There are roses, tulips, and a whole bunch of flowers I can't even begin to name.

I suck in my breath as a gigantic mansion comes into view. It's at least three stories high and has four large columns in the front of it like the White House. Before I can ring the bell at the delivery entrance, a blonde girl with big red glasses and one of those Eskimo coats opens the door.

"Rachel?"

"Yes," I say.

She's also wearing a black headset thingy that's plugged into a pager thingy clipped to her waist.

"Hi, I'm Michaela. Follow me."

She disappears down a pebble stone path that leads around the house into the backyard. We pass a tennis court, a really pretty pool, and one of those fancy Chinese ponds with goldfish. I press my lips together to keep my mouth from dropping to the ground. Michaela finally leads me into a guesthouse. And now I know why she's wearing the big coat. The temperature inside reminds me of the Ralph's frozen food aisle. Goose bumps break out all over my arms. If I hadn't known who the bosses were before, I'd sure know now. Two giant individual portraits of Victoria Rush and Lorne Henderson stare down at me.

I grin even though I have butterflies. Well, truth be known, it feels more like bats flying around in my stomach. And my palms are sweating so absurdly that it's actually visible to the naked eye. It's a condition I've had since I was six—all because Mom forced me to sing "Deep in the Heart of Texas" in the Little Miss Houston pageant.

"Why don't you have a seat?" Michaela smiles. That's when I notice she has brown teeth like she's been chewing Skoal for years. I try not to stare because she would be really pretty—if she got rid of the glasses and used Rembrandt.

She notices I'm freezing. "Lorne always wants his environment to be sixty degrees."

I look around the room. "He's here?"

"No. But we have to keep it this cold in case he pops by."

My hands begin to drip. I wipe them on my pants when she's not looking, then suddenly remember Dan's request not to get the clothes dirty. I pray sweat doesn't stain.

"As you can see, this is command central," Michaela says, all serious like Sipowitz, that huggable bear of a guy from *NYPD Blue*. "I'm Victoria's assistant and I am responsible for the day-to-day operations of Holly Pond Productions."

I hold the smile and wipe my hands again.

"This is a very, very important job. As you can imagine, I have received many résumés, but there was something about yours that caught my attention," she says.

My eyes widen. "Really?"

She studies my résumé carefully. After a few moments, I get nervous. What if there wasn't anything on there that caught her attention? What if she had me confused with someone else who had a better résumé? Panic attack! Panic attack!

"You worked at Starbucks, so you must be used to dealing with difficult customers," she finally says.

I'm so relieved. "Oh, yes. The general public can be very demanding, especially when they haven't had their first cup of coffee."

She smiles sweetly. "Victoria and Lorne are very demanding."

I expected that. They are Big Stars, after all. They don't have time for the little things.

"This job entails working in their home and making sure all of their needs are met. There are three of us here who will do whatever it takes to make them happy."

"Three?"

"Victoria has two assistants, and Lorne has his own assistant, Courtney."

I wrinkle my brows. "Lorne has an assistant? What for?"

"Lorne costars on *Mid-Life* now and he's, uh, very active."

"Oh."

"As you can imagine, this job requires one to wear many hats. And every day brings a new adventure, I promise. As Victoria's personal assistant you are expected to be at her beck and call, *always*. You might have to order her lunch. Or help rearrange her closet or help pack clothes for a trip. Whatever she wants you to do, you do."

Michaela takes a sip of water and picks up a thick, three-pronged, white looseleaf notebook. "This is the Book of Rules. Everything you ever wanted to know about Lorne and Victoria is in here: personal and medical history, religious preference, ex-spousal information, hobbies, etc. There are maps that show you the quickest way to get to any part of the house, diagrams showing you where everything is located, and lists of alarm codes, safe combinations, as well as pager, cell, and home phone numbers for anyone and everyone in their employ, including agents, lawyers, accountants, publicists, masseuses, hairdressers, manicurists, stylists, tarot advisers, etc. The Book of Rules is constantly changing and always being updated."

I gawk in awe at the massive book. It's even bigger than the Starbucks manual. And I thought that was big. Beans are hard to identify, ya know. Especially when you're trying to describe the difference between Ethiopia Lekempti and Ethiopia Sidamo. The only book I'd ever seen that was bigger than the Starbucks manual—until today, anyway—was *The Complete Works of William Shakespeare*.

"It's imperative that every assistant know the rules by heart," Michaela says.

I gulp and hope I'm up to the task. She smiles at me. "So why don't you tell me a little bit about yourself."

I've decided that her dirty teeth are killing me. Maybe she doesn't know Crest makes whitening strips now. Nonetheless, I relax somewhat and feel my hands stop perspiring for the first time since sitting down. "I'm originally from Sugarland, Texas—"

Suddenly the phone rings. Michaela hits a button on the pager attached to her waist. "Yeah?" Then she rubs her temples.

"Tell her the fastest a Learjet can travel to New York City is four and a half hours, and that's if you get a good tailwind," she says.

I uncross and recross my legs and feel my hands start up again. I carefully wipe them on my pants. I'm hoping Michaela won't notice. I have to convey confidence, not the nervousness of some sweaty schoolgirl on her first day of gym class.

Michaela takes off her glasses. That's when I notice she has really pretty eyes. Maybe she should go on *Extreme Makeover*. And for some reason she looks familiar, but I don't know why.

"I called every charter service on the West Coast. The Concorde no longer flies anywhere. *Yes*, Courtney, I'm *sure*."

I gaze out the window at the pool man. He's sprinkling a white powdered chemical into the pool. I envy how relaxed he looks as he picks up a large net and skims for leaves. I hope to be as relaxed as he is one day.

"Fine." Michaela hangs up, inhales deeply, and puts her glasses back on. "Sorry about that. You were saying?"

"I'm from Texas and moved here a year ago hoping—"

The phone rings again.

"Excuse me," she says. I shift uncomfortably in my seat.

"Tell her she can take something to knock her out. When she wakes up, she'll be there. She'll go straight to the Rainbow Room for the gig, and fly right back home."

The Rainbow Room? I had almost forgotten about Victoria's singing career, but maybe that was a good thing. Much as I hate to say it, she couldn't carry a tune if it was in a bucket . . . bless her heart.

Michaela turns her back and whispers, "How much Xanax has she had today?" She waits for an answer. "Why don't you find out and get back to me?" She hangs up and reaches for the Tylenol.

"Sorry about that. Courtney is filling in for Victoria until we find someone. As you can see, it gets pretty hectic around here."

"Yes," I say, trying to sound as if I'm up to the challenge. "I can certainly see that."

"So how do you deal with pressure?" she asks.

When the phone rings again, Michaela yells, "What?" Then quickly changes her tone. "Hello, Victoria," she says in a calm, soothing voice.

I sit straight up in my chair. On the other end of the line is Victoria Rush!

"Yes, four and a half hours with a tailwind. That's correct." She pauses to listen. "Of course I told them who you are." Her hands shake as she lights a cigarette.

No wonder she has brown teeth. She's probably a big coffee drinker, too.

"I don't think F-15s are allowed to take civilians anywhere. But I will check with the Air Force immediately." She hangs up and jots down the words AIR FORCE, underlining them twice.

The phone rings again. Michaela hits the button and says softly, "Hello?" Then, "Hi, Mary Jane."

Michaela listens for a second, then looks genuinely worried. "The

Rainbow Room canceled? How's that possible? How many tickets did she sell? Only six? Shit."

I guess that's not a good sign.

"I'll let her know," Michaela says and hangs up the phone. She looks at me. "So I think we're finished here."

My face drops. "Isn't there anything else you want to know? I type sixty-five words per minute, I taught myself Microsoft Word and Excel—"

"Can you answer a phone and run up and down stairs?"

"Sure."

"You'll be fine. When can you meet Lorne? He approves all new hires."

I'm so stunned I just sit there like a bump on a frog. Michaela stubs out her cigarette. "How about now?"

"Uh . . ."

"The job pays ten dollars an hour," she adds.

"Wow!" I've never made more than $7.50.

She scribbles down an address on a Post-it note. "When you get to the studio, ask for Courtney Collins and she'll take you to see Lorne."

"Will I get to meet Victoria?" I can barely utter the words.

"Probably not. She's not feeling well today, but if you get the job you'll meet her soon enough."

I try really hard to hide my disappointment. I tell myself that meeting Lorne will be just as exciting, in its own way.

Michaela hands me the slip of paper. "Do you mind showing yourself out? I have to make some calls."

"Not at all," I say. "And thank you very much. You won't regret your decision."

"I certainly hope not," she says.

Back in my car, I can't help shouting "Yes!" I pound the top of the ceiling with both fists, but not too hard. I don't want the dome light to fall off.

I GIVE MY NAME to the security guard at the front gate of the CBS Radford Studios. He scans his clipboard and after locating my name gives me a map and directions. When I pass through the gate, I feel like the bat that swallowed the canary. I walk by the enormous soundstages of some of my favorite TV shows. Large trucks carrying camera and lighting equipment drive past. Crew members hurry by, and important-looking men in tailored suits glide past in golf carts. I'm not sure, but that's either Whoopi Goldberg or that large male rapper who looks like Whoopi Goldberg. I spot parking spaces belonging to Jim Belushi and Jami Gertz. I see buildings that are divided into minioffices and large and small trailers that function as dressing rooms. All this activity. All this magic. This is my own little slice of heaven. I park and get out of my car, feeling light-headed. I follow directions and the map to a large beige mobile home with Lorne Henderson's name on the door. I knock.

"Come in!" a girl shouts from the inside.

I open the door and peer into a two-room office. The front room, the smaller of the two, contains a single desk and filing cabinet. There are black bags from Barney's and designer shoeboxes strewn about as a boom box plays songs from an oldies station. A vase full of red roses sits on the desk with an unsigned card that reads *I love you*.

"Are you Courtney?" I ask.

"Yes," she smiles. She's very petite, with reddish-brown hair and humongous boobs. She tosses the bags aside and asks me to make myself comfortable in the small chair facing her desk.

"I'm here to see Lorne Henderson."

Her cheerful demeanor vanishes. "What for?"

"I'm interviewing to be Victoria's new assistant."

She's totally relieved. "Oh, okay. What's your name?"

"Rachel Burt."

"So, where are you from?" She opens up the shoeboxes, which both have $450 price tags, and puts one shoe on her right foot and a different one on her left. Then she sits down on the desk and admires her feet.

"Texas, originally. I'm from a town located right outside Houston."

Courtney scratches her head. "Is that near Dallas?" But she gets distracted by the music. It's M.C. Hammer's *U Can't Touch This*. She hurries across the room and cranks up the volume.

"I love this song!" she emotes. "I danced to it at my first recital."

Courtney prances around the room, wearing one stiletto heel and a chunky platform tennis shoe. She's singing along and imitating Hammer's trademark moves. This is the weirdest job interview I've ever been on. I wonder if I'm supposed to sing along. I watch her dance around until the song ends. It's a very long song, and just watching her and her large breasts makes me very tired.

"So," she says at last, returning to her seat, "do you have any questions?"

"What's it like working for Victoria Rush?"

Courtney makes a face like she just bit into a bar of soap. "I don't work for her. I work for Lorne. I'm just filling in until someone gets hired."

"So what's it like working for Lorne?"

She breaks into a wide grin. "He's the coolest! Wanna meet him?"

BEFORE WE LEAVE the trailer, Courtney reapplies her entire face with makeup while I wipe my sweaty hands on my pants, again. The tops of my thighs are beginning to get damp. We drive to the *Mid-Life* soundstage in a golf cart marked "Property of Lorne Henderson." We walk inside and I feel like I'm in a meat locker again. I let my eyes adjust to the darkness and see a string of four familiar rooms. There's the living room where the characters spend most of their time. Next door is Victoria's bedroom. Next to that is the veterinarian's office where she works. Three cameras are set up in front of the kitchen. Enormous lights hang from the rafters. Across from all this is a set of aluminum bleachers where a group of writers and producers sit clutching scripts. Courtney approaches someone wearing another headset thingy. "Where's Lorne?"

"Try Victoria's trailer."

Courtney doesn't like this information. All of the color drains from her face, and she takes off so fast down a dark corridor that I almost lose her. Then someone comes barreling around the corner.

"Whoa, Courtney. Just the gal I was looking for!" Lorne Henderson winks. Oh my God. There he is. I try to act completely normal.

She deliberately steps away from him. "This is Rachel. She's interviewing for Victoria's new assistant position."

Lorne is stunned by Courtney's coldness but turns professional all of a sudden. He extends his hand. "Lorne Henderson."

I shake his hand firmly and notice his palm is as clammy as mine. He's also much shorter in person. If I didn't know any better, I'd think this was a Lorne Henderson lookalike who works at car shows and conventions. He's definitely more attractive on television. He's only thirty-five, yet he looks fifty in person. He has splotchy skin and a week's worth of stubble. But then he smiles, and I know I'm looking at the real deal. Lorne has the kind of grin that would make Bill Clinton nervous.

"We were looking for you," Courtney pouts.

"Victoria's having one of her spells. We should let her sleep it off. Let's go back to the set. Rehearsals are done for the day." Lorne lets us walk in front of him, but Courtney purposely strays behind.

"What were you doing in there?" she whispers.

"Calming her down, you know how she gets," he whispers back.

"I work for *you*, not her, and I don't like it one bit," she says.

"Can we talk about this later?"

We stop near the bleachers, and Lorne invites us to sit down. He cracks his knuckles and asks me, "So where are you from?"

"Texas."

"Ah, the Lone Star State."

"Do they have HBO in Texas?" Courtney asks.

"Yes," I say, and I decide right then and there that Courtney's as dumb as a bowl of hair.

Lorne closes his eyes and rolls his head around to stretch his neck. "Do your future plans include show business?"

I blush. No one important has ever asked me that. "I want to write."

He snorts. "Yeah, doesn't everybody."

He twists his torso to stretch his lower back. "I'm sure Michaela told you all about the job. It's pretty laid-back."

"Yes, she did."

"So when can you start?"

"As soon as possible."

"Good, that's good." He smiles at Courtney and taps his shoulders. "How about a little rub-a-dub?"

As she massages his shoulders, he says, "I'm sure I'll see you tomorrow, then."

I'm beaming. "Thank you so much. I'm really looking forward to this, Mr. Henderson."

"We're not that formal around here. You can call me Lorne."

I HAVE TO STOP back by the office to get a starter kit that includes all of the essentials: pager, cell phone, petty cash, and the Book of Rules. When I open the Book, the first thing I see is "Never look Victoria in the eye" in bold black letters. Then Michaela whips out a twenty-five-page legal document.

"This is a confidentiality agreement," she says and flips pages until she gets to the end. "Sign here."

"Shouldn't I read it first?"

"You'll get a copy. This is binding for seven years and basically means that once your employment ends, you are not allowed to talk about your experience with anyone, especially the media."

"Or what?"

"You will be sued at the rate of seventeen-hundred and fifty dollars per word in print or five thousand dollars per second on video, whichever applies. There's a chart inside the Book of Rules detailing all this."

I sign the document and she gives me a one-page release.

"I need your signature here as well," she says.

This page only has one sentence: *Victoria Rush and Lorne Henderson have the right to terminate any employee at any time and for any reason whatsoever.*

Michaela frowns. "Unfortunately, we have a lot of turnover here."

When she shows me out, she says, "So we'll see you tomorrow, then."

I grin. "Tomorrow."

"Don't forget to bring a coat!" she adds.

W HEN DAN COMES home from work that night, I leap from around the corner holding a five-dollar bottle of champagne. "You are looking at Victoria Rush's new personal assistant!"

Dan squeals with delight and gives me a bear hug.

"Hey, watch the suit," I smirk.

"That suit got you the job. Turn around. Let me see how it fits." I twirl around and wiggle my butt.

"I'd like to think my charming personality had something to do with it."

"Nah," Dan smiles.

I hand him the bottle. "Now open this champagne so we can toast."

He takes the bottle and goes into the kitchen.

"You were the one who said I'd get the job. God, I feel so good about this, Dan! This might actually be my ticket." I pick up the phone. "I have to call my mom. She's going to be so excited."

It rings five times before the answering machine comes on. "Leave a message, if you must." At the beep, I say, "Mom! I've got great news. Call me."

Dan retrieves two bright red plastic Solo cups out of the cabinet. "So what's Victoria like? Does she look really old in person?"

"She wouldn't come out of her trailer. But I met Lorne."

Dan pops the cork and fills both cups, then hands me one and raises his own in toast. "To Rachel," he says, beaming. "I always knew you'd take this town by storm."

"Thanks," I say, and I feel myself choking up. I can't believe it. *Me*. A little nobody from nowheresville. And I'm working for Victoria Rush.

"What are those stains on your legs?" Dan asks me suddenly. "That's not sweat, is it?"

GRIFFIN

AS PROMISED, the studio throws a soiree for Travis at the Viper Room, an appropriately named establishment for serpents big and small. A special last-minute performance by the rapper Ah'ight (a.k.a. Barney Clayton) adds to the bacchanalia. Argus-eyed stargazers swarm the sidewalk, waiting to get in. A trio of stoned skater boys try to figure out the exact spot where River Phoenix met his demise. Velvet ropes and no-neck burly bouncers keep everyone at bay. We await the doorman, who has yet to grace us with his presence. He is the keeper of the infamous list, the most important document at any private happening—the document that validates you as human being. It contains the names of the Chosen Few Hundred who are allowed inside these privileged bastions of ultrahipness, and if you aren't among them, well—your life counts for nothing and you should pack your bags and go back to Peoria, where your old job at Applebee's awaits.

When the doorman appears, everyone clamors for his attention. He stands there, chest puffed out, basking in glory, a well-coiffed Gucci figurine with headset and clipboard accessories. He swaggers toward one of the bouncers. "Do not let David Arquette in. I don't care if Courtney's with him or not."

The bouncer nods his fire hydrant–sized noggin as the doorman begins to randomly select guests. A few minutes later, I am confirmed and allowed to enter.

The place is dark and cool and filled with 250 of Travis's nearest and dearest, and those poor desperate hopefuls who aspire to be near and dear. The crowd's quite eclectic: malnourished fashionistas, X-game athletes, various band members from the rap rock music scene, and, of course, the *Queer Eye* guys.

Ah'ight's entourage—made up of five corpulent black men wearing sunglasses and Tommy Hilfiger paraphernalia—take up residence in the corner of the room. Their disdain for whitey is apparent as they keep a close eye on their leader. Exquisite potables flow from exasperated bartenders who'd rather participate in this extravaganza than serve the revelers. Drugs are intermittently exchanged through inconspicuous handshakes. All tabs are on the studio's dime.

I stand at the bar, smoking a cigarette. Travis is not in view, but his dissolute cronies, Pokey and Frog, hold court with some teen actresses from the WB. I finally spot Wonder Boy walking arm in arm with Ah'ight. They slither through the claque to a packed booth. Ah'ight leans in, mutters something, and the group scatters like stunned roaches in a suddenly well-lit kitchen.

It isn't until Travis and Ah'ight get comfortable that I make my way over. "How's it going, Travis?"

He looks up at me. "What's up? Have a seat."

Ah'ight glares at me when I sit down.

"It's cool," Travis says to him. "So finish telling me."

Ah'ight doesn't say a word. With hair extending one foot from his head, he resembles a pissed-off Buckwheat. He stares me down until I look away.

Travis explains, "Dude, he's cool. He's my manager."

I'm ecstatic that Travis thinks of me as his manager; now if only everyone else would. Travis explains, "Ah'ight's got a great idea for a movie for us."

"By all means, let me take notes," I quip and retrieve my notebook and Mark Cross pen.

Ah'ight starts, "As I was sayin', there's this nigga who's a cop and he kills white people in the line of fire. White boy runs from the scene of the crime . . ."

Here he pauses for dramatic effect and retrieves a nine-millimeter from his coat. He points it at me. "Pow! Whitey goes down!"

I jot down IGNORAMUS on my pad and nod. "I see."

Ah'ight's wide grin reveals a miniature Fort Knox. "White dude gets pulled over for no reason. Nigga ask to see his license and registration . . ."

He pretends to pull the trigger. "Bam! Dead cracker, yo!"

"Interesting," I say and write FUCKING PSYCHO on the pad.

The gun stays in my face for a few seconds longer until he finally decides to put it away. "It's the opposite of what happens when the PO-lice bust a cap in one of our asses, yo!"

Travis nods. "Dude, I like it." Then he looks at me. "What do you think?"

I cough. "What exactly would Travis's role be?"

My question elicits a gelid response from him. "He the only white guy the cop likes. Whatchu thank?"

"I think I'm glad you put that gun away."

Ah'ight's not amused. Before he retrieves the gun again, I say, "It's definitely an original idea."

"Who you tellin'?" he says.

"Why don't you see what you can do with it," Travis says to me before turning back to Ah'ight. "Griffin's the man. I'm gonna be in this movie about those high school kids that shot up their school. That's why they're giving me this party."

"Bling-bling," Ah'ight says and looks around the room. "Tell those niggas I got the soundtrack if they come up with something lucratable."

"Will do," I say and jot down BLOW ME.

I look at Travis. "Actually, the studio is giving you this party so you'll star in *Fire in the Hole*."

Travis looks at me strangely. "I'm not gonna shoot up the school?"

"This is a much better film," I lie. "You're going to love it."

"Will I get to shoot anything?"

I sigh. "I'll see what I can do."

Ah'ight's entourage pushes through the crowd toward us. They move en masse, like an approaching thunderstorm. Ah'ight glances at me. "I'll be in touch."

"Fabulous."

He hugs Travis before walking away. "Take care, dog. Peace."

Travis watches him with admiration. "That guy is multitalented. P. Diddy don't have shit on him."

"You are absolutely correct," I say.

Travis throws his arm around me. "Now it's time to *partay*."

Two hours later I'm stuck in a crowded booth with Travis, Frog, and two underage bimbos. Barely sixteen, the girls desperately try to appear older by wearing lots of makeup and cleavage-baring tops. Pokey sits in the booth adjacent to ours with his head and arms thrown back, the recipient of a phantom blow job from under the table. Frog excuses himself, and Travis sees this as an opportunity to make out with one of the girls. Then, because he's generous, he turns to the other one and gives her an equal chance.

I finish my beer and announce, "I'm out of here."

Travis pauses momentarily to remove his tongue from the girl's mouth. "Dude, the party's just getting started."

I yawn. "The party's over for me, man."

He extracts himself and jumps up. "Wait right here!"

We watch the youthful prince dart off and disappear amongst his loyal stoned subjects. "Where's he going?" one of the girls asks.

"No idea," I say.

"We're way past our curfew, Mandy," the other girl whispers.

"Who cares? How many girls can say they lost their virginity to Travis Trask?"

A disheveled and sweaty Pokey comes over and sits down next to me. "Dude, you know where I can score some blow?"

"No."

"Shit." He lights up a dirty bent joint the size of my pinky and struts away.

Five minutes have barely elapsed when Travis returns with another guy in tow. "Griffin, this is James. He cuts my hair."

"Hey, James," I say as the guy ogles me.

"He *is* cute," James says to Travis before sitting down next to me. He has a perfect blond coif and wears periwinkle eyeliner.

"You know what?" Travis tells James. "Give him a haircut, on me."

James's face lights up. "Sure."

"I don't need a haircut," I say.

James touches my hair. "I can do a little trim."

Travis pats me on the shoulder. "You can thank me later."

"I really need to go," I say quickly.

"Have another drink," Travis says.

"Yeah, honey," James coos. "Have another drink."

"Waitress!" Travis yells, back to cavorting with the girls.

James bats his tinted eyelashes. "So Griffin, tell me all about your fine self."

I move away from him. "I think you should know I'm in a serious relationship."

James winks. "So am I, honey. So am I."

I'M TRUDGING UP to my apartment when someone says, "Yo, G."

I look down to see Kenvin sitting in a chair near the swimming pool. For a second I'm flattered by the sobriquet he has bestowed me, but then I remember G is also cool black speak for compadre, buddy, or friend.

"Whassup?" he says.

"Isn't it a little late for you to be out?"

"Can't sleep."

"I can." I begin to head up the stairs.

"Grams says you're gay," he says.

Talk about cutting to the chase. I walk over to him and feel a long conversation is about to ensue. "That's true."

"You don't act gay."

I'm surprised by the boy's audacity but explain anyway. "Not every gay man is flamboyant. That's just a stereotype. Although it's an easy assumption to make, since you see outrageous gay men all the time on television and in movies. But we can't all be Steven Cojocaru. Thank goodness."

"You're not gay," he insists.

No one has ever questioned my sexuality before. When you say you're gay, people usually take your word for it. "I hate to disagree with you, but I've been gay for as long I can remember." I succumb to a cliché. "A leopard can't change his spots. Now, if you'll excuse me."

Kenvin shakes his head vehemently. "Nope. You don't fit the profile."

He's managed to pique my curiosity. I spin back around. "What profile?"

"It's the stuff that tells you about a person. Everybody's got one. See, you say you're gay, but according to the information I found—"

"What information?"

"High school and college transcripts. Medical records. Police reports."

"What are you talking about, Kenvin?"

"I'm talkin' about information, G. Information is power."

Really? All along I've been thinking *gay* is power. Maybe I've been misinformed.

"So you're checking me out?"

"I check out *everybody*," Kenvin explains. "You never know when it's gonna come in handy."

I'm definitely intrigued and more than a little nervous. "I see. You find anything interesting?"

"Lots of stuff." He looks up at the star-filled firmament. "You dated a cheerleader all four years of high school and were crowned Homecoming and Prom King. You played tight end on the football team and got a scholarship to Stanford. You pledged Sigma Chi there, got the clap from one of your girlfriends, and had a three-point-five GPA."

I'm blown away. Exactly how intelligent is this kid?

"Your first job was assistant manager at the Cheesecake Factory in Woodland Hills. You lived with another girlfriend for six months, but she went crazy, came at you with a screwdriver, and set your apartment on fire."

Lorraine! My god. The woman who forever cured me of women!

"That's got to be illegal," I say. I can't understand how he knows so much about me. Then I remember that he's building a computer for his "Grams."

"I ain't copping to nothin', G. But if you need the 411 on anyone, I can get it for you. For a small fee."

"Oh, really!" I say, and suddenly I'm channeling Liberace: "For your information, young man, you know absolutely nothing about me!"

"Come on, G. Relax. I'll keep it on the down low." He turns and heads off into the shadows. "And remember: if you need me, I know where to find you."

Rachel

I HAVE TO STOP at a newsstand on San Vicente Boulevard to pick up very important reading material for Victoria: *People* magazine, *US*, the *National Enquirer*, the *Globe*, the *Examiner*, and the *Star*. I carefully place everything into the back seat and do my familiar crawl to the driver's side. That's when the pager goes off. I've never had one because I thought that they were only carried by drug dealers and other people whose jobs were of similarly critical importance to the nation's health. The good news is that the beeping sound is coming from somewhere in the car. The bad news is that I don't have any idea where it is! I dig around the front seat and then the cell phone rings.

At least I know where the phone is. But then I discover a new problem. How in the world do you answer it? I press several buttons, and it doesn't help that my hands are their usual sweaty selves. The phone keeps slipping out of my hands as it continues to ring, while the hidden pager still goes off. When I finally hit the right button, Michaela hollers, "Rachel, are you there?"

I bring the phone to my ear. "Hello?"

"I just paged you," she says, sounding very upset. "Why didn't you call me back?"

"I'm in the car. I just left the newsstand and was on my way to the house."

"First lesson. Answer all pages instantly. I don't care if you're taking a dump."

I cringe. There's no need to get foul. "Uh, okay."

"There's been an update in the schedule. Lorne is out of town this weekend and Victoria had an emergency procedure done yesterday, so she's going to be really out of it."

"Is she okay?"

"She's fine and her painkillers are in the office. Now pay attention, this is very important. One Vicodin every four hours, *maximum*. That's it. No more. Whatever you do, don't give in no matter how much she screams."

"She's going to scream?" Now I'm frightened.

"She's not in pain, trust me. It's all drama. Do you have the alarm code?"

I review my notepad. "Yes."

"And you have the Book of Rules."

"Right here," I reply halfheartedly.

"There are just two things you've got to remember. Never look her in the eye, and don't fuck up. Got it?"

"Uh—"

"Okay, then," she says. "Bertie is already at the house and I'll be there shortly. I'll page you later. And Rachel, you better call back within ten seconds. I'll be timing you."

When the line goes dead, I put the phone down and continue on my way. Five minutes later the pager goes off again. This time I'm in traffic. I pull over and dial the number that's on the little screen. It rings once, and Michaela answers.

"Good job," she says and hangs up.

"Thanks," I say to myself. I had no idea how serious this was.

I drive directly to the house. I walk to the gate with my bag flung over my shoulder and my arms filled with papers and magazines. I manage to punch in the code on the alarm box and wait patiently for the gates to open. Once they do, I hurry up to the house. Before I can ring the bell at the delivery entrance, a large black woman opens the door swiftly, startling me. Some of the papers slip from my arms and slide down my waist.

"Rachel?"

"Yes." The papers fall to the ground.

"Pick those up and follow me," she says.

I scoop up the papers and follow her into the most glamorous kitchen I've ever seen. It's right out of *MTV Cribs*. It has white marble floors and countertops. All of the appliances are nice and fancy and state-of-the-art. There's even a brick pizza oven in the corner like at the California Pizza Kitchen. Again, it's freezing and I forgot my coat in the car. I exhale and expect to see my breath, like that kid from *Sixth Sense*.

"Your name's Bertie, right? You're the housekeeper."

She looks just like Weezy from *The Jeffersons*—but *mean*. She folds her arms in front of her and scowls.

"I read about you in the book," I explain.

"Then you probably know I'm here on my day off. And I don't like being here on my day off."

I did remember something about Bertie working only four days a week. The pile of magazines slips from my arms.

"You can put those there," she says, pointing to a black granite wet bar. "I'm here for two hours only. Victoria and Lorne are usually asleep at this hour, so it would behoove you to get as much done as possible before they awaken."

Behoove? I don't even know what that means.

"First things first. Place the publications in alphabetical order."

She goes over to the bar and sorts through the magazines.

"Tabloids on the right and magazines on the left."

I watch her overlap the *National Enquirer* with the *Examiner*.

"Are you writing this down? I don't like repeating myself," she snaps like an irritated schoolteacher. When she finishes laying them out, I notice a mistake.

"Shouldn't the *Star* be last?" I ask.

"The *Star* is the most important one. It's always on the top."

"But shouldn't the *Globe* come after the *National Enquirer*?"

"The *Globe* is Victoria's favorite magazine, so it has to come second."

"What about the *Examiner*, why does that come after the *National Enquirer* and the *Star*?"

"You ask a lot of questions," Bertie says.

"I'm just trying to get it right."

"Just put them in the order you see here. And don't ask so many questions. Lorne and Victoria hate that."

Bertie crosses the kitchen and opens the refrigerator door.

"The refrigerator must be fully stocked at all times." She opens the pantry and points toward an assortment of diet cola cans and vitamin water.

"The top of each can must be wiped clean and then placed in its appropriate row."

The uppermost shelves of the refrigerator hold nothing but diet drinks. Diet Coke, Diet Pepsi, Diet Sprite, Diet 7-Up, and Diet Dr Pepper are all lined up like little soldiers. The lower shelves are reserved for a variety of vitamin waters, arranged in alphabetical order—everything from Balance to Stress B. Each row has a little white label that identifies the specific beverage. In fact everything is labeled, even the obvious, as if someone went crazy with the label-making machine, or was thinking ahead to old age and the beginning of Alzheimer's. The butter tray is marked "butter." The egg tray holds nothing but eggs and is marked "eggs." Even the drawer that's already stamped "fresh meat" by the manufacturer has a little white label saying "fresh meat."

Then a couple of teenagers come into the kitchen. One of them is Matt, Victoria's fifteen-year-old son from her first marriage. He's holding hands with a teenage girl who's wearing an eyebrow ring.

Bertie fakes a smile. "Morning, Matt."

"Is Mom up?" The pine comb doesn't fall far from the tree. He has all of her facial features and original hair color.

"Not yet," Bertie says, holding the smile.

Matt gets two sodas from the refrigerator.

"Matt, this is Rachel," Bertie says. "She'll be working here, for now, anyway."

"Good luck," he says, but he doesn't say it like he means it. He and the girl disappear down the hall.

"He seems like a good kid," I say, mostly to fill the emptiness.

"He's a shit," Bertie says.

I T TAKES AN HOUR to get a complete tour of the house, and I can't help but wonder if I'll ever find my way around alone. It reminds me of the board game *Clue*, because there's a library, ballroom, billiards room, and conservatory—for real. Each room contains expensive antiques, silk Persian rugs, valuable artwork, and portraits of Victoria at all ages, each painted in a different medium. Others are actual photographs. The largest one, which was a *Vanity Fair* cover, hangs in the dining room. And there are phones everywhere, in hallways, bathrooms, the gym. Next to each one is a laminated miniature floor plan with a highlighted arrow saying, *You are here,* like at the mall.

The second floor is comprised mostly of bedrooms. After showing me Matt's room, Bertie gestures toward the others. "These bedrooms are for guests but they pretty much remain empty."

"Relatives don't come to visit?"

"Victoria is estranged from her entire family after the *incident*."

"What incident?"

Bertie sighs. "Someone has obviously not read the Book. It's all there in black and white on page four-twenty-one."

"I'm three-quarters of the way through," I admit.

The last stop on the tour is the master suite, which takes up the entire third floor. After climbing the stairs, Bertie gestures toward a set of double doors.

"This is where Victoria spends most of her time. If you think the Stairmaster is a tough workout, just wait until you make this trek a hundred times a day."

"At least my butt will be firm," I grin, but Bertie's far from amused.

She heads for the stairs. "Now I'll show you the office."

"In the guesthouse, right?"

She laughs for the first time that day. "You wish. Michaela just interviewed you there for show."

I follow her down and around a grand staircase that would impress the director of *Titanic*. When we get to the first floor, we walk through the kitchen and utility room, down another set of stairs, and into the office. Now I know what's so funny. The office is located in a stinky wine cellar that's even colder than the rest of the house! Goose bumps explode across every inch of my body.

Bertie points at the phone. "When Victoria or Lorne need something, they will use the intercom. You can talk to them by picking up and pressing here. These lines run throughout the property, so you can respond wherever you are."

She pulls a bookshelf away from the wall, where a small safe is concealed.

"Here's where we keep Victoria's medication. It stays locked up for obvious reasons."

She reaches for a prescription bottle of Vicodin and hands it to me. "This is her medication for today. And remember—"

"I know," I say proudly, cutting her off. "Only one every four hours."

She looks at her watch. "Well, that's it for me."

"But Michaela's not here yet!"

She walks away.

"Wait!" I run after her. "What if Victoria wakes up before she gets here?"

"You get her whatever she needs."

"But we've never met. What if she freaks when *I* answer her call?"

"She knows a new person was starting this weekend."

I begin to sweat. "Shouldn't you stick around, just in case?"

"I don't get overtime for coming in today. It's time for the baby bird to be pushed from the nest. Time to fly. Bye-bye."

Just like that, she's gone. I sit down in front of the phone and pray Victoria won't call.

An HOUR LATER, I'm shivering in the freezing cold wine cellar office and staring at the surveillance screens. Occasionally I catch a glimpse of a gardener or one of the maids. I flip through the Book of Rules and read several chapters entitled: *"What Lorne Likes to Eat," "How to Clean Victoria's Hairbrush,"* and *"Our Favorite Shoes."* There's even a whole chapter called *"Los Angeles Lakers 101."* From what I can gather, it's very important for all employees to have extensive knowledge about the team because Lorne and Victoria are season ticket holders. I know nothing about baseball, so I read this section twice and even try to ask myself a few trick questions.

I study the map of the house and imagine I'm in the garage and need to get to the screening room. Knowing there's more than one way to skin a cow, I trace several paths with my finger until I find the best way: enter the side entrance, go up the back stairwell to the second floor, sprint to the other end of the house, up another flight, and—bingo! Now, how about from the disco to the—

Suddenly a weak and tired voice blares from the intercom. "Bertie?"
It's Victoria! Oh my God! Panic attack! Panic attack! I drop the Book of
Rules, snatch up the receiver, and naturally push the wrong button.

"Hello," I holler. Dead silence.

"Bertie?" Victoria repeats, sounding just a little irked. Well, after all,
she doesn't feel well and I don't know how to answer her phone! I'm such
a dorkus!

I try a different line, nothing. Before I completely spaz out, I take a
deep breath and try to think clearly.

"Dammit," Victoria says and hangs up.

I have to act quickly. I know exactly how to get to the master suite. I run
out of the office like I'm on fire and shoot up the stairs in a couple of huge
leaps. I dash through the kitchen and living room, and up the grand staircase, three steps at a time. I'm completely out of breath when I get there. I
push the giant double doors open and step into an enormous sitting room
with a fireplace. Victoria hears me come into the room.

"Bertie?"

I follow a row of thick white columns toward the voice. A massive four-
poster bed draped with a muslin canopy sits in the middle of the room. An
entertainment center that houses a projection screen TV is built into the
opposite wall. When I round the corner, my heart literally stops beating.
Oh my God. There she is. Only she looks like she's been hit by a concrete
mixer. Her face is red and swollen and covered in a thick layer of Vaseline.
You can barely see her famous bedroom eyes. A cloth headband pulls her
copper-colored hair off her face, making her look like the cowardly lion.
She wears canary-yellow silk pajamas and is propped up against the headboard by a mound of pillows.

"Who the hell are you?" she barks.

Remembering not to look her in the eye, I bow my head subserviently
and stare at my feet. "Hello, I'm Rachel. Your new assistant," I say in my
best "professional" voice, but I can't help gushing: "I've been a fan of yours
since I was a little kid!"

"Where's Bertie?"

"She left an hour ago."

I really can't help staring at her even though her face is all messed up.
Victoria Rush is right here in front of me. Somebody pinch me!

"What's the matter? Haven't you ever seen someone after a chemical peel?"

I look away. "Can I help you?"

Oh, God! I sound like a salesgirl at the Gap.

"Yes, you can. Get Michaela on the phone and tell her to get her ass over here right away."

I look at her and then remember I'm not supposed to be looking at her. So I tell the floor, "She should be here any minute."

"Then get me my painkillers."

I gulp because they're all the way down in the office. "Yes, ma'am."

I take off like a character running for his life in a John Grishman novel. After retracing my steps exactly, I make it to the office in a matter of minutes, grab the medication, and book it back to the master suite.

"I'm back," I call out breathlessly. My heart is beating out of control like I drank too much coffee.

"Here you go." I take one pill out of the bottle and hand it to her.

Victoria snatches it from me. "Give me the bottle."

"Uh, Michaela said that you're only supposed to have one every four hours."

"I said hand them over," she hisses.

Fortunately, Michaela strolls in just at the right moment. "Good morning, Victoria. I see you've met Rachel."

"Where the hell have you been?" she snaps. I'm thinking the very same thing.

"You know I volunteer at the handicap center on Saturday mornings," Michaela says.

"Well, I'm in pain," Victoria whines.

"Then take your medicine."

"But it really, really hurts," she begs, using all the dramatic ability that must have won her all those awards.

"Okay, one more, but that's it." Michaela takes the bottle from me, pours a few in her hand, and gives one to Victoria. I'm stunned. I learned from *ER* that you can't just give an addict all the pills they want.

Victoria pops the pills, then whispers, "I need some water."

"Rachel, let me show you where the fridge is," Michaela says.

I know exactly where the built-in mini-refrigerator is because I studied the map. As soon as we turn down the hall, Michaela whispers, "I didn't give her another pill."

"But I saw you."

She pours a few pills in her hand. "There are also sugar pills in the bottle. They are marked with a small black dot. See?"

Sure enough, a few of the pills have a tiny dot on them. I'm relieved as we walk into the master bath, which is fit for a queen. The floor is that fancy marble again, and all the fixtures are gold-plated. There are his-and-hers sinks and toilets on each side of the room. There's also a sauna, a steam room, and a Jacuzzi as big as the kiddie pool at the Sugarland community center. Michaela grabs a Multi V vitamin water and we return to Victoria.

"There you go," Michaela says.

"Straw?" Victoria says in a babyish voice. I take one from the night-stand, unwrap it, and stick it in the bottle. She takes a sip and flicks on the television.

"We'll be down in the office if you need anything," Michaela says as we move toward the door.

Victoria is watching *Entertainment Tonight*. We hear the familiar *da-na-na-na-na-na* of the theme music.

"Dammit!" she hollers.

Michaela turns right back around and we head toward her. On the TV is a picture of her with her age posted beneath.

The announcer says, "Big birthday wishes go out to Victoria Rush, who is fifty-five today."

"Happy birthday!" I exclaim.

Victoria shoots me a dirty look. Oops. I guess she doesn't like birthdays.

"How do they know it's my birthday?" Victoria asks Michaela.

"It's in the public record," Michaela says.

Victoria changes the channel. "Call them right now and tell them never to air my age again."

"Right away," Michaela says, then looks at me. "Come on."

Once we step out of the bedroom, I ask, "Are you really going to call *Entertainment Tonight*?"

"Of course not."

"What will you tell Victoria?"

"I'll lie and tell her it's all taken care of."

I think about that for a moment. Isn't that wrong? She must see it on my face.

"This is Hollywood. Lying is *de rigueur*."

I nod, wondering what that last bit means or how to spell it. Then Victoria calls out, "Hey, Rochelle!"

I'm completely paralyzed. "Is she talking to me?"

"It's okay. Go see what she wants," Michaela says.

I slowly walk toward her. "Yes, Victoria?"

"Get me the Foot Buddy!" she shouts.

Michaela explains, "She loves to order crap off TV. Go jot the number down off the screen."

After getting the number, I march out of the bedroom and softly close the door behind me.

Michaela smiles. "Now that wasn't so bad, was it?"

"She didn't even get my name right."

"At least she was close. That's a good sign. It took her a month to stop calling me Sue."

AT THE END of my first day, I stroll down the driveway with my head held high. I always feel a sense of pride in a job well done. I'll never forget my first day at Starbucks. Even though I screwed up a couple of times—like forgetting to add chocolate syrup to the mocha drinks—it felt great helping all those people start their day. But now I'm Victoria Rush's assistant. Starbucks is nothing but a distant memory.

When I get to my car, a woman with long blonde hair and a short skirt throws a bag into a jeep parked in front of me. Then she turns around. "Oh, hi, Rachel. You startled me."

"Michaela?" I'm in shock. The glasses are gone and her teeth are no longer brown. "Where are your glasses?"

"I don't need to wear glasses. And the teeth are fake. It's quite a transformation, isn't it?"

"I don't understand."

"I don't want any trouble. Lorne has a wandering eye, and if I can look as unattractive as possible he won't even give me a second glance."

"But anyone can see how pretty you are whether you're wearing glasses or not."

My comment catches her off guard and she looks embarrassed. But now that she's all spiffed up she looks even more familiar than before. "Haven't I seen you on something?"

"I'm an actress. I've done a few things."

Suddenly it hits me. "You were on *Seinfeld*. You played the girl with the nose hair!"

She blushes. Maybe it's been a while since she's been recognized for her work. "Yep, that was me."

"That's so cool!" I marvel. "So was Jerry, like, funny the entire time?"

"He's okay funny."

I wrinkle my nose. "Just *okay* funny?"

"Michael Richards was much funnier."

Now *that* made sense. "Wow. That's so exciting. I can't wait to catch your episode on a rerun so I can tell everybody I know you."

She smiles. "Would you like to join me for a drink? It'll give you a chance to get to know some other assistants we work with. We meet every Thursday at Trader Vic's."

I can't believe my luck. I started a new job *and* I'm making friends. "I'd love to."

Michaela opens her door. "Why don't you follow me?"

"Okay!" I run to the passenger side of my car and crawl in.

Michaela

T RADER VIC'S is a Polynesian chain restaurant located in the Beverly Hilton. Its tacky theme is about as authentic as a high school production of the musical *South Pacific*. The reason we hang here is because it's always empty and they let us smoke. A bonus is that they serve killer drinks at a discount and it's so dark and unhip it's perfect for a bunch of assistants who don't want to be found. When Rachel and I stroll into the restaurant, Griffin is the first to greet us. He always goes out of his way to kiss me on the cheek. Most men do.

"How are you, Mick?" he winks. He looks like he stepped out of the Abercrombie & Fitch catalog with his perfectly coiffed hair, pastel-blue eyes, and unblemished complexion. His meticulous grooming habits SCREAM high-maintenance. He really is the perfect guy. Naturally he's gay.

"I'm great, Griffin. Meet Rachel, Victoria's new assistant."

Rachel steps forward, visibly nervous. "Nice to meet you."

Griffin shakes her hand. "Likewise. Survived the first day, I see."

"Yes." Rachel turns as pink as the J. Crew pullover she's sporting. I can tell she thinks he's cute.

"Griffin works for Johnny Treadway, Victoria's manager," I say.

She nods. "Oh, right. I read about him in the book."

"Ah, the infamous Book of Rules. I believe there are works of Tolstoy that are shorter," Griffin says. "Let's go sit down. Kecia has a table."

When we get there, Kecia's drinking a mai tai and munching on something in front of her. Large and in charge but with minimal attitude, she's a less annoying version of Queen Latifah. "Egg roll?" she offers.

"No thanks," we all say in unison and sit down. Griffin and I immediately light up cigarettes. I glance at my reflection in the mirror that's hanging over the bar. My face has a bloated corpse-dragged-from-the-river look. There must be something wrong with that mirror.

Rachel looks at Kecia. "Hi, I'm Rachel. Victoria's new assistant."

"Oh, Lord," Kecia says.

Rachel smiles uneasily. "Now, now," I say. "Let's not scare the poor girl."

Coco, the Malaysian waiter, comes over to the table. He's one of those cheerful, eager-to-please Asians with a permanent grin. He only knows two words. "Howdy. Mai tai?"

"Three, please," Griffin says.

"What's a mai tai?" Rachel asks.

"It's a big tropical drink with lots of liquor," he says. "You'll love it."

Rachel looks at the menu and makes a face. "Ten bucks? That's really expensive."

"You only need two and Coco is kind enough to give us a discount," Griffin says.

After Coco walks away, I look at Kecia. "How's Travis?"

"The same." She's a woman of few words because her mouth is always filled with food.

I glance at Rachel. "She works for Travis Trask."

Her eyes widen in shock. "*The* Travis Trask?"

"It's not that impressive, trust me," Kecia says sternly.

Rachel can't resist. "Is he as cute in person?"

"Oh, yeah. He's cute all right," Griffin says. "Cute as a hemorrhoid."

Coco returns with our mai tais. Then someone's cell phone rings. We all check our leashes. Rachel panics and searches through her things maniacally. Griffin retrieves his phone from his pocket. "Not me," he says.

The mystery phone continues to ring.

"Not me," Kecia says.

I search through my bag and my phone is the culprit. I don't check the caller ID. "Hello?"

"Sylvie?" It's my dad. Someone shoot me. "Have you heard from Ernie Finklestein?"

"Uh, Dad. I have to call you back."

Before he has a chance to respond, I hang up. I look at my nails. They are truly hideous.

"Will Courtney be joining us?" Rachel asks.

"Hell, no," I say and take a drag off my cigarette. "We don't like Courtney."

"Why?" Rachel asks.

Griffin looks at Kecia and me. "Care to field this one, ladies?"

"The girl really puts the *ass* in assistant," Kecia says.

"She's sleeping with Lorne," I tell her. "They went away together this weekend."

Rachel's dumbfounded. "How awful! Does Victoria know?"

"Of course she knows, but she doesn't care," I say.

"Then why does she stay married to him?"

"They never signed a prenup. She would have to shell out a ton of cash if they divorced."

Rachel's flabbergasted. "So she just allows Lorne to sleep with Courtney?"

"She's probably grateful she doesn't have to fuck him," I say. "Who would want to? He's disgusting."

Griffin laughs, but his phone rings and the laughter catches in his throat. "Excuse me," he says, stepping away from the table.

That's when Jeb arrives. He has all the crazed, frightening energy of the Tasmanian Devil. His tie is untied and still hanging around his neck. A cigarette almost burned down to the filter hangs from his mouth. I don't know why Griffin invites him. When I asked him about it he said he likes to keep the psychos close.

"Coco!" Jeb calls out. He mimes his version of a normal man drinking a shot. "Cuervo. Make it a double!"

He wedges himself between Kecia and me. "Ever fantasize about killing and dismembering the masses?"

Rachel is afraid—very afraid. He pulls his chair closer and breathes me in. "What's up?"

I inch my chair away from him. "Nothing."

"Nice skirt," he says, grabs my drink, and takes a large gulp.

Griffin returns to the table. "Hello, Jeb. How's the agency?"

"Wonderful," Jeb says. "I'm officially unemployed again."

"Damn," Kecia says, her mouth full of egg roll.

"I thought things with you and Randall Blume were finally going good," I say.

Jeb lights up a smoke. "Oh, they were going good all right. So good that the bastard stole my idea."

Griffin motions to Coco. "We'll take another round."

"And another plate of egg rolls," Kecia chips in. Trust me when I say she does not need any more egg rolls.

Jeb grabs my drink and takes another large gulp.

"I finally saw today's trades—"

"Don't tell me," Griffin says. "Your idea is going into production next month."

"Exactly. With fucking Jared from the Subway commercials attached to star!"

"Can't you call the Writer's Guild?" I ask.

Jeb snarls, flashing his teeth like a Doberman. "I don't need the Writer's Guild. Bunch of wimps. They always cave on everything. But don't worry. I'm going to get Randall. You'll see."

"So you got fired for no good reason?" Rachel ventures, looking nervous and sweaty. For a moment, I'd forgotten she was there.

"Who's the wizard?" Jeb asks.

"I'm Rachel. Victoria Rush's new assistant."

Jeb laughs out loud. "Let's see. You're what? Number two hundred and thirty-four?"

"Jeb!" I say. She doesn't need to know that. Christ.

"Why do I get the feeling that I'm not going to enjoy working for Victoria?" Rachel asks, rubbing her hands. I notice she rubs her hands—a lot. I wonder if she has OCD.

"Get this girl a pointy hat with stars," Jeb sneers.

Coco arrives with more drinks. We all sip from them eagerly. But Rachel wants an answer. Griffin decides to explain.

"Look, Rachel, the thing about Victoria is that she loves to fire people. She gets off on it. It makes her feel superior."

"A lot of people get off on it," Kecia says.

Rachel frowns. She looks so lost and out of her element that I actually feel for her. "That doesn't seem fair."

"This is Hollywood, kid," Jeb says, doing his best Bogart impression. "In this town, nothing is fair."

"Or logical," Griffin adds. "You've got to question the intelligence and credibility of a business that continues to employ Tom Arnold."

Rachel looks at me. "You've been with Victoria a long time. How come you haven't been fired?"

"I don't know. Unlucky, I guess. And I've only been there a year. Though it does seem a lot longer."

"Our length of employment should be measured in dog years," Griffin says. "I've worked for Johnny for three years but it feels like twenty-one."

Rachel slurps on her straw, quickly finishing her drink. "Maybe Victoria is looking for an assistant to reach out to her."

"She's beyond reach, girl," Kecia says. "Just do your job and hope she doesn't get sick of you."

Rachel removes the straw from her drink and chews on it nervously. "I'm going to try to be her friend. I've known people like that—not famous or anything, but full of anger—and you have to try to reach out to them."

"You cannot befriend the beast," Griffin says. "Nor should you try. These people are not your friends. They are your employers. And none of them are worthy of our friendship."

"Fucking assholes," Jeb says. "I'm going to reach into Blume's chest and rip his fucking heart out."

Rachel excuses herself and disappears in the direction of the ladies' room.

"How long do you give her?" I ask.

"Two weeks, max," Griffin says.

"Ten days," Kecia says.

"I think she likes me," Jeb says. "I'm going to show her the veins."

Jeb.

EXT. RANDALL BLUME RESIDENCE—NIGHT
CRANE SHOT STARTING FROM ABOVE AND SLOWLY MOVING DOWN
TO STREET LEVEL

This is an exclusive neighborhood complete with million-dollar houses, well-groomed lawns, expensive cars in circular driveways, and little people from foreign lands caring for the occupants and their spawn.

I pull to the curb a few homes away and kill the motor. I grab a smoke from a pack of Camels on the dash and stick it in my mouth. Lighting up, I keep my eye on the three-story Mediterranean. It's fucking huge, with six bedrooms and eight shitters. He can relieve himself in eight different places. Twelve thousand square feet of total luxury for three people. Nice. Though there should probably be a law against it.

TIGHT SHOT: Clock on car dash reads 8:15. Lying jackcock will be here any minute, just in time for dinner. His wife loves to cook. Her name's Ashley and she has a knack for it. She cooks the fancy shit: rack of lamb, beef Wellington, stuffed Cornish hens. Presentation is the key.

Whenever I used to run a personal errand for the jacklick, she'd open the door and I'd always find myself floored by her amazing looks.

"It smells so nice in here," I'd say. And it did, too. Who knew food could be such a powerful aphrodisiac? "You must be an amazing chef."

She'd blush—she looked even more beautiful when she blushed—and she'd tell me that I'd have to come to dinner sometime. But I never got invited. Not on her account, of course. I'm sure the asshole laughed when she suggested it.

Then I'd do what I had come to do—grab the cleaning, pick up the script he'd forgotten, retrieve the Blackberry—and be on my way. I always hurried. Something about Ashley made me nervous. She was, like, you know, The Dream. She was the girl I always wanted and the one I'd never get.

Okay. Here comes Blume now, behind the wheel of his convertible black Porsche. He's barely out of the car when the front door opens and Ashley steps outside, waving. She's been waiting for him. Jesus Christ, leave it to fucking Beaver. My first instinct is to duck. But then I realize she can't see me. I'm too far away. Besides, all her attention is focused on him. God, she's stunning. I bet she's rock hard under that J. Crew T-shirt and khaki shorts. She's got bluish-gray eyes with amazing lashes. This woman never needs mascara. Her hair shimmers and is the color of nutmeg. Her skin is velvety and supple. It's odd, though. She's standing there waving and smiling at the jacklick, and she seems kind of sad. I wonder what that's all about?

The kid dashes out from behind her. He's five and okay for a kid. Every time I come to the house, he chats me up. Not shy at all. Most kids are scared of me. He's so smooth it's scary. That's how they make 'em out here. Teach 'em to kiss everybody's ass, no such thing as sincerity. But Ashley once told me it was uncanny, the way he takes to me. She said he was very picky about people, so clearly I must be a pretty good guy. I almost died when she said that.

Blume pats his kid's head like he was a little dog or something. He's beaming. This is his life, and he's got it all: the fucking American dream. All we need is fireworks, apple pie, and the Stars and Stripes waving in the background. Cue Pat Boone. I hate fucking Pat Boone. But I especially hate Randall Blume.

Why the fuck am I here? Maybe I'll go to Barnes & Noble to pass the time. I always meet cute women in the self-help aisles. They're pretty damaged and all, but who isn't?

As I drive away, I find I can't stop thinking about Ashley.

Rachel ☺

THERE'S THIS REALLY BIG important meeting at Victoria's house during a "hiatus" week (that means they're not shooting). Griffin told me the *primary objective* (his words, not mine) is figuring out a way to save *Mid-Life* from cancellation. This is the first time I'm handling a business situation for Victoria. Michaela is usually in charge of all that. I'm mainly in charge of ordering stuff off TV. Just this morning I had to order the Abtronic, the Quick Chop, and the Perfect Fold. Some of the executive producers are coming over, so I've spent all morning making sure the refrigerator is fully stocked. I get out the nice glasses. Of course, every glass at Victoria's is nice, so it's hard figuring out which ones are the *nice* nice ones. I had to ask. I wonder if the producers want snacks. There's nothing in the pantry. Not even potato chips or pretzels. Then I remember Victoria doesn't eat much. In fact, I've never seen her eat.

"What the hell is this?" a voice suddenly bellows, scaring me half to death.

I turn around to see Lorne by the fruit bowl. "Is everything okay?" I ask.

He picks up a banana as his neck veins pulsate. "Does everything look okay?"

I know this is a trick question. Obviously, things are not okay.

"Bananas are supposed to be yellow. Not green, not brown, or any other color," he says.

I nod my head. But he's not done.

"And when I say yellow, I mean yellow all over. Not half yellow like this one." He thrusts the banana in my face. "Do you see the problem here?"

I nod again. He closes his eyes, exhales deeply, and puts the banana down. "See that it doesn't happen again."

"Yes, sir."

When the buzzer at the front gate sounds, I glance at the security cameras and see three people: Dustin Lucas, executive producer and head writer; Amber Lilly, co-executive producer; and Tyler Wanton, associate producer. (Their pictures are in the book.) I let them enter the compound—I love saying *compound*; it makes me feel like a Kennedy—and bound up the stairs from the office to greet them. At the front door, I give them a very friendly, "Good afternoon, y'all."

The producers mumble hello as they come in. It's not until I see them in person that I notice how young they are—just a couple of years older than me. They look cold and uncomfortable. I wish I had sweaters to give them. I show them into the ballroom, where they take seats at a big table that seats twenty. A glorious crystal chandelier hangs from the ceiling, its colorful prisms creating patterns throughout the room. I ask them what they want to drink in my chirpiest Starbucks voice.

"Jaeger?" Dustin Lucas says. Amber and Tyler laugh halfheartedly but look like they could *really* use a shot.

Dustin clears his throat. "Water will be fine."

"We'll have the same," Amber says, indicating Tyler and herself.

After thinking it over for a few secs, I decide to go with Balance, Focus, and Essential Vitamin Water for everybody. Then I summon Victoria and Lorne and return to the kitchen and hover near the marble bar, just in case I'm needed. When they come into the room, Lorne makes his way around the room, greeting all three producers as if he couldn't be happier to see them. Victoria sits down at the other end of the table without so much as a hello. Her face is still pink from the chemical peel. But she no longer has scabs. Lorne takes a seat next to his wife and begins the meeting with aplomb. "Victoria's not very happy."

Dustin starts, "We've been thinking long and hard about this." He has blond-dyed hair with black ends, and he squints his eyes when nervous. He hasn't stopped squinting yet.

"And?"

"We want to add a regular love interest to the show. Viewers love a good romance, and they absolutely adore Victoria, so it only makes sense that they would love her even more in love," Dustin explains, staring straight at Lorne. In fact, all suggestions are directed to him, not his wife, although it's always been her show.

As Lorne thinks about this for a minute, Tyler jumps in. He has chin-length hair that's tucked behind his ears. "We think a new veterinarian at the clinic should become the love interest."

Lorne's intrigued. "Hmm, that certainly sounds different."

Now it's Amber's turn. She has a pierced eyebrow and a smoker's cough, but she coughs so often that it might be a version of that weird thing I saw a special about on TV once: Tourette's Symptom. "We've also toyed with the possibility of a new roommate." *Cough cough cough.*

Lorne looks up at the chandelier as he thinks about this, too. Victoria studies her manicure. I'm not supposed to be staring, but I can't help it. She's wearing no makeup at all and still looks glamorous.

"Or a new wacky neighbor," Dustin suggests.

Lorne turns to look at Victoria. "What do you think, honey?"

Victoria sighs. "Who's going to play this brilliant love interest?"

Dustin seems relieved that she's actually open to the idea. He exhales deeply, and his eyes stop squinting for a second. "We're thinking that we should definitely go for someone the audience will immediately recognize, someone with major TVQ."

"Like when Tom Selleck played Monica's boyfriend on *Friends*," Amber says.

Lorne nods. "I love Tom Selleck. Let's get him."

The squints are back as Dustin jumps in. "Actually she was just using Tom Selleck as an example. We've got someone else in mind."

"Tom Selleck's not available?" Lorne asks.

Beads of sweat appear on Dustin's brow. "Tom Selleck's got nothing on the guy we have in mind. This actor is one of the most beloved stars of all time."

Lorne nudges his wife. "They're thinking *Magnum P.I.* Can you believe it?"

Victoria looks at her manicure again. Dustin's exasperated. "Actually, we've got someone just as big but better suited."

As Amber breaks into a coughing fit, Tyler shoots Dustin a weird look. "Maybe we should call Tom," Tyler says. "I know his people."

Dustin agrees. "Absolutely. He would be perfect."

Lorne slaps his hand on the table. "Great. I guess we're done here. Good job. I'll see you next week."

He pecks Victoria on the cheek. "I've got some things to do. I'll be back later."

When Lorne leaves, the producers waste no time in gathering up their stuff. They're almost out of the room when Victoria speaks. "Who were you going to suggest?"

They all turn around at the same time, careful not to look her in the eye.

"Who should play my love interest?" Victoria asks again. "You said you had someone great?"

They're afraid to say anything. It's so quiet you could hear a mouse toot. Finally Dustin addresses the floor. "That's not important. You liked Selleck, so we'll get you Selleck."

"I never said I liked Selleck," Victoria snaps. "And I especially don't like the way he wears his pants. Where does his waist start, anyway? Right under his armpits? What is wrong with that man?"

All of their faces flush. Amber coughs and looks down at her hands. "We were thinking about Pat Harrington."

Dustin and Tyler cringe as if she just pulled the pin out of a grenade.

Victoria thinks about this for a sec and then completely explodes. "Schneider? The fucking super from *One Day at a Time*? He's going to be the new veterinarian? The guy I fall in love with? Whose idea was that?"

"It was Amber's idea," Dustin and Tyler say in perfect unison.

Amber starts hacking so badly she can't breathe. Victoria stares her down like Montezuma turning someone into stone. "You're fired."

In between coughs, she tries to explain. "I realize now that Pat Harrington was a poor choice. But I've got a mortgage. How about someone else? I heard Emeril was ready to try another sitcom."

Tyler and Dustin hang their heads like puppies that peed on the carpet.

Tears spring to Amber's eyes. "*Please*, Victoria." She looks at Tyler and Dustin for help, but they keep their eyes on the floor. "Please."

"Don't ask me to repeat myself," Victoria says. "You know how I feel about repeating myself."

When Amber realizes she's going to hang on her own, she stomps toward the door. "I HOPE YOU GET FUCKING CANCELED!" she yells at the top of her voice.

The door slams in the distance, and the whole house suddenly feels as silent as a funeral home. All that's missing is a row of chairs and a casket and a little muted sniffling. Tyler and Dustin shuffle toward the door.

"We'll see you Monday, Victoria," Dustin says.

"No, you won't," she says.

They whip around to face their executioner.

"You're both fired, too."

I suck in my breath as the producers show themselves out. Wow! The assistants are right. Victoria does fire people a lot. I vow to go home and study the Book again even though I have most of it memorized already.

"Goddamned idiots," Victoria says when she enters the kitchen.

I stand at attention. "Can I get you anything, ma'am?"

"Nah," she says. She looks strangely pleased. In a good mood, almost.

From the corner of my eye, I see her get a Diet Coke out of the fridge, pop the can, and take a sip. With my head down, I stand there stiffly, awaiting instructions. My heart is beating rapidly and my hands break out into their usual clammy sweat. Then I remember from the Book that Victoria cherishes her time alone.

"I'll be in the office if you need me," I squeak.

"Can you believe they wanted Schneider for my love interest? Jesus Christ. Why not Arnold Horshack? That hack hasn't worked in twenty years either."

I'm not sure how to respond.

She slams her hand on the counter. "That's why TV sucks. You've got pipsqueaks in charge. Everyone was born after 1975. Do you know what Victoria Rush was doing in 1975? She was guest-hosting a brand-new show called *Saturday Night Live*. This obsession with youth is out of control."

I figure the appropriate response is to nod my head politely.

"Television was so much better when I started. Everyone was willing to take a chance. My first show took a full year before it became a hit. *Victoria* wouldn't have that chance today. They yank you after a few episodes if they don't see immediate results."

I again nod politely.

"What made my show and shows like *All in the Family* great was content. There was none of this politically correct bullshit that we have today. We talked about hot topics like abortion, racism, sexual discrimination, and birth control. We educated viewers in addition to entertaining them. Did you see the episode where I had the affair with the married black professor? Then got pregnant and decided to abort our interracial child? We were nominated for an Emmy."

I nod.

"Oh, we got a ton of shit for that one! We got letters, threats, and the NAACP claimed we wouldn't be so quick to abort the baby if it weren't biracial. Jimmy Swaggert tried to get station owners across the country to boycott our show. The Christian Coalition said we were promoting abortion as a form of birth control. Everyone thought we were crazy to go with that plotline. But that's why we did it—to get people talking."

I nod again. I can't believe I'm actually having a conversation with Victoria Rush! So what if she's doing most of the talking? She's Victoria Rush. She gets *paid* to talk.

"Today the most interesting thing you'll see on TV is the prepubescent hijinks of a couple of hormonally challenged jerkoffs on *Two Dicks and a Dog.*"

I've never seen that show. It must be on the UPM.

She picks up her drink. "Do you know where Lorne went?"

"He said he was going shopping," I say to the floor.

"Funny, he never buys me anything."

I don't know what to say.

"Where's Matt?"

I have no idea that I'm supposed to be keeping tabs on her son, but I think there's a clause about that very topic in Section Three of the Book. Before I'm forced to deal with my horrible mistake, Matt himself strolls into the room, reeking of pot.

"Hey, Matty," she says in a babyish voice.

He opens the fridge. "There's never anything to eat in this goddamn house."

She puts her hand on his shoulder. "Bertie will make you anything you want."

"I'm sick of Bertie's food. You know, most mothers cook."

"Would you like to go out to eat? Just you and me?"

"You must be fucking kidding," he says, and leaves the room.

I want to melt right into the floor on that one. That's just SO hateful. Victoria's face turns white as Liquid Paper. "I'll be up in my room," she says, trying to keep it together.

"Okay, Victoria!" I say with the enthusiasm of a chirpy cheerleader. And right away I realize that I must sound like a complete dork. I need to chill out. Victoria is just a normal person, after all. She's just as lost as the rest of us. Maybe *more* lost.

"Oh, and Rochelle," she says, getting some of that old snap back in her voice. "Bring me my tea and the newspapers."

"Yes, ma'am."

Sooner or later I'll have to tell Victoria what my name is. But for now, *Rochelle* is close enough. It's really not that big a deal, right?

A WEEK LATER, I'm supposed to be in the office manning the phones. But I'm sitting on the stairs outside the wine cellar because I just saw a mouse. I don't care how cute he is, I don't want Little Stuart keeping me company. Michaela has an audition somewhere. Things are pretty quiet. I served Victoria some pasta in a pine nut sauce for lunch. I had to pick out all the pine nuts because she hates the nuts but likes the pine nut flavor. Then I ordered her Nads, the Bagless Stick Shark, and the Showtime Rotisserie. The phone has only rung three times. The first call was Victoria's new publicist, who wanted to know about a benefit. The second was her hairstylist to confirm an appointment. The third was Courtney looking for Lorne. Besides that, things are pretty mellow. I go upstairs, where it's warmer, because I'm freezing—and I run smack-dab into Lorne.

"Do I have any messages?" he asks.

"Courtney called."

He nods. "Call her and tell her I'm on my way."

"Yes, sir."

He starts to leave but then spins around. "What's Shaq's free-throw percentage this season?"

Uh-oh. I think this is a Lakers question.

His face gets all mean. "Are you aware that you should know this?"

I feel my cheeks turn red. "Yes, sir. I don't know it off the top of my head, but I can find out and get right back to you."

He rolls his eyes and sighs loudly. "This is vital information. Call me in the car when you find out."

"Yes, sir."

He walks away and the phone rings before I can run off to research the Shaq question.

"Michaela?" someone says all urgent.

I recognize the voice right away. "Hey, Griffin. It's Rachel. Michaela won't be in until later."

"We've got a situation here," he says. I can already tell it's serious.

"What's going on?" I whisper.

"*Mid-Life* got canceled."

I suck in my breath. "Oh, my God."

"Where's Victoria?"

"She's having her tarot cards read."

"How much longer will she be tied up?"

I glance at my watch. "Half an hour."

"Okay, good. Tell her Johnny's coming over. I'll see you in a few."

He hangs up so fast that I barely have a chance to think. Where the heck is Michaela? I'm not telling Victoria the bad news. That's Michaela's job. I call her cell, but she doesn't answer. Then I page her. Five minutes go by and she doesn't call back. Hmmm. If I didn't call back, I'd be in big trouble with a capital T. Now I'm going to have to tell Victoria that Johnny's coming over without spilling the beans. Surely Victoria will ask me what the emergency meeting's about. I trudge up the stairs and linger outside the living room, unseen. Madame Bibka, tarot card reader to the stars, is in the middle of an explanation. She looks nothing like any fortuneteller I've ever seen. There's no headscarf or big hoop earrings. Instead, she wears a chic business suit with fancy pumps. She looks like a Russian Ally McBeal, though not as thin.

"The stars and moon mean a change is coming," Madame Bibka says in her funny accent.

Victoria's eyes widen. "What kind of change?"

"A big, big change. A life-changing change," Madame Bibka says.

Maybe those cards really *could* tell the future.

"Can you be more specific?"

When she flips over the next card, she mumbles, "Aaah."

"Aaah, what?"

"I see big changes in career and marriage both."

"The show's getting axed and I'm getting a divorce?!"

My hands begin to sweat. She's right about the first part, anyway.

"Madame Bibka don't say that. The *cards* say that." Smart. She blames the cards. That way she's not responsible for horrible predictions and bad advice. She should have been a lawyer.

As Victoria ponders this confusing information, or *mis*information, Madame Bibka puts her cards away. "Our time is up," she says.

"Okay, I'll see you next week, yes?"

"Yes," Madame Bibka says with a scary smile, then she turns and leaves.

I enter the room. "Uh, Victoria?"

She whirls around. "What is it?"

"Johnny's on his way over."

She's not pleased. "Did he say why?"

I remember what Michaela told me. *When in doubt, lie, lie, lie.* I feel all the blood rush to my face. "No, ma'am."

"I'm getting canceled. Madame Bibka was right, dammit! Johnny never comes over here unless it's something huge." She sits down. "I need one of my pills—*now*."

I run to the office to retrieve them. When I get back, Victoria is staring at the wall like a zombie. She's so still I can't even tell if she's breathing.

"Victoria?"

"WHAT?!"

I jump back, startled. Good. She's still alive. "Here you go," I say. I hand her a pill and a bottle of Stress B Vitamin Water.

Victoria wolfs it down and takes a swig off the bottle. "Get me a Diet Coke."

"Yes, ma'am." I walk over to the bar, set the pills down, and reach into the minifridge.

"From the kitchen," she says.

I look at her strangely.

"They're colder. Now hurry up. The show's about to begin."

When I return from the kitchen, the bottle of pills is now sitting on the coffee table in front of her. It's obvious she's taken more pills, but I have no idea how many. What if it was three or four or five or six? Oh, God. I don't know what to do. Maybe if I'm lucky she got mostly sugar pills.

"My career is over," she murmurs. "My show's canceled. The Rainbow Room canceled."

"Can I get you anything else?"

"The fat lady has sung," she sighs.

"A cool rag for your head?" I suggest.

"Stick a fork in me."

"Ma'am?"

"Now appearing for three weeks only: *Victoria Rush is Auntie Mame at the Burt Reynolds Theater in Jupiter, Florida.*"

I have no idea what she's talking about. I take the prescription bottle and tiptoe out of the room to call Michaela again. But she doesn't answer. I hang up and go back into the living room. Victoria's still talking to herself but otherwise she appears normal. By Hollywood standards, anyway. By Sugarland standards, none of this is normal.

I leave her alone and wait in the kitchen for Johnny and Griffin to arrive.

Half an hour later, the buzzer at the front gate sounds. I glance at Victoria on my way to the front door. She's sipping from a bottle of Bombay Sapphire Gin. She still seems okay, just a little upset. Who wouldn't be? When I open the door, Johnny steps past me before I can even say hello.

"Victoria?" he bellows.

"She's in the living room," I say. "Can I get y'all something to drink?"

Johnny stalks down the hall to find her. He doesn't seem like a nice guy at all. I look at Griffin.

"Don't mind him," he says. "The man has an inherent personality disorder that hinders his ability to be amiable." I'm starting to get used to the way Griffin talks. He's so smart. He was probably the valevictorian in his senior year. "How is she?"

"Not well," I say.

I follow Griffin toward the dining room and we hover by the doorway, straining to hear.

Johnny has cut right to the chase. "I've been on the phone with the network boys all morning, Victoria, trying to turn things around. But it doesn't look good. The bastards want to cancel the show."

Her only response is a loud sigh.

"I fought with them for over three hours," he says.

Griffin whispers, "He spoke to 'the boys' for ten seconds. He was at the spa, getting a hot salt scrub."

"They've got their heads up their asses, I tell ya," Johnny says. He sounds just like Jimmy Cagney, that little guy in those old gangster movies. My father loved Cagney. He had every single one of his movies. He used to go around the house talking like him, out of the side of his mouth: *What's that you say? All I'm getting for dinner is a lousy grapefruit? Well, here! Here's your damn grapefruit!* Maybe that's why my mother began drinking.

"What do those idiots know about art?" Johnny is saying. "They say the sitcom is dead, reality TV is dead, and that the future is all about 'niche programming.'"

"What the hell does that mean?" Victoria asks.

"I asked them that exact same question," Johnny replies. "They don't seem to know, either."

"Who . . . else . . . got canceled?" she wonders, struggling with the words. It sounds as if her tongue is too big for her mouth.

"I have no idea. But probably everybody. It's a bloodbath. Heads are rolling."

I peek around the corner. Victoria looks like she's about to cry. "Who knows about this?" she mumbles.

"The network and us. That's it. But it'll be in the Monday trades for sure."

She closes her eyes as if she's praying and begins to rock back and forth.

"What's wrong with her?" Griffin whispers.

"I don't know," I lie. I'm getting good at this lying business. I don't think her manager needs to know about the drug abuse.

Johnny steals a look at his watch. "But hey, there's an upside to this: we can go back to ABC and talk to them about that movie-of-the-week you didn't have time to do."

She opens her eyes suddenly, like she just got jolted with those paddle thingies on *ER*. "Wha—? Are you fucking nuts? That piece of shit!"

"Are we talking about the same movie? I'm referring to *Don't Touch My New Wife*, about the woman who is obsessed with her ex-husband's fiancée."

"I thought you meant *Water, Water, Everywhere*—about the psycho with the hand-washing compulsion."

"No, I agreed with you on that one. I don't think OCD is right for you."

"Why are we talking about this anyway, goddamn it?! Those fucking projects are beneath me. Do I look that fucking desperate to you?"

I hope Johnny doesn't answer that honestly.

"Tell you what, Victoria," he says. "Let's chat when you're feeling better."

"No," she slurs. "I wanna *chat* now, Mr. No Power Asshole."

Johnny stands, ignoring her. "I'll give you a call in the morning."

"Don't bother, loser!"

"Victoria, pull yourself together. It's not the end of the world."

"It is for you. You're fired."

"Griffin!" Johnny yells.

Griffin runs past me, into the room. "Yes?"

"We're leaving. *Now.*"

"Get out of here!" Victoria screams. She tries to stand but falls over the coffee table.

"Jesus Christ," Johnny says.

Griffin tries to help her up.

"Get your fucking hands off me!" she shouts, pummeling him with her small fists.

"Rachel!" Griffin yells. "I need some help in here!"

I hurry inside and kneel on the floor next to her. "Victoria?"

She turns her head to look at me. "Who are you?"

"I'm out of here," Johnny says, storming off.

Griffin again tries to help Victoria but she crawls away, hollering like a stuck pig. I remember that terrible scene in *Deliverance* where they did that sinful thing to that jolly red-faced actor, who I don't believe enjoyed it.

Victoria has managed to wedge herself between the coffee table and the sofa.

"Find Lorne," Griffin tells me. I cross the room and reach for the phone.

"Do I know you?" Victoria asks, staring at Griffin. She's still wedged against the sofa, but she's on her back now.

"I'm Johnny's assistant," Griffin says.

"Do you know how much money I've made that leech?" she says. "And that's the best he can do?! Some bullshit TV movie about a middle-aged has-been with some seriously loose screws?!"

Courtney's phone rings forever before she picks up, and she sounds all breathless when she does: "Hello?"

"Courtney, it's me, Rachel," I whisper, turning my back so Victoria won't hear. "Do you know where Lorne is?"

"Why would I know where Lorne is?" she says loudly.

"Victoria's show got canceled and she took too many pills and we need to find him."

She doesn't say anything for a minute. "I'll let him know," she says and hangs up.

I cross the room and whisper the news to Griffin. "She said she'd find Lorne."

"Why doesn't she look between her legs?!" Victoria shouts. "That's where she'll find Lorne, the little slut." Then she looks directly at me. "And brace yourself, Texas: you're next."

"That will never happen, Victoria," I say, trying not to cry. "I'm not like that."

"It's all over," she wails. "My career, my life. I'm finished."

Griffin's cell phone rings. He pulls it out of his pocket. "Yes?"

I can hear Johnny's enraged voice. "*Somebody* needs to get their fucking ass out to the car now."

"I'll be right there," Griffin says, hanging up.

I hand Victoria a throw pillow. "Why don't you put this under your head?"

She lifts her head and I slide the pillow into place. Victoria sighs and closes her eyes and says in a dreamy voice, "I'm dead. I can see a bright light up ahead. And Lord, I'm a-comin'. I'm going toward the light."

"I better split," Griffin says.

I walk him to the front door and burst into tears. "It's all my fault," I say, sobbing. "I left her alone with the whole bottle of pills. I'm so sorry."

"Rachel, relax," he says, touching my arm gently. "She's been like this for years."

"I'm going to get fired. I just know it."

"No one's getting fired. She'll be all right. She'll sleep it off and won't remember any of this, except the cancellation, of course."

"But Johnny got fired."

"She's fired him a dozen times. She will not recall this episode, trust me."

"Do you really think so?" I sniffle.

His phone rings. "I've got to go before *I* get fired."

I open the door for him. "Thanks, Griffin."

"Hang in there," he says. "This is as dire as it gets."

When I return to the living room, the phone begins to ring. I'm almost afraid to pick it up.

"Hello?" I say nervously.

"Victoria Rush, please."

She's sprawled out on the floor totally passed out. But it's not like I can say that. "She's not available right now. Can I take a message?"

"This is Maggie from Dr. Mitchell's office. The doctor would like her to come in as soon as possible to discuss some lab results."

I grab my notepad. "Lab results? Is everything okay?"

"The results are confidential. Dr. Mitchell doesn't work on Saturdays, but he'll make an exception for Victoria."

"Uh, okay. I'll make sure she gets the message."

"Thank you."

After hanging up, I glance down at Victoria. Her mouth's wide open and she's snoring. What if she's really sick? What if she gets sicker because she had all those pills? I decide to sit on the floor next to her until she wakes up or Lorne gets home, whichever comes first.

GRIFFIN

"**F**UCK THAT CUNT," Johnny growls from the back seat of his Mercedes.

I glance at him in the rearview. His jaw is clenched and sweat trickles down his artificial cheekbones.

"Jesus Christ, it's hot in here. I'm sweating like Michael Jackson at a day care center!"

I adjust the AC despite the fact that individual controls for his personal climate zone are mere inches from his grasp.

"Twenty years is a long time to put up with shit."

So is three years, asshole.

Suddenly he remembers something pertinent. "Have we been paid in full for the eight episodes?"

We? "Yes, we have."

"Like I was saying, fuck that bitch. I've got other clients. What's going on with Travis and the action flick?"

"He hasn't made a decision," I say.

"They threw him a fucking party! What's it gonna take?"

"I don't know."

"You're a fag, why don't you blow him? I know you've been thinking about it."

I'm so appalled at his effrontery that I slam on the brakes. Johnny flies forward and his forehead smacks the back of the headrest.

"Jesus Christ! Are you trying to kill me?"

"*Somebody* should always wear their seat belt," I quip, feeling the bile creeping up my throat. Lately my stomach has been doing an excellent rendition of The Montserrat Volcano Blues. I change the subject, hoping it might help. "Bart Abelman is auditioning tonight for a spot at the Aspen Comedy Festival."

He reaches for his seat belt. "Who?"

I look in the rearview. "The stand-up comic I told you about. I think we should sign him. He's already creating quite the buzz."

"I told you I'm not interested in comics."

"I know. But he needs representation and the sharks are circling. I would hate to see us lose out."

I pause to let the chum sink in. Johnny hates to miss the boat on anything, even if he's not on the dock to begin with.

He revives his finger-wriggling ritual and ponders. "Okay," he says at last. "Check it out and let me know. If he's really any good, I might reconsider."

"Done."

He has no idea, but Bart Abelman is already his client.

"And if he does get picked for the festival, I'm not paying your way, pal. You keep talking about 'we' and 'us,' so gamble with your own goddamn money."

Cheap bastard. "No problem."

I'm going to have to borrow from Mel again. I abhor living like this! Where's my damn Zantac?

I FINAGLE MY WAY through a swarm of people at The Improv. The crowd at the bar consists of comics on the lineup, others who wish they were, plus various managers and agents from firms across the board. The audience has been seated and is waiting for the show to start. They have no idea that they're about to see an important audition for the

U.S. Comedy Arts Festival in Aspen. It's a Tuesday night and about twenty-eight stragglers have wandered in, mainly tourists. Bart stands at the end of the bar. He has curly dark hair, a thin build, and droopy hang-dog eyes. I make my way over with my hand extended. "Bart, how are you feeling?"

"I'm a little nervous," he says, shaking my hand. "I've worked with a lot of these guys. Most of them are headliners. I'm just a feature act."

"You're all doing the same seven minutes. Don't worry. You'll be great."

"That's what I keep telling him," a woman chips in. She steps on my foot as she forces her way between us. A Virginia Slim 100 protrudes from a taut face surrounded by stringy auburn hair.

"I'm Anne Abelman, Bart's wife." She's barely five feet tall and her teeth are tiny but plentiful, like a piranha's.

I shake her hand heartily. "Griffin Marquette. Nice to meet you."

She takes a drag off the cigarette. "I hear you work for Johnny Treadway."

"That is correct."

She exhales the smoke into my face. "Is he coming?"

"He couldn't make it, but I'm here to watch Bart kill." I wink at Bart, who smiles.

An obese black woman suddenly horns her way in. "Hi, I'm Creama Wheat. I'm going up first. Don't miss me."

"Hi, Creama. Griffin Marquette. Looking forward to it."

She steps closer. "I couldn't help but overhear that you work for Johnny Treadway. I'm also looking for representation."

Anne steps between us and glares up and *around* Creama's waist. "We were in the middle of a discussion. Do you mind?"

Creama reaches into her purse. "Here's my card. Give me a call."

As she waddles away, Anne hisses, "The nerve."

"You're exactly right, Anne. I'm here for Bart and Bart only. Besides, I don't need to watch Creama Wheat to know that the funniest thing about her is her name."

"Johnny has a pretty impressive roster, doesn't he?" she asks.

"Yes, he does. Including your husband here."

She takes another drag off her cigarette. "Bart's been getting a lot of phone calls from other managers who think they can get him a TV show. Can you guys get him a TV show?"

I'm wearing a smile so unctuous it would make Johnny proud. "That's the plan, Anne."

"Bart's not afraid to walk away from you if he doesn't get what he wants. We've been in this business a long time and he deserves this."

"Honey," he says gently, "let's not worry about all that right now."

She shoots him a look. "You have to be very explicit about your expectations from the beginning."

Ah, the artist's meddling wife. There's nothing worse. And this one seems determined to make my life as difficult as possible. These people don't seem to comprehend that the pursuit of fame and fortune is a perilous endeavor under the best of circumstances, and that few marital relationships survive even the early part of the journey. I don't doubt that Anne has spent years listening to brainless jokes, traveling to dreadful gigs, and watching in horror as Bart's less talented colleagues achieve a modicum of success. It would be one thing if she empathized with her husband, but it's obvious that Anne has ambitions of her own. She is simply waiting to capitalize on his big break.

"What do you do?" I ask.

"I'm an actress."

Bingo! I smile, "Well, that's great. Bart, let me confirm your set time."

Moments later I glance over my shoulder to see Bart and Anne huddled together in furious debate. Hopefully this won't distract him from being funny. Anne storms off and Bart shuffles over, looking like a whipped cur. "Hey, man," he says, "I'm sorry about Anne. She gets a little worked up sometimes."

I go for a little of that over-the-top bullshit to set his mind at ease. "Bart, my man, don't worry about it. She's concerned about you. She obviously loves you very much."

"Yeah," Bart says, but he doesn't look too sure.

"How long have you been married?" I ask.

"Seven years."

"Wow, that's a long time."

"You're telling me," Bart frowns.

I can feel the man's pain. I know he's going to kill tonight.

Michaela

R ACHEL KIND OF GREW on me like mold on old food. I really can't explain it because we have nothing in common. She reminds me of a puppy—innocent, happy, easily pleased, and not too bright. And she likes to discuss my favorite subject: me. She wants to know everything about my career: gigs, classes, agents, costars, etc. My rehashed stories are really not that interesting—okay, maybe they are because they do star *me*—but she's so into them that I tend to embellish to give her some added thrills. She's kind of like the little sister I never wanted.

She's also a quick learner and has already lasted longer than I expected. Victoria's actually almost comfortable around her, which allows me to spend more time away from the office. I pack in as many auditions as possible. I get new head shots with my new name—Michaela *Liel* Marsh—printed on them.

About this time, I decide to expand my horizons, which means exploring relationships with other agents. Randall Blume is certainly very good, though he's not giving me the attention I need. I'm still fucking him twice a month, but he's losing interest, the BP notwithstanding. It's just a matter of time before he drops me. So I conduct a massive mailing and send my résumé and head shot to every A-list agent in town. I don't hear back from anyone.

Finally, one Saturday morning, something very interesting happens at the Farmer's Market. I'm over at the macadamia nut bin when I feel someone staring at me. I look over to see a designer-clad woman in her early forties with a very short haircut. She probably recognizes me from *Seinfeld*. She begins to follow me and then garners the courage to speak. "Excuse me?"

I turn around. "Yes?"

She's wearing a charcoal Susan Lazar suit and Burberry pumps. "I'm sorry to bother you, but are you an actress?"

"Yes, I am."

She checks me up and down. "I thought so. You are absolutely stunning."

The word LESBIAN blips on my gaydar.

"Thank you very much," I say and try to walk away, but she continues, "Would you like to join me for coffee?"

"No, thanks," I say.

The woman bites her lip and looks disappointed, naturally. But she reaches into her Hermès Kelly bag. "Here's my card. My name's Bonnie Adams and I'm casting a film for Barry Levinson. There's a part I think you should audition for. If you're interested, call me."

I change my tune immediately and extend my hand. "Hi, Bonnie. I'm Michaela *Liel* Marsh."

She takes my hand in hers. It's petite but firm. "Liel?"

"It's my Kabbalah name," I say coyly.

She's pleased with my answer. She runs her finger lightly over the top of my hand. "You sure you don't have time for a cup of coffee?"

I flutter my eyelashes and work it. "Sure, why not?"

One cup of coffee turns into drinks and dinner and then we end up back at her place—for dessert. I've never been with a woman before, so I'm a little nervous. At least Bonnie is well-groomed and very clean. She lives in a spacious two-bedroom condo in a high-rise on Wilshire. As soon as we get there, she pours us a couple of glasses of champagne and turns on the stereo. As Norah Jones serenades us, we step onto the balcony and check out the view.

"The city is so beautiful at night," she says.

"Yes, it is," I agree and take a big gulp of champagne. I'll need a lot more to drink to get through this. I'm wondering when she'll make her move. It doesn't take long. She puts her glass down and comes up behind me. I try not to flinch. She wraps her arms around my waist and softly kisses my neck. "Does that feel good?"

I'm reminded of my first sexual experience at fourteen with Saul Greenblatt in the synagogue on Park and 68th. He too, was concerned if it felt good. Of course, I actually never felt anything because he blew his load before unzipping his pants.

"Sure," I say, and I down the rest of my champagne. Bonnie's lips are thin and dry. Her hands disappear underneath my shirt and travel upward.

"You have a great body," she whispers.

"Thank you," I say as she caresses my breasts. I close my eyes, trying to get into it. But then I quickly reopen them because for some reason I envision my father watching.

"I need another drink," I say quickly. She grabs my face in her hands and kisses me. Her tongue softly explores the inside of my mouth. When she's finished, she says, "Come with me."

Bonnie leads me into the bedroom. "Make yourself comfortable."

As she disappears into the bathroom, I sit down on the edge of the bed. I'm far from comfortable. I fight the urge to run screaming out of there, but I've already come so far. Christ, I spent the whole day with the woman. I can't just leave now. If I piss her off, I won't be able to audition. And it sounds like a great one. It's an eighty-million dollar romantic comedy directed by Barry Levinson. Bonnie said I'm perfect for the female lead and he's looking for an unknown . . . so I'll stay. Seems a small price to pay, especially since it's going to change my life forever.

Bonnie comes back into the room, wearing a slinky number. "Is everything okay?"

"Sure," I say nervously. "Everything's fine."

She sits down next to me and touches my hair. "Have you ever done this before?"

Fuck somebody to get something?

"I've never been with a woman," I admit.

"Then lie back and get comfortable. I promise it will be something you'll never forget."

I feel like I'm in a bad porno. I smile weakly as she fiddles with the buttons on my shirt. I can get through this. I'm an *actress*. I'll just lie here and pretend Bonnie's my agent.

I SURVIVED MY FIRST lesbian experience. And I have to say, it wasn't that bad. Bonnie really enjoyed herself, especially after she got a load of my BP. I'm telling you, it's magical. Things got a little weird when she brought out that big black dildo, but I can do it again if need be. But I want to make something clear. Just because I slept with a woman does not make me gay. My index finger is the same size as my ring finger. My favorite TV show is not *The L Word*. I'm not bummed that Melissa Etheridge got remarried. I'm still into penises, thank you very much. When I left that morning, Bonnie told me to give her a call about the audition. Score another one for my little bald 'gina.

I have to have dinner with Dad again. It's time for his monthly visit. He's as regular as my period. We meet at Dan Tana's, a little Italian restaurant on Santa Monica Boulevard. As soon as we sit down, he starts in. "Are you sick?"

When in doubt, "I just got over the flu."

"I'll buy you some of that weight-gain powder that bodybuilders use. Put some meat on your bones."

"You don't have to do that, Dad."

I order an entrée that Rosie O'Donnell would dive into with reckless abandon: chicken parmesan with fettuccine alfredo. Between disgusting, fat-laden bites, Dad tells me that my mother has stopped talking to him.

"What did you do?" I ask.

He shrugs. "With your mother, one never knows."

I narrow my eyes. "You know."

He sighs and fesses up: "I told her I didn't want to do things with Herman and Mitzi Schwartz anymore."

I can't believe he finally told my mother how much those two annoy him. It only took him twenty years. "What did she say?"

"Nothing! She hasn't spoken to me in a week."

"I'm sorry."

"Sorry? This is the happiest I've been in years. I feel like a kid again."

I can't help giggling.

It doesn't take him long to get around to Ernie Finklestein again. I've heard from him three times since Dad's last visit, but I tell Dad that he never called.

"That's really strange," Dad says. "He was so excited about getting together with you."

"Maybe he was just being nice. He might already have a girlfriend."

"No. Ernie is single. Trust me."

"He could be gay. Think about it. He's a very natty dresser."

Dad looks at his watch. "Then we'll just have to ask him ourselves."

I don't know if I'm nauseous from the food or because of what Dad just said. "What are you talking about?"

"I took the liberty of inviting him to join us."

I want to die. "*Here?*"

"Yes, he had a business dinner, but he said he'd stop by when he was done. He's due any minute."

"*Dad.* Jesus. Why did you do this to me? I don't want to see Ernie Finklestein. I don't care if he's rich. I didn't like him then and I won't like him now."

"Stop being so dramatic, Sylvie."

"Shhh!" I look around to see if anyone heard.

Dad tsks.

I exit the booth. "I need to get out of here."

"Where are you going?"

"Home." I lean over and kiss Dad on the cheek.

"Sylvie—"

"Love you." I hurry out of the restaurant.

Outside, I hand the valet my ticket and wait. That's when I realize I'm a sitting duck. I'm the only person standing outside the restaurant and Ernie could show up at any moment. I reach into my purse for my Sally Jesseys and stained teeth. Then I pull my hair back into a ponytail. A Town Car pulls up in front of me. I shield my face with my bag and hold my breath as a man steps out. I'm afraid to look in his direction. He seems to be hesitating. Why won't he go into the restaurant already? Luckily my car shows up. I run over, get in, and drive off. I don't even look back.

Polaroid 86A08611A

Kecia

Kecia

I'M POLISHING OFF my third donut when the phone rings. "Hello?"

There's static on the line, but I can hear a male voice, smooth as a clean countertop. "Is Travis there?"

I've got one of those prickly feelings I always get when something big's about to go down. Like that Northridge 'quake. The night before it hit, I had the prickles all over. Then, boom! Four-thirty in the morning and all hell breaks loose. But that's a Pisces for you. I'm highly intuitive all the way. "Who's calling?"

"His brother Lenny."

Brother? Travis doesn't have one. This has got to be a prank call. Besides, this man don't sound white. He sounds likes one of those late-night R&B radio deejays, you know, hosting *Pillow Talk* or the *Quiet Storm*.

"He's not available. Can I take a message?"

"To whom am I speaking?" he asks politely.

"Kecia, his assistant."

"Hello, Kecia. I'm Lenny. Nice to meet you. Now that we've been properly introduced, could you find my little bro for me?" His voice is seductive but sprinkled with the right amount of menace. Something's definitely up. I close the donut box.

"How do I know you're his brother?" I ask.

"How do you know I'm not?" he teases.

I feel myself blush and get up to walk in the house. "Travis never told me about you."

Lenny chuckles wickedly. "What would you like to know?"

"How old are you?"

"I just turned twenty-eight."

"Happy birthday," I grin. What am I doing talking to a complete stranger like this? My horoscope today said I deserve *recreation and laughs*, but not to flirt with the wrong people.

"Thank you, darlin'," Lenny purrs. "Too bad you weren't there to celebrate with me."

My cheeks feel like I've been sitting in the sun. "There's always next year," I suggest. No doubt about it. I'm definitely flirting.

"Forget next year. How about tonight?"

"Say what?" The prickly sensation leaves my legs and travels up my spine.

"That's why I'm calling. If I hurry, I can make the four o'clock flight."

I gulp. "Where are you now?"

"Arizona."

"Let me see if I can find Travis for you," I say, putting him on hold. I find Travis in his bedroom. He's lying on his bed, looking at the pictures in *US* magazine. Sometimes I wonder if the boy can read. "Do you know that Christopher Reeve can move his toes?" he says, looking up at me. "Isn't that cool?" He can read captions, anyway.

"Your brother's on the phone," I say, and I hand him the receiver.

Travis tosses the magazine aside. "Len?" he screams.

I've never seen him so excited. He really *does* have a brother.

"Where are you? You're coming when? Wait 'til the guys find out! You're not going to believe my house! Did you see me win the MTV movie award for Best New Actor? I have so much to tell you!"

I leave him alone and return to the office. I'm rearranging the stack of scripts on my desk when Travis comes running in.

"Guess what?!" The boy can hardly contain himself.

"Your brother's coming," I say.

"Yep!" He grabs my hands and spins me around the room.

"I'm getting dizzy," I laugh.

"Sorry," he says and stops spinning around. "I'm just so stoked. It's been eight years since I've seen him."

"Why so long?"

"He was in prison. He just got released."

My face drops. I'd been flirting with an ex-con. My horoscope tried to warn me. The stars always know. "What did he do?"

"He killed a guy. But it wasn't his fault."

"Was it an accident?" I ask.

"No, Len killed the guy on purpose. The dude was assaulting this lady in a parking lot and he just snapped."

"So he has a bad temper?"

"He can't help it. He's had a tough life. After our parents died, we were sent to Social Services. Lenny was fifteen and I was only five. We tried to stay together but there were no foster families that would take the both of us. So we got separated. Lenny always ran away and tracked me down. Then we'd take off together. Eventually, we'd get caught and they'd separate us again. When Lenny went to prison, I ran away and started living on the streets. I'd still be living out there if this whole acting thing hadn't happened."

Sometimes I forget white kids are in the system, too. "I didn't know any of that about you," I say.

"Nobody knows, and I want to keep it that way," he says. Then he gets excited all over again. "Jesus! Lenny's back. From here on in, nothing and no one is going to keep us apart."

I don't know what to think. I'm happy for Travis, but I'm not sure I want to be working around an ex-con. Especially an ex-con I was flirting with. "Do you want me to have a limo pick him up?"

"Yeah, that'd be great. I also need you to call Delta and buy the ticket." He hands me a scrap of the magazine he was reading. "Here's all the info. There's a flight at four. Put him in first class."

"Sure."

I go off and call Delta and book Lenny's flight, and as I'm getting off the phone Travis walks in and tells me to take the rest of the week off. "I want to spend time with Len," he says, his voice cracking with emotion. "I can't believe he's back!" Now he starts blubbering like a baby. "My big brother's coming home! Thank you, God. Thank you for making our little family whole again!"

He runs off, still blubbering. I don't know what to say, but I know what I'm thinking: actors are about the damn craziest people on the planet

I RETURN TO WORK a week later. Usually there's all sorts off hangers-on at the crib, but the only car in the driveway today is Travis's Cayenne. I hurry through the gate toward the house.

"Morning, girl."

I turn around to find Lou hovering by the mailbox, with his damn cameras—all eight of them. And a brand-new Lakers jersey.

"Don't you get tired of hanging around?" I ask.

"Where's Travis?" he says. "He hasn't left the house in days."

"He had a tunnel dug under the pool that leads directly to the alley," I say. "That way he can leave without running into you."

"Really?"

I roll my eyes.

"Someone arrived late the other night with luggage," Lou says. "Must be stayin' awhile."

I don't say a word.

"Who's the mystery guest?"

"None of your business."

I hurry off and leave him there and reach the house and unlock the front door. Something about it feels intensely creepy. For one thing, there's no loud music reverberating off the walls.

I step into the foyer. The familiar smells—stale cigarette smoke, skunkweed, beer, sex—are all gone. Something else is in the air. And damn it if it ain't *bacon!* I can hear it frying. My stomach grumbles violently. Now I hear Travis's voice in the kitchen, which is very strange: I've never known him to get up before noon. Maybe I've stepped into an *X-Files* episode. I half-expect Mulder and that white girl to be lurking around the corner. I carefully walk toward the kitchen. Someone else is talking. The voice doesn't belong to Pokey, Frog, or any of the regular fools, so it must be that convict I spoke to on the phone.

I enter the kitchen. "Knock-knock."

"Hey, Kecia!" Travis exclaims. He's sitting at the counter and I can half-see the Mystery Brother at the stove. "Come on in and meet my bro."

I step through. The bro is barefoot and shirtless, tending to the bacon with his back to me. Every muscle on that perfect back ripples like water in a stream.

"Len—"

Len throws a dishrag over his shoulder and turns around. I hope someone's got my back because I'm about to faint. This man is Mac Daddy squared.

"—this is Kecia. Kecia, Len."

Lenny comes toward me with his hand extended, and oh my god! He's taller and leaner than his famous little brother, but they've got the same green eyes, sandy blond hair, and devilish smirk. He has to be a Scorpio. He comes closer, checking me out from head to toe, and I feel my heartbeat in my ears. I surrender my hand, which he kisses gently.

"Nice to meet you in person," he coos. The man is as hypnotic as a snake charmer.

"Are you hungry?" Travis asks me.

I can't answer. My panties are melting.

"Len makes the best omelets. You should try one."

"Uh, no thanks. I already had breakfast," I lie. I tell myself that I'm never going to eat again.

"Okay, but you're really missing out," Travis says.

I can't help staring at Len. I want to know what sign he is. If we're not compatible, I'll die. Either that or change my date of birth.

When I finally find the strength to tear my eyes away, I look over at Travis. "I guess you won't need this," I say, holding up a six of Mountain Dew and a box of Krispy Kremes.

"Nope," Travis says. "From now on I'm going to eat healthy."

"I need to get this boy into shape," Lenny says.

I grin and look away. I know Lenny's looking at me. And I'm afraid to meet his eyes because there's no telling what I might do.

"So, Kecia. How long have you been working for my little brother?"

Now I *have* to look at him. His back's against the bar and he's got his muscled arms crossed in front of him. The dishrag dangles over his shoulder. He looks like one of those studs on those sexy greeting cards. The kind you send your girlfriend that says, "Here's a hunk for your birthday."

"Almost a year," I say.

"That's great," he says, looking right at me. But I can't hold the look. Those sparkling emerald eyes are too much for me. I think I'm about to swoon. I try to look away, but I find myself staring at his abs. He has a perfect six-pack, or *twelve*-pack, or whatever the hell it's called. I feel like working them for a while. With my tongue.

"You sure you won't join us for breakfast?" Lenny asks.

"I'm sure," I squeak. Travis smirks. He knows exactly what big brother is doing to me.

Lenny goes back to the stove and I force myself not to look in his direction. I know Travis is watching me.

"Where's your friends?" I ask.

"Travis's going to get himself a whole new set of friends, right?" Len says.

"Sounds good to me," Travis says.

I feel like dancing on the ceiling, Lionel Richie–style. Big brother got here a week ago and already things are changing for the better.

"Kecia," Lenny says. "Tell me about Johnny Treadway and this boy Griffin."

"What do you want to know?"

"Who runs that show?"

"Well, Johnny's the boss, but Griffin does the real work."

"Why don't you call this boss man for me, and tell him me and Trav are coming to see him tomorrow?"

"Okay. I'll see when he's available."

"No, honey. With all due respect, that's the wrong approach. We'll tell him when to make himself available. Tomorrow, Tuesday. Eleven A.M."

"Okay," I squeak.

"Len wants to meet everybody I work with," Travis says.

"I'll take care of it right now."

I'm not halfway down the corridor when I hear Lenny say, "She's really cute."

That's it! No one has ever called me cute before. I'm definitely never eating again. I'm tired of looking like one of those fat, bad-tempered sisters I used to work with at the DMV.

As I come around the corner, I practically run into Marta.

"Sorry!"

Marta frowns. "What's the matter with you? Your face is all red."

"Nothing," I say. "I'm feeling *piqued*." I don't know what it means, but I heard it on *Will & Grace* the other night and it sounds about right.

"Someone just called for you," Marta says. "He said it was important."

"Who?" I ask, though I damn well know already.

"Joseph Somebody."

That's the IRS guy. Joseph Sanders. "Oh yes," I say. "My friend Joe. Did he say what he wanted?"

"No," Marta says, and I'm very relieved. At least the man was discreet. "I don't like the sound of this, Kecia," Marta continues. "Is this the same Joe who keeps coming by the house?"

"I don't know what you're talking about," I say, and hurry into the office.

Marta follows me inside. She knows I'm lying. "Why don't you tell me what's going on, *hija*?" she says impatiently.

"*Nothing* is going on."

Marta shakes her head and decides to drop it. She leaves.

I pick up the phone and call Griffin, and the office patches me through to his cell.

"Hey, Kecia," he says. "What's happening over there at this early hour?"

"Lot of things," I say. "Starting with Travis's brother."

"Travis has a brother?"

"That's right, Griffy. And you better not try to steal him from me."

Jeb.

EXT. RANDALL BLUME RESIDENCE—DAY

I am standing across the street from Randall Blume's house, a house that even in my wildest dreams I will never be able to afford. I couldn't even afford the fucking property taxes on this place. I'd probably have to scrimp and save and eat only once a day to pay the goddamn *utilities*. But the really weird thing is that I don't even know what I'm doing here. It's not like I'm the proverbial idiot returning to the scene of the crime—because I didn't commit any crime. Randall Blume committed the fucking crime. He fired me. After stealing my idea. But I'm going to get the bastard. Yeah. *That's* why I'm here: I'm *about* to commit the crime.

For a moment, I imagine myself driving a lemon-yellow Hummer through the massive front door. I race up the stairs and grab Blume's naked ass just as he's about to take refuge in the panic room, *without* Ashley and the kid. The man always looks out for himself first. I kick him in the nuts, hard, and make him beg for his life in front of his trembling family.

"You kah-vood!" I shout. "You shtinkin', sheefing kah-vood!" I'm trying to call him a *stinking, thieving coward*, but for some reason—in this particular fantasy sequence—I sound exactly like Governor Schwarzenegger. It's ridiculous. My whole life is ridiculous. I have to do something about all this anger in me. It's not healthy.

I'm unemployed again and I don't know what to do with myself. I was over at Barnes & Noble last night, cruising the self-help aisle, and I smiled at this cute brunette. Bitch tried to mace me. For *smiling*. But what was I expecting? Any woman who's looking for the Meaning of Life in a self-help aisle isn't going to be all there, is she?

Maybe I'll go for a run, say a quick ten miles. It's not like I have anything else to do. I turn and head back to my car, and just then Ashley's Range Rover pulls into the street. My back is to her. I hope she hasn't seen me. I put my chin down and quicken my pace.

I can hear her pulling into the driveway now, cutting the engine, getting out, and shutting the perfectly engineered door. "Jeb?" she calls out. "Is that you?"

I'M FUCKED.

Should have kept walking, but I have to turn around. Her voice is so goddamn mellifluous it's spellbinding. Doesn't she know I've been fired? Surely Blume told her. Maybe not. I wish I'd taken a shower. I turn and wave from the distance.

"I'm so glad you're here," she calls out. "Can you help me with the groceries?"

SHE DOESN'T KNOW.

I move toward her, thinking fast. "I was in the neighborhood. I thought I'd stop by to see if you had anything for the cleaners."

"How thoughtful." She opens the passenger door and unbuckles Junior from his car seat. He runs over and throws his arms around my legs. "Jeb!" he exclaims in that little-kid-always-hysterically-happy-way. "I have a SpongeBob snow cone maker. Want to see?"

"Sure," I say, gently extracting him from my body. He's a cute little bastard. He looks exactly like Ashley.

"Goody!" he squeals.

Ashley hands me two Gelsen's grocery bags and smiles. "You can't imagine how crowded that store was today." No, I can't. I can't even imagine shopping at Gelsen's. I mean, I like valet grocery shopping as much as the next guy, but I can't afford it.

"End of the week food rush," I say, returning the smile and wishing I'd brushed my teeth. She's wearing a light-blue V-neck T-shirt, short short khakis, and white tennis shoes. Her tanned legs are perfectly toned.

As I reach for the bags, she notices how shitty I look. "Are you feeling okay?" she asks. "I hope Randall's not working you too hard."

I'm afraid I'll kill her with my breath. I barely open my mouth when speaking. "I'm getting over a cold."

"Do you take Oscicillium?" she asks.

"Uh, no," I mumble. "Until now I didn't even know how to pronounce it correctly."

She laughs. "I'll give you some. It's amazing stuff. Works like a charm."

My mind launches into a perverted-nurse fantasy as we head to the front door. She digs into her Birken purse, retrieves her keys, and unlocks the door.

CUT TO:

INT. BLUME RESIDENCE—DAY

The interior is right out of *Architectural* fucking *Digest*. And there's always something new or different in the place. This time there's this like weird fucking Greek urn thing in the foyer.

"Is that new?" I say.

"Yes," she says. "Do you like it?"

"No," I say. I don't know what's come over me. I just blurt it out and suddenly I'm desperate to take it back.

But Ashley's eyes go wide with pleasure. "That's amazing! I hate it, too! Randall bought it, at that place near The Ivy. He thinks it's stunning."

"I could accidentally break it for you if you want," I say. "If he bought it with his Platinum American Express card, you're supposed to be covered for, like, thirty days."

"You are *too* funny!" she says, laughing wildly. She looks great when she laughs. I follow her into the kitchen.

"Here's my SpongeBob snow cone maker!" the midget announces. I didn't even know he was there. I walk over and admire it and tell him that he is one lucky dude; that I never had a SpongeBob snow cone maker when I was his age. He asks his mother if he can go watch TV.

"Okay, honey, but only for twenty minutes," she says. "I'm going to make lunch." Then she turns to me. "I know it's probably wrong, letting him watch so much TV. But it's not like we don't do plenty of other stuff."

"I'm sure he has a pretty full schedule," I say, knowing I sound like a complete jackass.

She begins to put the groceries away and I help her out. "Are you hungry?" she asks suddenly. "I'll be glad to make you a sandwich."

"Sure. I mean, if it's not too much trouble—"

"No trouble at all," she says.

The midget has returned. "Yay!" Junior claps his hands. "Sandwiches!" *Jesus, everything's a fucking celebration with this kid.* He's definitely a future producer.

I sit and Ashley looks over at us and smiles. "Do you like mustard or mayo?" she asks.

"Both," I say.

"Me, too," she says.

SHE WANTS THE VEINS.

The midget is trying to get my attention. "Jeb," he says. "Look. I'm going to show you my cards."

He begins to babble, but I'm having trouble focusing. Ashley is reaching for something in the fridge, in a drawer near the bottom. Oh my God, her ass is perfect! For a moment, I can't believe I'm really here. This has to be a dream sequence. Any minute now I'm gonna wake up in my non-air-conditioned apartment, sweating as I work myself into a frenzy watching the same Jenna Jameson video for the fortieth time.

CUT TO:
TITLE CARD OVER BLACK:
ONE HOUR LATER

The kid has eaten and gone back to the tube. I help Ashley put the lunch dishes away. "It's so nice to have some adult interaction," she says. "Don't get me wrong—I love being a mom—but being with a five-year-old twenty-four hours a day can be pretty exhausting."

"I'll bet," I say like a total lame-o.

"Randall's always working. Often late into the night. Don't people have lives in this town, or do they just put them on the back burner?"

The way she says it tells me that she's probably beginning to wonder about all the late-night meetings: like maybe there are no meetings.

"People are very driven in Hollywood," I say vaguely. "You have to be if you're serious about making it."

"You like working at Outcome?" she asks.

"It's not my first choice, but it's a way in."

"You mean you don't want to be an agent?

"God no!" I say, and I instantly regret it. "I mean, nothing against agents *per se*. But I want to write." *Per se?!* What—I'm gay now?

Her eyes light up. "You do? I had no idea you wanted to write."

"Well," I say, "That's the dream." I'm suddenly superembarrassed. I'm *never* embarrassed. What is wrong with me lately? This is what women must feel like when they're going through the so-called *life change*.

"What kinds of things do you write?"

"Screenplays mostly. But I've also had some poetry published." *Why did I say that?*

She's suddenly excited. "I can't believe that! I used to write poetry in college! I'd love to read your poems. Would you consider showing them to me?"

"Sure," I say. I can't believe she's actually interested. "I'll see what I can dig up."

"It's funny how you make assumptions about people. I never thought of you as a writer."

"What did you think of me as?"

"Oh, I don't know. You're, you know—with that body and everything— maybe an actor. Aren't writers supposed to be kind of nerdy and bald?"

I laugh. "You're very funny," I say.

She looks at me in a way that makes me want to kiss her, and suddenly I'm very nervous. I *do* want to kiss her—more than anything in the world— but I don't want to frighten her off. I can't believe what a terrific person she is. I had made all sorts of assumptions about Ashley—the Hollywood wife who married the rich asshole and ran with that girly Range Rover crowd—but it looks like I've been wrong.

"I, uh—I better get going," I say.

"Of course," she says. She looks disappointed. "I didn't mean to keep you."

"Thanks for lunch," I say, hurrying off. But just as I reach the door I hear her call my name. I have one of my mini–fantasy sequences: Ashley throws me to the ground in the foyer and asks me if I think I could ever love a woman like her.

"I almost forgot," she says, hurrying over. "Here's the Oscicillium. Take one of these little tubes every eight hours. Just let it dissolve under your tongue."

I take the three little vials from her warm hand and thank her.

"Don't forget to bring your poems the next time you stop by."

"I won't."

I walk into the yard in a daze. When I reach my car, I realize I forgot to get the stuff for the cleaners. I think about going back and ringing the bell, but the thought scares me. Ashley scares me. I feel giddy and light-headed, and I'm not even erect.

Polaroid C20786A08611A

Rachel

"RACHEL!"

When I open my eyes, I find Dan hovering over me with a dumb look on his face. "You've got a phone call."

I groan and pull the covers over my head. He interrupted my recurring dream about Stone Phillips and me ice-skating in Rockefeller Center.

He shakes me again. "Rachel!"

I rub my eyes. "What?"

He hands me the phone and shrugs. "I don't know who it is. But she said it was urgent."

I look at the clock—it's 7:30 A.M.—and reach for the phone. "Hello?" I croak.

"Rachel, it's Michaela. I'm sorry to bother you, and I know it's Sunday, but I need you to get to the house ASAP."

There's no saliva in my mouth when I swallow. "What's going on?"

"Lorne and Victoria got into a big fight last night. She's getting a restraining order against him and plans to make an announcement to the press in an hour."

"Oh my God."

"You were the last one to see her on Friday. Did anything unusual happen?"

My throat constricts. "What do you mean?"

"Besides her show getting canceled."

I knew Victoria taking all those pills would get me into trouble. I gulp. "She took too many pills."

"No, not that, either. Was there anything else that might have upset her?"

"Not that I know of."

"Phone calls, faxes, e-mails . . ."

Suddenly I remember! "Dr. Mitchell's office called. He wanted Victoria to come in and discuss some tests."

"Did he say why?"

"The nurse said it was confidential. I left the message for Victoria."

"I'm on my way to the house right now," Michaela says. "See you there."

I hang up and hop out of bed.

"Is everything okay?" Dan asks.

"I don't think so. Victoria's having a press conference in an hour."

I grab a pair of jeans and slip into them.

"Press conference? Are *you* going to be on TV?"

"I don't know."

I rummage through another drawer and throw a black T-shirt over my head.

"You're not going to wear that, are you? What if you're on TV? That color's all wrong."

The shirt hangs around my neck. "You really think I might be on TV?"

"Sure. There are always people milling around in the background at press conferences."

"You're right." I rip the shirt off. "Help me find something to wear. I have to take a shower!"

I run to the bathroom and turn on the water. As I strip down, I realize what I'm doing. Victoria is hurting and all I'm thinking about is my big television debut. Sometimes I can be so selfish. I turn off the water and put my clothes back on.

"I don't have time for this, Dan."

"Sure you do. But you better hurry. I'll get your makeup." He looks around the room. "Where's that blue button-down?"

"Dirty," I say and put the black T-shirt back on. Dan sorts through my clothes hamper until he finds it. "Here it is."

He holds it out in front of him. "It's pretty wrinkled. Let me iron it for you."

I'm already in the living room looking for my car keys.

"It won't take a sec," Dan insists, cradling the crumpled shirt in his arms. He's going to make a very good husband someday.

"I don't have time," I say, grabbing my purse. "I'll call you later."

"You're not going to brush your teeth?"

I run to the bathroom and shove my toothbrush in my mouth. "I'll brush on the way."

"But—"

"Call my mom! Tell her to turn on the news."

Beechwood Lane has so many cars and people on it that I have to park three streets over. Two police cars, one Westec security car, and several vans from *Hard Copy*, *CNN*, *E!*, *A Current Affair*, *Extra!*, and *Entertainment Tonight* are lined up and down Victoria's street, their satellite dishes pointing toward the sky. I wonder if Stone is coming. I would just die!

I weave my way in and out of a crowd made up of nosy neighbors, photographers, and television reporters holding notepads, microphones, and tape recorders. Local news helicopters circle high above.

A lady journalist in a pink and yellow suit talks to a camera. "I'm standing outside the home of actress Victoria Rush. She will be holding a press conference in half an hour. There have been conflicting reports on the nature of the conference and we will share details with you as soon as they become available. At the moment, there is rampant speculation that Victoria's marriage to Lorne Henderson is over. The LAPD is no stranger to this multimillion-dollar location, having been called here many times to quell domestic squabbles."

I push my way to the gate and find four Westec security guards blocking the way. Two police officers linger nearby, smoking cigarettes and flirting with a perky reporter. Just then, one of the news choppers flies dangerously low, its blades whipping around furiously and causing a windstorm. Baseball caps, tripods, and papers blow around wildly. People duck and curse, and one of the cops reaches into the squad car for a bullhorn. "Attention KCAL. You're flying too low and creating a disturbance," he bellows. "Clear the area immediately!"

The chopper banks hard and climbs, and the crowd resumes its vigil. I step forward.

"Can I help you?" one of the Westec guys asks me.

"I work here."

"Sure you do, kid. Now step back."

"I'm one of Victoria's assistants. Check with the house."

Several reporters hear this and hurry over. "Do you know what happened?" an intense guy with glasses asks me.

"No, sir, I don't," I say, turning back to the Westec guy. "Please, I really need to get inside."

"Step back," he barks. "I'm not going to ask you again." The way he says it reminds of Billy Fenton, who used to manage the Motel 6 just outside Sugarland. He used to come into Starbucks two or three times a week and take out his glass eye and scare people with it. But one day he dropped it on the floor and it smashed into a hundred tiny pieces. He couldn't afford to get a new eye, so he had to wear a patch just like a pirate, bless his heart.

I try calling the house. There's no answer. I dial Michaela's cell phone. Still no answer. Then a guy holding a big furry microphone hits me in the head with it and doesn't even say he's sorry. I give him a dirty look, but he just shoves past me to get closer to the gate.

A fat lady rushes over, red-faced and sweating. She's wearing a Universal Studios T-shirt and holding one of those star maps. "What's going on?" she huffs. She removes her sunglasses and wipes them on her shirt. "I've come all the way from Canton, Ohio. I've been a fan of Victoria's since forever."

An old man in silk running shorts adds, "She's still a looker, that's for sure."

Someone else counters, "If she has one more facelift, her eyes are gonna dry out."

I swear, some people can be so mean.

Polaroid 20786A08611A

GRIFFIN

I

'M COMPLETELY BAFFLED as to why Michaela insists on wearing this ridiculous disguise. The teeth and glasses are so vaudevillian, she could be headlining with Jackie Mason in the Catskills. She's fortunate that everyone in Hollywood is completely self-absorbed or her ruse would easily be exposed. Johnny paces around in front of us in Victoria's living room.

"You have no idea what this is about?" he asks Michaela.

"No, I don't," she says.

"You do work for the woman, don't you?" Johnny throws his hands in the air. "Jesus Christ. Why has Victoria called a press conference?"

Maybe she wants to tell the world about her larger-than-life human bowel of a manager. "Maybe she wants to tell the world her show is canceled. Or maybe she wants to sue the network for age discrimination," I say. "Or..."

Johnny's eyes widen. "If she files a lawsuit, that's it, instant retirement. No one will touch her. I think it's over anyway, but especially with a fucking lawsuit."

"I'm not filing a lawsuit, but thanks for the vote of confidence," Victoria says coolly, startling everyone as she enters the room. She wears a black silk designer suit with crocodile pumps.

"Nice threads," I whisper to Michaela.

"She had the outfit made last night."

"This must be some announcement."

Victoria's hair is swept into a French twist and she appears to be makeup free, which is unusual for a woman from the Tammy Faye School of Primping. Her face is a muted eggshell shade and her nose is dry and ruddy. Gray circles linger under her bloodshot eyes.

Johnny stands. "What's going on, Victoria? I'm very concerned."

I wince at his insincerity and reach into my suit pocket for a Tums, which I am now popping like Altoids. If these were prescription, I'd be a certified junkie.

"If Lorne did something to you, I'll make sure he pays," Johnny warns.

Victoria takes a seat on the chaise longue. "Has the press arrived?"

"Yes," he says.

"CNN?" she asks.

Johnny looks at me. Not since the murder of Nicole Brown Simpson has there been this much commotion in Brentwood.

I nod and say, "Every major network is out there, along with *Entertainment Tonight*, *Hard Copy*, and *Extra*."

"What about *Access Hollywood*?" she inquires.

Before I can respond, Victoria glances at Michaela. "Where's Matt?"

"I woke him a half-hour ago and told him to come down."

"Can you call him again?"

"Sure." Michaela leaves the room and returns momentarily.

We exchange nervous glances as Victoria sits rigidly on the chaise longue in a trancelike state. Matt finally decides to make an appearance. He skulks into the room wearing a wrinkled *Muff Diver* T-shirt and a pair of cutoff jeans.

Victoria swings her legs over the chaise longue. "Matty, come sit over here."

Matt shuffles to the other side of the room. "What's with the helicopters?"

"I'm going to make an announcement and I want you to be at my side," she explains. She reaches for his hand and tears well in her eyes. "I'm sick, Matty. Please. You're all I have left."

Matt takes a seat, but it's clear he doesn't give a damn about anything but himself. It strikes me that in that sense, he's exactly like his mother.

"T here she is!"

"Here she comes!"

Victoria, Johnny, and Matt make their way down the driveway, toward the waiting crowd. Michaela and I follow a few paces behind. Victoria is holding onto Matt's arm as if her life depended on it, and the kid is fighting the urge to yank free and run.

The crowd surges forward like a pod of killer whales closing in on an injured sea lion. The security guards and the police do their best to hold them back. Cameras whir and click, video rolls, and reporters rush forward shouting questions, their tape recorders held high above their heads.

"Victoria, what's this all about?!"

"Victoria—is the marriage finally over?!"

Suddenly I spot a familiar face among the restive throng. "Is that Rachel?" I ask Michaela.

She looks, but Rachel gets swept away in a crush of paparazzi and we lose sight of her.

"Victoria looks awful," someone says.

"What's wrong with her?" another asks.

The gate whirs to life, swinging slowly open, and the reporters surge forward, tasting blood. They're all shouting at the same time, and the cops have to struggle to keep them off the property.

Victoria, Johnny, and Matt approach the makeshift podium at the end of the driveway. Michaela and I lurk in the background.

"Is that her kid?" someone shouts.

"What's his name?"

"John."

"No, it's Jim."

"Matt," another corrects.

Victoria raises her arms, Moses-like, and the crowd eventually falls silent. She looks down at the bouquet of microphones in front of her and takes a moment. She works hard at appearing somber, though it's evident she's enjoying the attention. "I'm sure all of you are probably wondering why I called this press conference," she says finally, delivering the line with unusual equanimity. "I realize your time is valuable, perhaps more valuable than you yourselves realize, so I'll get to it without further ado." She takes a deep breath. "Last week, I went to see my doctor and discovered that I don't have long to live."

A cry goes up from the crowd, and there's genuine alarm in it. Even if you hate Victoria, and many do, this is a good time to let it go. I'm stunned. I look over at Michaela. She's as stunned as I am. Her mouth has fallen open.

There's a noisy barrage of questions, but Victoria once again raises her arms and calls for silence. "Please," she says. "I beg you. This is hard enough. Let me finish."

The crowd is unusually respectful. Then again, I guess the specter of death will do that to even the lowest tabloid reporter. I again catch sight of Rachel in the crowd. It *is* her. And she's crying.

"My marriage to Lorne Henderson is over. Mr. Henderson has been guilty of countless affairs during our marriage, and I have been guilty of ignoring them—because I loved him and because I wanted so much for us to make a life together."

The crowd is getting restless. They could care less about her marital problems. Victoria knows she's losing them, so she quickly adds, "Lorne gave me crabs."

A cry goes up from the crowd, but Victoria silences them again. "These are not your ordinary, run-of-the-mill, American crabs," she adds, "but a particularly virulent strain that has been traced back to Subotica, Yugoslavia. So far, none of the treatments have had any effect on the little buggers."

"But what is it you're dying of?"

"Yes! What do you mean you don't have long to live?"

"Do you have cancer?"

"Please. Be merciful," she pleads.

Be merciful? That was a bit much, extenuating circumstances notwithstanding.

"I intend to face the uncertain future alone, but I hope to do so with good grace and courage. In the meantime, and until my strength begins to fail me, I will go forth and try to do the best work of my career."

I'm actually moved by this last bit. I can't believe it. Michaela is clearly moved, too. She reaches over and squeezes my hand. I look over at Johnny, who's standing next to Victoria, trying to process the information. I can actually hear people in the crowd crying. Rachel is crying louder than all of them.

"How much time do you have?!"

"I don't know how much time I have," Victoria says, finally answering a direct question. "But I'm going to make the best of it. I want everyone to know that this setback won't keep me from working. In fact, I've decided to incorporate my real-life situation into *Mid-Life*. Victoria Penny will find out suddenly—just as I have—that she is dying. We will watch her live her life just as I intend to live mine, with quiet dignity."

Quiet dignity? This is what happens when actors write their own lines.

"My show will be the first sitcom to feature a lead character who has to contend with her own mortality."

The yelling persists and Victoria again holds up her arms, looking positively Christ-like this time. "I also want you to know that I've decided to donate a portion of my salary to charity."

When they're that vague, you know that portion is a fraction of a fraction. It will probably work out to about ten bucks for every million.

"Who are you wearing?" someone calls out. Everyone looks. It's that ditzy queen from *InStyle*, as inappropriate as ever.

"Carolina Herrera," Victoria says, losing herself for a moment. Then she thanks everyone for their support, steps off the podium, and turns toward the house. The crowd goes wild. The cops and the security guards struggle to keep the situation under control, but the area has become a veritable mosh pit. People are slammed every which way, expensive equipment crashes to the ground, and fights break out. As I turn to catch up with Victoria, I see a large woman punch a photographer in the eye, then yell: "That was for Princess Diana, you bastard!"

"This is awful," Michaela whispers en route to the house. "I can't believe this is happening. I feel horrible for her."

I don't know what to say. I look up and catch Johnny's eye, and he gives me a thumbs-up. *What the hell?* Then it hits me. There's no way the show's going to get canceled now. He's going to keep raking in his share until she croaks. He's probably hoping it's one of those long, lingering, painful illnesses. He's imagining the huge numbers we'll get when she's doing the show from a wheelchair and on a respirator.

Michaela hurries past me into the house and Johnny sidles over. "We're going to milk this puppy all the way to syndication," he whispers. I don't think I've ever seen him happier.

For the first time in my life, I begin to wonder if I'm really cut out for this shitty business.

Michaela

"First things first," Victoria bellows. "Turn off the god-damned air conditioning."

For someone who just found out she has a terminal disease, Victoria is eerily calm and professional. I don't understand it. I can be pretty unfeeling at times, but this is not one of those times. I am really totally wigged out. Of course, next to Rachel I'm completely composed. She was crying before she got past the security guards, and she's crying even harder now.

"From this day forth, the temperature in *my* home will never be under seventy-five degrees," Victoria declares.

Rachel runs to adjust the thermostat. I'm hoping she'll pull herself together. She's sweatier than usual. When she returns, the grief on her face has transformed into excitement. "You just got a call from Charlie Rose. *60 Minutes II* wants an exclusive!"

"What? I'm not good enough for regular *60 Minutes*? When do they show up? When I'm on my actual deathbed?"

In an instant, Rachel's sadness returns. Her eyes well up again. "I'm so sorry, ma'am."

Victoria looks away and asks for a cigarette. I reach for my pack and hand her one and she thanks me as I light it. "I haven't smoked in three years," she says. "Lorne didn't like it. But that doesn't matter anymore, does it?" She inhales deeply and chirps, "It still tastes great!"

I don't get this. I don't get it at all.

A moment later, Johnny pipes up: "So, Victoria. What's the next step?"

Victoria exhales, "I want to do as much press as possible. I'll guest star on *Will and Grace* and even go on *Hollywood Squares*. I'll write a children's book. I bet A&E will do a biography on me now. The only thing that will get me through this trying time is the love and support of my fans."

Rachel and I both take notes.

"Now that Lorne is out of my life, I want to rid this house of his things. Pictures, clothing, shoes, CDs, golf clubs, exercise equipment, cars. I want everything gone forever."

"Shall we have his things sent to him?" Rachel asks innocently.

Victoria stops pacing. "Are you crazy? Those things were bought with my money. He's not getting them back. Give it all to charity. I need the write-off anyway."

"What charity would you like us to send his items to?" I ask.

"Any charity will do. But maybe we can find a needy hospice right here in L.A. That would certainly be appropriate, wouldn't it? And I need to speak to Lebowitz as soon as possible. Tell him I want to file for divorce immediately, if not sooner. And Johnny—"

"Yes, Victoria!"

"Call the network. I want new writers and new producers. *Adults*, please. Youth is overrated, especially in this goddamn town. We need to get cracking on the 'finding out' episode."

"Finding out what?" Rachel says blankly.

"The moment my character finds out that she's terminal," Victoria says. "I want that to be the first episode of the fall season."

Everyone is staring at her. She knows that we are as desperate for the facts of this horrible illness as the unruly reporters, most of whom are still camped out front.

"I know why you're all looking at me like that," Victoria says. "And I'd like to share the details with you. Really I would. After all, every last one of you is like family to me."

Rachel tries unsuccessfully to stifle a sob.

"But I can't do it. I've decided to fight this battle on my own. And I'm not afraid. In fact, in many ways I feel stronger and more confident than ever. There's an old saying. *Live every moment as if it were your last.* I never understood it, but I understand it now. That's what I'm going to do, and that's what I suggest all of you try to do, too."

"How will the writers know what to write," Griffin asks, "if they don't know what you're dealing with?"

"Why do they need to know? If I tell them I have cancer, people who don't have cancer won't be able to relate to our show. I think it's enough that I'm terminal. It's enough for me, for God's sakes. You'd think it'd be enough for a television show."

"That's a good point," Johnny says. "The unknown is so much more frightening than the known."

"Exactly," Victoria says.

"I like it a lot," Johnny says, grinning like a retard. "In fact, I love it."

"Well, what are you waiting for?" she snaps. "Time is short!"

"I'm going straight to the network from here," Johnny says. "I'll call you the moment I have news."

He and Griffin hurry off. Victoria turns her attention to me and Rachel.

"Keep me posted on the interview requests as they come in," Victoria says, looking straight at me.

"Absolutely."

"I'm conflicted about Barbara Walters. I know she'll call, but don't you think she has diminished her status as a serious journalist by hosting that ridiculous *View* show?"

"I kind of like that show," Rachel says. "I love the *Hot Topics* part."

"I'm not sure about that chirpy new blonde," I say.

"Whatever. I'll make that decision when the time comes. Now come on," she says, moving toward the stairwell. "Stop lollygagging."

She leads us to the bedroom and into her gigantic closet, which is the size of a three-car garage. I catch my reflection on one of the mirrored walls and realize that I can lose the disguise. I can go back to looking hot. If I didn't know me, I'd want to fuck me. I whip off the glasses and take out the teeth and stick them in my pocket. But I'm not pleased. The lighting in here is hideous. I spy a new line on my forehead. Botox, here I come. I quickly look away.

Victoria slowly runs her hands over Lorne's suits. Then she opens up a drawer, takes out a T-shirt, and smells it.

"What's she doing?" Rachel whispers.

I shrug.

Victoria removes a pair of Lorne's boxers, inspects them carefully, and drops them. Then she opens all the drawers and tosses underwear, athletic wear, socks, T-shirts, sweatshirts, and shorts onto the floor. Her movements are swift and chaotic. She flings open the closet doors and continues her raid. Designer suits and jackets go flying. She chucks ties one at a time over her shoulder. Dress shirts and pants are ripped off their hangers. She has a crazed Faye Dunaway in *Mommie Dearest* no-more-wire-hangers look on her face. Rachel and I duck when she begins hurling shoes. Nikes, New Balance, Bruno Magli, Prada, and Gucci loafers fly over our heads and hit the opposite wall with a thud. Once she's done, she steps back to survey her handiwork. All three of us are standing knee-deep in Lorne's clothing. She places one hand over her chest and inhales deeply. "Call the maids."

When the three maids show up, they can't believe the mess. But their alarm changes to delight when Victoria tells them to take anything they want. "Your husbands will look *muy guapo* in these suits," she says, smiling.

For a moment, I think to myself, *She looks unusually happy for a dying woman.*

Victoria turns to leave, with me and Rachel close behind, and the maids pounce on the bounty like starving hyenas.

Victoria stops and turns to face us. She looks at me closely for the first time. With my disguise gone, she can see that something's not quite right. But she doesn't know what exactly, and she doesn't really care.

"You girls can help yourselves, too," she says, and we go back and join the fray.

Rachel rummages through the ties. "Which ones are the most expensive?"

"The Nicole Millers."

She picks out five of the gaudiest ones. "Wow! My roommate Dan will be *styling* and *profiling*. Not that he doesn't style and profile already," she smiles. She is *so* strange.

Everything in the closet is gone in a matter of minutes. The maids exit with their hard-won share of the haul, having left Lorne's side of the closet completely empty.

"There will be some well-dressed Guatemalan gardeners in El Segundo," I tell Rachel.

Victoria reappears. "Come with me."

We follow her into the bedroom. CNN is already showing footage from the press conference.

"I want all of this bedding burned. Who knows what else is lurking in there?"

Rachel and I look at each other. The bedding has to be worth ten grand—this is a *Dux*, for God's sake—and it would look very nice in my bedroom as long as it was crab-free.

"Are you sure you want us to *burn* it?"

Suddenly we hear Lorne's voice on the TV. We turn in unison as mobs of reporters descend on him at the entrance to the Peninsula Hotel. "I would like to state for the record that I am not responsible for Victoria's health problems," he says. "She is a drug addict with severe psychological problems. I have no idea why she's attacking me in this manner."

"Is it true you've had numerous affairs in the course of the marriage?" a reporter asks.

"No, it is not true. I am not now having an affair nor have I ever had an affair while married to Victoria. My biggest mistake was trying to love her."

"Oh please!" Victoria says. "I'm gagging."

"Did you give her crabs?" another reporter asks.

"I'm not even going to answer that question. It's beyond ridiculous. The fact is, Victoria is frigid. We haven't had sex in over two years."

Victoria flips off the TV. "Needle dick."

Rachel and I look at her.

"Wait till you get married!" she snaps. "I don't know a single married couple who still has sex. With each other, anyway."

We just stand there, frozen.

"What are you staring at?! Move move move!"

It's nice to see how quickly she's recovered. Too quickly, if you ask me. I'm beginning to think this terminal illness thing is total bullshit.

Polaroid C20786A08611A

JEB

Jeb.

EXT. STRIP MALL—EARLY MORNING

I'm on my way to the gym, still thinking of Ashley, when I find myself driving past the Korean-owned dry cleaners where I used to take the Blume family's clothes. Suddenly I have a wonderful idea. I pull a quick U-ey and park and go inside. The geek behind the counter knows me. "Ah, Jeb!" he says, which is the only part of his greeting I understand. "Da gama hoola kala berry klin!"

"Absolutely," I say, and he goes out back and returns with several items for the Blumes.

EXT. PAY PHONE—MORNING

I pick up the phone and dial Ashley.

"Hello?" Her singsong voice gives me a chill.

"Ashley, this is Jeb."

"Hi, Jeb," she says cheerily. *So far, so good.*

"I'm at the cleaners. Are you around? There's some stuff here for you and I'm happy to drop it off on my way to work."

"That is so nice of you, Jeb. And yes—I'll be here."

"My pleasure," I say. "See you shortly."

I hang up.

EXT. BLUME RESIDENCE—MORNING

I pull into the driveway and park next to the Range Rover. One last quick check in the rearview reveals nothing offensive. I'm clean-shaven and wearing cologne and a freshly pressed shirt. I grab the manila folder containing my poetry and retrieve the dry cleaning from the backseat. It takes Ashley a few seconds to answer the door, but when she does she's got a great smile for me. "Hey, Jeb," she says.

"Hey yourself," I say, holding up the clothes. "Where do you want these?"

INT. BLUME RESIDENCE—MORNING

"Right there is fine," she says, pointing to the coat rack. "I'll take them up later."

I hang up the clothes and hand her a manila folder. "My poems."

Her face lights up. "Oh, great! I can't wait to read them."

"Where's Jeremy?" I say. I can't believe I remembered the kid's name.

"He's at music appreciation class learning about Mozart's dramatic cantatas. I have to pick him up in an hour."

It figures. "Is there anything else you need?"

"Nothing I can think of," she says. "What about you? You have time for a cup of coffee?"

What the hell is going on here? Obviously, she still doesn't know her husband fired me. And now she's asking me to stick around. "Sure," I say. "I can stay for a quick cup."

She smiles that wonderful smile again. "Great."

I follow her into the kitchen and take a seat at the breakfast table.

"Randall has you busy even when he's out of town, huh?" she says.

Out of town? This is fucking sweet. "You know how he is. Always working on something."

She sighs. "I sure do," she says. She pours the coffee and offers me the cream and sugar.

"Just cream, thanks."

I can smell her perfume. It's something refreshing, green, like a cucumber. *That's pussy talk. I have to snap out of it.*

She brings me a cup and saucer and sits down. "Tell me something interesting, Jeb. About work."

I could start with her husband firing me. "At my level, it's not really very interesting," I say.

"Can I ask you something?"

"Sure."

She looks nervous. She takes a sip from her cup and her lip gloss leaves a perfect mark on the rim. "Does Randall get any strange calls?"

"Every day."

Her eyes widen. "From who?"

"Producers, directors, actors. They're all strange."

"Oh." It's not what she's looking for.

I narrow my eyes. "Spit it out, Ashley."

She takes another sip and is not sure how to say it. Deep breath. "I'm so embarrassed to be asking this, but do you know if he's having an affair?"

She's staring at me, hard. I feel like Buddha himself, on the verge of sharing the secrets of spiritual enlightenment with a very attractive disciple. "What makes you think Randall's having an affair?" I ask.

She plays with her right diamond earring. "I don't know. I have this funny feeling." She looks as if she's about to cry. "I'm sorry to put you in the middle of this."

I reach out and touch her hand. It's soft and smooth and feels like the skin on my ball sack. "As far as I know," I find myself saying, though for the life of me I can't understand why, "he's not having an affair."

He's just fucking whores and clients and any other strange piece of pussy that he can manipulate onto his veins.

Ashley tries to smile. "I guess I'm just being paranoid. Maybe I'm starting to imagine things. I have too much time on my hands. I'm sorry. You must think I'm a basket case."

"Not at all," I say.

"It's just, well—" She stops herself. She's fighting those tears again. I don't know what she was about to tell me, but from the looks of things this marriage is in trouble. "Do you have time for another cup of coffee?" she asks.

"Sure," I say. I watch her walk across the kitchen. She's wearing khaki capri pants and a short-sleeved white oxford shirt. She's barefoot, and her toes are painted coral. When she returns to the table, she sits and pulls one knee up to her chest. "Where are you from?"

"Laramie, Wyoming. You?"

"Tallahassee, Florida." She smiles. "I really miss it."

"California's not the same, is it?"

"Oh, it's not that. It's beautiful here. It's just that I miss my family. I don't see them as often as I want."

"Why not?"

"Randall would rather I stay here. He works so hard. I don't get it. It's like a pretend life. He hardly ever sees Jeremy. Even on weekends, if there's a birthday party for some kid or other, Jeremy and I always end up going alone."

It's the same old story. These fucking people. Why do they even bother having families? "Why don't you have your folks fly up and visit?" I suggest. "You seem to have plenty of room here."

"My father's sick," she says. "He doesn't travel well."

I wonder what Blume's problem is. She has a sick dad, for Christ's sake! What an insensitive prick.

She smiles brightly, trying to change the subject. "What do you like to do for fun?"

Her question catches me off-guard. I never have fun.

"I don't know. I work out. I like sitting in outdoor coffee shops when the weather's nice. I like hiking, too."

I don't know why I said that about hiking.

"I love hiking," she says.

Oh. Now I know why I said it.

"I bet you have a lot of friends," she says.

"Not really. I tend to put people off. I think I'm a little too intense." I can't believe I just said that. What is *wrong* with me? Do I think I'm in therapy? Do I really think she wants to hear this shit? I don't know why I don't just jump her right here, right now. It's clear she wants the veins. I have no idea what's stopping me.

"I don't have many friends, either," she says.

"I find that hard to believe."

"It's true. I don't have anything in common with the partners' wives. They're into shopping and lunching and nannies. I don't understand the nanny thing. Jeremy's my son and I want to take care of him. I never want to him to feel like I'm not there for him."

I try to think about her naked, with me on top of her, grunting and sweating, but the best I can come up with is me and her walking on the beach, hand in hand, with the sun setting behind us. Where did that come from? Suddenly I'm in the fucking Postcards from California business.

"I better get to work," I say. I'm nervous. I feel light-headed. Maybe I'm coming down with the flu. There's a bug going around. There's always a bug going around. If I hear one more person say there's a bug going around, I'll have to kill them.

"Do you mind if I ask you a personal question?" she says.

"What?

"How old are you?"

"Twenty-five."

Her eyebrows crinkle. "Wow. You're younger than I thought."

"How old are you?"

"*Much* older," she says, smiling coyly.

"You don't look a day over twenty-six."

She digs that comment. She smiles big and flutters her eyelashes. "That's one of the nicest things I've heard in a while."

She's having trouble meeting my eyes and, I'm having trouble meeting hers—so I get to my feet. "Thanks for the coffee," I say.

"You really have to go?"

"Yes," I say. Why do I feel like a nervous schoolgirl?

"By the way," she asks, standing and walking me to the door, "do you know anything about gardening?"

"Gardening?" It's clear she doesn't want me to leave.

"I want to start a little vegetable garden in the backyard, but I don't know what I'm doing, so I bought some books."

"I don't know much about gardening, either."

"This is so silly. I don't even know why I mentioned it. Forget it."

"It's not silly at all. We've gotta eat our veggies, right?"

"So you'd help me?

"I'd love to."

"I wouldn't want Randall to know. I know it's hard to believe, but I think he's a little insecure in that department."

"Hey. No need to explain. It's your little garden, and I'm your little gardening expert."

She laughs. She seems excited. I'm *beyond* excited.

"Maybe you could come by on your lunch break. We'd work in the garden and I'd make you a sandwich or something."

Or something.

"You know what?" I say. "That sounds really great. I can't think of a better way to spend my lunch hour."

What I wanted to say was, "Yeah, bitch! Get ready for the veins!" Talk about a Freudian slip.

Polaroid 003786 08611A

GRIFFIN

GRIFFIN

MENTALLY, I HAVE every reason to feel great. Physically, my midsection is burning like the oil wells in Iraq. Bart Abelman killed at the Aspen Comedy Festival. All the networks want him. NBC offered the best development deal. A development deal usually means a pilot will be written and hopefully shot. And a pilot means a chance at next fall's schedule or, at the very least, a midseason replacement. Johnny will be pleased with this information. He's been watching the media blitz on Victoria and he can't stop salivating. He's in such a good mood, in fact, that I've decided to make today the day I ask for my raise.

Stu, the security guard, greets me when I walk into the building. "Morning, Griffin."

"Good morning."

He steps from behind his desk. "I've got another idea for Travis. What if there were a pet serial killer on the loose?"

"Pet serial killer?" I reiterate.

"Yeah. Say there's this guy who was attacked by a dog when he was kid.

Maybe it disfigured him in some horrible way. So, as an adult, he's a drifter traveling around and offing pets."

I grin. "That is certainly very inventive."

"Thought so, too. Came to me last night as I was getting into bed. You know these ideas keep coming to me. I can't stop them."

"I would skip the treatment and go straight to the screenplay."

"Those were my thoughts exactly," he beams.

I step on the elevator. "Good luck."

I'm getting as good as Johnny at the lies.

Entering the office, I greet Judy. "How's it going?"

"Phone hasn't stopped ringing. Larry King is asking for an exclusive with Victoria. And I'm still in shock, frankly."

"I know. It's tragic. I can't believe it myself."

"This shows you how precious life really is. In the grand scheme of things, most of this doesn't really mean a thing, does it?"

We both bow our heads and share a moment of silence. Then it's back to business as usual.

"By the way," she adds as I'm about to head off. "Randall Blume called twice already. He wants to know if Travis has agreed to the comet project."

"*Meteoroid.*"

"He's coming by at eleven," she says.

"Blume?"

"No. Travis."

"What for?"

"I don't know. That was the message."

"And NBC called—" She pauses to rifle through the messages on her desk. "About someone named Bart Abelman?"

"Bart. Of course. The new client."

Her face lights up. "You found another hotshot?"

"I certainly hope so. Bart's coming by to meet His Highness. Damn, he's supposed to come by at eleven, too."

"I wouldn't worry about it. Travis is never on time."

"You're right."

"I'll let you know when Mr. Abelman arrives."

I stroll to my desk, put my things down, and hear the familiar hum of the tanning bed. I check my watch. He has at least ten minutes more. I pick up the phone and dial Travis.

Kecia picks up after the second ring. "Hemmllo?"

She always sounds as if she's consuming large quantities of food.

"Kecia, it's Griffin. What's this about Travis coming in?"

"I don't know nothing. You can ask him when he gets there."

"Did he read the coverage on *Fire in the Hole*?"

"Has he ever read anything?"

"It's two lousy pages," I say. Two pages of high praise for a nonexistent script. If somehow, miraculously, Travis actually commits, the studio will throw a million bucks at one of the usual suspects and have a first draft in Travis's hands in under three weeks. "This one's important," I continue. "I thought he might make an exception."

"I'd ask him, but I think he and his brother are already on their way over."

"His brother, too?" The minuscule hairs on the back of my neck stand at attention. "Kecia, what's going on?"

"Lenny's been back for a week. He's ten years older. They were separated when they were kids and placed into separate foster homes. It's pretty sad. If you ask me, it's got Movie of the Week written all over it.

"It's amazing," she goes on. "Lenny's been such a good influence. There haven't been any parties or drugs and his loser friends are gone. I'm telling you, for an ex-con, this guy is a godsend."

"Ex-con?" I pop a few Tums. "Let's take this from the top, Kecia."

"Why don't you let Lenny fill in the blanks? He's really looking forward to meeting Johnny."

"This sounds ominous," I say.

"And keep your hands off him," Kecia says. "He's mine."

"Wha—?" But she's already hung up on me.

Suddenly I'm wondering whether I should put off talking to Johnny about my raise. This could turn out to be a very full day.

"Griffin!"

It's Johnny. The day is about to begin. I hurry into his office and find him supine in his electric casket.

"Spritz," he barks.

I jump and grab the water bottle and spray him a few times.

"Has Travis committed to the comet movie?"

"We can ask him when he gets here," I say.

"He's coming to the office?"

"Yes."

"So the little bastard has finally come to his senses. Call Randall and tell him to get some contracts over here."

I figure I better break the news before he gets too excited. "Travis is bringing his brother along," I say.

"Brother? Who gives a shit about his brother? I've got a goddamn movie to make, Griffin. Stop wasting my time."

"I also have Bart Abelman stopping by for a meet-and-greet."

"Who?"

"The comic. He killed in Aspen."

"I don't have time for this. Spritz!"

I squirt him a few more times. "I spoke to NBC late yesterday. They're talking pilot."

Johnny turns to look at me, but he doesn't remove the electric-blue eye protectors. "I'm listening," he says.

"They think he's the funniest guy since Seinfeld."

"Jew?"

"Yes, I believe Bart *Abelman* is Jewish."

"It could be *German*, you know," Johnny says defensively. "Abelman," he intones, sounding like a Nazi. "And dis is his shtupid brudder, Dis-Abelman."

That was actually quite funny, but I fight the urge to laugh.

Johnny's fingers writhe. "This is all good. NBC has always had a thing for Jews. Moonves is Jewish, you know?" he says, proving once again he's not the sharpest cheddar on the cheese wheel. I choose not to correct him that Les Moonves is the president of CBS.

"I didn't know that," I say.

"He only looks Jewish up close. He photographs well."

"Lucky him," I say.

"Let me know when Herr Abelman arrives."

The timer dings and I lift the lid and hand him a towel. Johnny removes the eye protector and actually half-smiles at me, and suddenly I find myself pushing forward fearlessly: "Johnny, I'm not sure you remember," I say, "but today's the day we were going to talk about my raise."

Johnny pats himself dry, pretending he hadn't heard.

"Johnny?"

"It's been a year already?"

"Yes. I've been killing myself for you for three years. I've already brought you one superstar—and I think Bart is going to be as big as Travis, if not bigger. And this is series television. This is *real* money."

"Hey. You don't have to tell me, pal. You're preaching to the converted.

That no-talent putz Larry David was only a partner on *Seinfeld*, a *partner*, and he took home two hundred and fifty million dollars."

"That's what I'm saying," I say. "I am telling you that Abelman has the goods."

"What else do I have today?" he says, wrapping the towel around his waist and sitting at his desk.

I'm not going to let him change the subject. "I've done everything you've asked of me and more, Johnny," I say. "You asked me to give it another year, at which point I'd become an associate, with full benefits, an expense account, and a salary increase to six hundred and fifty a week."

The intercom buzzes. "Bart Abelman is here," Judy says.

"Send him back," Johnny says, reaching for his clothes. "We can discuss this later."

"When?"

"It's hard for me to think about your promotion when I don't know if Travis is doing this movie."

"How are these facts related?"

"I cannot in good conscience promote somebody who can't close a deal."

"What about all the hard work I've done to get us to this point?"

"That was single-A ball. You're in the big leagues now. You want to be in the starting lineup, I have to know what you're made of."

Before I can respond, Bart enters. I stand. "Hey, man, it's great to see you again. How's your wife?" My transitions to bullshit are starting to frighten me.

"She's good." From the way he says it, I can tell his wife isn't good and never was.

"NBC called today. They want to talk. They want to make an offer."

Bart grins. "Cool."

"For Christ's sake, Griffin, aren't you going to introduce me to NBC's Next Big Star?"

I turn around. "Bart Abelman, Johnny Treadway. Johnny, Bart."

Johnny pulls a lavender polo shirt over his head and extends his hand. "Pleasure to meet you." He shakes Bart's hand heartily. "Please. Have a seat."

Bart sits. I take the chair next to him.

"I understand you're funnier than Larry David," Johnny says.

"I don't know about that. I love Larry David. He's one of my heroes."

"Me, too. I've got all his shows on DVD. I can't get enough of that guy."

"Did you see the one with the sponge cakes?"

Johnny slaps his knee and laughs so hard it actually scares me a little. It's clear he has no idea what Bart is talking about. "Single funniest episode of television, network or otherwise, I have seen in my life," Johnny declares.

"The man's a bona fide genius," Bart concurs.

"So what's your thing?"

Bart's confused. "I don't know what you mean. I'm a comic. I pretty much just stand there and tell jokes."

"Great material," I chip in. "Very cutting-edge."

"So slay me," Johnny says. "Gimme a taste."

I can see that Bart is very uncomfortable—he's being called on to perform—and I suggest we all take a look at the *Tonight* show tape. "I have a copy at my desk," I say, standing.

"Why should I watch a tape when I have the real thing in front of me?" Johnny says.

Dead silence. Bart looks at me, wondering who the hell he just signed with. My stomach churns.

"To be honest with you—"

Judy's voice chirps over the intercom, interrupting Bart. I'm sure he's as grateful as I am. "Johnny," Judy squawks. "Travis Trask is here."

Johnny leaps from behind his desk as if electrocuted. He pats Bart on the shoulder and hurries toward the door. "I already know I love you. I'll have Griffin set up the meeting with NBC and we'll get back to you."

The moment he's gone, Bart turns to look at me, crushed. "I blew it, didn't I?" he asks.

"Not at all!" I say. "Johnny is very distracted today. Travis Trask is coming in to talk about a big project. There's a twenty-million-dollar offer on the table, and he's on the fence, and that kind of fence-sitting makes Johnny very nervous."

"I can imagine."

I realize I'm beginning to sound like all the other assholes in town, and I hate myself for it. "Don't worry about Johnny," I say. "I'm your point man here. The less you have to deal with him, the better."

"I'm so out of my league on this stuff. Maybe I should have tried a joke."

"It wouldn't have mattered. Johnny doesn't understand humor. His favorite comic is Emo Phillips."

"Christ. I hope you're kidding."

"Unfortunately, I'm not. But don't hold it against him. He's still one of the most powerful managers in town."

"I don't understand this business at all."

"Neither do most people. It's run mostly by morons, it's fueled by bullshit, and every aspect of it defies logic. But you don't have to worry about any of that. You just get out there and be Bart Abelman, and I'll cut a nice big swathe for you through all the shit."

As we step out into the hallway, we find Johnny moving toward us with his arm wrapped around Travis's shoulder. His oversized smile is threatening the safety of his cheek implants. The brother, the spitting image of Travis, is right behind them. Bart looks at the young movie star and immediately feels intimidated.

"Hey, Travis," I say. "How's it going?"

"Dude, good," Travis says and hugs me. "My brother, Lenny."

Lenny and I shake hands. He's got a helluva grip.

"You look great," I tell Travis. I say that every time, and with more conviction the worse he looks, but today he actually looks very good. He looks so well rested that his skin appears to be glowing. "Meet Bart Abelman," I say. "A hot new stand-up comic."

Bart extends his hand. "Pleased to meet you."

"Abelman! I saw you at the Laugh Factory. I almost peed my pants, man. You are too much."

"Thanks," Bart says, embarrassed. "That's very sweet."

"Let me know when I can catch your act again," he adds, then turns to me and lowers his voice. "James says hello. He's like in love with you, man. He wants to know when you're coming in for your haircut."

"Enough chitchat," Johnny says. "Let's get to my office. We have a lot to discuss."

He ushers Travis and Lenny into his office, then sticks his head out. "Burt, I'll be in touch."

Bart shoots me a desperate look. "You'll call me later, right?"

I smile to hide the embarrassment. "The minute I talk to NBC."

"Is anybody thirsty?" Johnny yaps, motioning me toward the fridge. "I've got everything. Wild cherry, orange, grape, fierce melon. Whatever you want."

"I'm good," Travis says, sitting down. Lenny glances at the tanning bed. One quick appraising look around the room and he has Johnny Treadway completely figured out.

Johnny snaps his fingers at me. "Peach."

I go through the ritual with the straw and squeeze him a drink before standing against the mahogany credenza. Lenny paces around the office, picking up various objects and then setting them back down, as if he's casing the joint. Johnny watches his every move, a tad nervous, and turns to face Travis with a tight smile. "So this is your big brother, Lenny," he says. "There was an interesting character called Lenny in that book about the mice by Steinway."

"Steinbeck," I say. "*Of Mice and Men.*"

"I didn't read it. I read the coverage. But it got three out of five 'excellents.' "

"You have some nice stuff here," Lenny says. "Maybe I'll come by after hours and clean the place out."

Johnny laughs nervously. He hopes Lenny is kidding, but he's not sure. "You're funny," he says. "You're funnier than that comic we just signed. Do you do stand-up?"

"No, I do not," Lenny says. He doesn't even crack a smile.

Johnny shifts uncomfortably in his seat. "So when did you get in?" he asks.

"A while ago."

"Are you enjoying your visit?"

"It's been dandy," he quips. He's studying a genuine reproduction of a tenth-century Chinese vase.

"Look, I, uh, the reason I called you here today is because I think *Fire in the Hole* will be the biggest movie of next summer. We've already got July 4th weekend. The budget on this film is monstrous and they're willing to pay you twenty million. So maybe I was wrong. Maybe we don't have a lot to discuss after all. Maybe this is a done deal."

"Let's get one thing straight," Lenny says. "You didn't call us here. We came here on our own. Are we clear on that?"

Johnny looks scared. "Of course. Yes. Absolutely."

"Let's begin at the beginning. This twenty mill, what's your cut?"

Johnny coughs once. "Fifteen percent. Industry standard."

Lenny sets the vase down. "Forgive me if I'm ignorant in the ways of Hollywood, but aren't those rates negotiable?"

"Not really."

"I find that hard to believe," Lenny says. "If I told you that you could only have ten percent, which is what the guys across the street are willing to settle for, are you going to tell us to take a hike?"

"What guys across the street?"

"Just answer the question, Treadway."

"Well, uh, no, not exactly. But I couldn't cut my rate. It's just not done. If I did it for Travis, I'd have to do it for everyone."

"Travis isn't just everyone. Ten percent of twenty million is a little better than fifteen percent of four hundred dollars a week."

"I'm not going to argue with that," Johnny says. He tries to smile, but even from across the room I can see that his forehead's beginning to get pretty damp.

"Okay. We're off to a promising start. You get ten percent, and it's a gift. And you'll treat it like a gift. Are we on the same page?"

"I think so," Johnny says. "I'll have to look at the contract."

"Fuck the contract. Contracts exist to be broken."

"This is highly unusual," Johnny says. "Travis, are you letting your brother speak for you?"

"Looks to me like he's doing pretty good, no?"

"What do you do for your big fat paycheck?" Lenny says. "From what my little brother tells me, your secretary here does all the work."

"I'm his assistant," I say, correcting him. Of course, I'm not going to make a federal case over semantics.

"Griffin is actually my associate," Johnny explains.

Associate? Am I hearing things? I am not. He fucking said it.

Johnny continues, "We are all a team here. I have many clients."

"Then they must be the ones getting the good scripts," Lenny says.

"Excuse me?" Johnny says.

"I read those two pages on *Fire in the Hole*. Who wrote that shit? Someone's secretary? And why didn't you send the script over? It must really blow."

"They're still polishing the script."

"Fine. We'll wait. We're in no hurry."

"You know, Lenny, I'm your team. And sometimes you've got to move fast. This is one of those times."

"Not for me," Lenny says.

"You want to explain it to him, Griffin?"

"No," I say. "Why don't you go ahead?"

Johnny wipes his brow. "Well, Lenny, as you said, you're not all that familiar with the business. One of the first things you need to know about Hollywood is that most of us are not interested in making good movies. We leave that to the foreigners. We are interested in movies that make money, and *Fire in the Hole* is already in the black. We don't even have a deal in place, and it's already making bucketfuls of money. Is that a beautiful thing or what?"

"I don't give a shit. My brother wants to make good movies. I've heard better ideas in the joint."

"The joint?"

Lenny sits on the edge of Johnny's desk and leans dangerously close. "I was locked up in the Arizona federal penitentiary for eight long years. Because some asshole pissed me off and I felt compelled to kill him. I don't like it when people piss me off. Motherfuckers who take advantage of my brother—that would definitely fit in the pissing-Lenny-off column."

Johnny doesn't know what to do. "I've never taken advantage of Travis."

"Where do my brother's paychecks get sent?"

Johnny mops his brow with his hand. "To the agency and then to me."

"Then maybe you can explain to me how my brother has made five million dollars in the last three years, and has less than four hundred thousand to show for it?"

"I'm afraid I can't explain that to you. The agency takes ten percent then I take my fifteen percent, and maybe a few dollars here and there for expenses, but the rest goes straight to your brother. Maybe Travis has trouble managing his money. Do you have trouble managing your money, Travis? I think he has a fairly expensive lifestyle. I understand he's paying that black girl a thousand dollars a week."

Kecia makes three times more than me?! Holy Shit!

"You know what," Lenny says after a pregnant pause. "I actually came in here determined to give you a chance. But I don't like you. You're a fucking parasite. You live off other people's talent. And your priorities are all fucked up. You think you matter, and you don't matter. The only thing that matters around here is my little brother. And I'm sure there are plenty of parasites in this town who understand that and will be only too glad to behave accordingly."

"I resent being called a parasite," Johnny says. "I discovered Travis—"

"*He* discovered me," Travis says, pointing at me.

"—and I have nurtured his career from day one."

Lenny places a large, heavy hand on Johnny's shoulder. "Well, my man, I'm officially relieving you of your duties."

"We have a contract!" Johnny squeals.

"I'd like to see it. If you don't mind."

Johnny turns to look at me. "Griffin," he says, but it comes out like a whimper.

I don't know how to play this. If I provide a copy of the contract, I will immediately expose the fact that three years have passed and that Travis is no longer officially a client. How am I going to save my boss's ass? My ass, too, come to think of it, since I officially became an associate about eight minutes ago.

"All our contracts are at the attorney's office," I say quickly. "We don't keep them here for, uh, security reasons."

Okay, so that last part was totally unnecessary and stood out like a pubic hair on a bar of soap.

Lenny's chilly eyes focus on me. "Can we get a copy faxed over here?"

Johnny gives me a nod, even though there's no attorney who has contracts. "Give him a call."

"I'll be right back," I say, and I move toward the door.

But Lenny picks up the phone on Johnny's desk and stops me cold. "Call him from here," he says.

"No problem," I say.

I move toward the desk, trying to ignore the burning sensation in my lower intestine, and pick up Johnny's phone. I dial my home number and press the receiver as close to my ear as possible to mute Mel's loud, singsongy voice on the answering machine. I need a name. Nothing's coming to me. My eyes frantically scan the room as I remember that great final scene from *The Usual Suspects*. I glance at the fridge. I spy Johnny's goblet.

"Capri, please," I bark into the phone. "Carlos Capri." Jesus Christ. Carlos Capri! I might as well have asked for Carlos Capri Sun! I cup my hand over the receiver. "They're transferring me to his office," I whisper.

Johnny looks at Lenny. "I know you're concerned, but I have nothing but Travis's best interests at heart."

"Sure you do," Lenny says.

I pause for the sufficient amount of time and then say clearly, "Is

Carlos in for Johnny Treadway?" I nod while listening to the phantom assistant. "Hmm. I see. Do you know when he'll be back? Okay. Have him give us a call. It's urgent." I hang up. "He went to lunch at Warner Brothers. He should be back at three."

I'm feeling somewhat proud of myself, except for that bit with the ridiculous name. But the "Warner Brothers" detail should have made up for it. Johnny gives me a dirty look and gets to his feet. "Gentlemen, unless there's anything else, I guess this concludes our little meeting."

"I want to see that contract," Lenny says. The guy is as cool as a cucumber. Nothing seems to faze him. I guess I'd be pretty cool, too, if I knew I could kill a man with my bare hands.

"I'll send it over as soon as we get it." Johnny says. "And Travis, while we're ironing out this little glitch, I want you to think about that twenty mil."

Lenny glares at Johnny. "The contract, girlfriend. I want to see the fax machine at Travis's crib spitting it out by three-oh-one."

They exit, and for once Johnny doesn't glad-hand Travis all the way to the elevator. Instead, he shuts the door and turns to face me, turning several different shades of red. "Capri?! What the fuck is the matter with you? Are you fucking retarded?"

He picks up the crystal goblet and throws it at me. I duck and turn around and the stapler bashes me in the forehead.

"Ow!" I say. "That hurt!"

"What the fuck am I going to do?" Johnny says.

"I'm not sure there's anything we can do," I reply, rubbing the injury. "His three years lapsed two months ago. Travis is technically not your client anymore."

"I told you to get new contracts drawn up!"

"I did. I have them in my office. Travis just never got around to signing them."

"Then change the goddamn contract. Make it five years."

"That's illegal."

"I don't give a shit. He doesn't know what he signed and he doesn't have a copy. The little idiot was living in a box under the Santa Monica Pier when I found him."

"When *I* found him," I say, correcting his mistake.

His squirming fingers go to work. "Fix that goddamn contract."

I don't move.

"Don't pansy out on me, you little faggot!" Saliva specks spray across his desk as he hurls more obloquy at me.

"Wouldn't think of it," I mumble. I go off in search of the contract, suddenly aware that my promotion depends on my willingness to commit a felony. I need a drink, *badly*. Thank God I'm going to Trader Vic's.

$Kecia$

M

ICHAELA, GRIFFIN, and I chill at our usual table at Trader Vic's. Coco brings us a second round of drinks. For the first time ever, my stomach ain't grumbling and I'm not eating egg rolls. And you know I live for Vic's egg rolls. It's Chinese comfort food.

"I find myself in quite the predicament," Griffin says, wincing as he takes a big sip of his drink. The boy is definitely trippin'. And that olive-sized lump on his forehead is turning a nasty shade of purple.

"Tell him you won't do it," Michaela says. She's wearing tight leather pants that my arms wouldn't fit into. The girl's got to have an eating dis-order. Throwing up must be her favorite hobby.

"He'll fire me," Griffin says.

"That's better than getting arrested," Michaela says.

"You shouldn't have to break the law for your boss," I say. Of course, I scored drugs for Travis more times than Monica blew Bill. Small amounts are misdemeanors in California. I draw the line at anything over an eight ball of coke.

"Why did Lenny Trask have to resurface?" Griffin sighs, looking at me. "And by the way, you could have forewarned me. I didn't realize he was such a prick."

"I think he's nice," I say. "I like the fact that he's standing up for his little brother."

"He's a convicted criminal, for God's sake. And it came through loud and clear: *I know a hundred ways to torture and maim assholes like you.*"

"Really?" I say. "He said that?"

"Not in those words, exactly. But it was there."

"I've never seen that side of him," I say, and I'm suddenly more turned on than ever.

Griffin can see it, too. He shakes his head, like he's disgusted with me or something. "Kecia," he says. "You need help."

My eyes flash angrily. "What did you say?"

"You obviously have some sort of bizarre fixation with this convict. It's clouded your judgment," he says.

I shake my head. My horoscope told me to avoid Geminis today. "You know nothing about it."

"You didn't see this coming? Travis fired his accountant and now he's trying to get rid of Johnny. Lenny will probably abscond with all of his brother's money. And you're oblivious because you've got some schoolgirl crush. Really, Kecia. I didn't think you were that desperate."

I *know* he did not go there.

Jeb arrives and drops into the seat next to Griffin. "Hello, all," he says cheerily.

He's looking a lot cleaner than last time. He looks *happy*, in fact. This is pretty strange because he's your stereotypical Aries: blunt, aggressive, and irritating. The butthead of the Zodiac.

"Aren't we in fine fettle?" Griffin says. "Don't tell us: you found a terrific new job."

Jeb signals for Coco. "Sort of."

"Where?" Michaela asks.

"I'd rather not say. But I'm an assistant to a charming, beautiful, kind, successful woman." We all look at Jeb, stunned. He's blushing. This boy's trippin', too.

"That's it?" Griffin says. "No details?"

"Well, you know my track record. I don't want to jinx it." Coco shows up and Jeb asks for a club soda.

Club soda? We again look at him like he's lost his damn mind.

"I need to cut back on my alcohol consumption," he explains. "So what's up with you guys?"

I look away, electing not to tell him I'm about to slap Griffin upside the head.

"Griffin's going to lose his job unless he breaks the law," Michaela says.

"Johnny wants me to alter Travis's contract. If I don't, we lose our most valuable client."

"You going to do it?"

"I don't know."

Then it hits me. He's planning to defraud *my* boss. So what if Travis is just a dumb, good-looking kid? He doesn't deserve to be played.

"Hey, y'all! Sorry I'm late." Rachel says, strolling up to the table. She's got to be the happiest white girl to come along since Cindy Brady.

"Gandalf," Jeb says to her. "You haven't been fired yet?"

"No, silly." Rachel says. "Look what Victoria gave me. We were cleaning out her closet and she doesn't want it anymore." She reaches into a Barney's bag and retrieves a fuchsia sleeveless sweater. "It's cashmere."

"That's beautiful," Michaela says through clenched teeth.

"The tag's still on it. It was $575!"

"She never gave me anything," Michaela says. The girl is pissed. I don't blame her. That's jacked.

Rachel stops smiling and puts the sweater away just as a white girl in shoulder-length braids approaches the table tentatively. "Excuse me," she says, squinting. "Is this the assistants' meeting?"

"Oh hi, Marilyn," Rachel says, excited as a wet-nosed puppy.

"Oh there you are!" the white girl says. "I didn't see you. My boss broke my glasses."

"On purpose?" I ask.

"Hard to say," the white girl replies.

"Everybody, this is Marilyn," Rachel says. "Marilyn, everybody. Marilyn is Alec Baldwin's assistant."

"I bet you could use a drink," Michaela says.

Marilyn smiles nervously. "Yes, actually I could."

"I recommend the mai tai," Griffin says, lighting another smoke. "It's fast and effective."

Someone's cell phone rings. I glance down at mine and see that I've missed another call from that brother at the IRS. The man ain't getting the message.

Rachel retrieves her phone and announces, loud and proud: "It's me!" She leaves the table to answer it and Marilyn orders a mai tai.

"So," Michaela says. "What's Alec like?"

"Is it okay to do this?" she asks, stammering. "I mean, do you guys, like, talk about your feelings and everything?"

Griffin looks around, "Feelings? I'm not sure I follow."

"Like in therapy?"

"It's more like an AA meeting," Michaela says.

And it hits me like a bolt of lightning. Michaela just nailed it. I mean, *really* nailed it. This thing really *is* like an AA meeting.

"That's right," Griffin says, very much on the same wavelength. "It's AA all the way. This is a support group for people who are saddled with impossible bosses."

"I'm glad I'm here, then," Marilyn tells us. "Rachel says you guys get together once a week, and I'm telling you right now—I'll be here every week."

"So how bad is he?"

"Pretty bad. I have to listen to him go on and on about how Kim broke his heart, and he can talk about her for hours, believe me. His other favorite topic is how come he's not a big star and has to take these little roles in small movies for a lousy hundred thousand a week."

"A hundred thousand a week?" Jeb says. "Poor guy. How can anyone live on that?"

Rachel returns to the table. "What's going on?"

"So," Michaela says. "You told Marilyn we ran a support group for assistants?"

"Was I wrong?' Rachel asks. "Isn't that what this is?"

Griffin goes into full-on AA mode: "Hello, my name is Griffin. And I'm an assistant."

I clap. The others join in, digging it.

"Hello, my name is Michaela. This is my first time here, and I'm very nervous. I'm an assistant, too. But I'm also an actress. And I have head shots with me in case any of you are interested."

We add a little laughter to the clapping.

"Hi. My name is Jeb. Until very recently, I was an assistant. It was a very difficult time for me, and I am still working on undoing the damage."

"Right on, Jeb!"

Then it's my turn. "My name is Kecia. I'm an assistant *and* I'm black. I used to work for the DMV, so I'm used to plenty of abuse. But being an assistant is in a class of its own."

Everybody claps and cheers, and Griffin signals for another round of drinks.

Then Rachel pipes up: "Hi, my name is Rachel. I'm an assistant, too. Before being an assistant, I was unemployed for a really long time, and I'm just thankful to have a job."

And damn if she isn't crying all of a sudden!

"I love being an assistant," she says, dabbing at her tears. "I'm here because I want to be the best assistant I can be."

Man, that girl is fucked up in ways I can't even begin to imagine!

Rachel

MICHAELA'S BOOBS look fake. Not that I go around and stare at them all the time, but today she's wearing a clingy T-shirt that makes them even more noticeable. Boobs aren't supposed to be as hard and perfectly round as baseballs. Now, I don't have any boobs of my own, thank you very much, but from everything I've seen and heard they're supposed to be on the soft side. Her boobs are about as natural as that fake fruit arrangement at Granny's house. I'm dying to ask her about them, but I just can't bring myself to do it. There are some things that are just too personal. So I ask her something else.

"How old are you?"

She grimaces. "It's not polite to ask a girl her age."

"I don't mind when people ask me. I just tell them twenty straight-away. No sense pretending I'm something I'm not."

"How old do you think I look?"

"Thirty-two."

She sucks in her breath. "I'm not that old. Do I look that old?"

I can tell I really hurt her feelings. I remember what she told me, *When in doubt, lie, lie, lie.* "Just kidding. You don't look a day over twenty-nine."

She doesn't like that one, either.

Michaela and I are hanging out on the patio. She's smoking a cigarette and I'm drinking a Power C Vitamin Water because I just don't get enough vitamin C in my diet. We're waiting for Victoria to finish up with Dr. Shazu. He's not a real doctor. He's an Indian spiritual healer to the stars who comes to see her once a week. His technique involves chanting and some sort of aromatherapy, and after he leaves, the whole upstairs smells like funky incense. I'm staring at the bright orange embers at the end of Michaela's cigarette. She really shouldn't smoke. It's not very ladylike. When she exhales the smoke through her nose, I wonder if she ever burns her nose hairs.

"Do you notice anything weird about Victoria?" she suddenly asks.

I blink. "I haven't noticed anything."

"That's what I mean. She's supposed to be dying, and I don't see her taking anything besides the usual Vicodin, Valium, and Xanax. She's popping them like tic tacs."

"Maybe there's nothing they can do for her. Maybe they're trying to make it as painless as possible."

"Well, what is 'it'?"

"'It' what?"

"Whatever's killing her."

"Shhhh. We'll get fired if she hears us talking about this. You know what she said."

Michaela shrugs, but she lowers her voice. "I don't know. This whole thing stinks. You've got every tabloid reporter in the country trying to break the story, and they can't come up with anything."

"*Weekly World News* thinks she was abducted by aliens and replaced by an alien impostor who won't survive in Earth's atmosphere for more than a few months," I remind her.

Michaela looks at me like I'm a loon. "I don't know if they're the most reliable newspaper in the country," she says.

"I had a Spanish teacher in Sugarland who said he was abducted by aliens," I tell her. It's true. His name was Señor Maldonado. He said they liked to poke and prod him with all kinds of objects and although he sometimes enjoyed it, for the most part it was *muy mal*.

"I'm telling you, it's total crap. She goes on Larry King and reminisces about her fucking career and talks about her hopes for the show now that it's taking off in this new and wonderful direction. But the minute he pushes her on the illness thing, she takes the mike off and walks."

"I thought that was pretty amazing," I say. "And she was very calm about it. Don't you think she looks sort of at peace with herself lately? I see it in her face."

"Don't be a dumbass," Michaela says. "That's the Botox."

"Michaela!"

We both jump to our feet and turn as Victoria steps out of the house.

"Would you mind paying Shazu?" she says. "He's waiting in the foyer."

"Sure thing," I say.

"No, not you, Rochelle. I want Michaela to pay him."

Uh-oh. What can this mean? Suddenly I'm very nervous. My hands begin to sweat.

"I'll be right back," Michaela says, and she disappears into the house. I look at my boss. "Can I get you anything, ma'am?"

"No. We need to talk. Come." I follow her back into the house. My stomach is all knotted up and I have to use the bathroom really bad, but I take short little breaths and hope the urge passes. I'm going to get fired, I just know it! I follow her all the way to the master suite.

"Have a seat," she says, indicating the big fluffy chair in the corner. Smoke from the burning incense fills the air. I have to fight the urge to bat it with my hands. I sit down and tell myself I won't cry when she fires me.

Victoria sits in the matching chair. She's staring right at me, which makes me even more nervous, if that's even possible. I'm trying to follow the rules by not looking at her directly, but it's hard to know where to look. My eyes dart around the room like a crazy person and I realize I'm making myself dizzy.

"My illness has made me rethink many things," Victoria starts.

Here it comes! And I've tried so hard to be good. I ordered everything she asked me to order, exactly as she wanted it! Why, only this morning I got the Pancake Wizard and those Carlton *"No Payments or Interest Till February 2007"* Sheets.

"I've been living a life of total excess for so long, but the truth is that Victoria Rush is really just a simple girl at heart," she continues. Her voice is so soft and gentle I'm worried I might nod off. "I grew up in Holly Pond, Florida, a small rural town with no fancy stores or restaurants. My family lived in a trailer. The highlight of the week was when Daddy took us to Dairy Queen on Friday nights."

She pauses and I feel like my intestine's about to explode. If I'm going to have to listen to the story of her life, it's all over for me. And for this chair.

"I've wasted so much money on frivolous things," Victoria says. "This room, for example. Do you have any idea how much I paid the interior decorator for this room alone?"

"No, ma'am."

"Well, I'm too ashamed to tell you. The old Victoria would have bragged about it, but the new Victoria is not like the old Victoria."

My stomach growls. I can feel the gasses in there bubbling and shifting. I hope she didn't hear them.

"You see that stupid giraffe?" she asks. I do see it. It's about three feet tall and made of ceramic and the poor giraffe has a crick in its neck like that real giraffe in the Santa Barbara Zoo that I read about. "I paid ten thousand dollars for that."

"Wow," I say. "That's a lot of money."

"Now tell me, Rochelle: what is the purpose of that thing?"

"It's decorative?"

She gets up, crosses the room to the fireplace, and picks up a china plate painted red and gold. "Guess how much."

I shrug.

"Five thousand. This paint is twenty-four-karat gold. Five grand for a stupid plate that you don't even eat off. It just sits there on a little stand, being useless. A so-called object of beauty."

She puts the plate down and picks up a five-by-seven gold picture frame that holds a snapshot of her and Matty. "Another object of beauty. Guess how much."

"Eight thousand?" I say.

Victoria shakes her head. "Nine ninety-nine. Got it at Wal-Mart." She strokes her son's face before replacing the frame on the mantel. "Now you tell me, out of these three things, what's more valuable?"

I didn't know there'd be a quiz. God! I hope I get the answer right. "The picture of Matt?"

"Exactly," she says and sits back down.

"Victoria Rush wants to simplify her life. She longs for the days when she did things on her own. She doesn't know how she became so helpless. Fame is funny that way. You work so hard to get to the top, but once you're there, you quit. You stop working on personal relationships, spirituality, and your oneness with the universe. We're all connected by the same cosmic force, Rochelle. Take it from me. How you tap into that force depends on your balance in life. Do you understand what I'm telling you?"

I nod, but I'm having trouble figuring it out. Am I or am I not getting fired?

"In short, Victoria Rush doesn't need all these people working for her."

There it is! The suspense is over. I feel my eyes well up with tears. I hold my breath again and look at the floor. I don't want her to see me cry.

"I've decided to keep you and get rid of Michaela."

My butt cheeks unclench, dangerously, and my head snaps up again. "What?" I say. I find myself looking directly into her eyes, and nothing bad happens.

"I haven't been too pleased with Michaela's performance lately. Besides, you and I are a much better fit."

My hands stop sweating. "Really?"

"Yes," she says. "There's something about you, Rochelle. I can't quite put my finger on it, but there's a simplicity there that makes you almost impossible to resist."

"Thank you," I say.

"Now please break the news to Michaela."

"*Me*?" The bowel cramp is back. "I'm supposed to tell her that she's fired?"

"You don't expect me to tell her, do you?"

"Uh, no, ma'am."

"Good. Now if you don't mind, I'm going to lie down for a while. This medication simply exhausts me."

I have to sit on the stairs for a while to get a grip. Victoria Rush said we were a "good fit." A famous person really likes me! But what about Michaela? She's my friend now. How do I tell her she's fired? When I get downstairs, Michaela meets me in the foyer. She's holding a stack of paper close to her chest. "Where have you been?"

I blink. "Victoria wanted to talk to me."

"What about?"

"Stuff." Now how am I supposed to come right out and say it?

"What kind of stuff?" she asks angrily. She's already mad at me.

"She wants to lead a simpler life," I start.

"And?"

"Balance her oneness . . . "

"What?"

I spit it out. "She only needs one assistant."

"Am I fired?"

I make a face like I have gas, which in fact I do.

"You've got to be kidding," she says.

"I'm sorry. I thought she was going to fire *me*. I'm as stunned as you are."

"If she's downsizing, why would she keep you? I've been here longer."

I whisper this next part. "She thinks we're a better fit."

"Has she ever had a conversation with you before today?"

"We've had lots of conversations."

"Like when?"

I don't answer. The truth is, I've never had a real conversation with Victoria. Until today, that is. But she's different now. Maybe the new, dying Victoria was able to peer within my soul and see what a great girl I am.

"I'm sorry, Michaela," I say. And I *am* sorry. But I'd be sorrier if it was me getting fired, so I'm also confused. I feel like a bad person, but I haven't done anything wrong.

"I don't know why I'm not angry with you," Michaela says. "Are you, like, completely clueless about everything?"

"That's a mean thing to say," I tell her.

"You're right," Michaela says. "I'm sorry."

"My English teacher in high school, Mr. Murchison, used to say I saw things 'differently' than other people. But I'm not 'clueless.' He said it's what made me a good writer."

"Don't tell me: you've written a script about a young girl from Sugarland who comes to Hollywood to make her mark, and about all of the charmingly odd characters she has to leave behind as she embarks on this voyage of self-discovery."

"Wow! How did you know?"

"Just a wild guess," Michaela says, rolling her eyes.

"A lot of it is about her relationship with her mother, who's an alcoholic. And about how hard it is for her to break free. I think good writing should resonate in unexpected ways."

"So you slept with him?"

"Who?"

"Your English teacher."

"No," I say. But I'm not very good at lying. "Well, *once*."

Michaela shakes her head, looking a little angry now. "Good luck, *Rochelle*," she says, then turns and walks off.

"I'll see you at Trader Vic's, right?!" I call after her, but she doesn't answer.

I don't know whether to feel good or bad now. I'm very confused.

"W"HAT CAN I DO to cheer you up?" Dan asks. I'm sitting on the couch with my knees pulled to my chest.

"I wish my mom would call. I've left her like a million messages."

Dan doesn't answer. I look up at him and I know what he's thinking. He's thinking that my mom is probably passed out at O'Herlihy's, the only Irish bar within seven hundred miles, in the pink cashmere sweater I sent her. I wonder who drives her home these days.

"Don't you ever miss Sugarland?" I ask him. "That crazy Irish bartender. The old gang at Starbucks. Señor Maldonado and the aliens. The half-Indian girl with the skin condition. The way Mr. Murchison cried whenever he talked about Shakespeare."

"No," Dan says, and he means it. "And she wasn't half-Indian. She just had a skin condition."

I don't know what to do with myself. I'm really happy I didn't get fired, but I feel bad for Michaela. It's hard making friends in this town, and I thought we were getting close.

"You want to go to the Mexican joint?" Dan asks.

"No. My stomach's still screwed up from my talk with Victoria."

"Rach, pull yourself together. I know you're upset about Michaela, but you didn't do this to her. Victoria picked you. It's as simple as that. Try to be happy, okay? You're in the business now."

"I'm never going to hear from film school," I whine. "They hated my script."

Dan reaches into the drawer and pulls out what's left of the weed. He begins to roll a joint. It's nice to have a friend like Dan. He knows me so well. He knows exactly what I need when I get like this. And I get like this a lot.

Mr. Murchison knew this side of me, too. He said I was sensitive, and that sensitive people often struggle with more than their share of depression.

"That's what makes you a writer," he told me. "And you know what Kierkegaard said about writers, of course."

"Who?"

"He said, 'The whole world can be divided into those who write and those who do not write.'"

"Which side is better?" I asked.

But he just shushed me. Then he closed the classroom door and turned off the lights.

GRIFFIN

D UPING AN EX-CON was relatively trouble-free. Lenny Trask wanted to see a contract. No problemo. I scanned the original, changed the length of service from three years to five, and printed a new copy, sans signature. All I have to do now is put pen to paper, and that's easy enough: I have forged Travis's signature a myriad of times on countless eight-by-tens for fans and members of the press. I never thought my job description would include white-collar crime, but what choice do I have? I must look out for number one. After I move up the food chain, I'll abjure criminal activity. Everyone knows I'm a good guy. As Johnny's employee, his demands are exigent and I'm forced to do what he says. I can't be held accountable. That's what I keep telling myself. Just like Eichmann did.

I bite my lip and sign.

Upon delivery of the document, Lenny examines it carefully, then hands it to Travis. "Is this your signature?"

As Travis inspects my handiwork, my belly twists.

"Yep."

Lenny points to a paragraph. "See that? Never give anybody five years of anything. Got it?"

Travis nods, looking appropriately cowed, and leaves the room.

"I hope for your sake this is legit," Lenny says.

My midsection reignites. "I can assure you that this contract is completely on the up-and-up."

He studies me carefully. "I'm sensing some nervousness here."

I tug at my collar. "Why would I be nervous?"

"You tell me."

"There's nothing to tell."

He slaps me on the back again. "Relax. I'm just fucking with you. I can tell you're a good guy. It's your boss I don't like."

Relief sweeps over me with such intensity that I almost hug Lenny.

"Len," Travis says, entering the room with an overstuffed backpack. "Are we ready?"

"As soon as we show Griffin out."

"Where are you guys going?"

"A little road trip," Len says.

"Just a couple of days, right?"

"Could be a couple of days, could be a couple of weeks, could be a couple of months, right, Trav? We're gonna play it by ear."

"What about *Fire in the Hole*?" I ask, and I can't keep the panic out of my voice. "I need a yes from you, Travis. And I can give you twenty million reasons to say yes."

"Come on," Len says, guiding me to the door. "Bring me something real."

"Okay, but how do I reach you?"

"It'll wait," Lenny says, throwing an arm around me and giving me a little squeeze. "If there's one thing I've learned in this life, it's that you should never negotiate from a position of weakness. And right now, you and Johnny are looking very weak. You need us, we don't need you."

"But we represent Travis," I protest.

"Sure you do. But fifteen percent of nothing is nothing."

He opens the door, grins like his little brother, and shuts it behind me.

I pop two Tums and get into my car and head back to the office. I don't know how I'm going to break the bad news to Johnny. But I'm not really thinking about Johnny right now. I'm thinking about Lenny. The guy is whip-smart. I could probably learn a few things from him. Of course, he's new to the business, so he could learn a few things from me, too.

I'm going to have to have a long talk with that man when he gets back.

"H E BOUGHT IT," I tell Johnny, trying to muster a little enthusiasm.

"Thank Christ!" Johnny shouts, and he dances from the tanning bed to his desk. He's got more than enough ardor for the both of us. "Get Randall Blume on the phone and tell him that *Fire in the Hole* is a go. We'll messenger the contract directly to Travis and then we'll call *Variety*."

"I wouldn't go that far," I say quietly. "He bought the forgery, but he's not even remotely interested in *Fire in the Hole*."

"What?!"

"It gets worse. Travis and Lenny are taking a little trip. Lenny said they'd be 'in touch.'"

"Little trip?! Who's running this show, anyway? Where are they going and how long will they be gone?"

"I can only answer one of those questions. The one about who's running the show. The answer to that would be Lenny."

"You get that son of a bitch on the phone now, or you're fired."

"Fired? Me? I don't think so, Johnny. There are only two people in the world who know the truth about Travis's contract, and I'm one of them."

"Are you fucking shaking me down, you little shit?"

"You did this to yourself, Johnny."

"You ungrateful little—"

"Let's talk about Bart Abelman," I say.

Johnny looks like he's having trouble breathing. He turns his back to me and counts to ten and tries hard to get his unruly emotions under control.

"That's the comedian we signed," I add helpfully. "Or, rather, the comedian I urged you to sign." Johnny doesn't turn around. It's taking a while. I guess he must be *very* angry. "NBC has committed to a pilot. They've sent over a list of show runners they want us to consider."

Johnny finally turns around. He's marginally calmer. "Just a pilot?" he says. "Why aren't we asking for at least six episodes?"

"I think that would be both unreasonable and unlikely," I say. "But I have faith in Abelman. I think this thing's going to fly, Johnny. And I think we'll find a nice part for you in the series."

"Not the pilot?"

"Maybe a walk-on in the pilot. To establish your character."

"Send Abelstein a nice bottle of wine," he says. "But not too nice."

"It's already done."

"Then call Randall Blume with the bad news on *Fire*. Maybe he can dig up another brilliant phantom script."

As I leave his office, it occurs to me that I work for a complete nincompoop. I get back to my desk and call Kecia.

"They're not here," she says.

"I know," I say. "But if they call in from the road, tell Lenny I really need to talk to him."

"So," Kecia says, and I can hear the smirk in her voice. "You hot for the boy, too!"

"You might say that," I say, and I hang up.

Bart and I have a meeting with two show runners at NBC. A show runner is exactly what the name implies—someone who literally runs the show, from the writing, to the casting, to the actual physical production, to the final edit. Other producers and network suits will eventually seep in to taint the process, but for now, we're on our own.

On the drive over to the network, Bart asks about the show runners. I tell him that I opted for two series veterans, both of whom got their start in stand-up. "They never made it on the circuit, but they're both very good writers, and I know they can deliver. I think you'll be impressed."

We meet the show runners in their temporary office, which is about the size of a trailer restroom and just as aromatic. Their names are Bill Daniels and Dave Lawry, and they look like you'd expect them to look: two grizzled guys who have been beaten down by a decade of bad notes. After the initial introductions, Bill wipes his glasses on his shirt and gets down to business: "So, Bart, NBC wants us to create a show for you," he says. "Do you have any ideas?" He keeps doing this weird little dance with his tongue, running it against his crooked incisor. I suspect that this is a side effect from an antidepressant.

"Well, that really puts me on the spot," Bart says. "I thought we were just going to toss ideas around."

"You first," Dave says.

"Are you guys fucking with my client?" I say.

"I'm sorry," Bill says. "We've had a bad morning."

"It started when they showed us our production office."

"Eighteen fucking years in the business, and this shithole is the best they can do!"

"I don't care about the office," Bart says. "I'm just glad we're here. I see this as a wonderful opportunity for all of us."

Bill and Dave exchange a look. Only someone new to the business would approach it with such innocence. If it weren't so heartbreaking, it might be refreshing.

But Bart is oblivious, thank God. "I've been thinking about this idea for a while," he says. "We can't do a show about a standup comic. That was *Seinfeld*. We can't set it in a bar. That was *Cheers*. I thought about a bowling alley, but there was a bowling alley in *Ed*. And it can't be about a Midwestern dork, because then we're into *Drew Carey* territory."

I'm impressed. Bart has been doing his homework. The show runners are impressed, too.

"I thought we should keep it real," Bart continues. "It's about a nice Jewish kid who was born and raised right here, in Los Angeles. The Valley, anyway. During the week, he and his wife work in a small hair salon, and they have all these crazy clients, and they're sort of like therapists. And they actually help people. But at home their life is sheer hell. They hate each other."

Now I'm beyond impressed. And so are Bill and Dave.

"That's good," Dave says.

"It *is* good," Bill agrees. "We never think anything's good, but this is very promising."

"Where did you come up with this?"

"What do you mean, come up with it? It's my life."

"You work in a hair salon?" Dave says, incredulous.

"I have to make a living, don't I?"

"What can you do about this?" Bill asks, running his hands through his thinning hair.

"Well, I can't promise you a miracle," Bart says, "but I'm pretty good at creating the *illusion* of hair."

We all laugh. This is good. I haven't seen this type of chemistry since high school.

"I don't know if we can work this into the story," Bart says, "but I'm an amateur magician, too." He reaches up and pulls my driver's license out of my ear. I can't believe it. How the hell did he do that?

"And I'm a pretty good pickpocket, too," Bart says. He holds up an old Timex. Dave looks at his wrist and realizes it's *his* Timex.

"Jesus," he says. "I think we have a show!"

TWO WEEKS LATER, I stop by Bart's apartment on my way home to see what he thinks of the first draft of *Abelman*, the show's working title. It's a very shabby apartment. It's in a part of Van Nuys that has not been gentrified and never will be. I find a parking spot about two blocks from Bart's place and make my way to his house. It feels a little strange, being the only white guy on the street. I whistle and smile and try to act like as if I'm not the least bit terrified.

Bart opens the door and lights up. "Hey! Thanks for stopping by!"

"Nice place," I lie. It's horrible. It overlooks an alley that seems to serve as the unofficial neighborhood dump, and I can hear the couple upstairs arguing.

"Can I get you something to drink?" he asks me.

"No, thanks."

"I don't blame you," he says. "You should be sober for the walk back to your car. This is a very dangerous neighborhood."

I look over at him and he laughs. "I'm kidding," he says, "and then again, I'm not kidding. But don't worry. I'll walk you back. The brothers know me."

"That's a relief," I say. "I was already dreading the return trip."

He laughs again. "So?" he asks. "What did you think of the script? Or do you want me to tell you what you thought of the script?"

I've got to hand it to the guy. He *is* funny.

"Why don't you tell me what you thought of it?" I say.

"I think it's great," he says. "I think we might have to soften the wife a little, but otherwise it's very good."

"That's exactly what I thought," I say. Bart laughs. I guess he thinks I'm making a joke.

"I only have one concern," he says.

"What's that?"

"All the acting," he says. "I'm a stand-up comic. I don't know if I can act."

I laugh, but I notice that Bart isn't laughing. He is genuinely concerned.

"I've never even been in a school play," he says. "Anne's the real actor in the family."

"Your wife?"

"She played Nurse Wilson on *General Hospital* two years ago. For about three months. She was very good, but her character was killed by a deranged patient, and they couldn't bring her back." Bart lowers his voice. "She asked me to ask you if she could audition for the role of the wife."

"I hate to say this, Bart. But I don't think that's going to be possible. We're looking for someone with a name."

"You've got to do something, Griffin. I beg you. Just get her a small role. Anything. Even one or two lines would be good."

"Okay," I say, sensing his desperation. "I'll see what I can do."

"Look at me. I'm so nervous my hands are shaking."

"You have nothing to worry about. You're going to be great."

"I just can't believe this. Last month, I was still cutting hair."

"And you'll be cutting hair again. On national TV. For a lot of money."

"At least that part I know I can do. Any stylist who tunes in will take one look at the way I hold those scissors, and they'll know I'm the real thing."

"You *are* the real thing, Bart. I wouldn't have pursued you so relent-lessly if I didn't think you had the goods."

Just then, Anne jets into the room. I wonder how long she's been preparing to make this Grand Entrance. It's clear she has spent hours put-ting on makeup to hide the fact that she's been spending time under a bridge scaring the three Billy Goats Gruff. "Hello hello hello!" she emotes. "I thought I heard voices in here!"

It would be hard not to hear voices. The whole place is about 400 square feet. I stand up and smile a big smile and shake her hand. "It's great to see you, Anne."

She glances at her husband and snaps, "Why didn't you tell me Griffin was here?" I feel like it's my job to protect my client, and I have to fight the urge to slap her, but I realize this isn't my bailiwick. "Did you offer our guest something to drink?"

"I think so," Bart stammers.

"He sure did," I say. "But I'm in a rush. I just came by to see how he liked the script."

"*I* have some notes," Anne says.

"Oh?" I was afraid of this.

"I think the wife borders on being a caricature. I don't know if that's what you had in mind for the show, of course, and I don't know where the writers got it, but she's not going to have many fans."

"You know what," I say. "I'm just a manager. This really isn't my area. I don't have a creative bone in my body."

Anne looks over at Bart, who averts his eyes and begins to play with the brass fasteners on the script. She turns her attention back to me. "Did Bart tell you he has absolutely no training as an actor?" she asks.

"He did," I reply. "Bart has been nothing but forthright with us. I'm putting him together with Phillip Bay, who is arguably the best acting coach in the business."

"Phillip Bay," she sneers, and it comes out of her like a hiss. "That hack? With all due respect, Griffin, I studied with him eight years ago, and even then his technique was dated."

"Who did *you* like?" I ask, forcing a smile.

"Well, I completed the Jason Paul workshop, and of course Gilbert Ohls's improv class is quite good . . ." She pauses to see if these illustrious names register.

"I'm afraid I don't know either of them," I say. "Are they local?"

"Yes. They're right here in Reseda."

"I see."

"Honey," Bart says, speaking very softly, "if Griffin says Philip Bay—"

"*If Griffin says! If Griffin says!*" she shouts. "Is that all I'm ever going to hear from now on? *If Griffin says.* He's not even a real manager, for God's sake. When are you going to open your eyes, Bart?!"

I feel like choking her. I glance over at Bart. He looks like he's about to cry.

"What are you going to do now?" she hisses. "*Cry?*"

Lizzie Borden had nothing on this woman—except height, maybe. If I were Bart I'd get rid of all sharp objects in the house. He can't even meet her eyes. Or mine. She glares at me again. "Did you talk about casting yet?"

"We did," I say. "Bart told me you'd like to read for the part of the wife, and I think it's a wonderful idea."

"You do?" she says. She's almost as surprised as Bart is. I can see Bart out of the corner of my eye. I believe those are tears of gratitude.

"Yes," I say. "It's not up to me, of course. Or Bart. You'll have to audition, along with everyone else, but I have a good feeling about this. After all, you know this character, or a less zany version of this character, better than anyone in the world. And you know Bart pretty intimately, too."

"That is so nice of you," Anne says, becoming another person entirely. "Is there any way I can thank you in advance for this opportunity?"

If I didn't know any better, I'd think she was offering herself to me. But maybe that snaky little thing she just did with her tongue is simply a nervous tic.

"Hey," I say. "Don't look at me. Bart's the one who's been doing all the fighting for you."

The minute I say it, I realize it's a mistake. I should be helping Bart get out of this horrible marriage. Instead, I'm brokering an uneasy peace.

"That's my Bart," she says, and it comes out like a threat.

"Well," I say, getting to my feet. "It was great seeing you guys. Bart, don't worry about the script. If the network likes it, they're going to bring a whole team of writers in to ruin it."

"Excuse me?"

"Little joke, Bart. The 'ruining it' part. The team of writers—that's standard procedure."

"What's wrong with Daniels and Lawry?"

"Nothing," I say. "And they're still going to be part of it. Probably. But, you know, NBC wants this to be the best it can be, and they're going to bring in a few really bright guys to sharpen it up, line by line."

"What a weird business," Bart says.

"Yes, it is," I concur, reaching the door. "Okey-dokey. You know where I am if you need me. Anne, when the time comes—good luck."

"Thank you, Griffin," she coos.

"Let me walk you to your car," Bart says.

"That won't be necessary."

"If anybody tries to fuck with you, tell them the Rabbi's got your back."

"Okay," I say. "I love it. The Rabbi's got my back."

I hurry to my car, trying hard not to look like a victim, and I realize I'm out of Tums.

Kecia

LENNY AND TRAVIS are back. But I have to keep it on the down low. They were only gone for a week, but they don't want me telling Griffin. Now this is jacked, because he keeps calling and won't let up. So I lie and can't help feeling bad about it. But I have to be loyal to the boss. He's the one signing my paycheck. Besides, things between Griffin and me still aren't right since he tripped out at Trader Vic's. Trouble is, I *like* the guy. If I didn't, I'd tell Lenny the truth about the contract. And part of me wants to. But I'd be ruining Griffin's life. And for what? Is the next manager going to be any better than Treadway? I don't think so.

Meanwhile, check out Lenny and Travis. I'm worrying myself sick with all these questions and they're carrying on like they don't have a care in the world. They're like two kids at summer camp. They work out every day, eat right, swim laps in the pool, and lay in the sun. The routine is doing wonders for Travis. He's sprouting muscles on his muscles. Whenever I hear one of them dive into the pool, I act like I need something in the living room. I wander over, hoping I'll catch me an eyeful of Lenny in his cute little swim trunks. I can't help myself—I'm a Pisces. Curiosity always gets the best of us.

Believe it or not, I'm getting into pretty good shape myself. And I don't have to work out, either. When you eat as much as I used to eat, all you gotta do is stop—and the el-bees start meltin' away. I'm already fourteen pounds lighter, and I feel *good*. It's not like I'm vain or anything, but I'm beginning to like what I see in the mirror. It makes a real difference. To *me*, anyway. I'm not judging no one else. I know sisters who look like they've got a couple of canned hams in their pants and they don't give a damn. In fact, some of them are proud of it. They go around in spandex so that everybody can enjoy their J.Lo's.

My big worry is I'll pull an Oprah. That girl's *always* had a weight problem, but the minute she slims down she finds her spirit and gets all fat again. That seesawing can't be good for you. I don't want to go there. I don't want to be that person.

Oh my God! There's Len, getting out of the pool and slipping into that plush white robe. I run back to the office, trying not to think about him. But that boy is sure yummy, and I'm crushing on him bad. One look at him and I lose my appetite. He's my very own private diet guru. I can't explain it. Even when he's not around, all I have to do is think about him and my hunger goes away. What is that boy doing to me? What is this feeling I'm feeling?

"Kecia?"

It's him. He ambles over and sits his fine self on the edge of my desk. "What's up?" he says, smelling all wet and clean in that comfy robe.

"It's all good," I say, trying to act casual.

He's staring at me so intently that goose bumps break out on my arms. Maybe he wants to ask me out. You know, try a little black magic. I suck in my breath and smile my best smile, the one that almost gives me lockjaw.

"You're such a sweet girl."

All the blood in my body travels to my face. "Thank you."

"And you really do a terrific job here."

I'm grinning like Al Jolson. I want to kiss him. My horoscope said today that vibes regarding work should be acted on immediately.

"But we're going to have to let you go," Lenny says.

Oh no he didn't.

"We really hate to do this to you. I've crunched the numbers and paying your salary is just not cost-effective. Until Travis does another movie, anyway."

I notice he keeps using the word *we*. I don't see Travis in here. I wonder if he knows big brother is firing my ass.

"What about Marta?"

"We're letting her go, too, for the same reason."

"I have bills to pay, Lenny."

He nods his head. "I realize that. So we'd like you to work for two more weeks. Then we'll pay you for an additional two. I think one month will be enough time to find another job. Don't you?"

"I guess."

He places his hand on my shoulder. "I'm really sorry, Kecia. But as soon as Travis commits to another project, we'll hire you back."

Yeah? When will that be, you ugly-ass white motherfucker? "Okay," I say.

He's almost out the door when he turns around. "By the way, I'll be out of town for a couple of days. Keep an eye on my little bro, would you?"

When he walks out of the room, I sit there in a stupor. No job, no money, soon I'll have no home. What about Marta? Where's she gonna go? What's a sister to do? I guess a sister can start by answering the ringing phone.

"Hello?" I bark. I'm not in the best of moods.

"Is Kecia Christy there?"

I recognize the brother from the IRS. Like he ain't got nothing better to do than harass my ass. I wonder if he's wearing that same cheap suit.

"No, she is not," I say, doing my best white girl impression. "May I take a message?"

"I have reason to believe I'm talking to Kecia Christy."

Damn.

"If this is she, I hope she realizes that this little problem isn't going to away by itself. And that in fact it's not so little."

I hang up. I've heard enough. I've got enough shit to deal with without this raggedy-ass bureaucrat breathing down my neck.

I'M WALKING to my car when Lou crawls out of the bushes, dragging his various camera bags. "Have a good night, Kecia," he croons.

I'm still so upset about getting fired that I ignore him, but when I reach my car I can't seem to get the door unlocked. Lou comes over to help.

"Allow me," he says. He takes the keys and unlocks the door like it was nothing.

"Thanks," I say, climbing in. He won't let me shut the door. I look up and scowl at him.

"You're looking good, girl. I can see you're in a bad mood about something, but you look *fine*. How'd you lose all that weight so quick?"

"*All that weight*? What? I used to be fat or something?"

"Did I say that?! Can't a man compliment a pretty girl without getting into trouble?"

He's got a point. Maybe he's not such a bad guy. Next thing I know, I'm blurting it out: "How much did you say we could get for a picture of Travis?"

His eyes light up. "Depends on what it is. Travis on Rodeo Drive is only worth fifty bucks, but Travis in a 'situation' could be worth thousands."

I crank the engine and my mind kicks back in. This is crazy! This isn't who I am! Where's my self-respect?

"Forget it," I tell him. "I didn't say that."

I yank the door shut, put the car in gear, and pull away.

A N   H O U R   L A T E R , while I'm working on my third Krispy Kreme, the doorbell rings. I figure it's the IRS guy, but when I steal a look through the peephole I see Lou outside. I open the door, brimmin' with attitude. "What the hell are you doing here?" I snap. "And who gave you my address?"

"I came to apologize," he says, and he sounds like he means it.

"For what?"

"For trying to suck you into my game."

I can't believe I'm hearing this. "You serious?"

"I'm not going to give you a big song and dance about how, once upon a time, I wanted to be a 'serious' photographer. That wouldn't be true. This is the way I make a living, and I enjoy it, and I'm not making any excuses for it. But I had no business making that offer. You're a nice girl and I know you're a nice girl, and I just came by to apologize."

I'm not sure I believe him. "You ain't messing with my head?" I ask.

"Damn, girl! What you think I want from you?"

"I don't know. I'm sorry. I had a bad day. I just got fired."

"You're kidding?"

"Come in. I think I got a beer if you want it."

"If you're offering, I'll take it."

He walks in and I shut the door behind him.

"Hell, this is some place," he says. "You live here all by yourself?"

"Yes. Marta's out back."

He struts into the den and notices Daddy's record collection. "You're a big fan of jazz, huh?"

"You could say that."

He carefully surveys the room. It takes him a few minutes before he notices the gold records and Grammys on the wall. He moves closer to get a better look. "Wait a minute! Your daddy was Eddie Christy?"

I nod.

"That shit's the bomb."

I go get his beer. When I come back, he's studying one of Daddy's albums. He looks up at me. "Your old man was a legend, girl!"

"He's a legend to me, too. Though I was barely six when he died."

Suddenly I find myself crying. Lou comes over and takes me in his arms. It's been a long time since a man has held me, longer than I care to admit. I keep crying, but it feels kind of good. And it feels *real* good being held. Damn.

Polaroid C20786A08611A

Rachel ¨

I SAW VICTORIA naked today. It kind of weirded me
out at first, but then I got used to it. She wanted me to wax her lower back.
She has these fine black hairs in a square right above her butt crack and
she absolutely can't stand them. I don't blame her. I knew this girl in high
school with a beard, Denise, bless her heart. It was really sad because if
she didn't shave every day she'd get a twelve o'clock shadow just like
a man.

I had to set up the massage table, which was a struggle, but the minute
I figured it out Victoria stripped right down and hopped aboard in the altogether. I gasped. I couldn't help it.

"What's the matter?" she asked in her mean voice, "Haven't you seen
a naked woman before?"

Well, I'd never seen a *famous* naked woman before—in person. But
that was this morning. Since coming to Los Angeles, I've grown in ways I
could never even imagine.

I wonder what she's doing now. I'm downstairs, waiting for the intercom to squawk, and when it finally does squawk I practically jump out of my skin.

"Rochelle?"

"Yes, Miss Rush?"

"Come up here."

I go upstairs, wondering what I've done wrong this time, and find Victoria wandering around in one of those little thongs. I try not to look at her body, although she's got a really good body for a woman her age.

"Look at me," she says, and she puts her face so close to mine that I have to step back a little. Her face looks like it's just been scrubbed clean. "You see any lines?"

"Ma'am?"

"On my *face*, Rochelle! Are there any lines on my face?"

"No, ma'am," I lie. There are a few lines here and there, but I don't want to hurt her feelings.

"Look closer," she says, and she sticks her face right in mine. There's something disturbing about a naked famous woman standing this close to me. It's not something you imagine happening in real life, but there you are. Her breath smells like boiled eggs. I take my time, studying her face intently. Her eyes follow my movements. "I really don't see anything," I say at last.

"Nothing?"

"Not really," I say. "No lines to speak of . . . But you do have a couple of gray eyebrow hairs." I don't know why I said that. I guess I wanted this investigation to end, and I didn't think it would end until I had something concrete.

"What?!" She is absolutely horrified.

"There's just a couple," I say.

She whirls around and glares into the lighted mirror. "Get me my tweezers!" she yells.

I hand her the tweezers and she begins to pluck away like a crazy woman. I try to tiptoe out of the room, but she stops me with what sounds like a bark. "Did I tell you to leave?" she snaps.

"No, ma'am."

She keeps tweezing. I stand nearby with my hands clasped in front of me like a scolded schoolgirl.

"Where's Matty?" she asks.

"He's at a friend's."

"Which friend? He has more than one friend!"

"Taylor's."

She folds her arms in front of her. "Did he clean his room?"

I blink. "I don't know."

"Why don't you go check?"

Matty's room is a total pigsty. Dirty clothes are all over the floor, his bed is unmade, and his trash can is overflowing with fast food wrappers and bunched-up wads of Kleenex. I report back to Victoria. "He didn't clean it."

She raises one of her newly plucked eyebrows. "I told him he couldn't go anywhere until he cleaned his room. Get him back here at once."

"At Taylor's? I don't know where he lives."

She opens up a jar of cream. "It's in the Book!"

Of course it is! I run all the way down to the wine cellar and look up "Matt's Friends" in the Book of Rules. The house is in a place called Thousand Oaks, which is really far from Brentwood. I go back upstairs and find Victoria rubbing a turquoise cream under her eyes and making that weird noise she makes to clear her sinuses. It sounds sort of like *HUNWAA! HUNWAA!*

I tell Victoria that the drive to Taylor's house might take a while, especially now, at the height of rush hour.

"Let that be a lesson to you," she says, and she makes that weird noise twice in quick succession.

"To me?" I ask, confused.

"In the future, you'll make sure he keeps his room clean."

"Yes, ma'am," I say. "I'm sorry. I'll be back as soon as I can."

"No," she says. "Sooner."

The drive to Taylor's takes over an hour. I have to ring the bell three times before anyone answers. Finally a teenage boy opens the door. He has black spiked hair and is wearing a studded dog collar.

"Is Matt here?" I ask.

"Who wants to know?"

"My name's Rachel. I'm his mother's assistant."

"Hold on," he says and slams the door. I can hear low murmuring voices on the other side of it. Then Matt comes out. "What do you want?"

"Your mother wants me to bring you home."

He's totally PO'd. "What for?"

"You didn't clean your room."

"So?"

"I'm just doing what I'm told. Now if you could come with me, I'd really appreciate it."

Taylor pipes in: "Dude, if you don't leave she might not let you go camping next weekend."

"Fuck!" Matt shouts. "You're right!" He storms out of the house and I quietly thank Taylor for his help. He responds by slamming the door in my face.

In the driveway, Matt stands near my car shaking his head. "You're taking me home in this piece of shit?"

"I know she looks bad, but she still gets me where I need to go."

"Does my mother know you're carting her precious son around in this?"

I hadn't thought about that. "No, I don't think so."

Matt walks around to the passenger side and opens the door.

"Wait!" I warn. "My side doesn't open so I need to crawl over on your side."

"Are you fucking serious?"

"Yes," I say and crawl into the car. He follows me in and shuts the door, and I ask him to put on his seat belt. He puts it on without an argument. He looks nervous, and I can't say I blame him.

"So, Matt," I say, pulling out and trying to make conversation. "What do you like to do?"

"I enjoy getting blow jobs," he says. "If you enjoy giving blow jobs, we could become friends."

In my book, that's a real conversation stopper. So I don't answer. I focus on the bumper-to-bumper traffic on the 101. There's a car in front of me with a license plate that reads RITUR. That's very clever. There are probably twenty thousand writers in L.A., so I'm sure there's a lot of competition for coming up with a license plate that tells people who you are. I try to think of other variations. WRI-TUR. RITER. IRITE4U. RERITE. Someday, if I'm lucky, I'll have one of those license plates. But I don't want to get my hopes up. I'm tired of going home and not hearing from film school about my script.

"I can't believe you don't have a radio," Matt complains.

I turn and look at the boy who likes blow jobs. "I have one. It just doesn't work."

"Why don't you get it fixed?"

"I can't afford to."

"Fucking loser."

"Matt," I say, and I say it with tenderness. "Why are you so angry?"

"Because you won't blow me."

"Do you talk to all girls in this crude way?"

"Suck my dick and I'll tell you."

"How would your mother feel if she heard you talking this way?"

"She wouldn't feel shit. She only cares about herself."

"It seems to me that a lot of this anger is connected to your feelings about your mother."

"Duh!"

"Where does your father live?"

"In San Francisco."

"That's nice. I hear it's nice up there. I've never been, but I've seen pictures. Is he remarried?"

"No. He's a big fag now. I think my mother fucked him up. He's got a boyfriend that kicks the shit out of him regularly, but he doesn't mind. I'm sure it beats living with my mother."

"I think you should give your mother a chance, Matt. She's changed a lot since she found out about her illness. Haven't you noticed?"

"Where the fuck are you from? You have a weird accent."

"I'm from Sugarland, Texas."

"Is everybody in Sugarland as gullible as you?"

"Gullible? I don't know what you mean. I think there are a lot of interesting and unusual people in Sugarland. And I'm sure we have our share of gullible people. There was this sandwich girl at the Starbucks, for example, who believed everything you told her. Like this one time someone told her that scientists cloned a sheep and named it Dolly. And she believed it!"

"Why are you telling me? You're a fucking bore! I can't believe I'm trapped here with you. I hope no one I know sees me in this shitbox."

We drive in silence for a few minutes. Or more like *inch our way along*. "You know, Matt," I say finally, "your mother is a wonderful woman and she loves you very much. I know for a fact that you're the most important person in her life. She'd be devastated if you left." I feel like Dr. Phil giving a wake-up call.

Matt looks at me. "Really?" he says.

"Yes," I say. "Really."

Matt smiles at me. It's the first time I've seen him smile. He's not bad-looking when he smiles. I feel good inside. My words must have made sense to him.

W HEN WE GET BACK to Victoria's, Matt jumps out of the car and goes directly to his room. I find Victoria in the kitchen, setting the table for two. She has the good stuff out: the fancy china, the sterling silver, and the crystal glasses.

"Can I help?" I ask.

She places silverware over two linen napkins. "No. I've got it."

"Do you want me to order something for you to eat?"

"I already ordered from the little Italian place that Matty likes. It should be here soon. Listen for the buzzer."

I'm a little confused because she never orders her own food. But it looks like she wants to spend some quality time with her son. I hope that the little chat Matt and I had in the car has softened his attitude to his mother. But I guess it hasn't. A few minutes later, he walks into the kitchen with a large duffel bag.

Victoria looks up and does her best to ignore the bag. "Hi, Matty! Dinner's almost here. I ordered you the four-cheese lasagna. Why don't you have a seat?"

"Can't. I've got a flight to catch."

The color drains from Victoria's face. "Where are you going?"

"Frisco. I just spoke to Dad. There's a ticket waiting for me at the airport."

My stomach falls to the floor. I'm totally responsible for this. My first urge is to hide, but I can't move.

"Why do you want to live with that shithead?" Victoria says shrilly, although it's obvious she's trying hard to control herself. "I thought you were happy here."

"I hate it here," he says.

Victoria throws her arms around him. "Don't do this to me, Matty. I'd die without you!"

"Why can't you behave like a normal person?! Why does everything have to be cranked to the fucking max?!"

He storms away, and she follows him to the door and falls to her knees, grabbing him around the legs. "Matt, my darling! My baby boy! I implore you! Don't break my heart like this. I can't go on without you."

"So don't go on," he says, and he lets himself out.

I am in shock. This is all my doing. "Do you want some water?" I blurt. I'm thinking she should go with Rescue vitamin water.

That's when I realize how stupid that question was. I could be really, really dumb sometimes. Did she want some water? She just lost her son. Why did I have to say all that to Matt? I'm such a DORKUS MANORKUS!

I am about to reach down and help Victoria to her feet when she springs up on her own. She's not crying anymore. "Thank God," she says with a big sigh.

"Excuse me?" I say, feeling deeply confused.

"I need a break from that monster. Let the butt pirate enjoy him for a while."

I can't believe this. That a mother would say such a thing about her own child! This little creature that was once the size of a pea, or smaller, and grew and grew and then popped out, covered in filth and slime, and started his very first day of life. Victoria can see what I'm thinking. "Don't look at me like that, Rochelle. If you're very unlucky, you'll be a mother someday, and you'll look back on this as a Seminole moment."

I think she means *seminal*, but I might be wrong. Maybe the Seminoles have some strange ritual involving adolescent children. I'll have to check it out later, on the Internet.

"I just feel bad for you," I say. "I know Matty loves you very much."

"And you know this how?"

"Well, back in Sugarland, there was a woman who lived across the street from my mother. And she had a son not unlike Matty, and about his age, too. There was a lot of anger in that boy, but he was out roller-blading in the rain one day and he got hit by lightning, and overnight he became a completely different person. Father Pete said it was a miracle. And for once I had to agree with him."

"You are a very strange girl, Rochelle."

"Yes, ma'am," I say. Suddenly I'm glad she's distracted, because I realize that maybe I shouldn't have told her that story at all. It ended badly, with horrible bloodshed and a long prison sentence, and I'm sure Victoria wouldn't want to hear about *that*. I suddenly find myself thinking about the portly, middle-aged man who moved into that same house a few weeks later, after a special crew came in and cleaned up the blood. He was a dog trainer. He had a business card with a drawing of a dog in a military uniform—a *well-behaved* dog, no doubt—next to the words *Chuck McGivillray / Dog Whisperer*. In the summer, he liked to walk around naked, with the curtains open. It was kind of off-putting. I'd look out my bedroom window and see this big pink man, moving from room to room, with his rescued dogs following him everywhere he went.

Victoria hurries up the stairs. "Call the restaurant and cancel the food," she says.

"Yes, ma'am."

I'm sort of sad about the way this day is ending. And I'm especially sad about canceling the food. I'm really hungry. I thought maybe Victoria and I could have had dinner together. It would have been nice. In some ways, I feel Victoria has the potential to become the mother I never had. Maybe subconsciously I pushed Matt away, but I'd rather not think about that: too scary. There are portions of my mind that are best left undisturbed.

I WAKE FROM UNEASY dreams to the sound of my cell phone ringing. "Hello?" I croak.

"Rochelle?"

The clock says 2:30 A.M. "Yes, ma'am?"

"I can't sleep."

"I left two Ambiens on your nightstand."

"I took them, and I took a couple of Valium, and nothing's working. Why don't you come over? I want to rearrange my closet."

"Now?"

"Of course *now*, you idiot. There's no time like the present. *Carpe diem* and all that."

"Okay," I say. "I'll be right over."

I get up, splash some water on my face, and dress. I'm thinking about maybe sharing this incident with the other assistants next week at Trader Vic's. I have heard many unbelievable stories at these meetings, and this one is right up there in the top two or three hundred in terms of outrageousness.

"Rachel?"

It's Dan. "Go back to sleep," I whisper.

But it's too late. He comes out of his bedroom, rubbing his eyes. "Where the heck are you going?"

"Victoria's."

"At this hour?"

"I took this job and I read the Book of Rules and I accepted all the responsibilities, which by the way are listed on page four hundred and seventeen, though not in any order I could figure out."

"This is crazy. This borders on abuse."

"Not really," I say. "I mean, comparatively speaking. I've heard a lot worse."

"I want to come to one of the Thursday things at Trader Vic's."

"I'm sorry," I say. "You can't. It's only for assistants."

"I really don't think you should go to Victoria's house. I think you should report her to someone."

"Who?"

"I don't know. Don't you have a union or something?"

"Of course not. We're assistants."

"The people at Ralph's have a union. The people who clean the department stores have a union."

"I have to go, Dan. She needs me."

"This is terrible."

"What?" I say.

"Do you realize this is exactly what you used to say about your mother?"

He's right. But then, my mother needed me, too. I'd like to get mad at Dan for reminding me, but he's the one who helped me find the courage to leave home. He told me, "Rachel, you have a life, too. You're a person, too." I've never forgotten it. I'm not sure I believe it, but I've never forgotten it.

"She's dying," I tell Dan.

"*People* magazine isn't so sure."

"What do you mean?"

"They had an article where all these so-called mental health experts felt she needed to come clean before the whole world began to question her crazy story."

Dan always puts the phrase *so-called* in front of the words "mental health expert." His father was one of three psychologists in Sugarland, but after that incident with Betty Schwartz, the high school principal, he had to leave town.

"How can you say that?"

"Even if she is sick, it's wrong to make you go over in the middle of the night. And what about all those long hours you've been working? You work six, sometimes seven days a week. Last night you didn't get home till midnight. And you're not even going to your screenwriting class anymore."

"I don't have time for class."

"This is wrong, Rachel. You're not an indentured servant."

I open the door. "I have to go."

He follows me. "I don't like it, Rach! I don't like it one bit!"

I run away. I don't have time to argue with Dan. And I'm no dummy. I know that in some ways he's right. Okay, *most* ways.

As I drive though the eerily empty streets on my way to Victoria's, I think about my situation. And sure, maybe she is taking advantage of me. But she's in pain, and someone has to be there for her, and it looks like I'm that person. I think there's something magical and maybe even a little miraculous about it, as Father Pete might say. Me, a little nobody from Sugarland, and I'm the one person in the world Victoria Rush can turn to in her hour of need. I used to watch her on TV. Never in my wildest dreams did it occur to me that someday I would actually become her best friend.

When I get to the house, I march up to the master suite, calling her name, but she doesn't answer. I tiptoe inside and find her in bed.

"Victoria?"

No answer. She might be ignoring me. She sometimes does that. I tiptoe a little closer.

"Victoria?"

Okay, now I'm concerned. But then I hear that high-pitched, kettle-like nasal snore. She's completely passed out and still holding the phone in her hand. I stare at her for a few seconds. Her hair's a mess and she has a little bit of drool coming out of the corner of her mouth. It's amazing how everyone looks innocent when they're asleep. Everybody looks like the little baby Jesus, probably even serial killers and that guy Jeb. If only some of these people could be permanently asleep, then the world would be a better place, if you want my opinion.

When I take the phone out of her hand, she snorts like a piglet. I freeze and wait a few seconds for the snore to return. When it does, I put the phone down next to all of her pill bottles. There sure are a lot of them.

"Good night, Victoria," I whisper and walk out of her room, gently closing the door behind me.

There's no sense going home, since I'm already there. So I lay down on the carpet, right outside her door, just in case she needs me.

GRIFFIN

WATCHING THESE GUYS soar through the air and slam-dunk brings me an indescribable pleasure. If the NBA ceased to exist, where else could you employ a seven-foot-tall skyscraper in sneakers? Hollywood, of course! And that's exactly the thinking that got Rodman and Shaq their studio deals. I'm lying on the couch in my boxers, watching the Lakers play the Kings, and it's heavenly. For the first time in hours, my stomach isn't throbbing. During commercials I flip to ESPN, where a pair of oversized mutants throw beer kegs over a brick wall in the World's Strongest Man contest. Earlier, they were pulling tour buses a hundred meters with their teeth. It's programming like this that makes me adore the medium.

There's a knock at the door. I reach for the remote and turn up the volume. The knocking continues. Groaning, I pull myself off the couch and amble to the door.

"Who is it?"

"Kenvin."

I open the door and peer down at the boy.

"'Sup, G," he says.

"How's my favorite homeboy hacker?"

"Dang, yo. I ain't no hacker. I have what whitey would call 'marketable skills.'" He breezes by me and struts into the living room and catches sight of the game. "You like hoops?"

"Yes," I say. "Some gay men actually like sports."

"Still stickin' with that gay thing, G?"

"What can I do for you, Kenvin?"

He picks up the remote control and looks at it. "I was hoping you could do me a favor."

The boy's audacity is mind-blowing. "Such as?"

He keeps his eyes on the remote. "You work for Travis Trask, right?"

I'm more surprised than suspicious. "How do you know that?"

He shoots me a look like I'm an imbecile of considerable proportions.

I sigh, "What's the favor?"

"My lady's real sweet on him, so I was thinking that maybe you can get me an autographed picture."

"Your girlfriend wants a picture of Travis?"

Now it's his turn to sigh. "She ain't my girlfriend. Yet. But if I give her this picture she might want to be. Ya know what I'm sayin'?"

"I know what you're saying."

"I figure in return, I won't tell nobody about your straightness. And make that autograph authentic. Don't you go signing it."

I should be getting more from this transaction, but the entire exchange strikes me as quite humorous. And how does he know about my forgery skills? I extend my hand. "Deal."

Like any consummate professional, Kenvin shakes my hand and leaves. Back to the game. The Kings are up by seven. Nine minutes left in the fourth quarter. The doorbell rings again. "You're pushing it," I yell. But this time another voice responds and it's distinctly female.

"Hang on. Just a minute," I say, leaping to my feet.

I open the door and Michaela walks in. "Oh, Griffin," she says, bursting into tears. "I'm so glad you're here!"

"What happened?" I stammer. "What's wrong?"

"You're not going to believe the day I had," she starts, taking a seat and lighting a cigarette. "Do you have an ashtray?"

"Use this." I push my can of Diet Coke toward her.

"After Victoria fired me, I didn't think it could get any worse. But now

I've lost my agent, too. I got a postcard, preprinted. There was a blank space for my name. One sentence. No phone call."

"Oh, Michaela, I am so, so sorry."

"I fucked that bastard twice a week, and he still dumped me."

Michaela is very hot for an older woman. A few years ago, I would have enjoyed congress with such a girl. But I'm done with women. Lorraine cured me. The fucking psycho. Who knew she was a borderline personality? Who knew she would come at me with a screwdriver and set my condo on fire?

"Why do you feel you have to sleep with people to get ahead?" I say, feeling like a gay priest. I wonder if I should send her off with a few Hail Marys.

"Come on, Griffin. Look at Marilyn Monroe. They passed her around like a collection plate, and she didn't seem to mind. After all, she got what she wanted, right?"

"What?" I say, confounded by her logic. "Being dead?"

"Okay," she concurs. "Maybe that's not the best example. But there are many women who fucked their way to the top."

"And many more who fucked their way to the middle," I say.

She lights another cigarette. "I even slept with a woman," she says. "I met this casting director who said she could get me an audition for a Barry Levinson film."

In my youth, this might have excited me: the thought of two women going at it, their bodies glistening with sheeny sweat, the air filled with their musky aroma. But the last time I had an erection was when I saw Bart Abelman on stage, and knew right away I had to sign him. Like I said, talent is a great aphrodisiac.

"Did you enjoy yourself?" I ask, but I'm not really interested. I'm doing this for Michaela. Because she wants me to ask.

"I guess," she says, taking another drag off her cigarette. "I basically lay there and let her do all the work."

"You're better than this, Michaela," I say. But that's just agent talk. I like Michaela, and I feel for her, but someone should tell her she's finished in this town. Maybe she should consider theater. There are two or three hundred small theaters in L.A., and no one ever goes to them.

"You think that's pathetic, don't you? That I slept with a woman?"

"Not at all," I say. Another lie. I think Michaela should find a nice boring husband, get married, move to Bel Air, and have kids. But I can't tell her that. It would break her heart.

"I can't be an assistant forever," she says, and I'm afraid she's going to cry again.

"And you won't be," I say. You'll be someone's dowdy wife, forever embittered by your shabby treatment in Hollywood. "I'll get you an audition for Bart Abelman's new pilot," I add. I don't know why I say this, and I regret it. Michaela has talent, to be sure, but so do ten thousand other pretty girls—on this block alone. The thing they don't seem to understand is that there's talent, and there's *Talent*.

"Bart Abelman?"

"He's a stand-up comic. Very funny guy."

"That really kills me. You get up on stage and tell a few jokes and they give you a network show."

"Come on. Chin up. You've caught a couple of bad breaks. Things will change." *Probably for the worse.*

Her hand is tremulous as she brings the cigarette to her lips. "Maybe I don't have what it takes. Have you ever been so sure of something and then found out you were completely wrong?"

"I'll have to think about that," I say. But I don't have to think about it. Sure, I've been wrong from time to time. I thought, for example, that I'd eventually get over the damage I suffered at the hands of that psycho Lorraine. I thought that with time and a little tenderness, I could become a normal, functioning male again. But it didn't happen. I'm not even remotely interested in sex, straight or gay. It's so messy. And some people smell really bad. No, that's not my thing anymore. All I want from life now are two things: power and control.

"I can't believe I got fired from *Friends*," she says, crying again.

And I can't believe she's still talking about that! I like Michaela, but damn it, she has to stop living in the past.

I'm trying to think of something nice to say, but luckily she's on a roll: "I'm still having nightmares God knows how many seasons later. I can't even say *years*; I'm so messed up I can only talk about fucking *seasons*. 'I went to Europe last season.' 'I have to find a new apartment before the end of the season.' Jesus, I'm losing my mind."

"You'll be okay," I say, but I'm hardly listening—I'm thinking of Bart Abelman's shrewish wife, and of all the damaged people in this town. I will not be one of them.

"Every time I hear that goddamn theme song," she is saying—and here she hums a few bars like an insane homeless woman with seven shopping carts—"I feel like drowning myself in that ridiculous fountain. *I* was Feebs. *I'm* supposed to be famous. I should have won that Emmy. Brad Pitt should be *my* husband."

"Jennifer Aniston married Brad," I point out.

She stands and begins to pace the room like a caged panther. I watch her smoke the rest of the cigarette, and I steal a look toward the TV. Wow! They're tied, with only one minute left in the game. She walks over to the mantel and picks up the picture of Mel and Roger in Palm Springs.

"Is this your brother?" she asks. "He looks just like you."

"Yes."

She studies the photo. "What does he do?"

I clear my throat. "He was a personal manager, but he died two years ago. A drunk driver ran him off the road."

She sucks in her breath. "How awful. I'm so sorry."

I nod as my stomach starts up again. I wish Mel would remove the picture from the mantle. Trying not to think about Roger is difficult enough. Seeing him literally rips my heart out. She sits down next to me and takes my hand in hers.

"Do you want to talk about it?"

"No."

I know she doesn't want to talk about it, either. She wants to talk about herself. But that's what's going to make me a success: I understand these things, and they don't faze me.

"I am so pathetic," she says.

Did I call it right or did I call it right?

"I'm old. I'll never be an actress. And I'll never meet anyone."

"What are you talking about?!" I protest. "Men would kill for a woman like you!"

"So, it's true, then! I won't be an actress?!"

You can never win with these people. "That's not what I said, Michaela."

"And no one will ever love me, either! How will they get past this?" she says, gesturing theatrically. "The plastic surgery, the bleached hair, the implants. Even if someone is able to see the real me, they wouldn't think I was pretty at all."

"I think you're beautiful."

"Sure. *You* would. But you're not a regular man. Regular men don't have feelings."

Out of the corner of my eye I watch the Kings sink a three-pointer, ending the game. Yes! Mel owes me twenty bucks! And I can certainly use it.

The door opens and, speak of the devil, in walks Mel. "Hi, honey, I'm home," he warbles. He never gets tired of that tired line.

"You owe me twenty bucks."

"The Lakers lost?! Oh, hi, Michaela! What are you doing here? You're not trying to seduce my boyfriend, are you?"

"I wouldn't dream of it. And I was just on my way out, anyway."

"Don't leave on my account. Griffin and I never have sex before nine."

She stands, ignoring him. "Thanks, Griff. You're a great friend."

"I didn't do anything," I say.

"I'll see you at Trader Vic's."

She waves and exits and the minute the door shuts Mel screams at me at the top of his voice, for her benefit: "You two-timing bastard! You've been with that dirty girl! How could you break my heart like this after everything we've been through?"

"Shut the fuck up, Mel," I say. "This isn't funny."

But Mel thinks it's hilarious. He collapses on the couch, laughing crazily, unable to catch his breath.

"Asshole," I say.

He's cackling so hard he can barely get the words out: "I thought I was protecting your cover. I *am* your boyfriend, right? Or am I not good enough for a seriously conflicted asexual?"

"Just drop it, would you? I'm not in the mood."

"Hey, I know what I look like. I know I'm not that attractive. I'm old. I have a receding hairline. My thighs are big. My ass sags."

"Mel, you're very handsome. Now please leave me alone."

He sits down and looks at me in that perky girlfriend way he has. "Come on, Griffy. Something's troubling you. Mel's here for you, as always."

"I think I need professional help," I say, and I'm only half-joking.

"I'm listening."

"I think I have made some very bad choices, especially lately . . . This whole gay thing, for one. It doesn't seem to be working. There are plenty of powerful gays in Hollywood, but they're not nearly as powerful or as helpful as I thought they'd be. They're just like the straight guys, maybe worse: they look out for themselves first and foremost."

"What do you expect, Griffy? That's human nature."

"It sucks."

"And you're right about their lack of power. Look at Dreamworks . . . S-K-G." He pronounces each letter forcefully. "The gay guy gets bottom billing. Maybe if it had been G-S-K they wouldn't have had such a disastrous year."

"There's something else," I say.

"What?"

"It's about Travis Trask. We didn't want to lose him as a client, so I altered his contract and forged his signature."

The color drains out of Mel's face. "Oh Griffy. Griffy Griffy Griffy. This is not good. This is not good at all."

Of course it's not good. I know it. And my stomach knows it.

Rachel

O, MY GOD! Today I met that Maury Safer guy from
60 Minutes. It was really wild! I wonder if he knows Stone? They came over
to do an interview with Victoria and you wouldn't believe all the people he
brought with him. There were producers, camera, lighting, and sound
guys, and a couple of PAs who were very nice and didn't look stressed-out
at all. Apparently Maury's a pretty mellow boss, probably because he's so
old. It took the cameramen a whole hour to transform the living room into
a ministudio. I had drinks and snacks set up in the kitchen and even went
up to Mr. Safer and asked if he needed anything. He said he'd appreciate
a cup of coffee, black. So I made a fresh pot and brought it to him in a cup
and saucer from the good china cabinet. I also mentioned that I used to
work in coffee and that he's drinking an Arabian mocha-Sanami that's
been aged for three years. He seems to appreciate my knowledge of beans
and after taking a sip says it's the best cup of Joe he's ever had. I don't
know why he called it Joe but he IS really ancient so I just played it off.

Before they start the interview, I run down to the office and try to call my mom. She loves *60 Minutes*. I really don't get that show. It's a little too serious. I'm more of a *Dateline NBC* fan, not just because of Stone, of course, but because it comes on a few times a week and they always have those court cases where you can call in and vote guilty or not guilty. I like to get involved. Mom's not home so I leave her a message.

Victoria is fine during the interview. At first, anyway. She's very frank about her marriage to Lorne and says she really loved him in the beginning, but their love faded after his infidelities.

"Will you tell us what you are dying of? Maury asks. And I guess this is the moment everyone's been waiting for, because the whole room goes totally still.

"I can't," she says.

Mr. Safer looks disgusted and gets a little hot around the collar. "Listen to me, Victoria," he says, trying to keep his temper in check. "The only thing you've admitting to having is crabs. Big goddamn deal. Every other person in this room has had crabs."

"Really?" she says. She seems confused, and I notice that her eyes are looking a little glazed.

He signals to the camera to get rolling again. (I love that word: *rolling*. I could say it forever.) "What I want to know," Mr. Safer says, and he says it with real intensity, "what the *world* wants to know, Victoria, is the rest of the story."

"What story?" Victoria says. She definitely slurred there. I knew she shouldn't have taken so many pills.

"This business about not having long to live," Mr. Safer says. I swear, he looks mad. He looks like he's going to whack her.

"I had a cat when I was a little girl," Victoria says. "His name was Pussy. That wouldn't work at all today, would it? Though on that show on HBO, didn't they have a guy called Big Pussy?"

Uh-oh. I think we're in trouble here. Mr. Safer's face is getting kind of red. Everyone is staring at Victoria. I feel like protecting her. I feel like running out in front of the camera and taking her in my arms and carrying her to bed. But there's no way I could pick her up.

"This is better than Farrah on Letterman," one of the sound guys whispers to his buddy.

"Victoria, are you with us?" Mr. Safer seems a little unnerved. "Earth to Victoria. Come in, Victoria."

"People have always depended on my kindness to strangers," Victoria says. I know this is not Victoria talking, because this sounds like something I've heard before—maybe even in high school, in Mrs. Eileen Mendt's class. Mrs. Mendt only wore black clothes and practiced witchcraft, but she almost got fired for posing seminude in *Wiccan Weekly*.

"Did you see the story in the current issue of *People?*" Mr. Safer says. I was hoping he wouldn't bring this up—I lied to Victoria yesterday and told her that the magazine didn't come—but I guess Mr. Safer is tired of being Mr. Nice Guy. "People are beginning to wonder—"

"Somebody get this shit off me!" Victoria bellows. She rips the mike off her silk shirt, taking half the shirt with it. Then she struggles to her feet, tottering, and walks off with one boob showing just like Janet Jackson at the Super Bowl halftime show. I hurry after her and help her up the stairs.

"This is one for the in-house reel," I hear somebody say. I can't believe I heard that. I can't believe they'd do that. I imagine this really long tape with all sorts of famous people suffering through all sorts of embarrassing moments, and I imagine the people at *60 Minutes* sitting in a back room and watching it and laughing. Please tell me the world is not such a horrible, cruel place. Please tell me people like that don't really exist.

I get Victoria into bed and she asks me to bring her fan mail. I tell her I will bring it up as soon as the film crew leaves.

"What film crew?" she says, but her eyes begin to close and I steal away.

I say good-bye to Mr. Safer and thank him for coming and apologize for things not going as smoothly as he had hoped.

"You have nothing to apologize for," he tells me. "It was one of the most compelling interviews I've ever done."

A S SOON AS they're out the door, I walk into the house and the intercom squawks. It's Victoria, demanding to know why it's taking me so long to bring the fan mail. There are only three letters today, but I bring them up and read them to her. The first is from a woman who wants an autographed photograph of her before she dies. (I think she should have left out the dying part.) The second is from a man who has written before to point out several plot holes in her show. And the third is from a little boy in Atlanta, Georgia.

Dear Victoria:

I'm only ten years old but my Mom says you're the funniest lady to ever be on TV. I'm sorry you're dying. I want to tell you not to be scared. I had a gerbil that died last month and it was hard for him but I spoke to him last night in my prayers and he agreed to be your pet when you get to Heaven. He said to look for him on the left side of the gate, and that Saint Peter knows he's there. His name is Tiger, by the way. You will love him.

Your friend,
Stevie Dunn

Suddenly Victoria begins to cry and I don't know what to do. I wonder if she's having a nervous breakdown.

Finally I have to crawl into bed with her and hold her in my arms until I get her calmed down. I hurry into her opulent bathroom and run some hot water over a face towel and bring it to her.

"Thanks," she says, and she says it real sweet-like.

I take the towel from her and she pats the bed and makes me sit next to her.

"I have something I need to get off my chest," she says. I think maybe she needs some more hairs removed, and I would be happy to oblige, but that's not it at all.

"What is it, Victoria?" I try to sound like one of those nuns in that Jane Fonda movie, but I couldn't buy Jane Fonda as a nun. I kept thinking of that hard body under her vestments, or whatever you call those robes they wear.

"I lied," she says.

"About what?"

"I don't really have a terminal illness."

I am too stunned to say anything. I cannot believe this.

"I *am* dying. I'll probably be dead in forty or fifty years, and God knows that's not a very long time. So that part of it is true."

"I don't understand," I say.

"What's to understand? I didn't want them to cancel my show."

I don't say anything. I'm in shock. I squeeze the little face towel so hard that it drips onto my skirt and leaves a huge wet spot.

"Why are you looking at me like that? Do you think I'm a terrible person?"

"No," I say. But it's such an awful lie that I have to correct myself. "Maybe a little."

"What should I do?"

I don't know what she should do. I'm just a girl from Sugarland, Texas. The biggest thing that happens in Sugarland is the habanero-eating contest every Fourth of July. It's muy caliente. People come from all over the world to compete. Last year this little runty guy from Venezuela won in record time. He gave a long, rambling acceptance speech in Spanish after, and my Spanish teacher from high school tried to translate, and apparently the little runty guy said that he did it for the people of his country, who were going hungry on account of that crazy bastard dictator-president, Somebody Chavez, but I'm not sure my teacher got it quite right, and after a while they had to drag the little runty guy off the stage.

"Don't just stare at me like that!" Victoria snaps. "What are you thinking about?"

"The habanero-eating contest in Sugarland."

"What?!"

I realize it was a mistake to say this, but I'm upset about what Victoria said. "I can't believe what you just told me," I say, my voice cracking. "I wish you hadn't told me."

"You can't tell anyone," Victoria says. "Do you understand?! If you tell anyone, I will hunt you down and kill you."

Wᴴᴇɴ I ɢᴇᴛ ʜᴏᴍᴇ that night, Dan meets me at the door. He's all grinning like the Chesterfield Cat from Alice in Wonderland.

"I've got a big surprise for you," he says with his hands behind his back.

"What is it?" I say, but I'm not interested. I am still in shock about what Victoria told me. I wonder if the witness protection program is as bad as they say it is, and whether it's true that some of the people who are said to disappear into the program don't get nice new homes in quaint little fishing towns, but actually end up dead—murdered by the very U.S. government agents that are supposed to be protecting them. After all, it kind of makes sense, doesn't it? These people disappear, and we don't know how.

"Close your eyes," Dan says.

"I don't feel like closing my eyes," I say.

"What is wrong with you?"

"I have a splitting headache."

"Just sit down and close your eyes," he insists, leading me to the couch.

"I don't want to close my eyes."

"I'm not going to ask you again."

I close my eyes and I feel him put a large envelope in my hands. I open my eyes. I have to blink twice. The envelope is from the UCLA School of Theater, Film, and Television. I'm in total shock.

He grins. "You'll notice it's a *big* envelope, not a little one. I think we know what that means."

I tear it open and quickly scan the letter.

Dear Rachel:

Congratulations. Everyone on the board absolutely loved your quirky screenplay, The Sugarland Shuffle. *We are pleased to offer you admission to the School of Theater, Film, and Television for the Fall Quarter 2004, and we are eagerly looking forward to meeting you.*

I can't believe I did it. If I didn't have Victoria's horrible secret weighing on my soul, I would probably jump off the couch and kiss Dan. Instead, I say, "There must be a mistake."

"What is wrong with you?" Dan says. "*The Sugarland Shuffle*; they said it themselves. Do you know how hard it is to get into the UCLA film school? You should be jumping up and down. You should be screaming from the rooftops."

"I think I'm coming down with something," I say. I get up and go into my room and close the door. Dan knocks on the door.

"What?" I say.

"Rachel, what the hell is going on?"

"Nothing. This is a lot to deal with, that's all." It is, too, though I know I must sound so ungrateful.

"Is there anything I can do?" Dan asks.

"No, thanks," I say. "I'll be all right."

"You want me to fill out the form for you?"

"What form?"

"For school, silly. You have to acknowledge the letter and let them know you'll be attending."

"I'll take care of it tomorrow."

"Are you sure you're okay?"

"Yes," I say, though I'm not. "I just feel a little flu-ish, and I'm worried about Victoria."

"I want you to stop obsessing about Victoria," he says. "I didn't drag you away from Sugarland so you could find a new mother."

"I am not obsessing about Victoria," I say, "and I know she's not my mother."

"Don't you see the similarities, Rach? Your mother is an alcoholic. Victoria is a drug addict. History is repeating itself."

"I know you mean well, Dan. And I'm grateful. But can we not have this conversation again?"

"Rachel, you're too nice for your own good. You're the most amazingly loyal person I've ever met. But you have to start thinking about yourself from time to time, and you have to start taking care of your own needs. Especially now. I am so proud of you for getting into film school."

"Thank you," I say.

"I'm here if you need me," he says.

"You're a wonderful person, Dan. I mean that."

I take off my clothes and get into bed without brushing my teeth. The world is so confusing. And people do bad things. And the Arabs don't like us very much.

I don't understand it. I would like someone to please explain the meaning of life.

I lie there for a while, lost in thought, then make up my mind. I pick up the phone and call Victoria.

"Hello?" she says. I can't believe she actually answers, but this is her ultraprivate line and I guess not too many people have the number.

"Victoria," I say. "It's me."

"Who?"

"Rachel."

"I don't know anyone called Rachel."

"*Rochelle*, then."

"Oh. Rochelle. Why didn't you say so?"

"I have something to say to you."

"What?"

"You have to tell the truth about your lie. I cannot keep this inside me. It's killing me."

"Listen to me, you little shit. I am warning you—"

"And another thing," I find myself saying, cutting her off. "I will not be spoken to that way."

I cannot believe I've actually said this!

"What did you just say to me?"

"You heard me."

"You little bitch! How dare you talk to me that way?"

"How dare you talk to *me* that way? You are not my mother."

"Do you know who I am?!"

"I know who you used to be," I reply, and the minute the words are out of my mouth I realize I'm being unnecessarily cruel. But maybe she needs that.

"You're fired!"

"I am sorry about that, Victoria. But not as sorry as you think. I've been here for you. You will not find a more loyal friend outside of Sugarland, but a person has to draw the line someplace, even in the sand." I feel like I've been waiting my whole life to say that, but mostly to my mother. Still, it kind of makes sense in this context, too. And I don't feel bad at all. I feel kind of lighter, actually. "I know you're going to find this hard to believe, Victoria, but I really care for you. I'm going to pretend I'm not fired. I'm going to pretend we're taking a little break from each other to regroup and pull ourselves together."

"I'm on the phone with a complete lunatic!" she bellows.

"I know this is hard for you, Victoria. When I was a little girl, my father had to face an important decision, too. He made the wrong decision, alas, and he died at the hands of the police in a hail of gunfire. They say he died laughing, and maybe that's true—he always said he'd get the last laugh. But I don't think he's laughing now."

Victoria hangs up on me and I set the phone back in its cradle. I feel oddly calm. In fact, I suddenly feel much better about myself and about life in general. First thing in the morning, I'm going to go down to that Starbucks in Brentwood, in case this trial separation from Victoria doesn't work out. I hear they're looking for friendly, personable people, people with partner potential.

GRIFFIN

WHEN I SHOW UP at Trader Vic's, I can't believe how many strange faces I see. The old gang is here, of course, but there must be two or three dozen new people. They've taken over all the tables on the west side of the lounge and a cloud of smoke hangs over everything.

"Well, well—what do we have here?" I ask Michaela.

She looks up at me and shrugs. "Beats me," she says. "I just got here."

I spot Rachel. She waves. There's something different about her. For one thing, she's grinning like a halfwit. I also see the girl who works for Alec Baldwin. Most of the others people are strangers, but I find a seat next to Kecia. "Who are these people?" I ask her. "What's going on?"

"I'm not sure," she says. "But I hear Rachel spent the last few days e-mailing everyone she's ever met in Los Angeles."

"I hear Victoria fired her," I say.

"That's not the way she sees it," Michaela says.

Someone is tapping on a glass. I look up. It's Rachel, just now getting to her feet. The room falls silent. "Thank you for coming, everyone. For those of you who don't know me, my name is Rachel, and I'm an assistant—although technically I'm on *hiatus* at the moment, as they say in the biz."

A dozen voices respond in unison: "Hello, Rachel!"

"For those of you who are newcomers, welcome. I'd also like everyone to say hello to Griffin and Michaela, who kind of started this whole weekly support group thing."

"Hello, Griffin and Michaela!"

This is very strange. My first reaction is that Rachel has taken this whole AA analogy a little too far, but then it strikes me that we probably need this. I know *I* do. I notice Michaela staring at me, perplexed. I certainly know *she* does. She needs all the help she can get these days.

"Griffin works for Johnny Treadway," Rachel says. "And Michaela works for —" She stops herself, not knowing how to finish the sentence.

"I *used to* work for Victoria Rush," Michaela pipes up, helping her out. "But I was recently fired."

There are various choruses of support from people who know what being fired feels like, which seems to be most of the people in the room.

"Who wants to start?" Rachel asks.

A thin, twitchy guy raises his hand. Rachel nods and takes her seat. Twitchy stands. "Hello. My name is Bill, and I'm an assistant."

"Hello, Bill," everyone roars back, myself included.

"I work for MGM. I have to be there by nine every morning, before anyone else, and I don't leave for home till eight, when everyone's already gone. And every night I have to take at least four or five scripts home with me, and read them, and have the coverage done before I come in the next morning."

People roar their approval and support. Bill takes a seat.

"So what do you do when your boss makes an unreasonable request?" Rachel asks, then looks at me. "Do you have any insight into that, Griffin?"

I shrug. "I try to do everything that is asked of me."

A large, orotund fellow gets to his feet. "My name is Eric and I work at Universal. What about breaking the law?"

The group gapes at me. "I guess that depends on the individual and what the request is."

"Every night at six my boss makes me take his Porsche along Santa Monica Boulevard and cruise for young boys."

Talk about your extreme example. For some reason I feel compelled to lapse into therapist mode. "How does that make you feel?"

"Totally gross. My boss is a child-molesting pervert. I don't want anything to do with it."

"You can always refuse."

"What if he fires me?"

I rub my chin. "That's the big question, isn't it? What is your occupation really worth? Is it worth your self-respect? If you can't look yourself in the mirror, then how do you get dressed in the morning?"

I mull over my own predicament. I haven't spent much time in front of the mirror, either, since giving Travis that bogus contract. If I were a superhero, I'd be Captain Hypocrite.

A pretty girl stands. "Good evening. My name is Deirdre. I'm an assistant in the development department at New Line." From the response of the guys in the group, they're very happy she's here.

"Hello, Deirdre!"

"Nice gams," Jeb whispers to me.

"So why do they treat us like idiots?" Deirdre asks.

"Although we are all fallible, there are some assistants who make Jessica Simpson look like a Mensan tainting the position for the rest of us," I say. "We must realize that having no requirements other than a pulse and a driver's license opens the door for all levels of idiocy in these posts."

"What about when there aren't any screwups, why do they still treat us like shit?" another guy asks.

"Unfortunately, there is no easy way to explain the complexities of this biz. But even if there were, it would still be beyond our ken," I say. Everyone gawks at me blank-faced.

I switch modes to elucidate. "Think of it as the most evil fraternity in existence. Most people start out as assistants, so once they reach the top, it's payback time. That's one of the perks of finally making it. It's your turn to make someone else's life a living hell, with bonus points for creativity and cruelty. I wouldn't be shocked if some executives sit around swapping stories, trying to top each other with all the barbarous and unusual humiliations they've inflicted."

The other assistants shake their heads at the injustice of it all. I take a big drink from my mai tai and feel my stomach twinge. How could something that used to bring so much gustatory pleasure cause so much agony?

"I'm not defending their actions, but this behavior comes from sheer paranoia. This industry thrives on a foundation of complete negativity.

The fault line running beneath our feet is a perfect metaphor for the business. Everyone's afraid they'll lose their job."

"I'm glad I came here tonight. I thought I was the only one going through all this," another assistant says.

"We're all in the same boat," Michaela says.

"We should form a club of some sort," Rachel says.

"I thought this was a club," someone says.

Rachel shakes her head. "We're not an official club with a real purpose."

"Girl, what do you mean?" Kecia asks.

Rachel's eyes are ablaze. "Why don't we form a union like in *Norma Jean?*"

"Who's Norma Jean?" someone asks.

"You know, the movie starring Sally Fields," Rachel says.

"Norma Rae," I correct. "And it was Sally Field."

I'm once again met with vacant stares. They have no idea who Sally Field is. Christ.

"Anyway, it's about this woman who worked in a factory where all the employees were treated badly," Rachel says. "So this guy from New York comes to town and convinces Norma Rae to help unionize the factory."

"Did it work?" Kecia asks.

Rachel nods. "Yep."

"We can't form a union," Jeb says, stating the obvious.

"Why can't we unionize? Every group in this industry has. Actors, directors, writers, crew members . . ." Michaela says.

"We are overworked and underpaid," someone else counters.

"Just like they said in the movie, if we all join together, we can become one voice. Then we can demand things like humane treatment," Rachel says.

"And fair wages!"

"A fit place to work!"

"Health benefits," I fantasize in my head, but then quickly return to reality. This is insanity.

"Wait a minute!" the assistant from Dimension Films interrupts. "There's no way this will work. Our bosses will laugh and then fire us. I don't know about the rest of you, but I can't afford to lose my job."

Marilyn adds, "If we try to shake up the system, every assistant will have to pay for what we're attempting. If we think it's bad now, what's going to happen if we threaten to unionize?"

"But if we succeed, they will all benefit, too," someone interjects.

Rachel nods. "That's all true. Norma Rae's coworkers got their wages cut and had to work more hours. Her friends hated her for it. She became an outcast and her father died."

I decide to speak for the first time since the union discussion began. "Does anyone have any idea how hard it would be to unionize?"

Blank stares. Dead silence.

I glance at the guy from Dimension. "There's no doubt about it. We'd get fired immediately, nothing would change, and our attempt would be futile."

Most of the group agrees with me.

Kecia shakes her head. "It's a damn shame we can't do a thing about it."

Then a fellow in thick glasses stands. "What if we *pretend* to have a union?"

"What do you mean?" I ask.

He looks around the room. "My name's Marty, by the way. I work at Sony."

"Hi, Marty," we all mumble.

"So say we have a fictitious union, we can get our actor friends to pose as representatives, and their sole function would be to scare the crap out of the worst offenders."

No one says anything. Marty turns red. "It was just a thought."

But suddenly the room crackles with unbridled enthusiasm.

"That's off the hook!"

"Could we really pull that off?"

"Might as well try. We don't have anything else left to lose."

I think this is a very clever idea, and warrants further investigation. I notice Jeb across the table. It occurs to me that it would be doubly effective if the fake rep happens to be a very strong, threatening man.

"What is the name of our union going to be?" Michaela asks.

Rachel jumps up. "I got it! THAG."

No one has any idea what the hell she is talking about, so she explains. "The Hollywood Assistants Group. Duh!"

O N M Y W A Y H O M E , I think about some of the things these assistants shared about themselves and their bosses, and it gives me strength. Some of the stories I could have done without—the girl at MGM who had to hold her boss's penis for him when he urinated, "tight, not too tight"—though of course in that case there were extenuating circumstances, since he had broken his arm in a motorcycle accident. And the one who had to clean out her boss's . . . No, that's more information than you really need.

Another guy got up and announced that his name was Charlie, and that he worked for Ron Howard, and everyone was waiting for the Big Reveal About Ron. Another myth quashed! Opie is an asshole. But no. "He's the best boss I ever had! I *love* him."

He was roundly booed, and I don't think he'll be back.

The evening had been both immensely entertaining and cathartic, and the fake union idea wasn't half-bad. These are my brothers- and sisters-in-arms, and they, too, are struggling with issues of self-respect. Just before I left, I took Rachel aside and told her how impressed I was.

"I just like people," she said in that quaint little Texas twang. "You can't tell how strong a bull is from the size of its horns."

That girl is definitely strange. I bet she used to go cow tipping with her friends. And she reminds me of someone in a movie. I don't know who exactly, though I'm sure it'll come to me.

On the drive home I find my euphoria tempered by this nagging business over Travis. I have committed an egregious forgery, and this is not the type of mistake one can simply ignore. Quite the contrary. The entire course of my career—nay, my entire future!—will be determined by my ability to deal with this delicate situation.

Kecia

TODAY MY HOROSCOPE SAID, _"Lucky you—sudden changes, societal power, and creative brilliance are all on your agenda."_ Can you believe that shit? I'm a no-job, no-crib, broke-ass sister and I haven't had a Krispy Kreme in three weeks.

"Hey, Kecia." It's Travis, coming into the office looking all melancholy and shit. "How you doin'?"

"How do you think I'm doing?" I say. Why stand on ceremony? What can he do now? Fire my ass? "I'm doing shitty."

"I'm sorry we had to let you go," he says.

"Not as sorry as I am."

"The minute I get my next movie, I'm hiring you back."

"And what am I supposed to do in the meantime? Not eat?"

"You know," he says, "now that you mention it, you're looking really hot. You been dieting or something?"

"No," I say. "But I knew I was going to get fired. So I started weaning myself off food."

"Really?

Jesus, I like this boy, but he is sure thick at times. Maybe that's the tradeoff. What the Lord gives you in good looks, he subtracts in brains. "I'm just kiddin' with you, Trav."

He grins that million-dollar grin. Correction: twenty-million-dollar grin. "I don't want you to disappear on me, all right? And I don't want you to hate me."

"I don't hate you," I say.

He shuffles through the large stack of scripts on my desk. "Have you read anything good lately?"

"Not in that pile."

He stops fiddling with the scripts. "I read *Catcher in the Rye*," he says.

"I loved that book," I say.

"Yeah. Griff told me about it way back. And it turns out Len read it in the joint. He said it was one of his all-time favorites."

"Did you like it?

"Yeah. Especially that bit on page twenty-seven where he's sleeping on the bench in Central Park, shivering in the dark and cold, and he gets bitten by the wolf."

"Say what?"

"The wolf, you know. Where he turns into a werewolf."

"Holden Caulfield turns into a werewolf?"

"I thought you said you read it."

"I read the *book*," I tell him. "I didn't read the script."

"There's no wolf in the book?"

"No! Of course not."

"I don't get it," Travis says. "That's the best part."

The doorbell rings. I glance over at the security monitor and see a truck from Party Rentals in the driveway, on the other side of the gate. I look over at Travis. He lowers his face like a guilty kid.

"What the hell's going on, Trav?"

"Nothing," he says, all shuffly-like. "I miss my friends. I thought I'd have a little party while Lenny was out of town."

"He's not going to like this."

"He's not going to know," Travis says.

I realize I don't want any part of this, and I tell him so, and I start gathering my things.

"I can't find the number of that caterer that makes that really good Thai food," he says.

If you ask me, that's no caterer. That's an escort service disguised as a caterer.

"You remember the names of those two little waitresses they sent over last time?" Travis wants to know. I swear, the boy is getting hot just thinking about them.

"Sure I remember," I say. "The little one with the big chest was called *Phun*. And the even littler one with the bigger chest was called *Thyme*."

"Yes!" Travis says. "You're exactly right."

I also remember what the two master chefs brought to the house in the way of food. One box of cold noodles and a second box of cold dumplings, both of which looked like they'd been lying around for a week. The dumplings weren't bad, though. This was back in the days when I was still eating anything you put in front of me.

They also brought a big bag of fortune cookies that were maybe the weirdest fortune cookies I'd ever seen. The first one I tried said, *"Kiss the person on your left."* The second one said, *"Remove an article of clothing."*

I give Travis the phone number and make my way toward the door. "I know you don't want to hear this, Trav, but I think you should call this party off. You've been doing real good. I hate to see you blow it."

"Don't worry about it," he says. "It's under control."

I leave the house and run into Lou. "Hey, Kecia," he coos. "How's it going?"

"Okay," I say. I can hardly look up at him. I'm so embarrassed at the way I fell apart the other night.

"What you doing Saturday?"

"This Saturday?"

"Yeah," he says. "Unless I gotta book a few Saturdays in advance."

"I don't have anything planned. Why?"

"How about I take you out to dinner?"

"Why would you want to do that?" I don't know why I say it, and the minute the words are out of my mouth I wish I could take them back. It's just that I don't have a very high opinion of myself. It's been a while since a man asked me out.

"Have you looked in a mirror lately?" he says.

Lou has a point. I *have* been looking in the mirror lately. The other day I looked in the mirror and bent over and looked even harder. And I'll tell you something: I liked what I saw. "What time you going to pick me up?" I ask.

"Seven-thirty," he says.

"I'll be ready," I say, and I sashay on over to my car. I know he's watching me, and I like it. J.Lo can keep her big butt. I wouldn't want something that size following me around all day. I like the butt I got now.

Later that night, I'm sitting in my house thinking about Travis and worrying about the boy. I know I don't owe him anything, but I decide I better go check up on him. I pull myself together and drive on over.

There's no sign of Lou outside, but the driveway and the street are crowded with cars. I make my way along and can already hear the music blaring. I'm sure the neighbors are thrilled.

I let myself through the front door and walk through a house that looks like it's been hit by a tornado. Marta ain't gonna be too happy about this. There are bodies here and there, and I hope they aren't dead.

I take a look out back, by the pool. The music is really cranking, and I count a good two dozen people shaking it up and clapping like they're watching some kind of show. I look closer. It's Phun and Thyme, of course. The caterers. They're standing on the diving board, dancing, taking it off. Those girls got breasts of steel. I wouldn't want to get hit in the eye by one of those.

I scan the crowd for Travis, and I can't find him.

I go back inside. I see Pokey and Frog, sitting in front of a pile of coke as big as an anthill. They're laying out lines on some girl's naked ass.

I make my way through the kitchen and see the familiar bounty from those so-called caterers. I grab one of the fortune cookies. *"Tell the hole room your biggest fear."* It's written just like that—*hole* without the w. My biggest fear is that the IRS is going to throw my black ass in jail. They say my daddy owed more than a hundred thousand in back taxes, and they're going to take the house if that's what it comes down to. I don't have a job, I don't have any money, and—from the looks of it— pretty soon I'm not going to have a place to live.

"You seen Travis?" I ask this model-looking guy in the kitchen.

"No," he says, in a swishy voice. "But I sure hope to."

Who are these people? Is Hollywood like some kind of mecca for weirdos or something? It's like you're strange, so you've got no choice but to make the trek west.

In the den, two guys and two girls are dancing and doing Skyy Vodka shooters.

"This is ruining my buzz," one of them says. "We better not be out of coke."

"Anybody seen Travis?" I ask. They all look up at me like who the hell invited the sister. I make my way into the back of the house and I can hear some serious humping going on in one of the bedrooms. I poke my head inside. The girl who costarred in Travis's last movie is taking on two guys at once, but neither of them is Travis. I hustle on down to the master bedroom and bang on the door. "Travis, are you in there?"

No answer. I pound the door again. "Travis?"

I turn the handle and push open the door. No one is in the room. I'm about to leave, but I notice a light in the bathroom. "Travis?"

I walk in and find Travis with his head in the toilet. I mean all the way *in* the toilet. You can imagine the shit I've seen since I've worked for the boy, but this is a first. "Travis!" I grab him by the back of the hair and yank his sopping head out of the bowl. He's not breathing!

"Travis!"

I smack him and I grab the phone on the wall and I hit 911 and beg for help. "It's Travis Trask," I stammer. "He's not breathing!" They tell me they're going to send someone over and to stay on the line because they're going to walk me through a number of emergency procedures. I'm shaking so hard I don't know what to do with myself.

"Where are you?" the operator asks me.

"In the bathroom."

"Is Mr. Trask with you?"

"Yes!"

"What's he doing?"

"Well he ain't fucking dancing, bitch!"

"I'm going to need you to calm down, Miss!"

My heart is going a million miles a minute and she wants me to calm down! I drop the phone. I go over to Travis and pound him on the chest, once, hard. He coughs and one of those damn dumplings comes shooting the hell out.

"Travis?"

He can't talk. He looks all disoriented and woozy.

Frog walks in, like he's on another planet. He takes one look at us and misreads the situation. "Everybody's getting laid except me!"

"Get the hell out of here!" I shout. "This party's over. The police are on their way."

Frog goes whiter than usual and takes off like lightning. I turn my attention back to Travis. "Travis? You okay? Can you hear me?"

He's still too weak to move, but he's coming around. "You saved my life, Kecia," he says in a hoarse croak. "You saved my damn life."

I did, didn't I? I can't believe it. I actually did save his life. I get a washcloth and run a little water on it and wipe his face and forehead. "I don't know what to say," he says in his weak voice.

"Hush. You don't have to say anything."

"I had this damn thing in my throat, and I kept trying to get help, and I couldn't talk or breathe, and everyone thought I was just jumping up and down trying to be funny. Then I ran in here to try to pound this out on my own."

"Hush up, now."

There's a commotion behind us. Two paramedics walk into the bathroom with their gear. Travis is still too weak to stand, and I don't see any need to move him at the moment. The guys move in and start checking out his pulse and stuff, and saying things about the color of his skin and the size of his pupils, but they don't seem too worried. They ask me to walk them through what happened while they finish checking his vitals, and they keep telling Travis that he's a very lucky man.

"I know," he says.

A couple of minutes into it, the guys are done. "This situation's been handled," the one guy says. And just then the other guy whips out one of those tiny digital cameras and takes a shot of Travis faceup on the floor next to the toilet bowl.

"Hey! You can't do that!"

They take off. I tell Travis I'll be right back and haul off after them. I run through the empty house and through the open front door and I can see them running down the driveway, toward the ambulance. All the other cars are gone—everyone sure cleared out in a hurry.

"Come back here, you bastard!" I shout, but I'm losing ground. I can already see that damn picture on the cover of *The National Enquirer*. I know I shouldn't care, but I do care. I can't help it. Say what you want about Travis, he's not a bad kid.

"Kecia!"

It's Lou. He's down at the end of the driveway, close to the ambulance.

"Stop those guys!" I say.

He gets to the ambulance first and the guy with the camera tries to push past. But Lou's about twice his size and he backs off. I reach their side, breathless. "He took a picture of Travis," I say.

"Who did?"

"That one."

Lou looks over at the guy. "Let's see the camera," he says, and he puts his hand out. I never noticed how big his hand was. What is it they say about big hands?

"Who the fuck are you?" the guy says.

"I don't think it matters," Lou says in a very calm voice. "I'm about twice your size and I think I'm going to enjoy stomping on your windpipe."

The guy considers this. He reaches into his pocket and hands Lou the digital camera. Lou checks out the picture and seems impressed. "This is good," he says. "Twenty-five grand easy."

He looks over at me. I guess he can see I'm worried. He drops the camera on the asphalt and smashes it twice with the heel of his boot. "Oops," he says.

"Motherfucker," the paramedic says.

"Get out of here," Lou says. "And be grateful we don't press charges."

The guys get into the ambulance and pull away. I look at Lou. "I can't believe you did that," I say.

"Well, you know how it is," he says.

"No, I don't," I say. "How is it?"

"I've been thinking about what I do for a living. All this running around, taking pictures of famous people and selling the good ones to the highest bidder. And I remember the kid I used to be. Eleven years old from Chicago. Skinny, ugly, kind of lost. And one day my daddy comes home from driving his cab and he shows me this big old camera he found in the backseat. He said he had spent half the day retracing his steps and trying to find the owner, but he had no luck. He said he was going to give me the camera, because he hadn't given me anything on my last birthday."

I can't believe Lou's telling me this.

"I thought I could become a famous photographer, an artist, but I found I had a knack for taking pictures of my friends in embarrassing situations."

Then it hits me: "Are you messing with me, Lou?"

"Yes," he says, laughing.

"Oh Lord—Travis! I forgot all about Travis."

I run back into the house, with Lou right behind me, and we find Travis propped up on his bed in a daze. I guess the boy got some of his strength back.

"Kecia," he says dreamily. "My angel." He turns to Lou. "Do you know that this girl saved my life?"

"It was nothing," I say, but of course I don't mean it. I'm really proud of myself.

"You're unfired," Travis says.

"Don't you think you should clear that with Lenny?"

"No," Travis says. *"There are some things a man's got to do on his own."*

This is a line from Travis's last film, and he delivers it just like he did in the movie. It sounds powerful. I've heard it a million times before, but it still sends chills up my spine.

"You sure you're okay?" I ask.

"I saw the light, Kecia," he says, all dreamylike. "It was a bright light, just like they say. *Blindingly* bright. And I started moving toward it."

"I don't want to hear that shit," I say. "I'm going to call Marta. We have to get this place cleaned up before Lenny gets back."

Polaroid CZ0786A08611A

Jeb.

EXT. BLUME BACKYARD—DAY

ASHLEY and ME adjacent to swimming pool with rosebushes, shovels, bags of dirt, and fertilizer. This has been the best week of my life, an entire week of lunchtime gardening. I arrive every day at one with plants and supplies, and every day I sit in Ashley's kitchen and have lunch with her. We've already managed to plant a small vegetable garden with tomatoes, herbs, cucumbers, and squash. I love it. I cannot believe it— me, Big Jeb, on my knees in the dirt, playing gardener—but I really love it.

I turn to look at her.

EXTREME CLOSE-UP: The back of Ashley's neck. Her hair is pinned up under a wide-brimmed sun hat. She has a perfect mole at the base of her hairline. It's the size of a speck of charcoal. I look away when I feel the veins tightening. That isn't what this is about.

"Should we plant all yellow and then pink," she asks me, "or should we mix it up?"

"We should definitely mix it up," I say. I like using the word we. It's like we're an item.

She backs up and surveys the area. "I think you're right."

Then she smiles. It just might be the most beautiful thing I've ever seen. It radiates more warmth than the sun on a ninety-five-degree day. More pussy talk. I've got to cut this shit out.

I'm so close to her I can smell her shampoo. I want to tell her I love her, but I think she knows. She's on her knees now. She looks across at me and smiles again. I can see down her shirt. She's wearing a peach-colored lace bra. I look away and tend to the rosebushes.

This is definitely weird. The first two days, we just worked. But on the third day she told me she had read my poems and cried in bed. She said that Randall had come home late, as usual, and found her crying—but that she couldn't tell him what she was crying about. "I can't really talk to him, you know," she had said. "I especially can't talk about my feelings."

W E W O R K in the hot sun for an hour, then go inside for lunch.

While we eat, or pretend to eat, Ashley tells me about her childhood, and about her romantic dreams, and about her lifelong search for her magical missing half. Nothing has turned out like she expected. "What happens if you look up one day and you finally find the person you've been looking for your whole life, but it's too late because you've already made a commitment to someone else?"

I don't really know what to do. Does she really want me to answer that question, and what exactly is the question? Or is she trying to tell me something? She is staring at me so intently that I have to look down, which is probably the wrong thing to do.

"Yes," she says in a voice that doesn't sound like her. "It's late. You better get back to the office before Randall starts wondering where you are."

I feel like a douchebag. Why don't I tell her the truth about the job? And, more importantly, about the way I feel about her?

I don't know why. I guess I'm still the wimpy kid I used to be.

I go off to my pretend job and feel seriously depressed until the next day at one, when I return. We work on the fuchsia, and there is obvious tension between us. We are both pretending that the previous day has never happened—that we have never talked about passion and romance and our search for the one person out there who would make us feel complete.

I look up. She wipes her face, leaving a dirt smudge.

"You've got some dirt on your face."

"Where?"

Instead of telling her, I reach up and wipe it with my own hand. And this is when I decide to tell Ashley the truth.

"I have a confession to make," I say.

BLUME (O.S.)

Ashley!

THE CAMERA PANS RIGHT to reveal RANDALL BLUME'S FACE. He looks simultaneously astonished, fearful, angry, panicked, and contemptuous. THE CAMERA PANS BACK TO ME for a reaction shot, then RIGHT AGAIN to reveal that the prick has a bouquet of flowers in his hand.

"Jeb," he says, his voice cracking. "What the hell are you doing here?"

"It's my fault," Ashley says, getting to her feet and jumping to my defense. "I asked him to help me with the garden."

Blume storms across the yard pointing at me. "You were fired!"

Ashley blinks. "W-what are you talking about?"

He puts a protective arm around her. "Are you okay?"

She steps away from her husband. "I'm fine."

"Honey, why don't you go inside?" he says in his prick voice. "I'll take care of this."

She looks at me, horrified. "Fired? What do you mean? Why didn't you tell me?"

"Because I didn't want to lose you," I say.

"What the fuck did you just say to my wife?" Blume snaps, whipping out his cell phone. "I'm calling the cops."

My fist is dying to make contact with his mouth. But now that I realize how pathetic Blume is, and how unhappy Ashley is, I know it isn't worth it.

I'm looking dead at Ashley. I'm trying to find the right words. "Ashley, I, I, I think I lo—"

"Police? This is Randall Blume. I need—"

I take off before he finishes his sentence. I feel like a coward and a loser. For a moment, I see myself at age forty, working at a 7-Eleven, where I will probably spend the rest of my miserable life. I'll probably have to wear a turban to blend in with my chirpy collegues.

I'VE BEEN CALLING Ashley for two days to try to explain myself, but she's not answering the phone. I don't know what to do. I really need to talk to her. I feel as if my life literally depends on it. I go over and park across the street and wait. An hour goes by. Then two. Just as I'm about to give up the hope of ever seeing her again, the Range Rover turns into the street and comes toward me.

It pulls into the driveway and I hop out of my car and see that she's alone.

"Ashley?"

She whips around, wary. "W-what are you doing here?"

"I need to talk to you," I say.

"I think you should leave, Jeb."

"Please, just give me two minutes. That's all I ask." She stares at me, which I guess means she's giving me my two minutes, so I stumble over the words: "I'm sorry I was dishonest with you, Ashley. You have no idea how sorry I am. For the longest time, I wanted to tell you the truth, and on one or two occasions I actually began to. But I couldn't bring myself to do it, because I didn't want to lose you, and you were all I had left."

"You expect me to believe that? You expect me to trust you? I shared all those intimate details about my marriage and my feelings and my life and my hopes and dreams, and it was just a big joke to you."

"Not at all, Ashley! It was never a joke to me. I've never been more serious about anyone in my life." I want to tell her I love her, but it frightens me. "I know you'll probably never forgive me, and I wouldn't blame you if you didn't. But I think you should know that these last few weeks together, the hours I spent with you—well, these have been the happiest times of my life."

I don't wait for her to answer. I don't want to put that kind of pressure on her. I turn and get into my car and drive away, fighting the urge to look into the rearview mirror and fighting tears, but not necessarily in that order.

I get home to my shitty little apartment. It's so hot inside I can hardly breathe. I lie on my bed, willing the phone to ring. But it doesn't ring. I drift in and out of sleep, dreaming uneasy dreams, then I get up and decide to write her a poem:

> *My beating heart, calls out:*
> *Do not let go of me*
> *Love is pain, Ashley,*
> *But for you I will endure anything . . .*
> *Anything but silence.*

As if in response, the phone rings. I reach for it. "Hello?" I say.

"It's Ashley," she says.

"Ashley!" I can hardly breathe.

"You owe me an explanation, Jeb. I want to know the truth, and I want you to start at the beginning."

So I tell her the whole truth. And an hour later I drive to Casa Del Mar and she's waiting for me in Room 862.

She opens the door and we stare at each other for what seems an eternity. Then she invites me into the harbor of her arms and we kiss.

Moments later, we're on the bed, naked, making love. I cannot even begin to describe how I feel. I feel as if I'm making love for the first time in my life. This isn't about the veins. It's about our two bodies, melding together, moving in perfect unison, as one.

I think to myself: *This is more happiness than a mere mortal can be expected to endure.*

Polaroid 620786A08611A

GRIFFIN

I'VE MADE up my mind. I go over to Travis's house to confess my sins. Kecia and Travis are in the living room with Lenny. There are two bags near the door. The mood is very somber.

"Is somebody going somewhere?" I ask, indicating the bags. I wince when I realize I just said *somebody* like Johnny.

"No," Kecia says. "Lenny just got back."

"You were out of town?" I ask.

"Did you hear what happened?" Lenny says, ignoring my question.

"Yes," I say. "Kecia told me she's been downsized. I hope you'll reconsider in the near future. I happen to think she's a terrific human being."

"Not that," Travis says, and he proceeds to tell me the whole incredible story, though I must say that I disbelieve the part about the dumpling actually shooting across the room and shattering the bathroom mirror.

"What an amazing story!" I say.

"What are you doing here, anyway?" Lenny says.

"I have a story of my own," I say. I reach into my briefcase and pull out both copies of Travis's contract, the real one and the one I forged, and I tell them exactly how I forged it. I also give them a signed affidavit, which is pretty much the story I've just told them, only in writing, and I urge them to get rid of Johnny, who is not the right person for them.

"I knew something was up," Kecia says. "Johnny left two messages this morning. He said he needed to talk to Travis and Lenny immediately."

"So Johnny's not my manager anymore?" Travis asks.

"No, he's not. You are under zero obligation to anyone but yourself."

"Why are you telling us this?" Lenny asks. "And I want the truth, man."

"I felt horrible," I say. "Johnny threatened to fire me, and I didn't want to find myself on the street again, especially after having invested three years of my life under him, so in a moment of weakness I made a bad decision."

Lenny is furious with me, of course, and he goes on about it for a bit: how I'm lower than pond scum, and how he loathed me and Johnny from the first day he laid eyes on us, et cetera, et cetera.

"I'm sorry," I say. And it's all I *can* say. I get to my feet.

"Oh, this is good," he says. "You stand there looking all contrite and shit, and I'm supposed to be so grateful that I tell my brother to sign with you because you fucked up but came clean and will no doubt be a stand-up guy from here on in."

"Not at all," I say. "I'm getting out of the business."

"Bullshit," Lenny says.

Travis tells him to stop harassing me. He says they should be grateful and just accept their good fortune, and then makes an obtuse reference to some kind of "blinding white light"—but the reference goes completely over my head.

"Honestly, Lenny—I'm done. I've left a letter of resignation on Johnny's desk."

"So what are you going to do?" Kecia asks me.

"I don't know. The weird thing is, I always wanted to produce, and maybe I will someday. But at the moment I'm thinking of opening up a pet store."

"You're fucking kidding me?!" Lenny says.

"No," I say. "I worked in a pet store all through high school. I know a lot about pets, especially reptiles."

"Really?" Travis says. "I always wanted one of those lizards where the eyes move funny."

"Chameleons," I say. "They're a little delicate. You might be better off with a bearded dragon."

"I should call the fucking cops on you," Lenny says abruptly, apparently tiring of this digression.

"I wouldn't blame you if you did," I say. "But I'd certainly appreciate it if you opted against it."

"Len, chill," Travis says. "Leave the dude alone."

"I'm sorry about everything," I say. "But at least you're free of Johnny."

"What about Blume?" Lenny asks.

"I'm not a big fan of his, either," I say. "He's very shortsighted. And he has no taste in material. It's not always about the size of the check. Sometimes the best offer is the one that pays the least."

"You're not leaving town, are you?" Kecia says as she walks me out.

"No," I tell her. "I'll call you. I might need somebody to buy me dinner from time to time."

"Hey, Griff—I always liked you, man," Travis says. "Don't be a stranger."

"Thanks," I say. "See you. And good luck."

"And sorry about that time I hurled in your car."

"Don't mention it," I say.

I get into my car, which still smells a little foul four months later, despite the three shampooings, and make my way over to Bart's. I get some dirty looks from the brothers on my way over, but it doesn't bother me. At the moment, I feel better than I've felt in months. I feel I could take on Stone Cold Steve Austin.

I ring the bell and hear Bart's faint voice through the closed door. "Who is it?"

"It's me. Griff."

He hesitates for a moment. "This isn't a good time, Griff."

"I'll make it short."

"Can't you just call me later?"

"No," I say. "This is it. There is no 'later.'"

There's no answer. I press my ear to the door. "Is everything okay, Bart?"

"Not really."

"Bart, I need you to let me in."

He fumbles with the lock and chain and cracks the door. Half his face remains concealed, but I can see that his left eye is swollen shut and horribly discolored.

"My God! What happened?" I push my way inside. I'm about to interrogate him further when I find Johnny sitting on Bart's ratty couch. He looks up at me and flashes a shit-eating grin. I'm shocked on multiple counts. One, that's he's even there. Two, that he found out where Bart lived and actually made the pilgrimage. And three, that he'd sit on that couch in his three-thousand-dollar suit.

"We were just talking about you, Griffin," Johnny says.

"I see you got my letter of resignation," I say.

"I suppose you're here to try to steal away my new favorite client?"

"Not at all," I say. "I actually came to talk to Bart, to see how he was doing. As you know, he's having serious misgivings about the pilot—"

"Yes, yes, yes," Johnny says, cutting me off. "He thinks he can't do it. He doesn't understand the process—all the writing and rewriting and dealing with the seventeen people who claim to be producers on the show. But we've talked about it. I'm here for Bart, and he knows it, and if he needs me on the set every day, well, I'll *be* on the set every day. Isn't that right, Bart?"

"Please tell me you're not buying this bullshit?" I tell Bart. I can't help but wince when I look at the eye. "Did Anne do that?"

He nods. "She auditioned. It didn't go well. They kept her waiting for an hour and cut her off after half a line."

"I'm sorry to hear that," I say.

"Are you? Johnny says that was your doing. That you told the producers to humor her because I have the misfortune of being married to her."

I turn to look at Johnny, aghast. "You're a piece of work, Johnny."

"Thank you. I guess. Now if you'll be good enough to leave, Bart and I have some rehearsing to do." This is too much. But indeed, I notice an open copy of the revised pilot script on Johnny's lap.

I turn back to Bart. "Bart, please. Don't listen to this guy. He's the most narcissistic, self-serving prick in a town that's filled with narcissistic, self-serving pricks. He didn't even know your name until two weeks ago."

Johnny frowns. "Griffin, I feel sorry for you."

"You said you didn't even like stand-up comics! I practically had to shove Bart down your throat."

"The lying continues," Johnny intones.

"Where is Anne?" I say.

"She's leaving me."

"I'm so sorry." I don't know why I say that. I guess you get so used to lying it becomes second nature.

"You should be. It's your fault."

"Bart—"

"I don't think we should worry about Anne at this point," Johnny says. "I have seen many Annes in my days, and I've seen them become the ruination of a great many men."

Ruination?! He got that word from me.

"Jesus Christ, Bart," I plead. "Listen to me. I know you don't want to do this show. I know it feels unnatural to you. And I don't think you should do it if you don't want to. You can make a great living as a stand-up comic, and *solely* a stand-up comic, if that's what you want to do."

"You know, Griffin," Johnny says through clenched teeth. "It's not too late for me to press charges."

"Fuck you, Treadway," I snap, my eyes never leaving Bart's tortured face. "You're a brilliant comic. Where is it written that being a comic isn't enough? You don't need a series, especially if you find it as banal as you say you find it—and frankly, I agree with you. All these endless rewrites and it's only getting worse."

Johnny gets to his feet. "Get out of here, Griffin. I'm not going to ask you again."

"Don't do it, Bart. If someday you decide to do a series, do a good one. Don't commit to something because a bunch of soulless, talentless assholes are telling you it's wonderful. You're smart enough to know better."

"Doesn't *somebody* have an appointment with the unemployment office?!" Johnny screams at me.

I'm crushed. I wish I could help Bart, but it looks hopeless.

"If you need me, Bart," I say, moving toward the door, "you know where to find me."

On the way home, I try not to think about these hellacious few weeks. I try to think about the future. I find myself driving past a pet shop on Wilshire Boulevard, and I go inside to have a look. They have a very cute baby bearded dragon. I used to have one of my own, Spike. They also have a beautiful ball python. I ask the kid in the store if I can take a look at it, and it promptly bites me. The kid is very apologetic, but the bite is superficial and stops bleeding in a few seconds. Maybe I should go to law school instead.

I'm driving along San Vicente Boulevard when I spot a Starbucks and realize I need a hit of coffee. I go inside and am stunned to find a familiar face behind the counter.

"Rachel! What are you doing here?"

"Nothing. I guess Victoria doesn't want me back."

"But *Starbucks*? I mean, seriously."

"I don't mind, really. I like people. I served Belizio El Toro a frappuccino yesterday."

I almost correct her but decide not to.

"And Donny Devito was in here a few days ago. Boy, I always knew he was short from his *Taxi* days, but it's a little shocking when you see him in real life. I wonder if he's part midget."

She's on a roll.

"And that Jewish fellow who looks like he's disgusted by everything, though he can't help it because that's just the way his face turned out."

"Gary Shandling." That one was easy.

"That's right, Gary Shandling. He was with this little British-sounding girl who kept asking him to admit that he loved her."

"Did he?"

"No. Not that I heard."

"Can I have a tall wet cap?" I ask.

"Good choice," she says. "Tall wet cap coming up!"

"Have you even heard from Victoria?"

"No," she says too quickly. "I haven't heard from Victoria. Have you heard from Victoria?"

"I hear they're having trouble with the show. The network isn't wild about keeping the illness vague. They think the audience isn't sophisticated enough to handle that much vagueness."

"I have to agree," she says tersely, and I notice an odd look on her face. "What's wrong?" I ask.

"Nothing," she says, turning away. "What could possibly be wrong?"

Now I know she's keeping something from me, something about Victoria. "The network is quite upset," I say, studying her face for clues. "But Victoria is being really stubborn. She doesn't really want to commit to one illness, despite the fact that they've given her three choices."

"What are the three choices?"

"Cancer, botulism, and AIDS."

"Wow," she says. "They all sound awful."

I take my coffee and have a sip, still wondering about her discomfort. "This is the best tall wet cap I've had in my life," I say.

"You want to know what the trick is?"

"Sure."

"Less water. Simple, huh? You want the coffee to be *restreto*. That's an Italian word that means 'tight' or 'restricted' or something. You know who I learned that from?"

"Who?"

"Pavarotti."

"Luciano Pavarotti?"

"Yes," she says. "He was on his way to Florida, on a road trip, and he stopped in at the Sugarland Starbucks for a coffee."

I don't know whether to believe this. It again occurs to me that Rachel reminds me of someone in a movie, and I know it was a hit movie, but I can't for the life of me put my finger on it. I notice a script on the counter in front of Rachel. "What's that?" I ask.

"My script."

"You write? I didn't know you wrote."

"That's why I'm here."

I feel bad for her. Every blockhead thinks he can write. The Writers Guild of America has ten thousand members, and at any given time ninety percent of them are unemployed. The strange thing is that those are people who actually sold something once upon a time. For every member of the Guild, there are ten new writers trying to break in. You do the math.

"What's it about?"

"It's nothing. It's just a story about growing up in Sugarland, Texas."

Now I feel really sorry for her. Every writer I know has some quaint, heartfelt, quirky little story in his bottom drawer about growing up in Poquott, Long Island, or wherever the hell it was he or she spent his or her "formative years." They don't seem to realize that nobody gives a damn about the first time they got kissed, let alone the time they fell out of the damn tree house. People want to be entertained. "That's great," I say, and I wait for my stomach to implode. But it doesn't implode. It occurs to me that I haven't popped a single antacid since I put my letter of resignation on Johnny's desk.

"Has anyone read it?" I ask.

"Only the people at UCLA Film School."

That and seventeen thousand other scripts, I think. I can't help it.

Sometimes I think negative thoughts. The business will do that to you. "Did they like it?"

"I guess," she says, her voice void of emotion. "I got in."

"You got in?!" I shout.

She looks at me, deeply perplexed, and suddenly I feel bad. I realize I've said it with such incredulity that I might as well be calling her an idiot. "I think that's wonderful," I say.

"Thank you," she says.

"Could I read it?" I ask. I don't know why I ask—I'm leaving this goddamn business—but I guess old habits die hard.

"Sure," she says. "You can have this copy. I'm just rereading it, trying to make it better, but I've read it so many times it doesn't even make sense anymore."

I thank her and take the script and head out, and it's only later, when I get home, that I realize I didn't pay for my coffee.

Michaela

BONNIE ADAMS CALLS and tells me she wants me to join her at a cocktail party at the Beverly Hills Hotel. "It's important for you to be there," she says, then adds quickly: "And by the way, I told Barry all about you over breakfast yesterday." So the Barry Levinson thing is still on! I can't believe it. I can't even believe I'm hearing back from Bonnie. It's true what they say about Hollywood. It's not dog eat dog; it's dog doesn't return other dog's phone calls. And it took her all this time for her to return my phone call.

At the hotel, the valet gives me a ticket and takes my car. I'm about to stroll into the lobby when I hear someone call my name—my real name.

"Sylvie?"

I stop and immediately tense up. Please, dear Lord. It can't be. When I turn around, Ernie Finklestein steps toward me. "I thought that was you."

"I look completely different," I say, struggling to keep the panic out of my voice. "How did you recognize me?"

He smiles. "Your father gave me your head shot. You look more beautiful than ever."

Of course I do. But Ernie looks exactly like he did when he was a kid, except for the Hugo Boss suit and the Bruno Magli shoes. This is not a compliment. He comes closer, smiling. I notice he's had work done on his teeth, thank God. I also notice his eyes, which are dark and soulful, and which I don't believe I had never noticed before.

"It's Michaela now, right?"

"Yes," I say.

"I called you—"

"I've been very busy, Ernie."

"No, no—please. You don't have to explain. I just wanted to say that the only reason I finally stopped calling you is because I was beginning to feel like a stalker. Of course, I still *think* about calling you, but now it's no more than thirty or forty times a day."

I notice he's smiling, so I guess he's kidding. I return the smile. "It's not personal, Ernie. Honest."

"And I'm not taking it personally."

"Well," I say, indicating my watch. "I have a meeting with a producer and I'm already running late."

"I'm here till Friday. The Sunset Suite. I'd settle for a cup of coffee. Then again, just standing here looking at you has been pretty great—so thanks."

My God. That really rattles me. I've never heard anything like that in my entire life. And the strange part is, he means it. "It was great seeing you, Ernie," I say.

"You, too," he says.

I expect him to wheedle and beg, but he just waves a friendly little wave, so I turn and hurry off. I race across the lobby and notice that a couple of bellhops have stopped in midconversation to gawk. This is good. This means I look hot. But of course I already know that.

I proceed down a long corridor to one of the Bungalow Suites. I knock. A moment later, a woman opens the door. I notice that she desperately needs to rethink the Dolce & Gabbana minidress she's squeezed into.

"Hi," I say. "I'm Michaela."

She looks the same age as Bonnie and has had her eyes done, too. "Michaela, of course. We've been expecting you. Come in. I'm Rita Patelli."

I know her name from somewhere. And then it hits me. She's the head of that newly formed studio. I'm impressed. Bonnie seems to know a lot of happening people. I wonder if Barry will be here, which makes my BP tingle.

I follow Rita into a room where three other women sit on the couch drinking cosmos. They wear peasant shirts, Seven jeans, and strappy designer sandals. Each one is thin, beautiful, and striking in her own way. One's a dark brunette, one's a redhead, and the third one has light brown hair. I'm the blonde who completes the quartet. We're a black sister away from the Spice Girls. I immediately notice all of their complexions and discover no fine lines or wrinkles. These girls have got to be underage. The redhead stands. On closer inspection, she looks as old as me. "Hi, I'm Daisy."

The brunette smiles, "I'm Leelee."

The one with light brown hair says, "I'm Trish."

I say hello to each of them just as Bonnie comes out of the bedroom. She approaches and kisses me on the cheek. "Michaela. So glad you could make it. Can I get you something to drink?"

"Yes, please. I'll have a cosmo."

I have a pretty good idea what's going on, and let's just say I'll need a lot of drinks to get through the evening.

Things START OUT normal enough. Everyone's chitchatting and drinking lots of alcohol, especially the teenyboppers. They keep making worried eye contact with one another, wondering why they are there. Then Rita Patelli brings out some coke. She sprinkles it onto the coffee table and draws out eight lines, two for each of us. Bonnie doesn't participate. She sits across the room in a chair, ogling us. After we snort the lines, everyone becomes livelier. Someone turns on the stereo. Rita pours more coke on the table so we can indulge. Bonnie calls me over.

"Nice party," I say.

She squeezes my hand. "I'm glad you think so. I want you to do me a favor."

"Sure."

"I want you to kiss Leelee," she whispers.

I raise my eyebrows. "What?"

She touches my face gently. "We need to get this party started. Go over and make out with her. Come on, do it for me."

I look over at Leelee. She no longer looks nervous. She's laughing at a story Trish is telling. She looks like a high school homecoming queen, but from a high school in a very remote farming community where people aren't bothered by the smell of manure.

"Go on," Bonnie pleads, running her finger over my lips.

"I don't want to," I say quickly.

Now it's her turn to raise her Georgette Klinger–groomed eyebrows. She takes another sip from her martini before speaking. "I wouldn't have invited you if I thought you didn't want to participate."

I choose my words carefully. "Of course I want to participate, it's just that I've never been in a group situation before."

"There's a first time for everything, Michaela," she says. "I know you don't want to disappoint me."

"I'm sorry," I say. "I'm a little nervous."

This comment seems to excite her. She whispers into my ear, "You won't regret it."

"Okay," I say, and I gulp the rest of my cosmo. My eyes tear up as the alcohol burns my throat. Light-headed, I stagger over to Leelee's side and sit down next to her. That's when Rita grabs Trish and Daisy and takes them into the bedroom. I look over at Bonnie. She's staring at me, smiling. She has a smile like a shark. I tap Leelee on the shoulder, and when she turns to look at me I kiss her on the mouth.

Leelee acts like she's been waiting for me her whole life, and it strikes me that Bonnie has choreographed this whole scene. Her tongue darts in and out of my mouth, and she struggles with the buttons on my shirt. I feel as if I'm being molested by a young Natalie Portman. Leelee's mouth is so wet it feels like she's cleaning my teeth with a Water Pik. Drool and slobber seep out of my mouth. I feel sick. I don't want to meet Barry Levinson that badly. When Leelee places her hand between my legs, I quickly move away. She looks at me curiously. Pink frost lipstick is smeared all around her mouth. "What's wrong?" she asks.

"I have to go to the bathroom," I say.

As I pass through the bedroom to get there, Rita Patelli and Trish are lying on the bed half-naked, pleasuring each other. I startle Daisy when I enter the bathroom. She's snorting coke off the top of the basin. Leelee's lipstick is all over my mouth. I look like a clown.

Daisy hands me the straw. "Want some?"

"Yes," I say, and snort up a two-inch line that stings my nose.

"Is this your first time?" she asks.

I squeeze my nostrils together and close my eyes. "If you're referring to this lesbian orgy, then yes. It's my first time."

She taps another smidgen of coke onto the basin from a vial. "How long have you known Bonnie?"

"A few weeks."

"And who were you supposed to audition for?" she asks.

"Barry Levinson," I say, numb with shock.

"Right. And Rob Reiner wants me to play the female lead in his next movie. He's looking for an unknown."

"Is that what she told you?"

"Uh-huh. Eight months ago."

I feel like I'm going to barf. I stumble out of the bathroom and walk past the bed and see Rita's head bobbing between Trish's legs.

In the living room, Bonnie and Leelee are locked in a 69. I see a nicely toned ass, Leelee's, no doubt, and wonder if mine would look as good in the same position. Then I feel awful for even thinking like that. I grab my purse and storm down the short hallway toward the front door. Bonnie calls my name twice, but I ignore her and let myself out.

Feeling queasy, I hurry down the familiar corridor, headed for the lobby. Then I remember what Ernie told me: the Sunset Suite. I feel compelled to visit him— maybe it's the Sylvie inside me—so I find my way to his room.

He answers the door in silk pajamas, clearly roused from deep sleep.

"Sylvie?!" he says, stunned. "W-what are you doing here?"

"I'm not sure," I say. "How would you like to take me to dinner?"

Kecia

I FINALLY BIT the bullet. I broke down and went to the Federal Building and met with that guy from the IRS and one of his fellow geeks. As they had been telling me for several months, Daddy owed more than a hundred thousand in back taxes, including interest and penalties. They said they were sorry, but there wasn't a damn thing they could do about it. Damn bureaucrats.

I was on my way out, trying not to go off in front of these horrible, heartless men, when the brother rushed out and stopped me at the elevator banks. He told me he knew this was a difficult time for me, and that he hoped I wouldn't hold the assessment against him personally, and he wondered if I would like to have dinner with him sometime.

I looked down at his hand and noticed a wedding ring. He quickly covered it up and said, "It's not what you think. We have an understanding."

Brother don't have to bark for me to know he's a D-O-G. "Have her call and clear it with me," I said, "and I'll be glad to have dinner with you." Then the elevator arrived and I got in without another word.

It was kind of flattering, to be honest. I can't go into a 7-Eleven without getting hit on these days. And I've got to tell you: I like it.

So here it is, two weeks later. I'm in the den, carefully packing up Daddy's records. The realtor lady told me she would have no trouble selling the house, and she put it on the market for $1.2 million. My daddy died penniless and in terrible debt, but at the end of the day it looks like he took care of his little girl after all.

I've been checking out condos near the beach, down in Marina del Rey, and I think that's where I'm going to end up. I'll need a two-bedroom, since I'm going to take Marta with me, and I've seen some pretty nice ones in the high sixes. That'll still leave me a little nest egg, which even I find hard to believe. I've gone from being broke and unemployed and harassed by the IRS to being practically a white person. It's scary. I can't wait for those monthly condo association meetings.

I find one of Daddy's ancient cigars behind a stack of albums. When I pick it up, half of it crumbles like the carcass of a dead bug. The label says Cohiba. I sniff it and still detect that tobacco aroma. I set it aside and try to figure out where to pack it away for safekeeping.

The doorbell rings. Lou walks in and kisses me like it's the most natural thing in the world. And it is. But it's nothing compared to what he did to me last Saturday night. There was some kissing, and a whole lot more. But I don't think the details are any of your damn business.

"Hey, baby," he says. "How you doin'?"

"I can't complain," I say. I look deep into his cinnamon-colored eyes and remember what my horoscope said: *"Save your energy for what's in front of you."*

I take him by the hand and lead him toward the bedroom. "Where we going, girl?" he asks. "I thought I was here to help you pack."

"I see what's in front of me," I say. "And I'm feelin' energetic."

"Huh?" he says, but he's not complaining.

Polaroid C20786A08611A

Jeb.

INT. ASHLEY'S BEDROOM—NIGHT

I look at Ashley, asleep at my side. The kid is staying with his father tonight, at the Four Seasons. It's his first official sleepover since Ashley told Randall that they were finished. I wish I had been there to see the look on his face when she told him that she was in love with me, the lowly assistant.

I hate Randall Blume and everything he stands for, and I don't want anything to do with this stinking business anymore. Right now, I'm weighing a couple of options. One, I become a personal trainer. And two, Ashley and I start a landscaping company together.

I am so in love with Ashley, and this was before I even knew that her father has about two zillion shares of Microsoft. He was one of the guys who started the whole thing with his good buddy Bill Gates, so money has never been an issue in Ashley's life, which is a good thing for me, as you can imagine.

Ashley says I can write all day every day if that's what I want, but I'm pretty sure I don't want to write. The fact is, I'm not a very good a writer. Everything I write, or try to write, sounds like something a real writer threw away. And all my movies always end exactly the same way: in a big fistfight in the final minutes, with the good guy walking away victorious but pretty ticked off, sort of like Gary Cooper at the end of *High Noon*. Then again, if you think about it, most movies end with a big fistfight, even the last installment of *Lord of the Rings*, so I'm not the only jackass out there.

I can't move into the house just yet because it wouldn't be healthy for little Jeremy. We want to ease him into it. He's got to get used to the fact that his father is not a good person, and he will, in time. Meanwhile, I'm just letting him know I'm here for him. The other day I took him fishing at this place in Agoura Hills. They have two stocked trout ponds, and for a while there we didn't get a lousy nibble, but then—bang!—the little bastard had one on the line. I helped him reel it in. I've never seen anyone so scared of a fish in my life. But it was a very nice experience. I am bonding with this young man, and I really like him. Sometimes, though, when the light hits him a certain way, he reminds me of his father. And those are tricky times for me. I almost feel like whacking the kid up the side of the head. But I never do, of course.

Early the next morning, Ashley makes me another wonderful break-fast: huevos rancheros with a side of lox and bagels. She has to go off to pick up Jeremy, bring him home, and get him ready for preschool, so I head back to my place to think about the day ahead. It's no idle day, either. I am doing something really strange this morning, and I'm a little nervous about it. I don't know if you remember the girl at MGM with the boss who broke his arm and asked her to hold his penis, "tight, but not too tight?" Well, her boss, Sven Norgaard, has been out of his cast for several months now, but it seems he still enjoys having his penis held. So I'm going over there to have a little talk with the guy.

When I arrive at the front desk at MGM, I say I'm there to see Sven Norgaard, and they ask me if I have an appointment. I say no, I don't, and then I show them my ID. There's a picture of me on the upper right, next to the words *Department of Labor*. Below that, it says *Bureau of Criminal Investigations*. I thought that was a bit much, but Griffin told his friend at the Warner art department to put it in there: he said it sounded "deliciously scary." His words. I would never use "delicious" in such a gay context.

I like Griffin. He's grown on me. Usually I stay away from those mud sharks, but Griffin doesn't bother me. I'm not even sure he's gay. He's never hit on me, for example, and I'm fag bait all the way. I kid you not.

The elevator arrives. I am escorted to Norgaard's office, and I walk past the desk of the young lady who has been subjected to months of penis holding. I can sense her tensing up, and I avoid making eye contact with her.

Norgaard has a swanky corner office. He gets to his feet and shakes my hand and I introduce myself—Peter Harwood, a name I picked myself (it was originally Hardwood, with a *d*, but Griffin thought I should drop the *d* because it felt a little obvious), and I get down to business.

"I'm afraid there have been some complaints about you, Mr. Norgaard," I say.

"Complaints? What kind of complaints?"

"Let us say they are of a sexual nature," I tell him.

"What?!"

"Let's not get excited, Mr. Norgaard. I don't like it when people get excited around me, and I'm pretty sure you wouldn't like it, either." This was not the best line in the world—I think I sort of stole it from *The Hulk*—but I'm not doing badly, considering that this is my first time and that I'm not an actor and that my principal qualification for the job is that I could break this guy in two like a twig.

"I'm going to call my lawyer," Norgaard says.

It's amazing. That Griffin is one smart guy. He told me that it wouldn't take long for Norgaard to reach for the phone and threaten to call his lawyer. If I was in the business, I'd want someone like Griffin to represent me. Because he's not only smart, he's devious, and those are two qualities I admire in a rep.

"Okay," I say, calm as can be. "That's your prerogative. But if you do that, I'll have to go through official channels and assign you a case number, and then of course it becomes 'official' and the media gets hold of it and it gets seriously messy."

"I don't understand," Norgaard says, setting the phone down. "You're not here in an official capacity?"

"Oh, I'm here officially, all right. But I'm also here in—how do I put this?— I'm also here in a 'friendly' capacity." I am very proud of that line. I'm going to have to remember it so I can share it with Griffin later. "I'm hopeful, and confident, that we can work this out before it goes any further, without destroying lives and careers."

Norgaard mulls this over. "Who complained?" he asks me.

"You know, Mr. Norgaard, I've been with the Bureau of Criminal Investigations for two years now, and I get that same question on every single investigation. The thing is, you're a smart man, and you know what you've done or haven't done, and as a result I'm pretty confident that you know the answer to your own question."

That was excellent. I delivered that whole thing exactly as Griffin wrote it down for me, word for word.

"I have my suspicions," he says.

"You seem like a good person, Mr. Norgaard. And I can see from the photograph on your desk that you have a lovely family."

"Thank you."

"I know that a great many things are racing through your mind at the moment. For starters, you are stunned that someone actually contacted us to complain about you. As far as you were concerned, it was a harmless little game. More importantly, at the moment, you are very upset with the person who filed the complaint."

"You're right on both counts," he says.

"Here's what I suggest you do, and believe me it's good advice. I suggest you find a way to promote this person."

"Promote her?"

"Absolutely. If you did otherwise, if, for example, you decided to fire this person, then I can assure you that the department will come down on you like a ton of bricks."

"I see," he says, and he doesn't look too happy.

"I will check in with that person in a few weeks; by the end of the month, say. If said person is satisfied with her advancement, I will personally see to it that this small peccadillo is expunged from your record, and you will never hear from me again."

"Is that a guarantee?"

"You have my word on it," I say. I reach over and shake his hand firmly, and then I let myself out.

I take the elevator to the lobby and cross into the underground lot and get into my car. I am feeling really good. As soon as I pull out, I call Griffin on my new cell phone.

"It's me," I say.

"How'd it go?" he asks.

"That girl's going to be running the studio within three years."

Michaela

So AFTER THAT horrendous experience with Bonnie and her little lesbo friends, Ernie Finkelstein and I went to dinner at Bastide. And I actually ate an entrée and didn't throw it up.

"Thank you for spending time with me," Ernie said. "I've been waiting for this day since I was nine years old."

He was so funny and so decent and so appreciative and so charming that I almost broke down.

When we went back to the hotel, he was a perfect gentleman.

"I'm not going to invite you in because I don't want to insult you," he said. "I know you're not that kind of girl."

I know I should have kissed him on the cheek and driven away, but I couldn't help myself. "Invite me in," I said. "For you, I *am* that type of girl."

Ernie loved the BP. He took one look at it and I thought *he* was going to break down.

For the next four days, I basically lived in his suite. I ordered room service, hung out by the pool, snacked, watched TV, snacked some more, treated myself to massages and facials, and waited for him to return from his various meetings. He was such a doll. He never returned empty-handed. A little dress from Neiman Marcus. A Marc Jacobs handbag. A suede jacket from Fred Segal.

At night he'd take me to yet another great restaurant, and order for both of us.

One time, when the steward brought the fancy French wine he'd ordered, Ernie took a sip, swished it around in his mouth, smacked his lips like a duck, and pronounced it totally unacceptable. "These grapes came from the west side of the hill," he said, looking very irritated. "They don't get any sun in the afternoon!"

It turned out he was kidding, and we all had a good laugh, including the wine steward, who a moment earlier looked as if he was on the verge of a heart attack. Ernie said the wine was so good his tongue was smiling.

The day before he went back to New York, I took him to the Louis Michael Hair Salon in Beverly Hills. They did a fabulous job. They didn't turn him into George Clooney or anything, but he looked seventy percent better: a nice Jewish boy with an exceptionally good haircut.

Life! What a confusing business! Ernie's only been gone for two days, and we talk on the phone three or four times a day, but I really miss him. I have a feeling Ernie is going to propose to me, and I think it's going to be soon. I hope so, anyway. For the first time in my life, I can imagine myself married, with kids. And that's a really big deal for me. I had always told myself that I wouldn't have kids till I was forty, when my life was over anyway, but suddenly I don't want to wait. I want a life *now*. And Dad! He's so proud that I'm eating real food and seeing Ernie, he's beside himself.

The other thing is, I have to be realistic. I'm probably not going to make it as an actress, and I'm tired of trying. I did the best I could and I came close a few times, but it's never going to happen for me. Is it painful to face? Sure, but what choice do I have? I may not be the smartest person in the world, and I'm certainly not the deepest, but I know there's more to life than Hollywood. And I'm sure I'll find plenty of drama in my brave new role of Hysterical Jewish Wife and Mother.

Ernie just called. He has to go to Paris on business, and he wants to know if I'll go with him. I've never been to Paris. I go to my computer and google *talking dirty in French*.

My my. This is going to be fun.

Ah, Ernie! Tu es grand comme un cheval!

GRIFFIN

RACHEL'S SCRIPT was without a doubt one of the three best scripts I have ever read in my life, and the other two were *Sunset Boulevard* and *Raging Bull*.

When I was done, when I turned that last page and set the script down on the bed next to me, I felt literally winded by the experience. I realized that I was dealing with a wholly original talent, and that my next move could change the course of her life *and* mine.

I further realized that I now knew, unequivocally, who it was that Rachel reminded me of. *Forrest Gump*. That's right, Rachel had written the female version of Forrest Gump, and she was Forrest all the way.

I called her at home as soon as I felt sufficiently recovered to talk to her intelligently about her script. "Rachel," I said. "I'm not going to mince words. I loved *The Sugarland Shuffle*."

"Really?" she asked. The poor girl. Clearly she was completely unaware of the magnitude of her gifts. "That is so nice of you! That is the nicest thing anyone has ever said to me."

"You are going to hear a lot more nice things from a lot more people in the weeks and months ahead," I said.

"Will it be anybody famous?"

"Until about five minutes ago," I said, pressing ever onward, "I was ready to leave the business. I was actually thinking of opening a pet store."

"A pet store! That's so amazing! My Uncle Rufus—he wanted to open a pet store, too! But he didn't have any money. So he started a mail-order tadpole business, and it took off. The man became a millionaire. What you get in the mail, see, are these two little live tadpoles, in these little sealed tubes of water. And you get a little tadpole aquarium, with these little mazes and slides for the tadpoles to enjoy."

"I know, Rachel," I said. "I read about your Uncle Rufus in the script."

"Oh of course!" she said. "I'm so sorry. I didn't mean to bore you."

"You're not boring me, Rachel. You could never bore me."

"It is so unbelievably nice of you to say so! Am I dreaming?"

"No, Rachel. This is me, Griffin. We are having a real conversation, and we are both wide awake. Though I'm probably more awake than you are."

"You are an incredibly nice man. The only homosexual I knew in Sugarland was the night manager at Denny's, down the street from the Starbucks. But he was married and had two kids and he was trying hard to fight his attraction to the short-order cook, this cute little black man called Slick."

I didn't have the heart or the energy to tell Rachel that I'm not really gay. Though I'm not really straight, either. I'd gone back to see my therapist, Barry, and we are trying to figure it out. Barry didn't seem to think there is anything wrong, per se, with my being undersexed, especially since I didn't seem to be clinically depressed, but he was troubled by the fact that I could get erect over talent.

"Let me ask you about this guy Dan," I said to Rachel, and I noticed that I was erect.

"My roommate?"

"He's real?"

"Of course he's real. We share an apartment."

"Has he read the script?"

"He *loves* the script."

I thought that was a little odd. Dan was portrayed as a very bright young man who operated well below his abilities, and who spent the bulk of his waking hours pursuing married women. Then again, he's the one who had helped Rachel's character break free of her alcoholic mother.

"Is everyone in the script real?" I asked.

"Yes," Rachel said.

It made sense. This stuff was so good you couldn't make it up.

"Let me ask you another question, Rachel."

"I will answer every question to the best of my abilities."

"How would you feel about having me represent this script, which I assure you I would do to the best of my abilities?"

"Trust you?" she said. "I would be honored."

Later that same day, I got a call from Bart Abelman. He began by apologizing to me for being too thick to understand that Johnny was a complete asshole, and then he begged me to get him out of doing the series. "I hate it. I hate everyone associated with it. I hate sitting around a conference table with six Jews, two Catholics, and a Presbyterian, and listening to them try to come up with funny lines. These guys are just not funny, Griff. Please get me the fuck out of here."

"I hear you, Bart."

"I just want to do stand-up," he said. "Is that so wrong?"

"No, Bart. It's not wrong at all." *I'm* the one who had been wrong. Bart and network television were not a good fit. That had been my mistake entirely. Still, if he wanted to go back to stand-up, and only stand-up, I would see to it that he made a good living at it. He was too talented not to.

"God, Griff—thank you. I feel so much better already."

"Don't worry about a thing, Bart. From here on in, I'll do the worrying for both of us."

"And by the way," he said, "do you know a good divorce lawyer?"

In the space of an afternoon, I'd gone from a prospective pet shop owner to a producer/manager. Then the phone rang again. It was Lenny Trask. "We have to talk," he said.

When I arrived at the house that afternoon, Lenny and Travis were waiting for me in the living room.

"Can I get you something to drink?" Lenny offered.

"A beer would be nice," I said.

As he went to retrieve it, I looked over at Travis. Jesus, he was handsome. Maybe I *am* gay. "How've you been, Travis?" I said. "You look good."

"And I *feel* good. Lenny and I had colonics this morning."

"That's wonderful," I said.

"I've never had a colonic before. It was pretty hot."

"I've never had one, either, but if it's as good as you say, well—I may just have to rush out and try it."

"Don't get nervous when you see that hose creeping up behind you."

"I'll try not to."

"But what am I saying?! You have plenty of experience in that department."

Lenny came back with the beer. I took it and thanked him and he sat down across from me.

"So you get your pet store yet?"

"Not yet," I said. "I'm sort of on the fence about it at the moment."

"Good," Lenny said. "Because I have a proposal for you."

"I'm listening."

"I want us to represent my brother."

"Us?"

"Yeah. You and me. Partners. Fifty-fifty."

"Fifty-fifty on Travis?"

"No. On everything. I want to get into the management business. I spent the last week meeting with agents and managers, from William Morris to Untitled Entertainment to I.C.M., and they're all morons."

"I'm not going to argue with that."

"So here's the deal. We commit to *Fire in the Hole*, take ten percent of the twenty million, and set ourselves up with offices in Beverly Hills. With Travis on the roster, and your knowledge of the business, we'll be drowning in clients in no time at all."

"I like everything you just said except that *Fire in the Hole* bit. It's a terrible idea. It's not even an idea, frankly. It's completely wrong for Travis."

"Do I get to shoot people?" Travis asked.

"Well, we need money, pal," Lenny said, ignoring his brother. "You know what they're getting per square foot in Beverly Hills?"

"I know we need money. And we'll get it. But not with that. Travis has talent. If we handle him properly, he'll be another Paul Newman."

"The salad dressing guy?" Travis asked.

"And I have just the script for him."

"What? *Catcher in the Rye*?"

"Holden Caulfield as a werewolf? I don't think so, Lenny."

"Werewolf? I don't remember that part."

"It's not in the book. It's in the script."

"What is wrong with these people?! They have to fuck up *everything?*"

"Don't worry about it. I've got a script called *The Sugarland Shuffle*. It's great, truly brilliant, and Travis isn't even the lead," I said.

"Say what?"

"That's right. The lead is a woman. Travis would play her best friend, Dan."

"Do I get to shoot people?"

"No, but you get to sleep with a lot of sexy married women."

"I could do that."

"I don't get it," Lenny said.

"Here's the way it works," I explained. "If Travis commits, we have a movie. And you and I produce that movie. Travis will only have to work two or three weeks, so we'll be reasonable. We'll ask for a million a week. Meanwhile, we'll look for the right action picture, and, when it comes along, we'll take the twenty mil."

"I don't know. Ten percent of two or three million isn't going to get us much in Beverly Hills."

"You're wrong. Plus, we don't have to pay for it. We'll get the studio to pay for it."

"Which studio?"

"Whichever one we want. They're all dying to be in business with Travis Trask."

"You sure about this?"

"I haven't been surer about anything in my life, Lenny. I need you to trust me on this. We're going to make a great team."

Lenny took a moment, then stood and reached out and we shook hands. "All right," I said, getting to my feet. "We have our work cut out for us. Call Kecia and tell her to get her ass in gear."

"It's Sunday," Travis said.

"This is Hollywood," I said.

Lenny walked me to the door. "I like you, man," he said. "And I think I can trust you. But don't fuck up. You fuck up, I'll make you my bitch."

Polaroid C20786A08611A

Kecia

LET ME TELL YOU how my life has changed since September. I wake up in a bright-ass condo in Marina del Rey. It's pretty fly, with high ceilings, a partial view of the ocean, and two spacious bedrooms. I haven't figured out what to do with the second bedroom yet. I was going to let Marta live there, but she went back to Mexico to retire. I helped her out to the tune of fifty thousand dollars, because she deserved it and because I could afford it: Daddy's house became the object of a heated bidding war.

Lots of mornings, I wake up with Lou next to me. I like that boy. I might even let him turn that second bedroom into a darkroom. I also understand this paparazzi business a little better these days. Lou isn't one of those guys who always go for the "compromising" pictures. Oh, sure, a liplock here and there is nice, and it pays the bills, but he's not going to be climbing no fence to get a shot of Julia Roberts, in the buff, screaming at her clueless husband. As far as Lou's concerned, he's performing a valuable public service. Everybody wants to see pictures of these Hollywood types, most of all themselves. If I can quote Lou, "They complain when you take their picture, and they complain louder when their picture stops showing up in *People* magazine."

The thing is, I know Lou's a good guy. How can I ever forget the day Travis almost drowned in the toilet, and the way Lou smashed that paramedic's camera right there on the driveway? That one shot would have fetched mucho green. But Lou didn't take it. He showed his true colors.

Now let me tell you about work. Griffin and Lenny partnered up, and they scored office space about ten minutes from my house, on the corner of Wilshire and Ocean Avenue. Griffin felt Beverly Hills was too congested, and too hot in the summer, and that the air quality sucked, and the boy is right on all three counts. We're way high up, with views in every direction, including the rooftop pool of that swanky building next door, where it seems like they got a clothes-optional clause in the damn lease. Every guy who comes by the office—agent, manager, delivery man, friend, looky-loo—gets all hot and bothered when he sees the kind of talent they got hanging at that pool.

And our offices—pretty damn sweet. All this custom-built furniture, in light-colored wood, with a plush six hundred-dollar chair at every desk. At the moment, it's just Griffin, his gay assistant, Charles, straight out of Harvard Law, and Lenny, and me. And we got this part-time kid, a brother, called Kenvin. He set up all the computers and all the phone lines and all the cable hookups, and he keeps everything running nice and smooth. We call him the *Information Officer*, since he's the guy to go to when you need anything on anyone, legal or otherwise.

Finally, saving the best for last, I have some big news. It looks like we're going into production this summer on our very first movie, *The Sugarland Shuffle*. Travis is taking a secondary role in the movie, mostly to show the town that he's more than just a pretty face, and partly to help get the damn thing made, and they're looking for the lead girl now.

Oh yeah. I almost forgot. You remember that lunkhead, Jeb? The one with muscles on his earlobes? He's engaged to the ex-wife of his former boss, and I hear he never has to work another day in his life. That's actually good for us, because every two or three weeks we need him to do a little job for THAG, which stands for The Hollywood Assistants Group. I can't tell you exactly what THAG does, or who's in it, but I can tell you that at one point or another every member was part of the fun at Trader Vic's—which is still going strong, by the way. Then again, I guess it won't hurt to give you a little hint. You ever see that movie *The Star Chamber*, with Michael Douglas? That's where these judges and lawyers become vigilantes because they're plain fed up with a system that's always setting criminals free on technicalities. Are you getting the picture now? We don't exactly execute people, but we try to steer them toward the straight and narrow.

"Goddamn it, Charles!" It's Griffin, yelling at his poor, tortured assistant again. He comes out of his office with a pen in his hand. "Does this look like a medium Uniball?"

"Sir?"

"I asked for a *medium*. You gave me a fine. The fine is scratchy. I *hate* the fine."

"I'm sorry, sir," Charles says with his head down

Griffin looks over at me. "What are you staring at?"

"Nothing," I say, and I smile kind of wicked. "Looks to me like this might be a job for THAG."

Griffin looks a little guilty, and he damn well should. We had a talk about this once: about the way everyone in this town seems to become corrupted by power. It's hard to figure out. Do they actually become corrupted by power, or is it that only the corrupt ones have what it takes to scratch and claw their way to the top? I don't have a clue, to be honest, so if you figure it out—well, be good enough to let me know.

"I'm sorry, Charles " Griffin says.

"I'll run over to Staples on my lunch break."

"Fine," he says. "Get me Gump."

That would be Rachel, his star writer. I don't know why he calls her Gump, and it's none of my business, but I'll tell you this: the name fits her perfect.

Polaroid C20786A08611A

Rachel

THE DAY AFTER Griffin called to tell me that he loved
my screenplay, which was maybe my most magical day since arriving in
Los Angeles, I got an urgent call from Dan. I was in the middle of making
a double mocha latte, and I finished it, then I asked Nugundu, the boy
from Botswana with the big white eyes, to please take over for a moment.

"I cannot do this, memsahib," he said in his cute little British accent.
"I do not know how to operate this infernal machine."

"It's only for a minute," I said. "If anyone comes by, just smile that
bright smile of yours and tell them you don't speak English."

"In what language, memsahib?"

"I don't care," I said. "Say it in Swahili if you want. And please stop
calling me that. This is America."

"I don't speak Swahili, memsahib."

I went out back and took the call. I knew this was against company policy, unless it was a genuine emergency, and I found myself in the difficult
position of hoping it was an emergency, but not a really bad one. "Dan," I
said, grabbing the phone. "It's me. What's wrong? Is it my mother?"

"It's your other mother," he said.

"What other mother?"

"Victoria."

"*Victoria?* Victoria called?!" I couldn't believe this. I hadn't heard from her in three weeks. I never expected to hear from her again. "What did she want?"

"I don't know," Dan said. "But she sounded desperate. She needs you to call her right away."

"I can't. I'm working."

"Rach, listen to me. The woman was wigging out."

So I called her, and she told me she needed me right away. I explained that I was no longer in her employ, and that I had a very promising job at Starbucks, with *benefits*, and that I would phone again when I got off.

"No!" she screamed. "I need you now! Do you understand?"

"I'll stop by after work," I said, and I hung up. I thought I could bring her a box of those really good new chocolates we just got in. I love chocolates.

After work, as promised, I drove over to Victoria's house. Victoria herself buzzed me in, which seemed a little strange, and on my way up the driveway I noticed that the garden looked a little shabby, as if it hadn't been tended in a while. I thought this was strange, too, but nothing prepared me for what I found inside the house. The place was a mess, especially the kitchen. There were cartons of leftover food everywhere, including from that wonderful Indian place on Wilshire, Akbar, and that amazing little Italian place on San Vicente, Pizzicotti.

"My God, Victoria," I said, trying hard to appear less shocked than I was. "What happened here?"

"I fired everyone."

"Even the gardener?"

"Especially the gardener. He was working for *The National Enquirer*."

I noticed a shattered mirror at the end of the hallway that led to the den. "Wow. How did that mirror break?"

"I broke it," she said. "I broke all the mirrors in the house. They make me look fat."

Of course they made her look fat. She wasn't fat by the standards of, say, Bradford, Pennsylvania, but by Hollywood standards she was obese.

"You broke all the mirrors in the house?"

"What is wrong with you?" she snapped. "Why do you repeat everything I say? Are you retarded?"

"Victoria," I said, and I stamped my foot theatrically to show her I meant business. "I will not be spoken to that way. And I will not have you speak ill of the retarded." I was about to tell her all about Davey Fuller, this little kid from Sugarland who loved to hide everyone's shoes. Every time I looked at his little face, with those thick glasses and everything, it broke my heart, because Davey Fuller wanted to be a writer, too. But then I looked at Victoria and I could pretty much tell that she wasn't in the mood for stories.

"Why did thou forsake me?" she said, softening.

"Excuse me?"

"Why did you leave me? I thought it was working out between us."

"I don't think we should talk about the past," I said. "I think we need to start by getting this place straightened out."

"Do you have any idea why I called you?"

"No."

"I called you because I can't stop thinking about you," she said.

This worried me a little. Michaela had told me about a really strange thing that had happened to her with a lady casting director, in great detail, and I didn't want anything like that to happen to me.

"I can't stop thinking about what you told me that day," she said.

"What did I tell you?"

"That I had to tell the truth."

Wow. This was heavy. "You've decided to tell the truth?"

"Yes," she said. "Call Randall and Johnny. I need them here for the press conference."

I went into the cluttered kitchen and picked up the phone and called Randall first. He wasn't available. He was on the phone with someone about his child visitation rights. Then I called Johnny. He had problems of his own.

I went back and told Victoria that neither of them was available. Randall had lost his wife, and Johnny had lost his most powerful client, Travis Trask. Plus Johnny had burned his penis on his tanning machine, and he was busy getting ready to sue the manufacturer.

"His 'most powerful client,'" Victoria said, looking at me all steely.

I realized I had insulted her and corrected my mistake: "*One* of his most powerful clients."

"Fuck them," she said. "They're both fired."

"Why don't we call Griffin?" I said.

"Who's Griffin?"

"You remember him. The good-looking guy who used to work for Johnny."

"The gay one? He doesn't work for Johnny anymore?" she asked.

"No," I said. "He'd been thinking of opening a pet store, but he changed his mind."

"What are you?" she said in her mean voice. "Fucking insane? I'm supposed to face the media with a pet shop owner at my side!"

"No. You didn't let me finish. He's a manager/producer now. Travis went with him."

"Why didn't you say so in the first place?" she said.

"I don't know. Stories come out the way they're supposed to come out. They kind of tell themselves."

Victoria shook her head and looked at me like I was the strangest thing she'd ever seen in her life. "Okay," she said. "Call him."

Griffin came over and we sat in the living room and talked it over. Then we made a few calls and within forty minutes there were about two dozen reporters and cameramen and photographers at the gates.

Victoria walked out to face them, with Griffin on one side and me on the other. Griffin asked everyone to quiet down. He said Victoria had a statement to make, and she was only going to make it once, and there would be no questions afterward, not even about fashion choices. I was impressed by the way Griffin handled it. I was glad such a competent young man liked my script and had decided to represent me.

Victoria cleared her throat. "I would just like to say that I lied about having a terminal illness. My lie was an act of desperation, and it came on the heels of two crushing personal blows. One, my husband didn't love me anymore. And two, my show was on the verge of being canceled. I don't for a moment think that these personal travails in any way justify or excuse my egregious behavior. But I am here today to beg my fans to forgive me, and to tell the world that I am prepared to face the future with no further lies."

The press went insane. They shouted questions and pressed up against the gates like a murderous mob, but Victoria didn't answer any questions. She turned around and we walked back to the house, the three of us as cute and tight as little soldiers.

"You were great," Griffin said. "You should be very proud of yourself."

When we got inside, we could still hear the reporters out there, caterwauling like wildebeests. I went into the kitchen to call a cleaning service, to try to get the house in order, and I made a mental note to myself to look up the word "egregious" the moment I got a chance. It seemed to be a big favorite of Griffin's.

That afternoon, when Griffin walked into his office, the network was already on the line. They were canceling the series. While he was thinking about how he was going to break the not-unexpected news to Victoria, Kecia told him that the Lifetime network was on the other line. They had seen Victoria on CNN, and they had been deeply moved, and they wanted to turn her dramatic story into a television movie. It would be a movie about self-worth, and about success, and about the vicissitudes of love, and about our desperate efforts to remain forever young. In short, it would be a movie about women everywhere.

Griffin called her with the good news, and it was the first time she didn't refer to the network as Vagina Vision. As far as Lifetime was concerned, it was a "go" movie. And it was Victoria's baby all the way. She would share executive producer credit with Griffin and Lenny Trask. The three of them would control every aspect of the movie: the script, the director, the casting, even the locations.

"And I'm already negotiating for a talk show," Griffin told her.

"A talk show?" Victoria exclaimed. "For me? On Lifetime? My very own talk show?"

"We could pull this together by next fall."

"Oh, Griffin. You're a genius. I love you."

"I know," Griffin said.

Two days later, when the story appeared in the trades, Victoria got calls from Johnny Treadway, Randall Blume, and seventeen other agent-manager types. This was her outgoing message: "If this is an agent or a manager calling about representing me, please fuck off. Anyone else, leave a message."

T HE FOLLOWING WEEK, Griffin took me to lunch at The Grill. It was really neat. Courtney Love was there and she appeared to be sober. And that dorky guy from *Friends* was there, looking upset because he suddenly didn't have a life anymore. I had watched the last episode of *Friends*, along with a billion other people, and I can't say I was impressed. I think it was trying too hard, although it did make Dan cry.

"This is the most expensive restaurant I've ever been to!" I told Griffin. And it was true. I couldn't believe they were charging nine dollars for a little bowl of corn chowder!

"Order anything you want," he said. "It's on me."

I wanted to order the twenty-eight-dollar swordfish, but I knew that was wrong somehow, on several counts, so I had the Cobb salad instead. I found it a little boring. They had a Cobb salad at the Denny's in Sugarland that was much better, and it was always changing, especially if Slick, the short-order cook, was pinch-hitting for the regular guy. He put all kind of surprises in that Cobb salad. You never knew what you were going to find!

"Do you want to know why you're here, Gump?" Griffin asked me.

"To eat lunch?" I said.

That was the day he broke the news: "We sold your script to Sony," he said.

"You're kidding!"

"And are you ready for this?"

"What?"

"I got you seven hundred and fifty thousand dollars."

I was in shock. I am not kidding. I couldn't believe that somebody would buy my script. I had really only written it because it was my life, and because I loved everyone in it, and to discover that someone actually cared was almost more than I could take.

"Mark this day down in your calendar. This is the day your life changed forever, probably for the worse."

"What?"

"Joke! Little joke. This is a great day, Rachel."

"I know. I'm just kind of like, boy, numb or something."

"It gets better."

"I don't know if I can handle any more good news."

"They're fast-tracking this thing. We have a creative meeting with the studio next Tuesday."

"Oh, I can't Tuesday. Tuesday I'm working at Starbucks during the morning rush, and in the afternoon I'm going over to help Victoria with some paperwork."

"Rachel, I don't think you heard what I said. You just made three quarters of a million dollars."

"I did?"

"Yes."

"Isn't that the money to make the movie?"

"Oh Rachel," he said, sighing and smiling sweetly. "My very own little Gump. I hope you never change."

I took Dan out to dinner at Melisse to celebrate. He had to cancel a date with this forty-four-year-old married woman he'd been seeing for a couple of months. She's very nice, and she has firm boobs exactly like Michaela's, but I really don't get it. For years now, Dan has been going on and on about me and my mother, who is back in rehab for the fourteenth time, but I wonder if he shouldn't be thinking about his own issues. On the other hand, maybe it's just me and the way my mind works. Maybe Dan just likes older women; maybe it has nothing to do with his mother at all.

"We should get a condo in Kecia's building," Dan said. "Wouldn't that be great?"

"Kecia paid eight hundred thousand for that place," I say. "Where am I going to get the other fifty?"

"It doesn't work that way," Dan said. "You put a couple of hundred thousand down and get a mortgage and then you're left with plenty of money in the bank."

"Wow! That is so neat! Who invented that?"

"I guess you won't be going to film school now, huh?"

"What?" I said. "Are you kidding? Of course I will. I have so much to learn."

"What are these little black things?" Dan said. "They taste like fish eggs."

"I don't know," I said. "They're called *caviar*."

ON TUESDAY I went over to Griffin's office, and we rode down to Sony together. There was a guard at the gate and he sent us right through and a valet took our car. I told Griffin I was very impressed, and that he must be a pretty important guy to them.

"It's not about me," he said. "This is all about you."

"No way," I said. That Griffin—he's such a kidder.

We went upstairs, and an assistant who looked like she'd been crying asked if we wanted anything to drink. She got us waters and ushered us into this amazing conference room. There were eight people waiting for us around the big table, and they all stood up to say hello. They seemed very excited to be there. Each one said his or her name, and said what they did at the studio—most of them were presidents or vice presidents or something—and they all said how pleased they were to be working with me.

"Before we start," the man at the head of the table said, "I would just like to say, Rachel, that I was completely blown away by the script. You have a talent for character that is beyond anything I've ever seen. I was wild about Slick, the little short-order cook at Denny's, and the married night manager who is in love with him."

"I loved the big pink neighbor," one of the women said. "The one who walked around the house naked, with all the lights burning—the Dog Whisperer."

They all began to talk at once:

"I loved Billy Fenton, the Motel 6 manager who liked to scare people with his glass eye."

"My favorite was Dan's father, the so-called mental health expert, and that business with Betty Schwartz, the principal."

"Don't forget the girl's father," another woman said. "He dies at the hands of the police, in a hail of gunfire, laughing the last laugh."

"What about Uncle Dwayne and those crazy Frankenstein cars he kept putting together?"

"I thought Pavarotti was great. The way he explains the finer points of making a good cup of coffee. Maybe we can get him to play himself?"

"What about the half-Indian girl with the skin condition?"

"Or Mr. Maldonado, who believes he was abducted by aliens!"

"Or the boy who was struck by lighting when he was roller-blading in the rain!"

I couldn't believe it. These nice, thoughtful, caring people had taken the time to read my little screenplay, and they loved it.

Life was a truly miraculous thing. I was in Hollywood. Me, little Rachel Burt, who was Employee of the Month at Starbucks twice, but who had never been voted most popular, or smartest, or most charming, or anything at all, and these wonderful people were going to make my movie!

ACKNOWLEDGMENTS

So I FEEL like I need to thank everyone I've ever known, met, or bumped into now that this book has become a reality. We're talking former writing instructors, friends I've lost touch with, my entire kindergarten class, the guy who bought me and my girlfriends Jolly Rancher shots last weekend, etc. Obviously I have to pare down the list down, so here goes:

Many thanks to my agent, Jessica Papin, for her guidance, vast publishing knowledge, perseverance, and, of course, discovering my query letter in the slush pile and asking to take a look. My editor, Aliza Fogelson, for her sound advice and wonderful, intuitive editing. Lina Perl, for first acquiring the manuscript, Jennifer Suitor, Jason Puris, Judith Regan, and the rest of the Regan Media team for their professionalism, dedication, and nonstop enthusiasm.

Special thanks to my dad for great teeth, artistic genes, and teaching me all about football; and to my sister, Erin (aka Midge), for her sense of humor and constant wisecracks. I'd also like to thank the fabulous people in my life whom I have way too much fun with: Allyson Burt, Laurie Wilkes,